SHAKE H

North Beach, San Fra

beat scene is changing. The Narco Squad are coming down heavy. One particular narc, Lieutenant Carver, really has it in for Lee Cabiness. All Cabiness wants to do is jam on his sax, score some weed and hang with the action. He had a thing going with Jean but that's cooled off, and now she's going with that flashy pimp, Randozza. One night Cabiness's friend Furg introduces him to Clair Hubler, a slumming rich girl who wants to hire them for a private party. She's got an anti-guy vibe but you never know. But all Furg wants to do is score some junk to find out what all the excitement's about. Naturally he thinks of Sullivan, the local junkie playwright. But Sullivan has a problem—Carver is using him to set up his friends. One summer in North Beach, they all collide. That's when things get crazy, real crazy.

IT'S COLD OUT THERE

JD Bing is out from San Quentin, just trying to get by selling encyclopedias—but he's not very good at it. In fact, he's getting desperate. Kristie has just lost her aerospace job and is holding herself together so tight she's beginning to lose touch with reality. Grove is a quiet young man who gets by selling clever little cartoons to the papers, trying to work up his nerve to ask out Kristie. When Bing comes around their apartment building in a last ditch attempt to sell, their lives are forever changed. Because Bing has entered a world of backstabbing winos, lonely check-kiting old men, cocktail waitressing divorcees, bullying counterfeiters, impotent ex-generals and crazy street people. It's a California underground—life on the fringes. And as Bing soon finds out, he was safer in prison.

MALCOLM BRALY BIBLIOGRAPHY

Felony Tank (1961)
Shake Him Till He Rattles (1963)
It's Cold Out There (1966)
On the Yard (1967)
The Master (novelization of the film Lady Ice, 1973)
False Starts: A Memoir of San Quentin and Other Prisons (1976)
The Protector (novelization of the film, 1979)

Shake Him Till He Rattles

- - - - - - - - - -

It's Cold Out There

BY MALCOLM BRALY

Stark House Press • Eureka California

SHAKE HIM TILL HE RATTLES / IT'S COLD OUT THERE

Published by Stark House Press
2200 O Street
Eureka, CA 95501, USA
griffinskye@cox.net
www.starkhousepress.com

SHAKE HIM TILL HE RATTLES
Copyright © 1963 by Malcolm Braly. Copyright renewed 1991 by Kristin Braly

IT'S COLD OUT THERE
Copyright © 1966 by Fawcett Publications Inc.

Introduction copyright © 2005 by Ed Gorman

ISBN: 1-933586-03-6

Text set in Dante. Heads set in Pike and Dogma.
Cover design and book layout by Mark Shepard, shepardesign.home.comcast.net

The publisher would like to thank Knox Burger and Craig Tenney for all their help in preparing this book for publication.

First Stark House Press Edition: February 2006

0 9 8 7 6 5 4 3 2

TABLE OF CONTENTS

Introduction

BY ED GORMAN

Malclom Braly (1925-1980) was always a special case in the world of crime fiction.

He was one of very few crime writers who knew the turf first-hand. He spent seventeen years inhabiting such institutions as Folsom State Prison, San Quentin and Nevada State Prison, a not unexpected fate for a boy who was dumped by his parents at an early age and was raised in various Dickensian welfare system dumping grounds—i.e., foster homes and reform schools.

He wrote three of his four novels while still in prison encouraged by an important and wise editor named Knox Burger who bought and published them. He wrote his masterpiece, *On the Yard*, after leaving prison. During the last decade and a half of his life, he saw his work not only widely read but widely praised.

Shake Him Till He Rattles is, in some regards, even more interesting in some ways than *On the Yard*. In the course of it he explores the intersection of the so-called beatniks and criminals. After all, Neil Cassidy, Jack Kerouac's sainted icon of all things beat, was a pretty hard core car thief. Braly also gives us the portrait of the sadistic cop as only an ex-con could. So the ex-con protagonist and the bad cop play cat-and-mouse right up to the nightmare finale. The novel shows us San Francisco just a few years away from the hippie explosion. Everything is in place for the rebellious years to come. Braly paints in searing colors.

For me there's a lot of Charles Willeford in *It's Cold Out There*. Both Willeford and Braly give us tours of down-and-out America that few writers ever have. And there's that same sad laughter you hear in the fiction of both men. And both writers usually toss in a successful man or two who likes to work out his kinks on the fringes of society. And both frequently use The Iconic Woman. She is not only The Great Beauty, The Great Lady, The Great Heartbreaker, she is also The Great Mystery. And she is never more mysterious than she is here, largely because she may also be clinically insane.

This is another ex-con story, this ex-con, sweaty, confused, terrified of being dragged back to prison, is for me the saddest of all the Braly characters. He lives in unrelieved fear; his goals are so humble they're almost pathetic. And humble as they are, they seem impossible to achieve.

If I had to describe these two books musically, I'd say that *Shake Him* is cool but melancholy jazz on a chill rainy San Francisco night, while *Cold Out There* is honky-tonk, red neon on a gravel parking lot where a couple of drifters are stomping on each other over an argument both are too drunk to remember.

Ladies and gentlemen, Malcom Braly.

Cedar Rapids, IA
November, 2005

Shake Him Till He Rattles

BY MALCOLM BRALY

To Bobbie

chapter one

Lieutenant Carver turned off Broadway, up Grant Avenue into North Beach. His hands tightened on the wheel of his unmarked police car, but he didn't notice the reflex or the accompanying tension at the hinges of his jaw because his eyes were flicking restlessly as he tried to watch both sides of the street.

He prowled slowly, taking a grim pleasure in the knowledge that, in spite of the unmarked car, he would be recognized. He pictured the waves of invisible shock moving out around him, vivid as electricity—the wake of a shark, he fancied.

His headlights skipped and flared in the wet street, merging with the reflections cast by the yellow windows of the little oddball art galleries, the obscure-book stores, the red smears of neon from the hectic overcrowded bars, and the light seeping through the green shades of the second-floor bedrooms.

Carver's experience and imagination penetrated all the windows. He smelled out what might be happening in the secret rooms of North Beach, and he didn't like what his sharp bent nose offered him. He saw the Beach as a parade of unashamed degeneracy. A world turned upside down with its ass painted to please.

Through the large windows of the coffee houses he studied his quarry. Most of them wore old clothes, deliberately shabby, khakis, denims and army-surplus jackets. The girls dressed the same as the men; they would be indistinguishable from the back, except for the loose hair around their shoulders. There were exceptions to the uniform—a number of young men in very tight slacks and sweaters—and he passed a light-skinned Negro standing in a doorway who wore an immaculate riding habit, jodhpurs and polished knee-length boots. Another group brought Carver's gorge up, hot and fast. Three grotesque celebrants from some private masquerade wandered arm in arm. Their finery was half muffled in dark raincoats, but they were still masked and glittering with theatrical jewelry, impossible to identify as to gender, except that they were so aggressively female they must have been male. Finally there was the large floating body of tourists. looking drab and ordinary in their soft-colored conventional clothes. They carried hastily-wrapped abstract paintings, probably "poured on" the day before. Cameras dangled at their middles like a sad third eye. An apt symbol, Carver thought, since intercourse between these people seemed primarily visual. Everyone watched everyone else, and he watched them all—protecting some, dragging others out of their flamboyant disguises, their lying poses and reducing them to the common level of decent fear and humility.

He watched the faces blurred in the rain, the faces in the windows, the sullen eyes sliding away in parked cars. He made careful note of those faces he already knew, adding others for the first time, underscoring those he'd already seen too many times.

He parked above the corner of Grant and Green, noticing that the street sign had been reversed again. The third time in two weeks. The Grant arm of the sign, canted and tipsily misdirecting, pointed up Green Street. Goddam irresponsible savages!

On the corner below him, the original coffee house was open. Settling back, he lit a cigarette and blew smoke at the windshield, watching the door. After a while two men and a girl came out. They were typical. When the rain hit them, they laughed and ran across the street into a small jazz club called The Hoof.

Carver knew the club. It was little more than a beer-and-wine license tacked up in an empty room. The opening door released a blast of music like a brass jack-in-the-box.

The hand holding his cigarette jerked in a stifled gesture of disgust. Ash powdered on his black suit and he brushed at it absently, thinking about the musicians over there…. Cabiness over there. The thought of Cabiness smouldered in his mind like fire in wet rags, obscure and sullen. While the ecstatic singing of Cabiness' alto sax jittered in his ear, he tried to frame an excuse for calling the goon squad to turn The Hoof inside out. But he had orders that casual raids were out for awhile. Even against musicians. And they were the worst of the whole useless lot. The original carriers of the Beat infection.

He noticed a single man turning the corner, walking quickly, full of nervous haste. Here's one, he decided. Rolling the window down, he called sharply. The man hesitated, thrown off stride. His face flashed, narrow-eyed, grayish-white in the rain. Then he shrugged slightly and moved over to the side of the car.

"Yeah?"

He was an older man than Carver had expected. The rain had plastered a thin wave of hair across his forehead, but his mustache was thick, full and glossy like a wet beaver pelt. He wore a plaid mackinaw with the collar turned up.

"What're you doing around here?" Carver asked.

The mouth beneath the mustache crimped scornfully, but the eyes were small and wary.

"What's it to you?"

Carver snapped the door open causing the man to jump out of the way. He extended his open card case showing the round Special-Squad shield.

"Get in," he said curtly.

The man took another step back. "Now hang up! There's a limit to what—"

"Get in!"

Reluctantly the man slid inside.

"Close the door," Carver ordered. When he was obeyed, he put the car in motion, heading on up Green, shifting for the steep flank of Telegraph Hill.

"What's your name?"

"Sullivan," the man answered in a tired voice. He was sitting as far from Carver as he could, leaning against the door with his arms crossed high on his chest. His nose in profile was bold, heavy, and triangular. On his wrist he wore the kind of thick leather band affected by weight lifters. Carver studied him out of the corner of his eyes, noting the resigned posture, the arrogant stoical face.

"What's an old fart like you doing around North Beach? After some of that young tail?"

Sullivan continued to stare straight ahead where the rain had blistered on the windshield. "You tell me. You seem to know all about it."

"If I were you I'd play it very cool," Carver said evenly. "You have been dealt a piss-poor hand."

He continued in silence to the top of the hill and parked on the gravel apron below Coit Tower, close to the stone safety wall. Beyond the wall, the hill, choked with brush, dropped abruptly for three-hundred yards, down to a shallow flat where the factories and warehouses shouldered each other towards the dark waters of San Francisco Bay.

Light brushed the windshield and Carver squinted, identifying it as the revolving searchlight on Alcatraz Island.

"You ever think of those poor bastards over there?" Carver inquired pleasantly, pointing out at the dark mass of the Federal prison. "Just a thousand yards from all they dream about. They can see San Francisco from the cell blocks. At night this hill is lit up like a cross between Christmas and the Fourth of July."

Sullivan nodded with a pretense of interest, but it was obvious that he was just waiting it out.

Carver was in no hurry, "—The ironic part of it is that all the tourists come here to stare at the prison through those telescopes, and if the prisoners had telescopes they'd be staring back. Now you figure out what that means, if anything."

Carver chuckled and looked around at the deserted parking area. "Too wet tonight, but ordinarily this is a good place to do up a joint. You ever make it up here?"

"No," Sullivan said shortly.

"No? Well, pass that for now. What's happening tonight?"

"I don't know. Nothing, I guess."

Carver showed his small teeth in a quick meaningless smile. "There's always *some* action. You look like you know what's happening."

Sullivan turned abruptly. In the shadows his mustache seemed black as a splash of paint. "Jeezus, you're cute, aren't you," he murmured bitterly. "A hip cop. If you're so hip, you ought to know where everything is."

Carver settled back, his face quiet and smooth as something carved from rock, but inside a spark was beginning to jump. Deliberately he lit a cigarette, taking his time over it, before he turned back to his prisoner.

"Sullivan—if that's really your name—I'm going to tell you a story. It's kind of a square story, but I like it. It makes a nice point.

"There were these two cops, burglary detail. Pretty good cops, even though I can't seem to remember their names. Anyway, they'd been after this same bastard for months. They knew he was real wrong, but they never could make him. He was more than half-slick.

"One night they stopped him for a shakedown, just to roust him a little, and, of course, he was clean, being a careful type. But that night he made the mistake of getting in their faces, rubbing it in their chests about how they couldn't get anything on him. So they just decided they'd had it with him.

"They took him to a poultry market down the block, smashed a window, grabbed a chicken out and put it in his hand.

"Then they told him, 'All right, chicken thief, you're under arrest.'"

Carver started laughing, throwing his small head back, obviously enjoying what he considered an excellent joke. He sobered suddenly and turned to Sullivan.

"You wouldn't want to be a chicken thief, would you? That's a hell of a jacket to carry."

"I knew some fuzz like that in Chicago," Sullivan replied mildly. "They're both doing twenty years. Rape and Robbery. It was a hell of a shock to their Captain—"

Before Sullivan could finish, Carver had the police sedan in motion again, plunging down the hill. They drove in silence back through North Beach where the streets were crowded with eager cabs drawn by the 2:00 A.M. closing hour. The changeover was being made from the bars to the after-hours places; others were starting the excited roll to various beds. It happened every night at 2:00—the city chose partners and, sometimes, mixed doubles.

The police sedan crossed Broadway and skirted the edge of Chinatown. Sullivan held his face in the shadows where he couldn't be seen from the street. His fingers were gripped tightly in the rough cloth of his mackinaw.

When they were passing through the dark brick throat of the police garage Sullivan broke.

"Okay," he agreed.

"No," Carver denied him coldly. "Too late. After I book you, I'll try again with someone else. I've got all night."

"Hold on," Sullivan protested, grabbing Carver's arm. "I'll steer you. Square business."

Carver pulled his arm free and finished parking on the oil-darkened concrete. It was an illusion, but the temperature seemed much lower in the garage; maybe because a white ambulance sat like an iceberg in the gloom. Carver switched off the ignition and turned to Sullivan.

"It's funny you don't even care how I'm going to charge you. What's the matter? What're you sweating?"

Sullivan looked at the rows of dark sedans, the empty elevator waiting to climb the five stories to city prison.....

"Give me a pass. I'll put you on to something."

"What?" Carver demanded harshly, coming in the open to bargain hard.

Sullivan paused. His hands worked together compulsively for a moment. His fierce profile and heroic mustache seemed foolish now. In the lines around his eyes, Carver read the message of accumulating fear, fear with deeper roots than this night's roust.

Sullivan began to snitch with humble earnestness, like a salesman who has lost faith in his product. He told Carver about a new meeting place, where the hard-core of the really hip hung out.

"—It's out-of-the-way, and it's kept pretty quiet. The musicians go there to session—after hours—you know?"

When Sullivan said musicians, Carver immediately thought of Cabiness, and he nodded alertly and asked, "Is there action there tonight?"

"Every night. It's the place to be right now. You know?"

"Yes," Carver mused. "How about Cabiness? A head who pretends to blow a horn. Know him?"

"Yeah. Like you know people on the Beach."

"Does he hang out at this place of yours?"

"Maybe. But I don't think I've seen him there. He'll make it though. He makes all the scenes."

"Yes," Carver agreed sourly. He switched on the ignition. "We'll take a look." Under his coat he loosened his service revolver. "No tricks," he warned Sullivan.

This time they went out around North Beach, then, on Sullivan's direction, cut back to Columbus Avenue a few blocks above Fisherman's Wharf. They parked on the dark side of the street. Above the buildings a neon fish blinked against the sky.

"That's it." Sullivan's voice automatically adjusted to a whisper even though there was no one in sight. "On the corner. See the place that looks like a warehouse? The pad's in the basement."

Carver studied the seemingly deserted building, a dark shell of stained concrete, sitting on a corner next to an overgrown vacant lot. It was outside the
spiritual limits of the Beach and he hadn't picked up any rumbles on it, but
he knew everything floated on the Beach, drifting ahead of police surveil-
lance and the crowds of tourists.

"You're too smart to try to burn me, aren't you, Sullivan?"

"It's no burn. There's action in there. You'll find a lot of them holding."

"They think this place is cool?"

"It probably was," Sullivan said without inflection.

"Uh-huh."

Carver leaned forward intently as a couple crossed the street below them.
They merged with the shadow of the building. A moment later a stain of yellow light flushed on the sidewalk, and a faint whiff of steamy music fell
sharply back to silence.

"See?" Sullivan pointed. "It's in the basement."

Carver nodded.

"Can I cut?" Sullivan asked quickly.

"Wait a minute." Carver leaned closer. "What is it? Can't you stand a
pinch?"

Sullivan hesitated, then, "Sure. But who wants to spend a night in the slammer?"

"I don't quite buy that. You split too easy."

Carver paused, studying the sharp bones of Sullivan's cheeks, the drawn
flesh of his neck. Then he asked softly, "You hooked? Maybe you're going to
be sick pretty soon? Is that it?"

"I'm all right."

"Sure you are. You're fine. Here—"

Carver unlocked the glove compartment and felt behind a long flashlight.
He came out with a tightly folded piece of paper, creased into a small plump
envelope, and tossed it into Sullivan's lap.

"That's the stuff I was going to find on you."

Sullivan stared at it. There was a sharp difference in his face, but he didn't
move to pick it up.

Carver continued, grimly now: "You take that over there and be generous
with it. Give away at least half of it. The rest you can keep. But make sure
that if Cabiness is there, he gets some. Give him plenty. Then you'd better get
out. You understand?"

"I can't do that," Sullivan said, and he sounded like a different man; the flip
edge was missing from his voice—it was neutral and weightless. "I'll stink all
over the Beach. I live here."

"That's your problem. Pick it up and get started. And don't chisel! If you do
a good job get in touch with me. Maybe you can earn some more. Is that

clear enough for you? Maybe you won't have to worry about getting sick."

Sullivan had been listening with his head down. His eyes seemed closed. Now he shook himself with a harsh tension as if he were trying to throw off a bad taste. He picked up the packet, dropped it in his pocket, and slipped out of the car without another word.

Carver watched him run across the street against the rain, and for the first time he noticed that Sullivan was wearing tennis shoes. They seemed grotesque on the feet of an aging man.

Addicts! Carver thought savagely. For a moment his small white face was twisted by a fierce aversion that he made no effort to understand—

Then he reached over and turned on the police radio.

chapter two

Lee Cabiness and Boyd Furguson hugged the buildings along Columbus Avenue. It didn't help much because the wind was still and the rain fell straight out of a closed sky. They were Indian-file, Furg leading.

Cabiness had his jacket collar up, but the precaution didn't catch the rain that dripped off his hair and down his back, feeling twice as cold there as it did against his face. Characteristically, he was only half aware of the water down his back, because he was wondering if his horn case leaked, and if it did, would the rain spoil the seat of his pads. New pads were a luxury enjoyed by musicians who took the trouble to work steady. It was considerable trouble to take. But, Cabiness reminded himself, trying to blow a horn full of muffled notes and agile squeals was trouble of a different color. Step right up and pick your trouble. He smiled, putting his interior debate aside. Either the case leaked or it didn't.

It was only 10:30; they'd left the gig early because they'd grown drug with blowing for one drunk (who at the end of each tune re-requested "Red Sails In The Sunset," apparently unable to grasp the obvious conclusion that they had no intention of ever playing "Red Sails In The Sunset") and a pair of lovers, chewing on each other's face in the gloom of the back tables.

Cabiness was still a little high. They'd turned on in the can before they left The Hoof, going with the last joint they had between them. He'd stood for a long time with his face pressed against the cold plaster wall, listening to the distant roar of the toilet flushing, singing something under his breath he vaguely remembered as:

> "The pot, the pot
> The goddam pot
> It's not much,
> But it's all I've got...."

And the song had gone to an accompaniment of brilliant implosions of blistering reds and sulphurous yellows; now it had all faded to a somber blue.

"Where is this place?" he called to Furg.

"Just a few more blocks."

Cabiness grinned. Furg and his discoveries. Furg's idea of a large charge was three teenagers beating on oil-drums in a vacant lot, which might be all right if they could beat in time, which they usually couldn't.

"It'd better be something more than that lame's party you took me to last week," Cabiness shouted.

"It is, Lee-boy. Man, is it ever."

Furg was grinning back at him, his eyes squinched against the rain, a home-ly country grin. Furg was raw and bony, over six-two, with a narrow rusty face and eyes so clear and blue they seemed almost girlish. He had a good grin. It couldn't have changed much since he was a hill kid asking some little chick, "Wanta see my frog?"

So now Lee was going to go look at Furg's frog rather than try to find Jean. If that made sense, the quality eluded him, but he always had a ready pride for his capacity not to make sense.

They came to the end of the block, losing the protection of the slight over-hang; then they went splashing across the street through the long blue reflec-tions of a distant light. Russian Hill rose above them, a black shoulder tat-tooed with the pale yellow of scattered windows.

Cabiness looked up at the tall gray apartment buildings, weathered by the rain into the almost meaningless forms of an abstraction. They seemed life-less and melancholy, structures raised by an alien race, an old tired race los-ing its energy in a slow downward spiral. Cabiness frowned. How could peo-ple live up there in those upholstered cocoons? He despised comfort, com-placency. He wanted to swing.

Across the street he followed Furg around the side of an empty windowed building and down a short flight of steps. They stopped in front of a rusty fire door. Through it they heard the rush of uptempo drums. That sounds tasty, Cabiness thought.

Furg slapped the metal door with the flats of his hands, banging out two perididdles—tatataDum! tatataDum!—and after a moment, creaky and stub-born, the door rolled to the side. Music roared out.

Sullivan stood in the opening, his mustache barred beneath his big nose. His lips flexed briefly in a cool greeting.

"Hey there, old Sully," Furg said. "What's happening?"

"Plenty. Make it." Sullivan stood aside to let them in. Jeezus, he looks sick, Cabiness thought, as he stepped into the concrete room. He caught an instant impression of smoke and shiny faces. Then he really heard the music and dug his elbow into Furg's side. "These cats are honkers," he said mockingly.

A huge spade tenor player was blasting B-flats off the low ceiling; he was so big his tenor seemed the size of an alto, and his face was screwed up in a manner that made it appear that he was eating the instrument rather than playing it. The entire rhythm section was one skinny kid with half a set of drums, but he cracked them like cannon. A trumpet player stood to the side, fiddling with his valves, waiting his turn. Sweat glistened on their faces, dark glasses flashed.

"Yas, Lawd!" Furg mimicked, throwing his hands up like a hill preacher. "That's A-men music."

"I'm not going to blow," Cabiness said. "Not with honkers."

"You guys want a taste?" Sullivan asked quietly behind them.

Cabiness turned in surprise. "When did you start dealing?"

Sullivan shrugged, looking at the floor. "I've got a little extra."

"The writing's not doing much, huh?"

"It hasn't budged. How about it? You want a hit?"

"What you got?" Furg asked.

"Good stuff. *Schmeck.* "

"No, man," Furg shook his head rapidly. "That's too rich for my poor country blood."

"I'll trust you," Sullivan said automatically. His voice seemed numb and mechanical, and Cabiness shifted uneasily.

Furg grinned and slapped Sullivan on the arm. "In that case, let's step out back and try yore wares."

"Come on, Lee," Sullivan offered.

"I don't think so. I can't cut heavy. I'm going to see if I can find some pot."

"Why don't you try this?" Sullivan urged, patting his pocket.

"No thanks. I know what I want."

Sullivan shuffled a little, and then, with a peculiarly joyless expression, he said, "You're lucky."

"Hold my axe, will you, Lee-Boy?"

He took Furg's trombone and watched them shove through the crowd, heading for a far door. Okay, Furg, you dumb Kentucky bastard, have a ball. He turned back to the party.

Whoever was paying the rent on the basement—if anyone was—hadn't done much more than rig up a light, a naked hundred-and-fifty watt bulb strung over a pipe, and set up some makeshift furniture. The cement walls were dirty and water-stained, and up near the ceiling someone had scrawled the motto: BIRD LIVES!

It was in black letters, dashed on with a big brush, and celebrated the resurrection of Charlie Parker, the first Beat Saint.

Someone else with a red crayon had contributed: SCOWL! YOWL! HOWL! BOWEL!

Probably derived from Ginsberg's *Howl*. His place in the hagiology hadn't been computed since he had the misfortune to be alive.

At one end of the room a dismantled furnace lay on its side, with vent pipes stacked up around it like the skeleton of a teepee.

There were over thirty people pressed together in the room. Cabiness saw the same people he was always seeing, those who made a point of being on the inside hub: fellow musicians too cool to join the honking contest; painters; a near-famous poet; and half the cast of one of the current little-theatre hits, out of costume, but still made up; as well as a good scattering of just talkers and hangers-on, and probably an occasional office girl or young accountant from the Shell Oil Company, nervously waiting for the orgy to start and meanwhile straining to maintain a supercilious smile.

A man named Harvey seemed to be acting host. He wore a shapeless suit coat and a beret. His beard was three weeks gone in a thin curl around the edge of his jaw, and his face looked wet and soft. He handed Lee a glass of wine and smiled loosely.

"That's good wino music, huh? Ain't that good wino music?"

When Cabiness didn't answer, Harvey grabbed his arm and shook it clumsily. "Ain't that good wino music?"

Cabiness smiled and said, "Sure."

"Damn rights! You goddam rights!" Harvey nodded proudly, his eyes squeezed almost shut. Then he wandered off, leaning to the side.

The wine was thin and tart. Cabiness sipped it, listening to the tenorman wind up with a piercing squeal way off the top of the horn. Probably a G-Sharp. The guy must have a jaw like a vise. The musician snatched the saxophone out of his mouth, giving everyone a big smile like Louis always did.

Cabiness found himself smiling back, but the crowd barely acknowledged the end of the tune. It was hard to move a Beach audience. They were always careful to under-react. No one wanted to be caught digging the wrong thing, and it wasn't always too clear which was which.

He circled the outside of the room looking for Jean, but she wasn't there. Some slob got in the sugar bowl. For a moment he thought of making a stronger claim on Jean, moving in with her, or the other way around, but he wasn't sure it wouldn't get sticky. He liked Jean and it would be a bad scene to be drug with her.

He started talking to an orange-haired girl named BeeGee, and out of the corner of his eye, he watched an over-dressed blonde, who seemed to be watching him. BeeGee had a tired white complexion and intense green eyes. She played piano sometimes and could swing like a man.

"You working?" she wanted to know.

"Just on the weekends," he told her. "At The Hoof."

"I'll have to pick up on you," she said, crossing her thin arms on her flat chest.

"We're not getting much down. It's just Furg and me, and whatever rhythm drops in. We're the only ones who make any bread, and we're supposed to keep quiet about it."

"I know," she said scornfully. "The suckers. They think you're supposed to be happy to play for nothing, while they charge double for that piss they call beer."

Cabiness grinned at her anger. She didn't look like much, but she was a down chick. He put his hand on her shoulder.

"You want to make it tonight?"

"Oh, I don't know," she said. "I'm kinda off men for a while."

"Well, we could turn on and play some sides?"

She grinned. "In that barn of yours?"

"It keeps the rain out."

"Just barely. I don't think so, Lee. If I go up there we'll end up making it, and I don't really want to. I got another thing going."

"Okay," he agreed easily, but he was still conscious of disappointment. BeeGee suddenly looked better. He remembered her boy's butt and thin legs, how she shook with her own intensity.

He looked back to where the blonde had been, but she was gone. She would have been too much trouble anyway. He talked idly with BeeGee until Furg came back.

He was full of excitement. He picked Cabiness' glass out of his hand and gulped from it.

"Hi, BeeGee," he said in a quick aside; then to Cabiness, "Come on, we've got some action."

"Good. What happened with Sully?"

"Later. Come on, and try to watch your lousy manners, because this is special."

BeeGee grinned and said, "Easy."

Across the room, two girls were sitting on a green park bench, probably lifted from Neurotic Park up on Columbus Ave. They made an alien island against the wall. It wasn't only that they were expensively dressed, but the instinctive habit of their faces belonged to a different part of town—Seacliff or the Marina, money and manners.

One was dark and severe looking, handsome more than pretty, and the other was the blonde he'd been watching. Her hair was smoothly worked and fashionably tinted. She wore a low-necked black cocktail dress and was playing with a decorative umbrella, delicate as a wand, the sort of thing that sold for seventy-five dollars in The City of Paris. He thought she was a toy, and it wasn't until she stood, in response to Furg's clumsy introduction, that he caught the flash of intelligence in her deep blue eyes. Wise eyes, marred with a faint hint of aggression. Maybe a little too direct and watching.

Clair Hubbler, Furg called her.

"*Hu*-bler," she corrected automatically. "How are you, Cabiness? I wanted to meet you."

He shook her small firm hand and listened to the other woman's name—Carla Saunders—and acknowledged her brief nod. She remained sitting.

Furg was a boob. He obviously thought they were going to make it with these two, and these kids just as obviously made it with each other.

"Did Furguson tell you what we want?" Clair Hubler asked.

"No, he told me what you didn't want."

That puzzled her. A faint angry line appeared briefly on her smooth fore-head. "Could you just take it straight for a moment? I think it will be worth your while."

"All right," he agreed. "What do you really want?"

He could have been pleasant, but this time disappointment made him sour. He'd run into so many dykes lately, it was either a lousy average, or a sinister symptom. Furg was sending him anxious signals, and Carla Saunders watched him out of a somber arctic face, marking one more arrogant male for potential humiliation.

"Do you—hire out?" Clair Hubler asked delicately.

"You mean, do I get paid?"

"Yes, of course."

"Sometimes. I'm not prejudiced against it."

"Good," she said firmly, as if they had just decided something. "We'd like you to play at a private party. Both of you."

"Why us?" he asked quietly, simply because he wanted to know.

"They dug us at The Hoof," Furg put in.

"Yes," Clair added briskly. "We were quite impressed with your conception, and when we saw you here, we decided to ask you to play for us." She smiled. "I'm impulsive sometimes."

The word "conception" hit Cabiness wrong. He suspected the words connected to music. He suspected the people who used them so fluently. What did they think they were saying?

She read his hesitation instantly. Her expression altered subtly, and sex came flooding up like a bright glaze. It was quite pretty on her face, and he forgot what it was covering.

"I don't mean to irritate you," she said. "Perhaps I didn't ask the right way. I don't know. But I sincerely would like you to play for us… it wouldn't be anything formal. Just like you were playing in that club."

Well, that did it. He couldn't refuse a job that wasn't outright mickey-mouse. Not as broke as he was. To say nothing of how broke Furg was. But he discounted the other suggestion that danced obliquely in her eyes. Apparently she was used to getting her way, one way or another, but the black-haired bull glaring beside her looked like a major obstacle, and anyway he didn't like the smell of patronage they both gave off. The girl was the kind who described things as "interesting" or "amusing," and he had a hunch that the chance to interest or amuse her would be more work than fun.

"Can we make a deal?" she asked.

"I don't see why not."

"Good," she said with what looked like honest enthusiasm. "That's wonderful."

Furg grinned and sat down on the bench beside Carla Saunders. He must have thought this was the one he was going to get, because he put his big raw hand on her knee. She jerked away with a muffled expression of disgust.

And just then a girl screamed.

At first Cabiness thought it was in response to the hoarse moaning of the tenor. Then he was caught in an ugly beat of silence. The drum faltered. A man swore. The metal door rattled violently, and an amplified voice dominated the room:

"Stay where you are. *Don't anyone move!*"

A small man in a black suit stood in the doorway using a portable loud-hailer. Two large men stood behind him. Carver. Cabiness' stomach turned over.

"Oh, Christ," Furg mumbled dismally. "Wouldn't you know it."

Clair Hubler grabbed Cabiness by the arm. "What is this?"

"Vice raid."

"Vice? What vice?"

"Dope."

Her face went white, and she tugged aimlessly at the front of her dress. Carla Saunders had jumped to her feet, and she was glaring angrily at the vice cops as they moved into the room. Their commands snapped over an angry murmur.

"Furg!" Cabiness whispered urgently. "Are you holding that crap from Sully?"

Furg was fumbling through his pockets, staring at Carver. He didn't seem to know what he was doing.

"Dump! Get rid of that stuff."

The single light went out. The darkness staggered everyone for a moment. Then there was a rush of hidden motion.

"Freeze!" Carver's amplified voice blurred in its own echoes.

Flashlights lashed out, rushing briefly over frightened and angry faces, to spot the two entrances with their combined light. Both doors were already blocked by cops with drawn guns. No one was getting out.

At least I'm clean, Cabiness told himself. Something brushed him roughly in the darkness. He heard the tall woman say something in a low voice. Then he was aware of Clair's hand clutching his arm again. It amused him. Her self-sufficiency had seemed so complete.

The moment of shock passed quickly, and from the sounds almost everyone seemed to be waiting quietly. Except the vice squad. They were charging around trying to get the lights on, and somewhere a girl was crying. Not loud; the low sobbing of shame. Cabiness winced angrily. What a lousy drag.

Someone succeeded in tracing the plug. The light came on, and everyone had moved back along the walls. He saw the big tenor player, with his saxophone dangling across his front like a golden zigzag. His dark face was glum, his lips fixed in a meaningless smile.

Cabiness glanced at Clair Hubler. She smiled nervously, making an effort to re-establish her composure. She released his arm, running her hand up to do something to her hair.

"Does this happen all the time?" she asked brightly.

"No, but too often lately."

He was on the point of making some complaint against Carver, when he noticed Furg was gone. At first he thought he might have moved to some other part of the room, but a quick glance disproved that. Furg's head would have stuck up.

"Do you know what happened to Furguson?" he asked. Clair looked blank.

"No, where'd he go?"

"Beats me."

The vice squad was busy lining everyone up facing the wall. Carver roamed back and forth, snapping mad. Even after everyone had obeyed he continued to shout, "Face the wall," monotonous as the single cry of an angry bird. Cabiness knew Carver hadn't seen him yet. When he did there'd be some crap.

He stared at the dirty concrete, watching the fingers of rust streaked on a broken water pipe. He tried to think that Furg had slipped through one of the doors before the flashlights had flooded them. Not too much chance. The cops knew what they were about. Give them that.

He could hear the noise of a shakedown starting. "Turn around. Get your hands up. Spread your legs." They were going through with it even though the moment of darkness had given anyone who needed it the time to get clean. The time to get rid of whatever they had—horse, pot, bennies, red-birds, yellow jackets, Christmas trees, perrys, dexies, or rainbows—any of the dozens of drugs on the growing palette of illegal stimulation. Time to throw it on the neutral floor where it could belong to anyone—or no one. That's why Carver was burnt. He was going to come up with an empty net.

Following his line of thought, Cabiness checked the floor around his feet. His boredom blew out in a flash of panic. Six inches from his canvas shoe was a roll of joints held with a rubber band. They'd been crumpled and dropped. Instinctively he edged away a few more inches, but it was no good. They were standing facing the park bench; if he could kick them under the bench, there was a chance they would go unnoticed. But if he was seen kicking them.

He looked around. Carver was watching. Not him. Just watching for some-one to point themselves out for special attention.

He'd had it. Carver would bury him so deep they'd have to pipe in daylight. He found himself remembering the last time the Narco had picked him up and how his stubborn pride has caused him to make a dangerous and resourceful enemy.

Carver had snatched him up on Grant Avenue in broad daylight for no rea-son that Cabiness could ever figure, except that he just happened to be in the wrong place at the wrong time. If you were on the Beach and you weren't obviously a tourist, you could be in trouble any time the Narco saw you. And if you were a hardhead, as Cabiness admitted he was, you could make a little trouble go a long way.

He'd been on his way to Jean's, his mind, for once, quiet and empty as summer sky, when he sensed the dark sedan sliding along the curb beside him. Instinctively he glanced at the driver and met Carver's eyes. Hot dog, he thought, and went on walking until he heard the siren, turning so slowly it sounded like a groan. He shrugged and walked to the side of the car.

"What's your hurry, Cabiness?"

"Sorry, I don't have time to talk to fans."

Carver smiled: "From what I hear your fans don't talk anyway, they just make odd noises, that is when they're not on the nod."

"Yeah, they're awful," Cabiness said quietly. "Well, what's it going to be?"

"You holding?"

"Not likely."

"I hear different."

"All right, you hear different. What's it going to be?"

"You'd better get in."

"Is this an arrest?"

"Not yet." Carver leaned over and opened the door. "Get in. We'll talk about it."

They drove in silence, ending at the Embarcadero, where Carver parked alongside the frayed heads of the great pilings. At the nearest pier, a stained white ship named *The Kyper* was loading drums of tallow. Carver got out and went to look down at the water. In a moment Cabiness joined him. Below them floated the remains of someone's lunch—a torn paper bag and wads of wax paper, surrounded by a planetary system of orange peel.

"Crummy bastards have no respect for their city," Carver said.

Cabiness grunted. A breeze stirred his hair and he found the smell of salt and oil vaguely exciting. He wished the Narco would get on with it.

Carver, however, was taking his own time. "You people are like that," he said. "You louse up whatever you get near. You take and you never put anything back. North Beach used to be a nice Italian neighborhood. Now look at it. A girl goes down there at 16 and by 18 she's a veteran whore with a habit a mile long. But I don't suppose that means anything to you."

"It might," Cabiness said. "It would depend on the girl. Some girls manage to be whores in Columbus, Ohio, and, from what I hear, they even get habits there. What's all this got to do with me?"

"That's what I want to know."

Cabiness remained silent.

"I hear you're The Man." Carver prodded.

"Someone's putting you on."

"You stand a shakedown?"

Cabiness lifted his arms. "See for yourself."

"You make it too easy," Carver said. "Let's try it down at the squad room where I can give you the attention you deserve."

Cabiness lowered his arms and stood looking at Carver, making no effort to disguise his feelings.

"Come on, move," Carver snapped. "This isn't funny any longer." Then Narco stepped back and placed his fingers inside his coat, obviously intending to emphasize the reality of the gun hidden in its blind of special tailoring; unconsciously, he fell into the classic pose associated with Napoleon. Cabiness smiled bitterly and re-entered the car.

Ugly stories filtered out of the Narco Squad Room, and Cabiness, not without some surprise, admitted he was afraid. I don't know why I go to these parties, he told himself with rueful sarcasm, I never have any fun.

The squad room was quiet. A thin gray-haired cop, standing at the front counter, was writing a report. He glanced at Cabiness, then Carver, and looked away. His expression was sour.

Inside there was one other person. A kid in sport clothes sat tilted back in a swivel chair with his gray bucks crossed on the desk. His hair was long and combed into a glossy duck's-butt, and he wore a heavy mustache in the style called Viva Zapata, because it resembled the mustache worn by Marlon Brando in his role as Zapata, the Mexican revolutionary.

Cabiness had difficulty realizing that this kid must be a cop. He looked like a Mission District punk, he even gave off the same spiritual smell, and it was easy to imagine that if he hadn't become a cop he would be just exactly the kind of person he was taking such trouble to imitate. He spoke to Carver.

"What's shaking, Daddy-O? You catch yourself some poor grasshopper?"

"Save it," Carver said sharply. "And I still haven't seen a report on that Haight Street connection."

"Yes sir," the undercover agent said mildly, but he still didn't move his feet.

Carver took Cabiness into a question room. It was nothing but a plywood booth, windowless, bare-walled. A heavy wooden table almost filled it, and four mismatched chairs sat as they'd been left by the last people to use them.

"Let me see your arms," Carver said.

Cabiness rolled his sleeves up and looked away when he felt the Narco's moist fingers on his flesh.

When Carver was satisfied that Cabiness' veins were unscarred, he asked, "You don't skin-pop, do you?"

"No," Cabiness said.

"You turn on some way," Carver said with certainty. "You're not kidding me. Strip down."

"What?"

"Take your clothes off. And I mean everything. Bare-assed."

Cabiness struggled over each button, fighting the impulse to tell the Narco to shove it and take whatever the consequences might be, because having his head whipped on seemed an easier thing to endure than the systematic humiliation Carver was imposing.

Loosen up, you stubborn bastard, Cabiness told himself. You can't let this creep see he's getting to you. That's probably how he gets his kicks.

Cabiness managed to undress quickly, folding his clothes neatly on a chair. Carver handled him as if he were livestock, going over his legs from his ankles to the insides of his thighs, examining his feet and neck. He even had Cabiness stick his tongue out and curl it back towards his nose so he could examine the hidden veins at the base. He even poked around in Cabiness' mouth with the eraser end of a wooden pencil, while Cabiness looked at the ceiling and forced himself to stand quietly.

Carver finished with the pencil and wiped it carefully with his handkerchief. He slipped the pencil into his inside breast pocket and said, "Bend over and spread your cheeks."

"What?"

"Bend over. Turn around and bend over."

Cabiness obeyed, bending from the waist, automatically he grabbed his ankles.

"Spread the cheeks of your ass," Carver instructed. "Come on, I said spread them. Don't worry, you don't appeal to me."

Carver started laughing, an odd little laugh that came in short bursts with long pauses between them. Cabiness listened uneasily. Then he felt the Narco's finger prodding the rim of his anal sphincter.

"A bath wouldn't hurt you," Carver said.

"You *are* still looking for needle tracks, aren't you?" Cabiness asked. He felt the sweat turning cold in his armpits.

Carver started pushing in with his finger. "Smart users wouldn't shoot anyplace else," he said. "That is, until they collapse the veins in there and are forced to use something else. You might just be that smart, Cabiness—" Carver pushed sharply. "—You don't act it, but that might be your shuck."

Carver started chuckling, his finger still busy. "You hear about the guy who was getting his prostate massage when he just happened to notice that the doctor had *both* hands on his shoulders."

Carver pulled his finger free and went to wash his hands. He was still laughing at his own joke.

Cabiness straightened up. "Is that it?" he asked, indicating his clothes.

Carver stopped laughing and the amusement drained out of his face. "I'll tell you when to get dressed," he said. He studied Cabiness for a moment, shaking his head. "I didn't figure you for a grasshopper. I knew you were going some route, but I didn't think a high-school kick like pot would move you. Who's your connection? Baby Calderon? Neal Flannery? What about Chilene up on 16th and Mission?"

He had bought pot from Neal Flannery, and he hoped his involuntary start of fear at Carver's accurate guess hadn't betrayed itself through the impassive expression he was trying to maintain.

Carver sat down in one of the chairs and was silent for a few moments. He squeezed the end of his nose as if that helped him concentrate. Then he turned back to Cabiness.

"I want you to get something straight. I'm going to bust you. I don't much care what for, but I'm going to bust you for something. It may take a week. It may take a month. It may take six months. But one of these days I'm going to find you wrong, and when I do I'm going to bury you, unless—"

Carver paused, letting the "unless" dangle. He took out his handkerchief and wiped his palms.

"—unless you co-operate with me and help me clean up that cesspool you live in. You're a big man on The Beach, aren't you? They trust you, respect you, tell you their secrets. With that kind of pipeline, I could have that whole area cleaned out in a few months. Don't bother to look so grim and noble. Any decent citizen would be glad to do what I'm asking you to do. Do you know that we've had dozens of people, both men and women, volunteer to go into North Beach as undercover agents to help us break up the narcotics rings and the sex orgies—"

Cabiness smiled. "Imagine some pure citizen making such a sacrifice—an undercover agent at a sex orgy. A sense of civic responsibility like that makes you think."

"It should make you ashamed," Carver said grimly. "It should really make you ashamed. But you're going to help out whether you want to or not."

"No, I don't think so," Cabiness said deliberately. "If I wanted to be a goddam bull, I'd be one, and I'd get paid for it. And I'd wear a uniform so anyone who just itched to make trouble for a cop could find me without looking too hard. And I wouldn't go easing around pretending I was something other than what I was, and I wouldn't—"

"That's enough! That's just about enough! Now look, boy, I'm not *asking* you. I'm *telling* you and you'd better—"

"I can't seem to hear you, man. Talk louder."

"All right," Carver said, breathing hard. "All right, if that's the way you want to play it."

"I'm no goddam snitch," Cabiness said. "I never have been, and I'm not likely to start. And you sure as hell aren't going to turn me out. Particularly *you*. You stink just about as bad as anyone I ever ran into, and, personally, I'd rather—"

Carver slapped him.

Cabiness put his hand to the side of his face, not because he was hurt, but because the feeble, awkward and, somehow, petulant blow surprised him. He smiled. Then, watching Carver's eyes, he gradually stopped smiling.

All right, big mouth, he asked himself, how much trouble do you think you bought this time?

He got part of his answer half an hour later when Carver booked him for vagrancy. It was as much as the Narco could do for the moment. It was pretty good. A municipal judge found him guilty of the charge and sentenced him to thirty days in the city prison.

Now, standing inches from the bundle of sticks someone had thrown away, Cabiness remembered the pale glossy set to Carver's face as he told him off, he remembered what he'd seen, floating free for an unguarded moment, in the cop's depthless eyes. A hatred so intense he couldn't understand it. Why me? he sometimes asked. He didn't know the answer.

He called softly to Clair Hubler, indicating the bundle on the floor. She located it and looked back with a mild question in her eyes.

"Be ready to kick it under the bench," he whispered, "I'll cover you."

"What is it?" she asked, whispering herself.

"Pot—marijuana."

"Oh," she said softly, understanding.

"Kick it under the bench," he insisted. "As soon as I move."

He was going to do something to deflect Carver's attention, and without waiting any longer, he turned and stepped out in such a way as to place himself directly in front of her. Alerted by the motion, Carver pivoted. His lips thinned.

"Get back there, and face the wall."

Woodenly Cabiness turned around. His gut rippled when he saw the pot still in the same place. He adjusted his steps so he stopped with his foot on it.

"I'm sorry," Clair whispered. Her eyes were vague, and that single change made her look like a helpless ball of fluff.

"Shut up," he said dully. He sensed Carver directly behind him like a six-inch circle of cold in the middle of his back. For several moments he stood anxiously, aware of the lump under his foot as if one foot were inches higher than the other, propped up on a fused stick of dynamite. Dynamite was nothing. It would only blow his leg off. His armpits were wet, and the insides of his palms slick with tension.

Then behind him he heard Carver say, "Stampher, shake this guy till he rattles."

"All right, turn around." Cabiness didn't move.

Stampher was a big young cop in sports clothes, with a solid white face and pale blue eyes. His lips looked wet. He asked Carver. "Is he special?"

Carver grunted. He was looking at Clair Hubler. "What are you doing here, miss?"

Clair smiled demurely, still with the same baby-stare. "We're just here to see the sights. We're seeing more than we bargained for."

"I told you to turn around," Stampher said.

He pivoted carefully on the foot that covered the pot. Carver was looking at Clair's billfold as she brought out identification. His manner had changed. She didn't bear the markings of his accustomed quarry.

Cabiness avoided Stampher's eyes, while he felt the cop's hands on him. He was thorough, patting the seams of his pants and jacket.

"Empty your pockets."

He had a door key, half a pack of cigarettes, book matches given away by someone named Stuart who was running for councilman, a note from Furg he'd found pinned to his door three days ago (on the back of it he'd jotted down the chords to "You Stepped Out of a Dream"), eighty-seven cents in change, and a wallet flattened and curved to his rump. Stampher seized on the wallet. Going through it he came up with a pawn ticket.

"What's this?"

"My clarinet."

"*Your* clarinet?"

"Yes, my clarinet."

"Why'd you hock it?"

Cabiness shrugged: "Why do people hock things? I needed the money."

"How are you going to make any money if you hock your instrument?"

"I don't blow it. I haven't used it since I quit going with bands."

"Yeah?" Stampher made it nasty. "What bands did you ever play with?"

"What the hell, man. You wouldn't know one band from another."

"Try me."

"Joe Elastic and his rubber band."

"Take your coat off and roll up your sleeves."

Cabiness stripped off his jacket, and started to dump it on the park bench, but Clair reached over and took it, folding it on her arm. Carver's eyes flickered with surprise.

The room was emptying. A man and a girl were being held. He was smiling numbly, but she was looking at the floor, biting her lip. The kid was tearing down his drums. Above him Bird still lived.

Stampher found a small white scar on the inside of his arm. An old puncture. "What this?" he demanded.

"Blood donation."

Stampher winced, moving his wet mouth in disgust. "Can't you do better than that?"

Carver stepped back. "What've you got?"

"He's been donating blood to the Red Cross," Stampher said with heavy sarcasm.

Carver nodded bleakly: "The Red Cross must have half the blood in North Beach."

"I didn't give it to the goddam Red Cross," Cabiness said angrily. "It was a private donation, and you know goddam well that one scar doesn't mean a thing."

There was silence for a moment. Then Stampher said reluctantly, "He's clean."

"You sure?"

"He's clean, sir."

Carver dismissed Stampher, and the young cop moved on. Carver turned back to Clair and Carla. "You can go," he told them. He went on to give them a little lecture. Cabiness took his jacket back. When he put it on, he subtly exaggerated the necessary motions, and at the same time he lifted his foot carefully and kicked backward. The bundle of joints slid away on the traction of his rubber sole. He turned around to pick up Furg's horn. The pot was out of sight.

Suddenly he realized that he was going to make it out of here. Involuntarily he took a deep breath.

Carla was walking to the door, but Clair was standing, fooling with her umbrella.

"You'd better go," Carver said.

"I'm with him," she said.

Carver looked sour, but he jerked his head at Cabiness. "Move on."

But before he'd taken a half a dozen steps, he heard "Cabiness!" and turned to see the little cop motioning him back. For a moment he thought the pot had been discovered, but Carver just smiled, a tight shrunken smile, humorless as the grin of a cat.

"Maybe next time, huh, Cabiness? You know I'm not a hot-shot musician or anything like that, but I take a certain pride in my work. I like to think I win the big ones." He touched his temple. "And you bother me. You've been up to bat for a long time. I keep wondering when you're going to strike out. You know, I've got a file down at the division with your name on it. Later on tonight I'll write in there that you were caught in a raid where narcotics were found. If a file like that gets too big, I like to be able to tell the captain something, even if it's only that you left town—"

Carver watched him blandly, still smiling. Then his face went dead. "Cut out before I book you for vagrancy."

The girls were waiting outside. The rain had stopped and the first of the morning's fog was a quiet mist in the street. Another cop sat in a police sedan at the curb. The trumpet player was heading up toward Russian Hill with his horn under his arm. Sullivan was leaning on a telephone pole across the street. Cabiness called to him, but he turned and walked away.

Carla was a few feet from Clair. From her expression some quick words had been exchanged, but Cabiness didn't give a damn now. The encounter with Carver had left him shaky, and he was worried about Furg. It was just luck that Carver hadn't asked him why he was carrying two horns.

Clair had lost her air of fuzziness. She suggested they go somewhere, have some coffee, and fix the details, so he suggested the Coffee House. Clair had her car around the corner, a big square imported job of some obscure make. Beloita. Cabiness had never heard of it. He held the door for her and looked at her ankles, smaller than his wrists. The back of her neck seemed fragile. He caught the unhappy fixed face of Carla Saunders in the shadows and went to sit in the back.

"How'd you happen to find that place?" he asked.

Clair answered: "We followed the crowd over from that club you play in." She paused, turning a corner; then, "Quite an experience."

Cabiness cut off a sarcastic reply.

Apparently they'd never made the Coffee House before. They looked over the beat-up old tables and the second- and third-rate paintings, brushed past the near-pornographic photography, and decided it was all interesting.

Cabiness didn't pay much attention to them. Jean was sitting in back, drinking a cup of tea, talking to Leon, the night counterman. He enjoyed looking at her when she didn't know it. Then he saw her free of her reactions to himself—as a new girl for a moment—enjoying her tall solid body, her long straight back, and pillow breasts. Her heavy red hair was loose around her shoulders, and her round white arms were bare in a sleeveless blouse. Even across the room he could see the pale disc of her vaccination. He smiled thinking of the flaw Michelangelo had made in the statue of Moses.

From the way Jean was moving her head, she was angry about something, running it down to Leon, and Leon leaned on the counter, his heavy quiet face absorbing everything and never showing anything.

But when she saw Cabiness coming up behind her, she instantly smiled, her dark eyes tilting up, and reached for his hand. "Hey, man, where you been? I thought I'd missed out."

Her wide mouth still carried some of the lipstick she wore at work, part of her cocktail waitress' costume. It made her look different, faintly gilded and unnatural.

"I was by after two. You weren't home."

"I know," she admitted. "There was a hang-up at work. What've you been doing?"

"Furg and I went on an expedition. Ran into Carver. Among other things—"

Her face clouded and she started to say something, but then she caught sight of Clair and Carla. She was grave during the brief introductions, and Cabiness thought, Jean could outclass these two in all departments.

Clair remarked: "I like the way you do your hair."

And Jean replied, "I don't do anything to it except brush it. Is that what you mean?"

"It looks so natural," Clair said with an ambiguous undertone.

"Coffee all around?" Cabiness asked.

Carla nodded stiffly. Clair said, "Let me look," and followed him to the counter. The Coffee House wasn't cheap. The prices bristled for people just like Clair. She looked over the imported goodies, deciding on a pastrami sandwich. She sat down while Cabiness watched Leon put the sandwich together. He pulled the eighty-seven cents out of his pocket and looked at it. He didn't need to get his wallet out. He knew there was nothing in it. Thoughtless bitch.

"A dollar-twelve," Leon said.

Cabiness turned: "Jeanie, do you have four bits."

"Sure, Lee," and she reached for her purse.

Clair got a funny, half-embarrassed look on her face, and said, "Oh, let me."

But he scowled and took Jean's dollar bill. After he paid Leon, he shook the balance of the change in his hand for a moment; then dumped it in his jacket pocket. Rolls and instant coffee in the morning.

Talk faltered. Carla sat like a wooden Indian, staring at a platter of cold cuts behind the glass of the display case. Clair tapped on her cup with pink fingernails, and nibbled at her sandwich. Her eyes were oblique. Cabiness exchanged wry glances with Jean. At the next table he could hear two old German men discussing Nietzsche in heavy accents. Old slew-foot Nietzsche. Bombed out of his gourd by the nowhereness of it all.

He tried to turn the conversation back to the gig, but Clair went vague again—her best trick, it seemed—and there were some things she was still undecided about. Where could she reach him? Didn't he have a phone? He was lucky to have an address. He watched while Clair copied it into a small, red leather notebook. He went right below someone named "Cookie."

He yawned and asked Jean if she wanted to go home. She nodded firmly. "Let's."

Clair looked quickly from one to the other, and asked, "Do you have far to go? We can run you by."

Cabiness was on the point of refusing, but Jean smiled: "That's very sweet of you."

They drove down to Broadway in silence.

chapter three

Jean Diamanto unlocked her room, frowning critically at the stale unaired smell. The place was too small to cook in, but the decision to do something about it was smothered in the weight of a dozen previous postponements.

She left the door ajar. Her light cast a bright sliver on the floor of the dark hall. Lee was downstairs. Still talking to the Lily Maid. She'd called him back for a last private word. Coy bitch. She was really trying to burn the candle at both ends—literally, figuratively, symbolically, and the hell with it—

Jean shrugged away a twinge of uneasiness. She washed her face, brushed her hair out and tied it into a pony tail. She was still at the sink when Lee came in. He stacked the horn cases inside the door, and asked, "What'd you think of that?"

"She's lovely."

"No, the car."

"Well, it's conspicuous."

She smiled over her shoulder and saw the light shiny on the hard angles of his cheekbones as he bent to kiss her neck. A quick kiss of habit. How long had it been. Only six months?

In spite of herself Jean asked, "What else did she want?"

In the mirror she caught the white beat of Lee's familiar grin, splitting his thin intense face. "She just wants to play games."

"I'm hip. She offers a fair field for the encounter."

"Too cramped."

She went on fixing her hair, taking more time over it than she ordinarily would have. In a moment she heard the bedsprings creak.

"Why so brittle?" he asked.

She chose to misunderstand him. "I just asked what she wanted. What's brittle about that?"

"She wanted to know if I needed an advance."

"Oh," she said softly. "And?"

"I told her no."

"That was foolish. Still I'm glad you did."

"I dug it myself."

She turned and smiled fondly. He was such a collection of sharp angles. Long bony arms and legs with big hands and feet. He had a full, almost Latin mouth, light hazel eyes, and his short hair was beginning to go out a little at the temples. It was a hard, knowing face but with surprising shifts of immaturity that caught her unaware and squeezed her heart.

She walked over to the bed and put a kiss in the hollow of his temple. His hand went to her hair.

"Hang on," she whispered against his cheek. "I'll make some sandwiches."

"You don't have to *always* stuff food into me."

"I like to. It makes me feel feminine."

He smiled dryly. "For feminine read motherly. If you were any more feminine, you'd be illegal."

"Did you eat dinner?" she asked bluntly.

"No—"

"All right then."

Her kitchen was smaller than a good-sized closet, a shallow dent in the wall packed with an old bent-legged hot plate and a square refrigerator with a coil on the top. She lit the hot plate, then stepped out to ask Lee if he wanted coffee.

"No, milk," he said quietly, without looking up. He was holding one of his shoes. She glanced at it and saw that the canvas top was beginning to pull away from the heel.

"Don't worry," she said on impulse. "I've got some money."

"What?"

"I said I've got some money. I picked up a lot in tips tonight."

His eyes slanted up at her from beneath his dark brows, and she knew she'd made a mistake. Sometimes his face was almost grim, the lines in his cheeks like the scars of tension.

"That's your money," he said flatly.

"Ours," she countered.

His eyes drifted away from hers. He said carefully, "Strictly speaking there is no 'ours.' I already owe you too much and you earn it too hard."

"Carrying highballs on a little tray? It's killing me."

"Don't try to snow me, Jeanie. I know what you put up with in that hole. I've played in enough of them. What were you bitching to Leon about?"

"Oh, that. Nothing really. Some clown who came on stronger than usual."

"What clown?" he asked pointedly.

She gestured aimlessly, wishing she hadn't mentioned it. "You don't know him. Anyway he didn't get out of line. Just persistent."

"What's his name?"

"You're a little persistent yourself. All right. John Randozza. Does that mean anything to you? He's some kind of wheel among the Italian boys. He's got big white teeth, curly hair, and he can't understand why I don't quiver when he smiles at me."

For that matter she didn't understand it herself. Randozza was a big graceful man with quiet good manners. Well, she was just all bitched up behind Lee. She knew he occasionally balled other chicks on the side, but he was the only one who could turn her on.

Lee was grinning at her satirical tone. "I didn't mean to bug you. I forget how capable you are. A good fast middleweight."

She chuckled and slapped her solid hip in response to the routine joke. But for some reason she found herself comparing her own heavy body to Clair Hubler's slender elegance. Why was it so important Lee play at her party? Lee was a good sax man, but Jean wasn't convinced Clair Hubler knew it. Lee's advanced style puzzled more people than it pleased. She had the sure instinct that the girl would pitch at Lee in some way.

She made peanut-butter sandwiches and poured milk into old jam jars. She gave Lee two sandwiches and kept one for herself.

"Peanut butter is all I had."

"Peanner butter is elegant," he said, mimicking *Pogo*.

They ate comfortably, talking idly. Then Lee started describing the raid, and her growing sense of disturbance came on her again.

"I'd like to break that hillbilly's neck," she said.

"It wasn't Furg's fault. That can happen anywhere on the Beach, and you know it. Carver and his buddies are going to push it to the point where there won't be anyone down here but snitches, tourists and undercover vice cops. The snitches will rat on each other, the vice cops will go around trying to get the tourists to buy some pot so they can bust them, and the tourists will be thrilled to their socks thinking they've seen a real, hope-to-die dope fiend. Meanwhile all the swingers will have taken off for Venice or the Apple. Somewhere where there's a little privacy." He paused, then added, "'Carver told me to get out of town."

"Oh," she said in sudden dismay.

"Don't worry. I'm not going."

Reluctantly she murmured, "Maybe you should."

"I'm hip. But I'm not going to." He shook his head, chewing slowly. "It's a weird scene."

"You'd better be careful."

"If I can't smoke a little pot and blow my horn, what's there to be careful for?"

She wanted to say, there's me, but she shrugged the question off. You couldn't argue with Lee. He was too quick-tongued. She put the empty glasses in the sink and rinsed them. Then she unzipped her skirt and stepped out of it.

"Are you going to stay all night?" she asked as she walked over to the cardboard wardrobe.

He paused, lighting a cigarette. "I should look for Furg, but I don't suppose I will."

"He's a big boy," she said tartly, slipping out of her shoes.

"He's a big hick, but I like him."

"I like him, too, but I don't feel any impulse to mother him."

Lee laughed, and she paused with her fingers on the buttons of her blouse.

"What's funny?"

"I don't know. Association. I thought of you as a mother hen; then I saw Furg's knobby knees hanging over the edge of your nest."

She grinned. "I don't think I want Furg in my nest."

"I don't want him there, either."

She finished undressing, taking care to do it without awkwardness because she knew Lee was watching. Enjoyed watching. She rose on the balls of her feet, placidly coping with the snap on her bra, her elbows outspread like the wings of a white bird. Her breasts dropped a little, and she lifted one of them on the palm of her hand.

Too heavy. One of her nipples was inverted. Blind. A doctor had told her that if she had a child it might pop out.

She walked, toeing in deliberately so she'd sway, over to the bed. She rested her knees against the edge, pulled the rubber band from her pony tail, and shook her hair out. It dropped in a choked mass over her shoulders. She watched Lee unbuttoning his shirt.

"Is that all you?" he asked.

She smiled. There was still a sense of strangeness in it. She found herself thinking, maybe this is as close to married as I'll ever get. And maybe this is the right distance to be. Never completely certain. Never sloppy. But she didn't quite convince herself—

Minutes later he asked her if she was ready and she opened to receive him. They found their old rhythm, but he seemed almost perfunctory, and she caught it from him as easily as at other times she caught his excitement. There were too many odd vibrations loose in the room.

She drifted on a pleasant plateau, waiting for him to help her climb, and after a while he did. As a technical exercise. She remained almost as conscious of the sharp stubble on his cheeks as she did of the journeyman job he was doing on her. She flushed bright pink and tumbled over gently with a little sigh.

"Lee?"

"Mmmmm?"

"Why would you have to go to Venice or New York? Why don't we just leave North Beach and live in some other part of San Francisco?"

"What? What for?"

"Well, there's Carver. He probably wouldn't be on your back if you weren't around the Beach. And then, this is kind of a dead end for you. You play all week for nothing just to make a few dollars on the weekend—"

"But I'm playing what I want to. That's an expensive privilege."

"Oh, I'm not trying to say it's not a lot of kicks and all, but it doesn't seem to be leading anywhere."

She sensed him raising up on his elbow. His eyes were angry. "Where would you like to be led?"

She refused to react to the edge on his question. "I think I'd like something solid. I know it sounds draggy, but this is beginning to wear a little thin. Look at this dump. Nothing works right around here. Yesterday I found a cockroach as big as my thumb. Oh, that's nothing. I know. But it's not great, either, like I used to think when I first hit the Beach. My first room was nothing but a mattress on the floor over in the old Monkey Block, and I thought it was the end. I thought if you weren't broke and scroungy you were a terrible lame. But I don't feel like that any more."

She saw that he was looking at his corduroy jacket lying in a heap where he'd tossed it.

"Oh, Lee, I didn't mean you, or anything about you. I think about you just as if you were myself."

He didn't respond for a moment. Then he said soberly, "I'm never going to make anything blowing. You know that, don't you?"

"No, I don't. There's a group in the Jazz Lounge right now. There isn't one of them that's the musician you are, and they brought them up from L.A. at a five-hundred-dollar-a-week minimum."

"Jeanie, it's not that simple. It's a question of vogues, and how many people toss your name around. The average person comes to hear a name, not a musician, just like he goes to the flicks to see a star not a story. Look at Kovin, for crissake, he's the best tenor man on the coast, and all he has in his kick is a wad of pawn tickets."

"He doesn't try," she flared. "All he wants to do is blow that horn of his. I bet Ann has to feed him—"

She broke off suddenly, fumbling for an apology. She saw his mouth tighten.

"Like you do me?" His voice was tainted with bitterness.

"I didn't mean that, Lee."

"It's what you said. Where's the big difference?"

She stared at him angrily. Why should she apologize? He *was* the same as Kovin. Both of them horn-proud. Wasting their talents playing in cheap little clubs for their Beat followers. Pursuing some indefinable and therefore pointless ideal. To swing at a pitch that approached mindless emotion. She didn't pretend to understand all they thought they meant by it.

"All right," she told him bluntly. "Have it your way. It's what I said."

Twice before he left, she was again on the verge of apology. The quarrel frightened her because it had rushed too suddenly, flaming on too small a point, betraying the unguessed depths of its origin. Watching the angry abruptness with which he put on his clothes made her feel defenseless, vulnerable. North Beach relationships weren't durable. Passing things. Just kicks. But she couldn't quite carry it off like that. She closed her eyes.

When she heard the door shut, she reached over and turned off the light. For a while she listened to the traffic on Broadway. The trucks rolled by in the early morning. Trucks full of lettuce, potatoes, and apples coming in from the Northern counties, bound for the produce center in the Battery. They pulled over the Golden Gate bridge, down Van Ness, through the tunnel to Broadway, and under the window of Jean Diamanto.

chapter four

Leland Frederic Cabiness was born to a half-Spanish father and an English mother in Willows, California, in the fall of 1932. The Leland was for his mother's brother, and the Frederic for Chopin. His mother was a piano teacher, and the one responsible for his name. But in time Lee decided that he'd been let off easy. His younger brother was named Sergei Wassilievitch, after her other hero. He switched that round to Sergy, Wergy, Wash-the-Bitch, but the best his brother could do was Lee-land.

He grew up in a small white house three blocks from an irrigation canal, a long slow muddy stream, sluggish in grassy banks and crossed by a number of wooden bridges that boomed with the wheels of farmers' pickups. In summer the bridges were so hot you could hardly walk on them barefoot, but the bottom of the canal was a cool cloudy green filled with dim furred rocks. In the different times of his boyhood, the canal bank held frogs and lizards, then girls in bright bathing suits.

When his mother started him on the piano at the age of five, his father scratched his thinning hair and said, "What the hell, Agnes, he's only a kid." But she replied music was a joy in anyone's life and undertook to prove it some nights with grim and mechanical renditions of favorite Chopin and Rachmaninoff works and the recitation pieces she had learned in her own youth. Pieces with improbable names like "Bagatelle," "Scenes From the Panama Exposition," or "Blue Water, An Indian Romance."

It was a long time before the piano was anywhere near as good to him as the irrigation ditch. But in time two things happened that brought music alive for him. One was the first Woody Herman Band, and the other was a recording of Vladimir Horowitz playing "The Stars and Stripes Forever." It was even more years before he made the connection between these two very different kinds of music—that they both swung like mad—but without having any word to put to it, he knew that was what he wanted to do.

He asked for a saxophone. His mother wouldn't hear of it; he was doing so well on the piano, and in her pinched conception of culture only the piano, or possibly the violin, was acceptable. His father, who in his youth had popped his fingers to the hoarse periods of Dirty-Dog Wayne, was inclined to be more tolerant, until he inquired and found out how much even a secondhand saxophone cost. That put an end to it for a while.

He didn't grow up a herd boy. Neither was he a loner. Going into his teens he palled around with a buddy named "Droopy" Pearson—named after the cartoon dwarf, not the cartoon dog—a gnome-like boy, a year older, who played the trumpet... Droopy could sail through the "Carnival of Venice Variations" like they were the F scale, and never miss a note, and never interpret one either. Droopy, the robot trumpet player, the high-school bandmaster's favorite and delight. For Droopy there was nothing between the notes on the score and the sounds that came out of his horn. There was no Droopy in there at all. But to Cabiness, from the first summer he worked and bought an old tenor saxophone, the written notes competed unequally with the sounds wakening in his own head. The written notes were only a road map, indicating where he might travel over the vast country implicit in the chords. But he took a lot of detours before he really set out to explore that country.

Before he was out of high school, to his mother's highly vocal dismay, he was playing with the Art Baker Five. Baker was a gum-chewer. A drummer in the early athletic style of Krupa and Buddy Rich. He flipped sticks like a juggler, cocked his face in a calculated simulation of orgasm, and took fifteen-minute drum solos. After the first few minutes the solos disintegrated into a formless clamor, but the faceless crowds in the high-school gymnasium screamed their approval and delight. Cabiness got slightly hooked on all that love. He wore an engineer's cap when they played "Night Train."

Still later, he wore a kitchen mop dyed yellow and helped to sing "Windshield Wiper, Putty, Putty."

Later yet, he wore a wine velveteen jacket, two sizes too small, with black satin lapels, and played "My Happiness," "The Bluebird of Happiness," "Happiness is a Thing Called Joe," and "I Want to Be Happy." All of which didn't make him happy. The streak of the artist in him was demanding more of his time. Selfish and blind, it didn't care about money.

By that time he was playing alto. The great altoists of the late forties and early fifties—Bird, Johnny Hodges, Sonny Stitt—had inspired him, and he put down the tenor in favor of the smaller horn. He was valuable to the small-time hotel bands he played with. He was a good sight-reader, with excellent tone and sense of phrase, and if in his occasional solos he wandered a little far into left field, that was all right. Some people liked it.

When one of the bands he was on came to San Francisco to make what the leader anxiously referred to as the big time, Cabiness decided to stay. The band ran out of money and folded inside of a month, but not before Cabiness tasted the jam sessions in the Fillmore and North Beach. He listened and he played, and he knew he should have been in San Francisco three years earlier. He wasn't sure why he hadn't been. He knew one thing. He was through with mickey-mouse bands.

A weird thing happened after he'd been in San Francisco about six months. He was living in North Beach, stretching his money, and even so it was almost gone. Then one night he fell into conversation with a beautifully dressed Negro named Simes, who turned out to be the road manager for the

Earl "Fatha" Hines big band. They were auditioning for their next tour, and
Simes insisted that he show up for a tryout... "Baby, the way you blow, Fatha
will come unglued."

"Does he hire gray studs?"

"He hires musicians," Simes replied without inflection.

The auditions were held in a narrow hall on Green Street. When Cabiness
came in, the band was already set up on the stage. They were in shirt sleeves,
sitting on wooden folding chairs. And they were cooking! He sat down to listen. Now they can blow, he thought; this is where they weed out the little fel-
lows.

When the tune was over, two men stepped down, a tenor and a trombone,
and two more came out of the first rows. They sauntered across the stage,
playing it cool, with their axes dangling, but Cabiness knew how much it
must mean to them.

They auditioned half a dozen before Fatha seemed satisfied with one of the
trombones. Then he was looking for a second tenor. Solo spot. One of the
hearts of a jazz band. I could switch back to tenor in a week, he told himself.
He decided to wait until last so he'd know what he would have to best. He
twisted nervously and put his horn case on the floor between his feet. He
knew he should unpack, but for some reason he didn't.

Then Fatha was squinting out into the darkness and smoke, calling, "Any
more?"

He didn't move. Hell, who am I kidding? I can't play with these guys.

Simes caught him as he was going out the door, his dark face half hurt, half
puzzled. "Why didn't you blow, man? I hipped Fatha to you. He was waiting
to dig you."

"I changed my mind," Cabiness said slowly. "I don't want to go on the road.
I got a thing going—here in the city—you know?"

"Man, dragsville! They got chicks all over."

"It's more than that."

Simes smiled, still showing disappointment. "Well, if you're hung up,
you're hung up. There's nothing to do about that. We'll be back in six
months. Maybe you'll feel different then."

"Maybe."

But he didn't. Because there wasn't any girl, or any one girl. Jean was as
close as he ever came to taking it big, and he didn't run into her until he'd
been in San Francisco two years.

He stood for a moment in the doorway of Jean's building. Still hot. She was
turning square. No. That was a stupid expression. But she *was* looking wist-
fully at the big crapped-up merry-go-round. She wanted to ride on the San-
forized, dust-resistant and infinitely sanitary plastic leopard. She wanted to

grab for the gold ring, still not convinced they were all brass. It was a ride he had no use for. The admission was too high. Don't knock, he cautioned himself like an old Rotarian, just choose. And if Jean's choices were becoming different from his—

Angrily he put a period to his thoughts. Where was the sweat? North Beach's greatest natural resource was willing girls... and tricked-up derelicts... and phonies....

Balls! He stepped out into the fog with a horn case in each hand. He'd better make it home before the heat stopped him. One horn case was an invitation to them. Two would excite them unbearably.

He glanced into the all-night hot dog stand on the corner of Broadway and Grant. The nightman sat reading behind the counter, and a Filipino, wearing a gray gabardine topcoat and a maroon sport shirt, played the pinball machine. No Furg.

The Coffee House was dark except for a single light lit below a black-marble abstraction sitting in the front window. The piece was entitled "The Interstellar Kiss of Molly O'Shea," and priced at an unabashed thousand dollars. No one wanted "Molly" that badly. People snuffed out cigarettes in her oddly placed cavities.

He went a half block out of his way to check the Bird's Nest. A new after-hours club, named in an obvious attempt to profit from the Charlie Parker myth. It was housed on the site of an old Chinese market, and the smell of rotting vegetables seemed ground into the wood. They'd knocked out the shelves and counters, moved in some unmatched tables, a coffee maker, rented a piano and hired a kid to play it. Now they were waiting. Hoping the magic would happen. Hoping the night people would lead the numb herd of tourists into the Bird's Nest.

Furg was sprawled out next to the piano drinking a bottle of root beer. Cabiness was intercepted by a bushy-headed man with his hand out. "That'll be a dollar," he said, with a thin hustler's smile. Then he saw the horn cases, and his face altered as if a recognition signal had been exchanged.

"You blow? You wanta blow some? It's okay." He gestured at the piano. "Haley there can play anything you call."

"I'm beat. I'm not going to stay."

"That's okay. Come in anytime. No charge. You can always play here."

"That's nice of you," Cabiness said dryly. "I might come in and run some scales."

The man nodded briskly, not getting it. "Great. Just great. We're trying to build the place up."

Furg was grinning as he came over. "What'd Dino want?"

"A dollar."

"You give it to him?"

"I didn't have it. I told him I played first Kazoo with the Symphony. He was impressed. He let me in for nothing. Here's your horn."

"Thanks. Dino's sharp. I bet he knows who you are."

"If he's sharp he fooled me. What's he got in here he thinks is worth a dollar?"

"Nice piano."

"Yeah," he glanced briefly at the young piano man; then turned back to Furg. "How'd you slip that trap?"

Furg tilted his root beer, killing it. He peered at the empty bottle, twisting his face into a caricature of country foxiness. "Now that was *really* something. I wasn't about to dump the stuff Sully gave me, so I hid in the furnace. Damn near choked to death. It's full of soot—about an inch thick. Dig." He held up his arm and the back of his sleeve was smeared. "Ruined my goddam shoes too."

"Yeah, but you're not in city prison."

"Man, I'm telling you I'm not. Anyway, it was kinda kicks. I could hear Carver running around out there like a blind dog in a meat house. He lean on you?"

"Some."

"Lee-Boy, you mark me. That cop's going to jail you and throw the key away."

"Not if I stay clean."

"Crap. You're not foolish enough to believe that." Furg tipped his bottle again, but it was empty. "What happened to that high-tone blonde?" he asked.

"She cut home, but the gig's on."

Furg smiled slyly. "She's got eyes for you."

"She can keep them."

"Wisht I could be so choicey."

Cabiness didn't answer. He looked around the poorly-lit room at the scattered couples. It seemed dismal. The piano struggled unevenly with the four-ayem lassitude.

"I'm going to make it," he told Furg.

Furg stood up too. "Might as well."

The streets were empty and quiet. They walked quickly past the dark windows. A block away the buildings were nothing but vague shadows in the fog.

Furg pulled a twist of paper out of his pocket. "Wanta help do this stuff up?"

"What're you carrying it around for?" Cabiness asked uneasily, automatically looking around.

"No 'fit," Furg explained. "I thought I was going to use Sully's, but he had the jumps so bad he couldn't stand still."

"Sully ought to stick to writing plays. What a giant boob! Well, what're you flashing that stuff for? You know I don't have a 'fit."

"You know what, Lee-Boy?" You sound kinda bogus."

"Bogus?" Cabiness demanded. "What's bogus about not wanting to get busted? You think they're kidding about that crap? What do you think happened to Anson and Red-Dog? Or Lee Wilson? Or Charlie Falco? They're all in San-Damn Quentin. You think they're having a lot of kicks over there?"

"All right lay off, just lay the hell off!"

Furg was sullen, but he dropped the paper back in his pocket. He was silent for the space of half a block. He held his thin head sideways, one shoulder dropping with the weight of his trombone. Then he gestured out over Nob Hill and beyond where the city of San Francisco lay sleeping.

"Why do you s'pose they're so interested in us? I could go all year and never worry about what they're doing over on Market Street, but they're forever poking into our business."

Cabiness smiled: "They're afraid they've got cancer."

"They've got something."

"Yeah, but they think we're the cancer."

An old black Chevy pulled into the street a block ahead of them. It brushed them with its lights and swerved straight toward them, braking inches from the curb. A girl in a sweatshirt leaned out.

"Hey!"

It was Kovin and Ann. They were an odd couple, even on the Beach. Ann, plain as a boy, with an intense wooden little face, bristling with competitive femininity, and Kovin, bald and nearly forty, an odd mixture of saint and fraud, believing in magic and spells, seeing visions, addicted—all the backlash of his large talent.

"What's happening?" Ann asked. Kovin nodded from behind the wheel, his sharp face almost lost beneath the brim of his hat. The motor of their old car still labored with a dull whine. Furg slapped the top.

"It's a miracle," he announced solemnly.

"Not too hard," Ann warned.

"Oh, no," Furg burlesqued, throwing his hands out in mock horror. "This thing's a death trap."

"Get in," Kovin invited.

Ann opened the back door. "Come on. We'll all go together."

"I'm going home," Cabiness said.

"We'll take you," Ann offered.

"We'll never make it," Furg protested, going on with his fun. "We'll be stranded in the desert—buzzards!" he predicted in a portentous voice, lurching up on his toes, and flapping his arms, craning his long neck and making a dismal croaking sound.

"Come on," Ann said. "You sound like a sick sheep dog. I don't see you driving."

"If there's anything I can't stand, it's a talky broad."

"It's the school teacher coming out," Cabiness said. "They get in the habit of being right."

Ann smiled. "It's easy enough. I've got the book."

They climbed in, stumbling over a bulky machine propped between the front and back seats. They barely had room to sit because Kovin's tenor was in the corner of the seat.

"Annie, what's this damn thing?" Furg asked.

"It's a lawn mower," Kovin answered, peering around, the shadow of his hat a harsh curve on the pallor of his cheek. "Do you know where we could off it? I got to make it pretty soon."

Furg kicked the machine. "That don't look like no mower I ever saw."

"It's a power mower," Ann explained. "We've been trying to sell it all over the Beach."

Cabiness settled back and rubbed his forehead. Another night on the Toonerville Trolley. The large question up for debate is, why don't I get tired of it?

Ann was kneeling on the front seat, leaning over to talk to them, spinning one of the wheels on the mower. The sweatshirt was several sizes too large for her; the loose front obscured the slight curve of her breasts, and the sleeves were rolled back off her thin wrists. She swayed to the side as Kovin backed around.

"Where'd you get it?" Cabiness asked.

She smiled, her big front teeth glinting violet in the dim light. "Kove found it."

"Up on Russian Hill," Kovin added. "Some boob left it on his front lawn. So I swung with it."

"I'm hip," Cabiness said. "Where's the door?"

"The what?"

"His front door. Didn't you get his front door?"

There was a beat of silence. Then Furg chuckled.

"That's not really funny, Lee," Ann said in an altered tone.

"I'm hip, it's not."

"I've got to get on," Kovin said without looking around.

Furg spun the other wheel and mused, "The big lawnmower caper... you know, I bet Tree-Top'd take this thing."

"You think so?" Kovin asked.

"Sure. He's got boss connections in the Fillmore. He can turn stuff like this."

Kovin had been headed down into the produce center where Cabiness lived, but now he turned abruptly and started for the Fillmore.

"Hey," Cabiness complained. "I meant it. I want to make it home."

"Don't be a bringdown," Ann told him. Switching around she opened the glove compartment and shook a couple of pills out of a small brown bottle. "Here."

He recognized the vertical score and dense white texture. Why not? But he shook his head, before he had time to answer himself.

"Whew! What a stiff," she accused him, releasing a flicker of malice. Cabiness shrugged and shifted deeper into the seat. He should have walked home.

"This is Lee-Boy's night to be moral," Furg explained. "But don't ask me. Whatever you do, don't ask me."

Ann held the pills over, and Furg picked them up one at a time, popping them into his mouth.

"'Goodbye blues,'" he sang. "'Goodbye fo' t'night.'"

"Where's Tree-Top's pad?" Kovin asked.

Furg broke off to answer. "Up on Eddy. In the twenty-hundred block." He went on singing as the car turned through the deserted streets. They passed a street-cleaning machine. It was rolling slowly, gushing a sheet of black water edged with ragged gray foam. Furg stuck his head out the window and shouted "Goodbye blues" at the uniformed driver. The driver stared down at him coldly. Their car lights shimmered in the wet street.

"Did I tell you about the Indian?" Ann asked.

"What Indian?" Furg obliged.

"The one that went around scraping all the moss off the North side of the trees and pasting it on the South side, muttering, 'The bastards killed all the buffalo.'"

Furg grunted sourly, and Cabiness chuckled. Kovin announced, "She's been dropping that lemon all day."

They turned onto Eddy, and a moment later Furg pointed out a thin, mustard-colored building jammed between two others. Cabiness went in with Ann and Furg, while Kovin stayed behind to watch the stuff in the car.

Moving quietly through the dark narrow hall he was aware of a strong sour smell. The floor creaked under the thin carpet. A broken scooter leaned against the wall. An old building. The very nails were probably tired. Ann walked close to Furg, her hand on his arm.

Furg stopped at a door with a slanted numeral "8". He put his ear to the crack, then smiled broadly and knocked.

"Ol' Tree's got action," he said.

They heard a bed creak. Silence. Furg knocked again, louder. The bed groaned and they heard footsteps, the soft plop of bare feet on a wooden floor. The door opened a few cautious inches, and a dark, almost blue face appeared way up near the top of it. Tree-Top was close to seven feet.

"Yeah?" he asked in his light husky voice.

"We got something for you, Tree."

Tree grunted softly, looking deliberately at each of them, pausing at Ann, nodding at Cabiness. His face was so heavy and dense, its only possible expression seemed a solemn dark watchfulness.

"I know, man," he told Furg, "but it's late."

The bed creaked again, and a slurred voice from inside asked softly, "Who is it, baby?"

Tree-Top looked down at them. "You dig?"

"Get loose, Tree," Ann said. "This is a chance to make a nice taste of money."

Tree-Top smiled, his teeth brilliant. "Tha's right, girl." The smile vanished. "Just you dudes in this?"

"Kovin's out in the short."

"Okay. What you got that's so important?"

Ann laughed quietly. "You'll have to see it."

"Okay," Tree-Top agreed. "Bring it into the basement, whatever it be."

He closed the door, and as they started down the hall Cabiness heard a murmur of feminine complaint, and Tree-Top answering sharply, "Hush, girl."

Tree-Top came down the basement stairs wearing a soft white topcoat. His feet and legs were bare, and the exposed vee of his chest gleamed blue in the electric light. He didn't say anything. While Furg and Ann watched anxiously, he walked all around the mower, then stooped and opened the housing. It wasn't possible to tell what he thought of it.

What a role, Cabiness thought. Bet he has a lot of fun playing it. Cabiness walked over to lean against the heavy gray washtubs.

Tree-Top straightened up and slipped his hands into his coat pockets, looking up as if some decision might be written on the ceiling. Then he said, elaborately casual, "I got a friend might like that. Just might."

Furg kicked one of the rubber wheels. "How much would he like it?"

"Hard to say. He ain't ever seen it."

"How much you think?"

Cabiness turned one of the sink taps, and a trickle of water ran out of a short length of red hose. He let it run on his hand, then held his wet palm to his forehead. I should have taken Annie's pills.

Ann was following the debate with lively interest. She stood with her stomach pushed forward, her thumbs hooked in the back pockets of her jeans. The cold light was gray on her face.

Finally Tree-Top said, "Twenty."

Furg scowled, then grinned slyly. "Tree, you oughta wear a mask."

Tree-Top shrugged. "Tha's it. Take it or move it."

"That thing's worth two or three hundred dollars," Ann said angrily. "What're you trying to pull?"

Cabiness jerked the tap shut. "Come on, Furg. Take it and let's get out of here."

"Crap," Furg said. "He's playing us for fools."

"And you think he's got us figured wrong?" Cabiness asked wearily. "Tree knows this thing's hot. And he knows we're going to take the twenty dollars. He always knows exactly how much to offer, don't you, Tree?"

Tree-Top smiled. "Fellow wants a little taste of stuff, he don't argue too long. You not getting hooked, are you, Lee?"

"No. This is Kovin's prize. I just want to get home."

"Twenty?" Tree-Top asked again.

> "Goodbye, blues
> Goodbye fo' t'night.
> Come, pretty baby,
> Come—treat me right."

Furg was still singing, wide awake now. He'd sold Sullivan's stuff to Kovin for half of the twenty. Now he snapped the two fives and stuffed one of them into Cabiness' breast pocket.

"Thanks, Furg," he mumbled sleepily.

His thanks seemed to embarrass Furg. He grinned off to the side and punched Cabiness lightly on the shoulder.

"Hell, that ain't nothing, buddy. Bread ain't nothing. We'd a had more except for that burglar, Tree. There's a cold dude."

"We went to him. Remember?"

Furg didn't answer.

Cabiness smiled. Good old Furg, he mused drowsily, his head bumping softly in the corner of the back seat. Furg claimed he'd never been off his daddy's farm before he went into the Army, and that the Army had given him shoes and taught him to play the trombone. He liked to say he still didn't have much use for the shoes, but, man, he sure did learn to love that trombone. Cabiness didn't buy the story whole. He suspected that Furg was the author of his own myth; that he wanted to be a genuine character like the Eskimo psychology student, or the Cambodian prince who blew bongos and wore a gold medallion as big as a fist. So Furg played the shoeless hill boy, but Cabiness thought he'd probably been a Dixie musician even before he went into the Army. He knew for certain Furg had spent five years in one of the Army's best bands. Top 'bone. Boy could read flyspecks on the wall....

He woke to Furg's hand on his shoulder and stumbled out of the Chevy. The sky was beginning to gray and, with a tightening in his chest, he looked up the face of the old building. Had he really expected the light to be on? In the eaves above his window the chipped enamel letters spelled out: TEPPELO'S MACARONI FACTORY.

The four of them crowded up the stairs, and he admitted he was glad they were coming up with him. The air of his pad hit him with a flat staleness. He flipped the lights and dumped his horn beside the door.

Ann looked around, her thumbs again hooked in her back pockets. Cabiness thought of her teaching English. It was a hard picture to animate, but a true one. She taught adult continuation classes in the big Marina night school.

"This is double wild," she said enthusiastically.

Cabiness glanced around the big shadowy room with a pucker of distaste. He actually lived in a corner of it. The machines that had mixed the pasta had been here. The holes where they were bolted were still in the floor, and the boards were oil-soaked. The sink stood isolated in the middle of the room where the wall had been ripped away from in back of it. The empty loft stretched around the small island formed by his couch, his wooden boxes full of books and magazines, the GI foot locker he kept his clothes in, and a cheap record player. He had one chair and a faded blue rug, worn through in places to the hemp backing.

"Yeah, this is too much," Ann repeated. "What's the damage?"

"Twenty a month. Lights are a few dollars more." He stripped off his jacket and threw it at the foot locker. He plugged in the electric heater and lit the hot plate. "Have kicks. I'm going to get some sleep."

He settled on the couch, but he didn't close his eyes right away. He watched Kovin over by the sink getting ready to fix. The match under the spoon licked out into the shadows of the loft, and Kovin looked like a grotesque parody of the intent chemist. Furg and Ann were talking quietly, leaning against the foot of the couch.

"Anyone want a taste?" Kovin invited, not very heartily, busy tying off with one of Cabiness' dish towels. No one answered. Kovin shrugged and hit. He hadn't taken his hat off.

Cabiness heard Furg telling Ann, "That was going to be my cherry kicks."

"You've never used before?"

"Nope."

"Why don't you pass then? It's got Kove all fouled up."

"Sure, sure," Furg agreed. "But I figure I owe myself a little taste just to see what the shouting's all about. I'd mortally hate to overlook something. You see if I'd always listened to folks, well, I'da never even got hip to diddling. Everyone said it were an awful thing to do, but all the same it seemed like everyone was doing it—"

Furg broke off and chuckled, "You follow me?"

"Furg, you're eloquent."

Their voices drifted off into a blur. After a while a record started. A slow, burnt-out blues—the kind Furg would pick—full of a mournful, faintly self-pitying, Southern melancholy. A single tenor like a blue river, winding and winding, sadder than hell—

Lee lowered imperceptibly into a dream of fragmentary and super-colored images. He was wailing somewhere in a huge auditorium, and everyone in the audience was Clair Hubler. Thousands of her. And they weren't listening. Their cold faces froze him. Then he was on the street, and Carver's hand was coming toward him. Carver's arm was stretching—his face a tiny white dot, glimpsed through the fingers of the rushing hand, cold as the silver face on a nickel. The arm was stretching, dwindling like a giant rubber band. Carver was yelling something—

"It's all right, Furg. Kove doesn't care."

"You sure, baby?"

"It's all right. Come on, it's all right."

There was a gasp and a long sigh. Cabiness turned over and went back to sleep.

chapter five

Clair Hubler was full of discontent even before she opened her eyes. She lay realizing she'd edged, almost without transition, from a dull formless dream into consciousness. What's today? What can happen today?

Her dissatisfaction galled her. So pointless. Still, sometimes she felt as if she were hopping across the Sahara on a pogo stick. Not to get to the other side, but just back and forth. Gravely passing other people who were hopping along, too. Smiling and saying, *Good morning, Mrs. Thompson. Good morning, Sally. How's Roger? Still hopping up North? It must be nice to hop up North. They say the climate's wonderful. Not quite so dry as it is here. . .*

Clair threw the blankets back and sat up. Across from her she saw a blonde, heavy-eyed girl in a blue nightgown. She threw the mirror girl a little grimace of love. Still watching her reflection she stood up and pulled the nightgown over her head. For a moment the pale blue-edged softness of her body pleased her. She moved closer to the glass and looked at the creamy round of her belly, faintly creased by the bunching of her nightgown in sleep, the firm structure of her narrow waist, the gentle slope of her breasts—

Then the blunt fact of her coolness blotted out the pleasure. What good was this wealth when she couldn't enjoy spending it. What good were the sweats and noises of her partners when she remained limp and cool. Frightened and ashamed of her automatic control, and yet, perversely, a little proud.

She left her nightgown on the floor. Carla would pick it up. She went in and started to shower. The bathroom was immaculate. There wasn't a trace of Carla's use of it as she'd prepared for work early this morning, and Clair read a subtle reproach in the gleam of the wash basin.

She stepped under the warm water. Maybe if she had to work, as Carla did, it would give dimension and contrast to her days. But her father had relieved her of that necessity. He'd done that much before he died. But was it a good thing? Sullenly she viewed the cliché. All she had to do was enjoy herself, and that simple aim daily proved more elusive. Recently she'd started to tinker with sensation.

Last night. She remembered throwing away the marijuana before she'd had a chance to use it. And that musician had covered it up. A hero. He'd fallen on it like a soldier in a first-world-war movie falling on a hand grenade. A strange man. There was a kind of ruthless negative quality in his face that was at odds with his romantic gesture. A useless gesture, too. She would have simply denied knowing anything about it. They couldn't have done anything.

Out in the apartment she heard the front door and the rattle of heels. Carla, home for lunch. She stuck her head out of the shower and called, "I'm up. Fix me something."

"What would you like?" Carla's voice came back.

"Oh, anything. I don't care."

When she came into the kitchen in her bathrobe, Carla bent to kiss her, but she turned her head slightly and took it on her cheek.

"What's the matter?" Carla asked, masking any hurt she might feel behind her near-perfect composure.

"I don't know. Nothing. I suppose I'm just tired."

The kitchen was full of the smell of fresh coffee. Carla poured her a cup while she waited in the breakfast nook, looking out the window. Far below in the thin sunlight the pigeons wobbled around the Union Square fountain.

Carla placed her cup in front of her along with toast and eggs. "Well, I hope you've satisfied your curiosity as far as North Beach is concerned."

"I thought it was interesting."

"Interesting? We could have gone to jail. I don't think that would have been interesting."

Clair sipped her coffee and frowned into the cup. "We were in no danger. Even if Lancelot hadn't jumped to our rescue."

"Lancelot?"

"Oh, Carla, don't be dull. The musician, Cabiness. He covered up for me. You saw it."

Carla smiled sternly. "I'm not quite that dull, Clair. I just question whether he did anything for you. I imagine he thought he might be blamed himself."

That rang of too much truth to be denied, but she was piqued that vanity had misled her, and she refused to admit it. Carla shrugged and asked dryly, "You think he was taken with you?"

"It happens all the time," Clair replied. She heard the smug tone of her voice, but it was too late to retrieve it. She stared at Carla until the older woman's eyes wavered, and she covered herself by buttering a piece of bread. Carla was lunching on some kind of dismal broth. Clair was weary of the procession of health foods that fed Carla's appetite for self-denial. The bread she was buttering was some off-brand, tasteless as sawdust.

"You don't deny that?" Clair challenged, pressing her advantage.

"Of course not, dear. In my position how could I? But I imagine that your musician has his hands full with that big girl he went home with. I don't think she'd leave him much energy with which to speculate."

Clair pushed her plate away, the eggs untouched. Carla was becoming tiresome. The situation, never positive, was turning negative. It was almost time to tell her the experiment was over. And unsuccessful. But that much she wouldn't tell.

"Well, maybe I'll check his battery," she said with deliberate vulgarity. "I'm going over this afternoon and see him."

"Whatever for?" Carla asked coolly.

"The party. Have you forgotten?"

"No, but I didn't think you were serious."

"I am now." She paused significantly, and added, "And I think he can get me some more marijuana. I still want to try it."

"Is it really necessary?"

"If it was necessary, I wouldn't want it."

Carla looked away for a moment. Then she started gathering the dishes. Before she stood up to leave the table she squeezed Clair's hand, and her sober expression softened for a moment.

"Promise to be careful?"

chapter six

Cabiness woke with a mutter of protest. His mouth tasted foul and his eyes were gummy, squinted against even the thin light that filtered through his dusty windows. He had slept hard. And not long enough.

Furg was grinning down at him. "That broad's out front."

"What broad?"

"What broad?" Furg repeated mockingly. "How many have you got lined out? That groovy blonde from last night."

"Oh, her."

"Yeah, her. I didn't think you'd want her to see this mess, so I asked her to wait."

Furg was still big-eyed from the stimulant he'd taken the night before, but Ann was asleep on the floor with an extra quilt over her. Her jeans were thrown to one side and her sweatshirt to the other. Kovin was folded up in the only chair with his hat over his face.

"Looks like a flop house," Furg added.

"So?" Cabiness asked yawning. "You think this chick's the Queen of Spain? Let her in."

Cabiness had his shirt off and was washing when he heard the tap of her heels on the old boards. He grinned wryly into his cupped hands and splashed water on his face. He shook his head vigorously and turned. "Hang up. I'll be done in a minute."

Clair was staring at Ann. Enough of her was visible above the quilt to make it apparent she was naked. At least to the waist. She was sleeping with a small smile, and it worked an honest miracle for her face.

Clair broke away from Ann and stared at him for a moment before her expression came under control. "I wanted to talk to you," she said tightly.

"Sure. Soon as I brush my teeth."

"He just got up," Furg said helpfully. "We were out cattin' around most of the night."

Clair had taken in the rest of the loft. "What a strange place to live."

"It does what it's supposed to do," he told her, squeezing a line of toothpaste along the brush. "It's cheap, too, and that's the important thing."

"Yes," she replied without conviction. She remained standing, obviously not at ease, and just as obviously unused to the feeling. She wore a simple pale-blue linen suit, striking a contrived chord with her eyes, and her fine hair was brushed straight back off her forehead. Her style was simpler and more effective than the one she'd employed the night before. She was a good-looking girl and aware of it, but probably unaware of her odor of complexity and willfulness. Still she looked good.

Cabiness smiled at the care he was taking to define this girl, to explain her to himself, and that way rob her of her female power. Avoid a bad scene was the way he thought of it.

Furg started talking around Clair, telling Cabiness what a weird night he'd spent. "Everyone crapped out on me. Even Annie. I listened to just about all your sides, and that damn Kovin was snoring. But you know, that crazy sonofabitch even snores in meter. And I guess about a zillion trucks went by outside."

"Vegetable trucks. They're moving all the time after midnight."

"There was sure enough of them. I kept hearing them roaring in the street while Annie and I was making it. It was nutty. You know, that's a crazy little broad. I mean it. She's too much."

Kovin stirred in his sleep, mumbling something, some wordless complaint drifting out of his unconscious. His hat had fallen to the side, tipped on his shoulder, and his bald head was exposed and vulnerable. In sleep his face wore a quiet agony like the death mask of a saint.

Cabiness glanced at Clair. She was fidgeting, and her face was smoky with mortification. He realized that when Kovin woke up he would have to fix, and that was more than this girl should see. He put on a clean shirt and picked up the same corduroy jacket he'd thrown down the night before. "Let's go," he told her. "I've got to get some breakfast."

Clair nodded and walked quickly to the door, her eyes skirting Ann as they would a mess on the floor, just seeing enough to make sure she didn't step in it.

"You coming?" he asked Furg.

Furg glanced at Ann and smiled. "I'll catch you later, Lee-Boy."

"If you cut out, lock up. I don't want the pad torn up again."

On the sidewalk, Clair turned to him. "That little scene was right out of *The Grapes of Wrath*."

"I don't know. I don't read. Anyway you invited yourself."

Her mouth tensed with some retort, but she abandoned it, and in a different tone of voice asked, "Where do you usually eat?"

"The Coffee House."

"Then let's drive. I've got my car."

The workday was already over in the produce center. The iron grates were drawn and locked before the empty stalls of the wholesalers, and the broken vegetable crates were stacked in the alleys. An old Italian, thick as a tree stump, methodically swept down the gutters with a push-broom that looked like an enlarged version of his own mustache.

Her car was parked around the corner, elegant as a wolf hound. Cabiness remembered his snatch of dream from the night before, and he was smiling as he slid onto the leather seat.

"What's so funny?" she asked crisply.

"Several things. It was nice of you to call on me."

"Don't flatter yourself. This is business."

"I had a feeling it would be. Well?"

She waited until she had the car into the street, rolling smoothly on Montgomery; then she turned to him, her eyes deliberately remote. In the daylight it wasn't an effective pose—her face was too youthful, too untouched.

"Do you smoke marijuana?" she asked.

He couldn't help laughing. There was something so prim in her voice, a grammar-school accent.

"Oh, dear me, no," he said.

She stared at him levelly. "You're not as funny as you think you are."

"I couldn't be."

"When you get all through being whippy, will you answer my question?"

"All right," he said gravely. "I've been known to smoke it, but I don't recommend it."

She smiled her disbelief. "Do I look like a policewoman?"

"A policewoman wouldn't. But aside from that, what's your interest?"

"I want you to get me some."

"You're a bold dolly—" He broke off. "I'll be a sad bastard. That was your stuff last night!"

Something in the street seemed to need her attention.

"Wasn't it?" he demanded.

"I thought you knew it was mine. I meant to thank you."

"Of all the lame stunts."

She drove in silence for a while, absorbing his reprimand. Then she asked, "What should I have done?"

His anger had slipped away as quickly as it had gathered. Nothing had happened. Unless you could count the fact that his name was now filed more indelibly in the black-and-white brain of a vice cop named Carver. His name had been there anyway, but now there was another star behind it.

"I don't know," he said. "If you're going to throw something away, throw it. That's all. Look, it's easy to get the idea that stuff's harmless, like sniffing furniture polish or something, but they're deadly serious about it. If you don't believe me, read the newspapers."

The Coffee House was empty. It had just opened; they took a table still damp from the counterman's rag. "Just coffee," Clair volunteered, and in her averted eyes she made unconscious recognition of her pastrami goof. He brought coffee and rolls for himself and ate, listening to her talk about the party. She was going to borrow a friend's place in Sausalito because her apartment wasn't large enough, and he remembered to ask whether a piano would be available. Yes, her friend had a concert grand. So that was all right, they could use full rhythm if they could find decent people. He thought of BeeGee on piano. She'd raise some eyebrows. Clair was going on, and a certain air of mischief filtered through her routine explanations, as if there were going to be something cute about this party. Maybe she thought the jazz would shock some of her guests. Cabiness didn't pursue it. He was reading other signals in her blue eyes.

"It's at Seven-eleven Bayroad," she concluded.

He nodded, thinking that the seventh of the B-Flat scale was A, and the eleventh was E-Flat. A, E-Flat.

"Do you want to write that down?" she asked, motioning toward her purse.

"I'll remember."

The sound of the door drew his eyes, and he saw Sullivan entering. He looked drained. The only thing in his face which had the appearance of health was his mustache. It was glossy, a startling black, like dyed hair on a corpse. Sullivan's eyes passed Clair with indifference, but they stirred when he saw Cabiness.

"Lee," he said vaguely and passed by.

"What's the matter with him?" Clair asked.

"What do you mean? You know him?"

"No. It's just that he looks so sick."

"That's about it. He is sick. And incurable."

They were both silent for a while. Then she cupped her chin and bent her eyes on him, letting a little heat trickle into her fashion mask. "Are you going to get me the marijuana, or am I going to have to get it somewhere else?"

"You're sure?"

She nodded. She really wanted it. It wasn't just a game with her. Or it was a game, but she was the kind who went for the dangerous ones. Lots of people did. Like Furg, they wanted to know what the shouting was all about. Weed had been magnetized by the very forces that sought to suppress it.

"I know you can get it," she persisted.

"How much do you want?"

She opened her purse and took out her wallet. She handed him a bill. He realized it was a hundred. "Half of whatever this will buy."

"And?"

"I don't expect you to do this for nothing."

It was so goddam bald. She couldn't keep pleasant. She had to throw her weight around. She'd bought pot, at least once before, so she must have known that twenty dollars would have been plenty.

But precisely why did he give a damn? No one was betting on the sweepstakes taking place in the transparent brain of Lee Cabiness. He wasn't even betting himself. And who did he think he was to be immune from ordinary wants? And who did she think he was to stage this little demonstration of control?

He folded the bill once and stuffed it in his shirt pocket. "When do you want it?" he asked coldly.

"Could you bring it the night of the party?"

"Anytime you like."

"The party will be fine."

He lit a cigarette, staring at her. She closed her purse and smiled uneasily. "Well, I've got some things to do." She paused, then, "I thought we were going to be friendly—but we seem destined to rub each other the wrong way."

"I don't think it's important," he replied.

"No, probably not." She stood up. "Well, until Thursday night?"

He nodded.

He watched her through the window as she pulled away in the low convertible, her yellow hair bright above the cream car, in style with the green leather seats and old-fashioned metal-bound headlights.

Cabiness, he told himself, you're turning into a shabby bastard.

He went over to the Angelo Real Estate Company and broke the bill paying a month's rent. Then he walked down to the big Sherman and Clay and bought a box of alto reeds and a bottle of key oil.

A block from the hall of justice on Kearny Street, Carver passed him in a black police sedan. Carver rapped his horn and nodded—almost cordially.

chapter seven

Sullivan met Carver a mile from North Beach. He couldn't say it had been an honest struggle. The weight against him was too crushing, and from the first Sullivan had known it was only a matter of time until he called the Narco Division. The good assassin reporting for duty.

Carver was parked beside a playground watching two little girls compete to see which one could swing the highest. They arced up in the early evening sky, screaming with the thrill of self-induced fright.

The Narco was freshly shaven. A cast of talc still clung to his cheek. He wore a gray suit with an unpatterned dark-blue tie. Sullivan slid in beside him, sheltering his sick face in the upturned collar of his mackinaw.

"That was nothing last night," Carver said coolly, his gray eyes steady and pinched with distaste.

"It wasn't my fault," Sullivan said quickly. "I did what you told me to."

Carver flicked his chin with his thumb and studied Sullivan. "You shot it up already, I suppose?"

Sullivan nodded, unable to take his eyes away from the small round clock set in the glove compartment. It was stopped at 11:30.

"You're at the hog stage now," Carver continued in a soft monotone. "It doesn't really do any good any more. You're just shooting to keep even, but you keep hoping you might get that old flash, the one you used to get, so you fix a couple of times an hour—"

Carver broke off. He took out a cigarette and pushed in the lighter on the dash.

"All right. I can use you," he said briskly. "And I'll keep you from getting sick. But that's all. I'm not putting out any protection. You get busted, you ride it."

The lighter popped out and Carver reached for it.

Sullivan understood that Carver hadn't been asking for an agreement but was telling him how things were going to be. A captain formulating orders for a private bound by stronger allegiance than any army.

Sullivan waited with his hands clenched in his jacket pockets. Waited to hear what he had to do in order to get what he needed. His life was reduced to a proposition that simple. There were still rooms in his mind where he knew a kind of regret, rooms in which he wondered about the family he'd left in the East, rooms where he groped after the lost meaning of an unfinished play he was trying to write. But the doors of these rooms had been slammed and sealed by the over-riding need that mastered him. Sullivan had been a complex man. But he was no more Sullivan. Sullivan had gone hissing out of his ruptured veins.

Carter blew smoke out the open window. In the playground one of the little girls was shouting, "I was too higher! I was too!"

"Who's the big connection in North Beach?" Carver asked.

"There is no big connection," Sullivan replied dully. "That's funny-paper stuff. Maybe at one time there was, but you've got everyone on a panic kick. Every once in a while someone drives South, over the border at TJ or Mexicali. They sell about half of what they bring back to pay for the next trip. You know all this."

"Yes," Carver agreed. "That's about the way we see it. And I think you're going to be one of those connections. Only you won't have to go to Mexico. I'll supply you. And you'll set up who I want set up. . ." "

Sullivan listened to the details. He had to. But he could only think, how much longer before he gives me something and lets me go. There was a Standard Station in the block below. That's where he'd head. Right into the can-
—

He realized Carver had asked him a question. "What?"

"Cabiness. What about him?"

"Nothing. He wouldn't go. His partner did, but he froze on me. He's not a user."

"I don't care about that, he's wrong, wrong clear through," Carver said. "I want him, and I'm giving you the job of putting him where I can get him."

Carver flipped his cigarette out the window. Sparks jumped where it hit the cement. The two little girls were running off, arm in arm, through the growing dusk. Faintly, from the next block, there was the sound of a mother calling, "Suzie, dinner's ready... Suzie...."

"Okay," Sullivan said. "I'll keep trying." At this point he didn't care what he said. He couldn't keep his eyes off the glove compartment thinking of what might be in there.

Carver followed his glance with an expression both of pity and disapproval; then he reached over and unlocked the glove compartment. "Here," he handed Sullivan a folded envelope. Sullivan felt its plumpness and drew in his breath with sharp pleasure. Quickly he opened the door on his side. "See you," he said vaguely, already moving.

"Don't forget Cabiness," Carver called after him.

Sullivan nodded, still moving towards the oasis-like glow of a large Standard Station on the corner. He entered the men's restroom and slipped into the single booth, bolting the door behind him. He lowered his pants, in case anyone else came in, then sat, and unfolded the envelope Carver had given him. At least four good fixes, he calculated, and raised the powder to his tongue to see how deeply it had been cut. He tasted sweetness, and touched his tongue again, searching for the reassuring bitterness of a high heroin content. Only sweetness. Oh, Jeezus, he thought miserably, it's milk sugar, nothing but milk sugar, Why would Carver do this to him? Some crazy joke? Or a mistake. Yes, Carver'd given him the wrong stuff. Sure. That was it. The wrong envelope. Envelopes all look alike.

He rushed out of the restroom and almost sobbed with relief when he saw Carver's car still parked where it had been. He started running and ran all the way back. He stooped and looked in the window. Hey, he started to say, when he noticed that Carver had one leg crossed over his knee and was holding the ankle of that leg as if it were causing him great pain. His eyes were dull, his shoulders hunched, his breathing quick and shallow.

"Hey, what's wrong?" Sullivan asked. Then he noticed the spike half-hidden in Carver's hands; the needle was buried in one of the large veins that cross the ankle bone, and he realized what he had taken to be pain was really ecstasy as Carver experienced the "flash" that follows a good fix. He started to back away, and when he realized that Carver's eyes were on him and that now the Narco was really seeing him. He held out the envelope full of milk sugar.

"This is cut down to nothing," he said, almost in a whine. "I can't get on with this, not even if I shot the whole piece at once. This is nothing. Go on, taste it. It's nothing."

Carver brushed the envelope aside and removed the needle from his vein, repacking it in a little leather box. "I'm a diabetic," he said, easily. Sullivan realized that all of Carver's anxieties were washed out with the stuff in him; the policeman literally couldn't worry, or formulate the possible consequences of exposure. Everything was fine. Everything was wonderful.

Sure, Sullivan thought, a diabetic. But who ever heard of anyone mainlining insulin?

"Here," Carver said, reaching back into the glove compartment, "I must have given you the wrong piece." He brought out a similar folded envelope. "This is good." He laughed softly. "I took it off one of the biggest connections in the Fillmore, and all the way downtown he kept saying about how 'Hit just didn't seem right for the po-lice to end up with that *good* smack.'"

Sullivan took the envelope and backed away. He started walking rapidly along the sidewalk. He turned once to glance back. Carver was just sitting looking out at the park; he appeared to be smiling.

If you had the sense you used to kid yourself you had, Sullivan told himself, you wouldn't stop moving until you were on the other side of the Rocky Mountains. And then stop just long enough to rest, and get going again. If, he repeated dully. This time he went into a Shell Station.

chapter eight

Cabiness saw Jean several times in the next few days, but she always avoided his eyes. Once from the stand in The Hoof he recognized her out in the crowd. She was with a tall dark man he'd seen several times in front of the Bocche Ball on Broadway. He thought he recognized John Randozza from her description of him. So that, he thought, seems to be that. But he admitted to himself that he missed her.

Wednesday night Furg talked him into going to the Bird's Nest after 2:00. Furg baited him a little, his eyes a sleepy blue, telling him Kovin was blowing over there, and it was pretty rough on saxophone players.

They were packing up after a dead night in The Hoof. Cabiness snapped his case and straightened. "Kovin's Kovin, and I'm me."

"Sure, Lee-Boy. Wanta make it?"

"Might as well."

In the street they started out to walk the three blocks up Grant Avenue. Across from them the gartered neon leg in front of the Sorrento Pizzeria kicked tirelessly, and at the Cobana a ruffled drummer beat out a soundless stroboscopic pulse. Ahead THE RED BEARD flashed out of the darkness once a second. A motorcycle roared in the street, and three people passed them laughing at the funniest joke of the night.

"Did you hear about Jean?" Furg asked.

"What about her?"

"She's been going around with a cat named Randozza."

So he'd guessed right. Cabiness shrugged.

"Randozza's a fish," Furg added.

"How do you know?"

"How do I know weasels suck eggs?"

"Don't give me that phony hillbilly crap," Cabiness snapped. "What do you know definitely?"

"Just what Annie told me. She and I saw them together last night, and she ran it down to me. Randozza tried to turn Annie out when she first hit the Beach—"

"A cross-eyed Eskimo wouldn't try to turn Annie out. As a whore she'd starve."

"You don't need to get salty," Furg said sullenly. "That's what Annie told me. Make whatever you want out of it."

"Jean wouldn't waste two minutes talking to a fish."

"Whatever you say, Lee-Boy."

They were silent crossing a street. A crowd had gathered in front of the Coffee House. Some kind of loud debate was taking place inside. The voices rose between the bursts of laughter and applause. The boy with the cycle sat by the curb, gunning his motor and watching the girls in the crowd.

"I'd play it quiet with Ann," Cabiness told Furg. "Kovin's liable to come out of that fog he's in long enough to see what's going on, and he'll probably try to nut you."

Furg let go with a slow razzberry. "Kovin couldn't nut a sick chicken. Besides, he don't care nothing about the sex end. He thinks Ann is something to warm his feet on."

"That's what she told you, huh?"

"Yep."

"Okay. You play it your way."

"I will."

Cabiness went on scowling for a moment... then he smiled and banged Furg on the shoulder. "All right, don't get pissed off. We're not too hot at giving each other advice, are we?"

Furg smiled back. "I reckon not, man."

There was a better crowd in the Bird's Nest. It was obvious why. Kovin was leaning against the piano, his dark hat slanted over his eyes, his sharp pale face intent around his mouthpiece. He was playing a slow ballad—"Laura"—and the piano man was pushing out hushed chords behind him, probably glad to be backing a musician of Kovin's caliber.

Ann waved to them from a table near the piano, smiling mostly at Furg. Dino nodded and passed them automatically. They moved over and sat down.

"Listen to the Man," Ann invited.

Kovin raked them with his eyes and blew a little riff in greeting. The crowd was intent. The only sound, other than the music, was an occasional muffled clink of crockery as some one set a cup back into a saucer, or knocked an illegal bottle against the table. The underwater faces were hushed in the dim light: glint of shadowed eye, or soft curve of mouth—

Whee-Owww, Kovin's horn said. Whee-Ohhhh! Laura is a pixie-bright, moondust chick, who will never—neverneverNEVER—grow old.

Then he sighed off, drifting out the end of a diminished chord, and the piano went a couple of beats further, still not quite resolving. Cabiness smiled. These were the moments that plugged up all his questions.

There was a murmur of pleasure through the room, and someone said softly, but emphatically, "Work!"

Kovin was king. He unsnapped his horn and put it on the piano top. He came over to the table and straddled the remaining chair, folding his arms on the back. Close up, Cabiness could see that his eyes were soft and contracted. All anxiety rubbed away.

"That was real pretty, baby," Furg said.

Kovin smiled dreamily, rubbing his chest.

"How was school tonight?" Furg asked Ann.

"A drag," she said with elaborate wryness. "Same as always. But I had a little help tonight. Some nutty little helpers. Redbirds."

Cabiness laughed. "Jeezus, if those cats at the school board ever get hip to you, they'll come unglued."

"I play it cool," Ann said. "I pound the English language—what I can remember of it—into those numb inflexible heads, but I won't do it sober. Not if I can help it."

"Amen," Furg mocked her.

But she just smiled at him. "I mean it."

She wore one of Kovin's shirts and an old black raincoat, but her hair was brushed smooth, and she had a hint of lipstick on her small mouth. Kovin, crouched in his warm hole, seemed oblivious as to what was going on.

Dino came up with some set-ups. His smile was enthusiastic. "Too much," he told Kovin. "They couldn't hear anything like that this side of the Apple."

Kovin was king. He took it calmly. He knew he was the best. Dino turned to Cabiness. "You cats going to blow?"

"I don't know. We've been playing most of the night."

"Why not?" Ann protested. "The three of you can really swing."

The people at the next table had been picking up, and one of the girls leaned over. Cabiness knew her. She was one of the casuals on the Beach, and he'd made it with her before he'd hung on Jean.

"Oh, you've *got* to blow," she said. "*Please.*"

She made it real broad, and everyone cracked up.

Cabiness stirred angrily. He wasn't a goddam entertainer.

Ann asked, "You're going to play, aren't you, Furg?"

Furg grinned and started unpacking his horn.

"Come on, Lee," Kovin challenged. "Let's play a little head up. Blow fours. You know?"

Cabiness knew it would turn into a cutting match, and Kovin would blow him through the door. Kovin was a head-hunter. When he blew with another saxophonist he always contrived to turn it into a duel. All right, why not?

Cabiness took his horn out. An old silver alto, scratched and worn. It looked beat out, but actually it was a fine instrument. Hand-crafted to last in a one-room French factory over fifty years ago. He settled the strap, wet his reed, and noodled an almost silent scale. Furg was checking his slide, running it back and forth, watching the long reflections blur in the oil. Kovin stood waiting.

"'Donnalee'?" he asked, and without waiting for their acceptance he told the piano player, "Donnalee," and stomped it off at a killer's tempo. The piano sailed into an intro.

"Donnalee" was an old Charlie Parker original played against the chords of "Back Home In Indiana." It was always played way up and was one of the showdown tunes. The ones they played when they wanted to see who could really blow and who was shucking.

They roared through the intricate line. The thirty-two bars vanished in a blur of sound, and Kovin grabbed the first solo, arcing out into the silence of the break on the shadowy ladder of an alien arpeggio, slamming back into the chorus with a furious propulsion, spinning like a fierce bright wheel, kiting higher and higher. Hard bop at its hardest. Someone shouted, "Go!" The reflection of the beat came from all over the room.

Over the piano Cabiness caught a moving figure and saw that it was Jean. Randozza was right behind her. His handsomeness was almost operatic: heavy black hair, a strong arched nose and large square teeth. He squired Jean, drifting gracefully behind her, holding her chair, helping her off with her coat—full of what Cabiness instantly labeled as phony charm. But Jean seemed to like it. A big girl, she liked feeling small and helpless. Cabiness realized that for the first time, and he couldn't understand how he'd missed it. But if he had known it, would he have filled that need? He knew that he wouldn't have.

There was a slam of applause as Kovin finished his solo, dying quickly as Furg picked it up. Ordinarily the tempo would have been too fast for trombone, but Furg could cut it. His slide was a blur of light and his narrow head was laid to the side, his face a fist of concentration. He put out a line both intricate and percussive. Hoarse grunts and shattered clusters of notes way up on the top of his horn.

Cabiness wet his reed again and ran the keys silently. He glanced at Kovin. Kovin was slouched and unmistakably challenging, smiling and scat-singing under his breath. Cabiness had the choice of playing one of his familiar and half-rehearsed solos, or just to let himself go and see how he felt about the chords, the night and himself. He knew that the magic of improvised music, while obscured and bound by as many rules and superstitions as any magic, was essentially inexplicable. He pushed away the temptation to play it safe and blow the clichés certain to move the audience. He didn't want to see himself as a subtler and up-to-date version of Art Baker, the acrobatic drummer of his youth. He would go on trying to mint the new words of a vigorous art right in the moments of its long birth.

He stepped forward in the applause for Furg and let go. He stood erect, his horn held straight in front of him, and his expression was one of faint worry. The chords were as familiar to him as they were infinite in their possibilities. He set out to re-explore them.

What he found was an implacable energy and excitement, set in a meter that moved forward in an eerie three-legged gallop. The first "Go!" was as exciting as the crack of an Olé! in the bullring.

"Cook, Lee-Boy!"

He grabbed air around his mouthpiece and reached for an impossible note, caught it, swelled it, tumbled off it and shot down his horn like a skittering silver bug—bright, manic, sharp-angled as hell—

The applause cracked. People were yelling. Furg was bobbing with enthusiasm. "Cook!" he shouted again.

Jeezus, he thought, that was a good solo. *Jeezus!* And he filled with a pure twelve-year-old joy.

"Fours," Kovin called, and immediately took the first four.

In "fours" the solo is tossed back and forth like a medicine ball, a different man taking it up every four bars, each player in turn seeking to match and add to the contribution of the man before him. This framework quickly exposed the inferior or mediocre musician, and it was Kovin's obvious intention to bury him. Understanding this, Furg laid out at the end of the first chorus.

Cabiness accepted. They faced each other, just as if their horns were clubs, each spitting their four bars right into the other's face. Recklessly Kovin pushed the beat, setting the tempo faster and faster.

Cabiness didn't try to think. Everything he'd ever felt or understood about music was loose in his synapses. He continued to let himself go, and because he didn't care about the contest, he found that he was winning it. He realized that he was clean and away, blowing his best. The crowd sensed it too and began to shout its approval.

Then Kovin understood and immediately began to falter. His articulation slurred and his intonation became sketchy. The tempo he'd forced turned against him, and his last four was nothing but a series of guttural honks. He signaled his resignation by going into the out-chorus, and Furg stepped back to join them as they rocked the tune home.

"Hey!" Furg exclaimed. "Man, did you wail! What got under you?"

Cabiness shook his jaw to relax it and dropped his hand on the piano player's shoulder. "You were making it," he told him.

The piano man smiled, wiping his face with a balled handkerchief. He shook the fingers of one hand as if he'd just burned himself. "You cats whistle," he said with open admiration.

"Let's take 'Stablemates'," Furg suggested.

Cabiness nodded agreement and looked around at Kovin. But Kovin was breaking his horn down. "Hey, Kove," he said in protest. "What the hell? We're just getting started."

"Like it's late, man."

He saw Kovin's eyes move under his hat brim in a venomous and hurt expression, and he watched Kovin pack his horn into the old black case, covered with astrological signs crudely rendered in orange poster paint.

Smeared with rain and wear. They seemed dismal and foolish. Why couldn't you do well without making someone else look bad? he asked himself. Why was everything so goddam expensive?

"Come on, Annie," Kovin said.

Ann was engaged in a silent communication with Furg, and Kovin repeated with a rasp of petulant irritation, "Come on, Ann, let's make it out of here." He glanced around the club. "This bunch wouldn't know real jazz if they had it smeared on their chests."

Cabiness turned away feeling oddly guilty. The horn was "it" for Kovin. The only edge of the real world that penetrated the clouds of his addiction, and that was where he did his only true living. Cabiness had to remind himself that he hadn't invited the cutting match. Why louse up music with that kind of feeling? If they had to, they could stand in the alley and throw rocks at each other. It would satisfy the same impulses and be a more wholesome expression of them. Anyway it was a fluke. He hadn't really blown Kovin down. Kovin was fouled on junk. His anxieties were stunned, and his talent had lost its sharp edge.

Cabiness unsnapped his horn. And without realizing what he intended to do, he turned and looked directly at the table where Jean and Randozza were sitting. He caught her eyes on him, brooding and intense. She looked away at the moment of contact. Randozza smiled and beckoned him over.

"How are you, Jean?"

She was wearing a little flat hat like the lid of a sugar can. Her mouth looked dry.

"Fine, Lee. And you?"

This was the Beach. You didn't take things big. Or, at least, tried to avoid that appearance—it wasn't cool. And to be cool was both fundamental virtue and prime commandment. But Cabiness noticed, with a painful irony, that they had both instinctively fallen into the quiet formality of an older and safer language.

Randozza was standing with his hand out. "That was some set," he offered. "I just wanted to tell you."

He shook hands, feeling the solid strength of the other man's grip, and matching it. Randozza was dressed very quietly in a suit of some soft dark material, his bold white collar crisp against his tan. You didn't tan in San Francisco. Not even in the summertime. When Randozza withdrew his hand, Cabiness saw a heavy silver link the size of a quarter. Red fires glimmered in the eyes of a miniature heraldic lion. Sheer corn. But Jean was wearing what he knew to be her best dress. Together they were right out of *Esquire*.

Cabiness shrugged uncomfortably with the acute visual image of his own wrinkled jacket and dirty T-shirt. There was more that didn't show. He hadn't changed his socks in three days because he'd forgotten to pick up his laundry.

He hadn't shaved for two days. He'd taken his last bath at Jean's, and he wasn't sure where he was going to take his next since he didn't have one, and—

What did all that matter? But he found himself thinking of those things in the brief moment when he looked at the smooth conventional gloss of the couple sitting before him.

Jean was gravely shifting her cup in her saucer as if it were important to have it sitting just right. Randozza sat down and dropped his hand on the back of her chair in a casual gesture of ownership. "Did you ever think of trying to make some real money with that talent of yours?"

"I do all right," he said tightly, conscious of the pucker of displeasure that marred Jean's forehead. Does she still care? Or does she only want to win an argument?

Randozza smiled tolerantly. "What do you call all right?"

"Whatever I call it, that's what it is," he said, and it was such a natural exit line that he couldn't miss it. He nodded. "Well, I've got to make it."

Randozza called after him, "If you change your mind, look me up."

Whatever that means. Go jump in the dollar machine and let it press all the juice out of you. You'll come out looking like those depressed men with the empty smiles who play for—Jesus save me—Lawrence Welk.

Furg was gone. Off with Kovin and Ann probably. A third wheel on a broken scooter. He took his horn apart, cased it, and left without looking back.

On the way home he stopped twice and tried to get a line on some pot. As much for himself as for Clair Hubler, but he didn't connect. Everyone was jittery and evasive, if not openly scared. And the Beach came tumbling down, he thought. This life is ending here. But he hated to consider moving on. Going where he was unknown.

He found himself thinking of Clair. A slightly overripe peach. He tried to define the faint dark taste, but he couldn't decide whether it was pleasant or unpleasant.

chapter nine

Jean decided she liked John Randozza. She found him interesting and complex. She was so used to the Beach people, that it seemed she read their glass heads like a broker at the end of a day of quiet trading; but in Randozza she sensed the hint of booms and panic, and there seemed to be a shift of purpose behind everything he did and said. But the precise purpose never emerged clearly. She could never be satisfied that she'd guessed what he was after. She was convinced that his motives, like cunning spies, operated behind many different disguises and didn't tell each other where they lived.

Besides this, she liked his courtesy, his easy charm, and—reluctantly—the money he had to spend.

She pulled her eyes away from the door and stopped her imagination from reaching after Lee. He was gone.

"That was a big thing, wasn't it?" John asked.

She looked into his large face with the curiously quiet eyes. "Yes," she replied.

"Is it over?"

"I think so—"

"Good. You know why? That fellow's heading for a dead end. In another ten years he'll be a joke. The only thing that excuses the life he's leading is his youth, and when that's gone—what is he?"

It shocked her to hear her own complaints against Lee stripped bare of any affection, but she didn't argue. She'd talked the subject out in her own mind. Now she wanted to forget it.

The life had left the club with Kovin, Furg and Lee. The light piano wasn't strong enough to hold a focus, and people were leaving. Going home or up to the Fillmore and Bop City, or downtown to Sam's 259 Club. John squinted at a half-pint in the dark, shaking it.

"Let's finish this and move on," he said, tipping the bottle over her cup.

The lukewarm coffee and whisky tasted like brass, but for some reason she gulped it down and then bent over the table coughing. It felt like she was trying to cry, but she didn't know what the hell for.

"Easy," John said, his hand firm on her back. "Come on, I'll take you home."

That was what she wanted, wasn't it? His hands lingered on her shoulders as he helped with her coat, and she looked up and back to smile at him. His silent eyes tugged at her, and she shivered and started out.

It was only a few blocks, but John unlocked his car. She settled into the big seat with pleasure. It was better to have a car. It was childish to think otherwise. Maybe it wasn't the most important thing in the world, but it was satisfying to ride the few blocks down Grant Avenue in the new convertible, lifting her hands to the kids standing around in front of the Coffee Shop, feeling the rush of the night air on her face. It was like a high-school dream, simple and uncomplicated.

Her only negative thought when John started to follow her upstairs was that her room was so small and dull. But she didn't really care. Her head was buzzing pleasantly, and she laughed softly when she couldn't quite manage the key and felt his hands taking over.

She switched the light on and turned to him, murmuring, "It's not much of a place."

But he was setting the night latch. He's direct enough, she thought. Then she realized again how big he was. Even bending, his broad back was above the level of her eyes. She felt a warm softening begin in her.

John tossed the key on the table and measured her with his eyes, deliberately looking her over. She straightened and smiled, feeling the impulse to turn so he could look more fully.

He put his hands into his pockets. "Strip," he said flatly.

"What?" she asked uncertainly. He'd never kissed her. Never put his hands on her in any but a casual way.

He frowned, getting one hand back out of his pocket so it could smooth the hair over his ear; he patted absently at one of his dense waves, seeming to test it for springiness.

"Strip," he said. "Take your clothes off. That's clear enough."

Jean felt a nip of anger and unconsciously she squared her shoulders. "I will—when I'm ready."

She sensed the motion to her side and quickly stepped back. Randozza, his hand open to slap, missed her and swung clear around, carried by his own weight. He recovered and scowled. "Don't push me," he said.

"Don't push you?" she demanded indignantly. "Don't *you* push me."

Randozza was busy settling his coat, disarranged by his wild swing; he unbuttoned the single button, then rebuttoned it. "I was just putting you on," he said, without looking up.

"Sure," Jean replied, uncertain whether she believed him. "You know any more funny games like that? I haven't laughed so hard in years."

"All right, forget it. I just wanted to see how *real* you are. Whether you'd admit to yourself and me at the same time just what it was you brought me up here to do, or whether you'd have to back in, so you could tell yourself later, 'Well, I just got carried away.'"

"Christ," Jean said wearily. "I haven't heard crap like that since I left high school. Next you'll be telling me I'm not a real woman, that I must be frigid, or a bull-dagger, or something."

"Let's just drop it, huh, baby? You know you turn me on. Maybe I'm just trying to give myself a little protection because I think you'd like to get back with that musician, Cabiness."

"That's finished, all finished."

"I'd like to think so, baby." He moved next to her and put his fingers inside the neck of her dress. She didn't resist him, but the beginnings of excitement she'd felt before didn't return. He ran his thumb slowly up and down the side of her neck.

"Do you want a cup of coffee?" she asked.

"Hummmm?" he murmured.

"Coffee. Do you want some coffee?"

"I can't even remember what coffee is," he said.

Jean laughed, and felt his hand pushing deeper into her dress, feeling warm and pleasantly firm against her hidden skin. "That was a silly thing to say—strip!—did you read that somewhere?" She started laughing louder. "Come on, did you?"

Randozza didn't answer. He was smiling down at her, but his amusement seemed forced. Then she was aware that he had both hands on the neck of her dress, pulling her up so she was on tiptoe, leaning in against him. Her collar grew tight across the back of her neck; then she heard the shriek of ripping fabric, and cold air hit her stomach.

"I said, strip!" Randozza whispered. "And, baby, I meant it."

Jean opened her mouth to say something out of her confusion, she didn't know what, but instead she caught her breath sharply and was suddenly so weak for Randozza her legs wouldn't hold her. She threw her arms around his neck and sagged against him.

"That's the way, baby. That's fine, just fine." His hands were busy with her. "We just had to get that straight, that's all." He lifted her easily and put her on the bed, the short way, so her head hung down the side and all she could see was the painting on her far wall as it looked upside down.

"That was my best dress," she murmured, not really caring but noting a fact.

"You could have dresses that would make that one look like a burlap bag," he said over her. She waited, but then he was moving back, and in a moment she felt his mouth.

"I don't like that," she said. "I'm simple. For me the nicest distance between two points is a straight line." She chuckled, and watched his face as it appeared again above her. She felt his weight. Then it started.

When she opened her eyes afterward, she was dumbfounded to see Randozza up, dressed, and carefully brushing lint from his suit. He noticed her eyes open and winked at her as his hands were moving to adjust his tie.

"The greatest, baby," he said. "Really, the greatest."

"Thanks," she said with a trace of dryness. "Are you leaving?"

"Yeah, I got to take care of business."

He took some money out of his billfold and dropped it on the kitchen table. "Get yourself a couple of new dresses. I'll pick you up for dinner tomorrow."

"Okay," she said. "What time?"

"Just wait for me, baby, I'll be by when I can make it."

She nodded, looking at the swell of his deep chest and the square set of his heavy shoulders, still quite obvious even when, as now, he was wearing a suit. A crazy-looking man, she thought and remembered how hard his arms had seemed beneath the urgency of her fingers. Randozza had his comb out and was stooped down in front of her mirror so he could see. He combed his hair carefully, disarranging it twice before he got it the way he wanted it.

My tiger's vain, she thought gently. And corny, she added.

After he'd left, Jean lay awake for a long time trying to understand what it was she'd learned about herself during those few moments it took John to tear her dress.

chapter ten

Cabiness turned, swaying onto the approach of the Golden Gate Bridge. He was at the wheel of Ann's car. Furg had borrowed it, but Furg didn't have a license. BeeGee sat between them, and Motion, a quiet, perpetually angry bass player, slumped in the back seat with a horn wedged in over the top of him.

Cabiness watched the weather-stained cement piling dropping off to the water far below. Ahead, the orange suspension tower grew larger and larger, and the foot-thick cables seemed to spin in the darkness. Yellow fog lights went by like slow explosions above them, and far below in the black vault of water, small green and red specks moved slowly on the bows of invisible boats.

"Too much," Furg said quietly, but Cabiness didn't amplify. He was thinking of the pot under the seat. The bridge was a natural police trap, with State highway cars constantly on duty at either end. He thought he suffered more from nervousness than fear, but his guts were heavy and his hands tight on the wheel.

It had been late afternoon before he'd finally connected. Someone had steered him to Sullivan. It should have been a jelly-bean transaction to Sullivan, dealing schmeck like he did, but Sullivan had hung him up until almost 8:00 o'clock over a couple of cans of pot. How they loved the mysteries and formalities of their trade... leave twenty bucks in the hollow oak and blink your lights three times... the stuff will be hidden in the third volume of Gibbon's *Decline and Fall* in the public library. Sullivan was playing a bigger role than he ever attempted on the stage.

As they approached the toll gate, Furg asked, "Anyone got a quarter?"

"It's thirty-five now," Cabiness said, and handed him a dollar. He stared straight ahead as the money passed. But the toll taker had long since seen everything in automobiles that was ever likely to be crammed in one. "What a gig," Furg remarked as they speeded up again. He dropped the toll receipt fluttering from the side of the car.

"Watch the cars go by," BeeGee murmured in some kind of agreement. She was entirely in black, and her orange hair flamed around her white face.

The first buildings of Sausalito appeared above the shore. Cabiness smiled. This is just where Clair Hubler would give a party. A nice airy-fairy musical-comedy sort of Bohemia. He drove into the small town and found Bayroad. True to its name it followed the curve of the water. Cabiness slowed down, looking for the address on the little white houses backed down to the bay.

When he realized they were past it, he braked and looked back. He laughed out loud.

Their destination was a ferry boat.

"Crap," said the bass player from in back. "Ain't that cute."

"Holy smoke," Furg murmured half mockingly, but BeeGee was enthusiastic.

"That's crazy," she said. "What a place to live."

Cabiness backed the old Chevy to where a small ramp led across to the wooden half-oval lip of the ferry. The boat wasn't beached. It was secured to pilings by ropes as thick as a man's arm.

Clair appeared at the head of the ramp in a white cocktail dress.

"And there's the ferry princess," BeeGee punned tartly.

"Prince, I'm afraid," Cabiness said, but marked as he said it how good she looked. Like something expensive, finely wrapped.

When they piled out he lifted the seat and shook the two Prince Albert cans out of an old grease rag. The ramp swayed as he crossed it, and Clair smiled, a controlled smile, but not quite social. When he held the cans out to her, she quickly put her hands behind her back.

"Not now. I haven't any place to keep it."

Cabiness tapped the top can. "This is not gingerbread."

"I know. I'm sorry. But this isn't my boat. I wouldn't want to bring anything like that aboard. You understand, don't you?"

He nodded curtly.

He put the cans back under the seat, hiding them deeper because the car wouldn't lock. The others were making it onto the boat, the bass player last, holding his horn over his head, probably getting that special feeling of importance that playing a gig gave. Coming like gypsies with their esoteric skills and equipment—hardened, wise and childish.

He found them setting up in a corner of the big central room. The original hardwood benches were gone, and the lunch counter had been converted into an elaborate kitchen-buffet affair, paneled and louvered, a hollow island full of dense white kitchen equipment. The home beautiful, on land or sea. The rest of the room was painted black, gray and ocher, and the clusters of furniture were old knobby stuff that had started life with very different expectations. Now, refinished in fashionable shades, the furniture hit Cabiness with the same bitter taste he experienced seeing the little ducks dyed for Easter. The round nautical windows were unchanged, overlooking the water as they always had.

BeeGee was banging an "A" on a mottled-gray concert grand, and Furg was adjusting his horn to the pitch of the piano. The bass player was looking for some place to put his bag, muttering under his breath. He finally gave up and threw it under the piano.

Clair was standing with an older couple, and Carla was beside her, looking as stiff as she had the other night, but with the addition of a black swollen quality he could sense but not define. Clair called him over and told him the guests were beginning to arrive. She didn't offer to introduce him to her friends, and they looked their polite curiosity.

Cabiness found himself reluctantly conscious of the picture the group created. Furg was in rumpled suntans, the collar and sleeves buttoned tight like a farmer, exposing three inches of bony wrist; BeeGee, with her baggy black sweater and chalk face, looked like the movie impression of Dracula's helpmate; Motion, the bass player, wore shades and a duck's ass haircut, his thin lips sealed with general and relentless bitterness against a whole world that didn't swing.

BeeGee started playing Errol Garner's "Misty" and Furg picked it up. The sound of Furg's horn was enough to scatter his depression. Nutty! Furg's 'bone was a brass bowel hooked in his nervous system, completing some rare equation of heart and body. Furg was a child, a vagabond child, a fey and travel-torn minstrel barely suffered in the halls of the minor barons. But, whether they knew it or not, Furg was necessary to them, to breathe into their lives the vital stuff of myth. Furg was the outsider come to tell them who they were, to tell them how shiny and grand the ordinary uses of their days could sometimes be.

Cabiness unpacked his horn.

The party was about what he'd expected. People were coming in. Pink, clean examples of college and social Bohemia, mostly young and some white-haired, tanned and professionally young. They were roughly thirty per cent queer. He saw Clair moving around. In her white dress with her pale hair she looked chilly. He caught her smile coming and going, like distant sunlight on ice.

Liquor was beginning to move out from the buffet in brown tumblers and frosted glasses. Gasoline-colored martinis, the correct white onion speared with a bright toothpick.

They were talking. Not loud yet, just greeting each other, catching up, but still talking. Furg put down a couple of irritated honks and ended with a raspy hokum lick. Cabiness knew he was drug already, but they were getting paid. They had a right to play what they wanted, but they had no right to demand listeners.

"Let's take something way up," he suggested. "Let them know we're here."

They went pounding into the furious chart of "Room 421," a jazz tune, probably created and named in some very early pot-bound hour in room 421 of an on-the-road hotel, the boys blowing with towels stuffed in the bells of their horns.

Sure sound and energy stilled the busy glasses. People looked around, catching some of the contagion. Cabiness took his solo first; finishing it quickly, he turned it over to BeeGee. She got off a cloud of luminous moths, sending them into a sky etched with the needle-bright points of complex and dissonant constellations.

Some of the crowd gathered around. So they were doing a little better than those sad old bastards with mustaches, who sat behind the potted palms and sawed out nameless waltzes. Some of the younger ones were patting their feet. Cabiness saw white bucks and lancia slippers, open toes and sandals, all tricked obediently into the beat. A big freckled girl was grinning and snapping her fingers soundlessly, pushing her head forward on her smooth unfreckled neck, rocking her hips slightly with her shifting weight. But for the most part, people stood listening for a while with an abstracted judging look on their faces, then moved on to do whatever they did at parties.

When they took their first break Cabiness went out to the car and rolled some joints out of Clair's pot. He sat behind the wheel and smoked one, and he felt better when they started to play again. Better or different? Who cared? He didn't care.

On the next break he headed for the double glass doors that led to the old observation deck. Clair stopped him. Calling his name. He watched her swaying, staccato, high-heeled walk, the linen ripples swirling from her hips. He felt a flicker of excitement and rebelled against it.

"We're taking a break," he told her.

"I know that." She looked sulky. Her eyes seemed darker than he remembered. "I meant to ask you before, but do you usually get paid before or after?"

"Don't sweat it. We usually don't get paid at all." Then on impulse he added, "You don't owe me anything."

She wasn't slow at all. Her hand clenched, and she said, "That's altogether different."

"It was too much money."

"I don't think so. There was some risk, wasn't there? How are you going to put a price on that?"

"It was about as dangerous as a trip to the Safeway."

"I don't believe that," she said firmly.

He watched her a moment until her eyes wavered. Then he gestured at the glass doors. "Can I go out there?"

She smiled. "Certainly. They live downstairs. It's all made over. Would you like to see?"

"No." He put his finger on her elbow. "Let's make it out on the deck."

The air was still warm and the sky and the bay formed a single sheet of darkness with a double moon broken only by the slightly darker soft folding of hills on the far shore. There was a lot of white sundeck furniture, but she

walked through it to the rail and leaned there with her arms crossed. From
under the boat came the flat concussions of small waves; the air was strong
with salt.

He snapped the ends loose on one of the joints and lit it, taking the first
deep drag, getting it going, and then he passed it to Clair. She accepted without comment and started to smoke it like a cigarette. He showed her how to
take some air with the smoke.

"That's strong," she said breathlessly.

It wasn't, but it was all right. "It's some of yours," he told her.

They passed the dwindling cigarette back and forth until someone stuck
their head out the door, and Cabiness snapped the roach out into the water.
The head said "Oh" and withdrew.

Clair looked at him curiously. "I don't feel anything," she said. Then she put
her hands to her temples and started laughing. She ran her fingers into her
hair and held her head tightly. She was still laughing.

He took her elbows and looked into her face. She stopped laughing. Her
skin was very smooth and soft, warmer than the air, and he shifted his grip
to her upper arms, holding her too tightly. Almost like a reflex her head went
back and her mouth parted. He wanted to taste her different textures.
Explode her cramped spirit.

Instead he asked quietly, "When did you decide to have this ball? The night
you hired us?"

She didn't answer. Her face was still, shadowed, but somehow moonlight
found her lower lip, lighting the furrowed smoothness. A big red neon was
heart-beating on the far shore, and above it was the ghostly flicker of a drive-
in screen.

"You know, you've got too much money. And besides I don't like you very
much."

She still didn't say anything. It was too dark to read her eyes, but it was obvious that she was waiting for something to happen—high, clear and drifty—
waiting for something to happen.

He kissed her. Irritated enough to kiss her roughly, to lift her by the arms
onto her toes and push his mouth harshly into hers. For a beat her lips stayed
cool, then her mouth opened, warm and wet. She sighed along his cheek and
leaned into him, limp and passive. He forced the flat of his hand over her
breast, and she made a low sound in her throat. He kissed her again and tried
to kiss her quietly, but she wouldn't have it. She grabbed his head, and pulled
his mouth down on hers hard. Then the pot nudged him powerfully and he
didn't care.

When they came apart, she said, "I've got a room downstairs."

"I'll ask!" he flared. "I'm not a goddam stud."

He could see the pinch and spread of her nostrils, heard her breathing heav-

ily, then she was answering him in that cool detached logic that pot sometimes brings right along with the clash of nerves.

"—and I'm not sorry if I don't have to worry about money, and I'm not sorry
if I've dented your pride. If it was what it should be, it wouldn't dent so easily."

He took a deep breath and answered in the same detached tone. "If you
want to be ringmaster, you'd better get one of those varnished, half-pansies
in there. I don't care much about planned recreation."

She put her hand on his arm. "Please, Lee. It doesn't mean anything—nothing happens." That was as much as she could say. She sketched a futile gesture in the air and asked, "Do you know what I mean?"

She caught him completely off balance, because he knew she was trying to
say something very difficult, something she probably hadn't attempted to say
before. Her openness engaged his sympathy, and also he couldn't resist the
role she'd cast him in.

He reached up and put his hand along her face. "Where's your room?"

She led him back along the side of the boat, down a wooden ladder, and
along a white hall into a featureless guest room with two women's coats
lying side by side on the Hollywood bed. He picked up the coats and held
them inquiringly while she turned the spread down.

"Carla's," she said briefly before her face was covered with the flash of her
dress. She came out pink and white with violet underwear, softer and more
vulnerable looking than he had expected, and while she loosened the faintly
medical-looking straps that held up her stockings, he lit the last joint, handing it to her deliberately to stop the graceless and determined preparations
she was making. He waited until she was lost in the smoke before he loosened her bra and ran his hands beneath it.

"Oh," she breathed and he saw her stomach flutter. Sense of wonder, he
thought. That's what she needs. Not the overbrisk heartiness of a girl-scout
project. He switched on the bedlamp and turned off the overhead lights. The
small room went amber. She was laying half off the bed, still smoking. The
glow of the coal flushed on her face.

They passed the joint until the room was full of thick orange haze that they
moved in languidly, hot as salamanders, drifting to their certain burning.

When the door opened, it didn't make any sense, didn't penetrate until the
cold air fell on his back, and numbly he broke his rhythm to see Carla standing a foot into the room, her mouth a thin twisted line, her eyes sick with disgust.

"Oh, you bitch," she got out with great effort. "You little bitch!"

Clair's face was swollen with blood, her eyes dull, still inward. Instinctively
Cabiness pulled his hips back, but she grabbed him fiercely and told the other
woman, "Get out."

Carla made a noise deep in her throat, throwing her hands up in a strained awkward gesture. Then she was stumbling towards the bed trying to hit at Clair under Cabiness.

"Filth! Rotten filth!"

He grabbed her wrists, but she tore loose and clawed his face before he managed to hold her, bent almost to her knees. Clair slid out the other side of the bed and stood leaning forward, her hand caught in the soft flesh of her belly.

"You miserable freak," she spat at Carla. "I was going to make it. Do you hear that? I was going to make it."

"Shut up!" Cabiness told her sharply. He turned to Carla, sagging forward against his locked fists. "Are you ready to leave?" he asked quietly.

She looked up at him, her stern eyes shattered, and he could see into the part of her where everyone is small, alone and afraid. She nodded and looked away.

When he let her go, she straightened and walked out without closing the door. When he reached for the knob he saw her leaning against the wall of the white galleyway. She was either sobbing or trying not to throw up.

When he turned back, Clair was on the bed, her legs open.

"Not here," he told her.

"Why not? That didn't have anything to do with you and I."

"Maybe not," he admitted. "I take things pretty much as they come, but I don't think anything's going to happen here."

Clair sat up and threw her head back. "All right. We'll go somewhere else."

She gathered up her underwear and wadded it into her purse. Then she slipped her dress on and picked up her coat. Cabiness dressed quickly and when he was finished she handed him the money to pay off Furg, BeeGee and Motion. It was too much, but he didn't refuse for them.

Furg didn't bother to hide an amused grin. He danced the bills on his big palm and said, "Tell me I can't call 'em. All that crazy bread."

And as Cabiness left, he started blowing funky blues, the trombone squalling in rut.

When they were back in San Francisco, he asked, "Where do you live?"

But she shook her head. "Carla might be there already. She'll be moving out, I think. Let's go to your place." She sat close to him with her hand on the inside of his leg staring straight ahead, with her eyes still half closed. He suddenly thought he liked her after all, and, when he pulled her big car up beneath the MACARONI sign, he paused to kiss her.

When they broke, she asked, "Have you got it?"

He patted his jacket pocket. The cans clicked against each other.

"Good," she said, and he could hear the catch of excitement in her voice.

He was checking her car to make sure it was locked, when he heard, "All right, Cabiness. Hold it right there."

Carver was alone. He came quickly across the street with his gun out.

chapter eleven

The bust was different than the last one. It surprised Cabiness. He'd expected Carver to rage or gloat, but the Narco handled him with weary contempt, and Clair seemed too startled to put up a fuss.

Now in the booking room of the city prison, a stern young sergeant made a calm efficient recording of his certain guilt. Then Carver pulled him aside to shake him down. They went behind a wooden screen that would hide the middle part of his body from Clair, who was sitting on a bench across the room. She was holding up. She'd fallen back on a dead formal tone, calmly accepting what she made clear was a disagreeable experience.

"Strip down," Carver told him, standing back to watch as he piled his clothes on a bench provided for that purpose. Carver picked up each article and went over it. He knocked his shoes out and examined the heels.

"Your socks, too."

Cabiness stripped them off, standing gingerly on the cold cement. Carver lifted his leg as he would examining a horse, running his fingers over the small veins of the ankle. A feeling of humiliation forced its way through the icy reserve Cabiness had imposed in himself. This was something he couldn't get used to. Again he felt the cool fingertips on the inner curves of his buttocks and flinched automatically.

Carver snickered. "Don't worry."

There was buzzing in his ears; above it he was aware of a thin whisper of music from a radio and the voices of two jailers arguing over a play at cards.

"All right, put them back on."

As he was dressing, Carver asked him, "What's the story on the broad?"

"No story," he said, automatically moving to protect her.

"There could be quite a story there." Carver smiled faintly as he looked over the screen to where Clair was sitting. Her hair was still tousled, but the blush of heat had left her face. "Nice piece. Is she a head?"

Cabiness drew his belt tight. "I doubt it."

"She wasn't going to turn on with you?"

"I might have tried that if I couldn't make it any other way. But why waste grass?"

Carver looked doubtful. Cabiness was dressed now, ready to get on with it, anxious to put off the moment when he would have time to think. He caught the scent of fear through the stale routine of the arrest, but he wasn't ready to deal with it even though he knew it would come for him a long time before sleep.

"Sit down a minute," Carver said.

The Narco sat alongside him, holding his hands crossed lightly on his cocked knee. The smooth moldings of his face seemed edged with gray. A gray man all over. Without passion. A regulator.

"You've had a long run," Carver told him, and he thought, here we go again. "But you look clean as far as heavy goes. That's where the real heat is. As for one pothead more or less..." Carver made a limp gesture as if he were shooing something away, "no one really gives a damn."

Cabiness held up his hand. "We've been through this—"

"You could walk out. Tonight."

"There's no point in kicking a dead horse. I don't know anything, and if I did I wouldn't tell you. So let's take it from there."

"Okay!" Carver stood up. "Okay, you just play it like that, and there's no way you're going to stay out of Q."

"This is my first offense," Cabiness reminded him.

"First offense? Crap! Do you know what your probationary report's going to look like? Known police character for over a year... Numerous arrests on suspicion... Refusal to cooperate with the police. You're jammed right. You better send over and have some of your buddies pick you out a nice quiet cell because you'll be there. You'll be there, and be there."

Cabiness didn't say anything, just stared at Carver, watching a muscle ridge in the cop's marble cheek.

Carver walked over and told the jailer, "Put him in the hype tank." The Narco was beginning to talk to Clair as the jailer led him out into a metal corridor.

He remembered the hype tank. It was the coldest tank in city prison, and it was deliberately kept that way. For some reason that he couldn't penetrate, the jailers seemed to hate addicts. It seemed to him like the old hatred of sex, inverted desire, and they were punishing for a pleasure they could imagine too keenly. He didn't know. But he did know that an ordinary thief or murderer never had to take the calculated abuses that addicts endured. There were no blankets, or even mattresses, and the only form of medication ever issued was aspirin. Cigarettes were forbidden, and the commissary wagon that served the other tanks didn't stop. It was bad enough that users picked up for other crimes would lie in the main-line tank with towels stuffed in their mouths so they wouldn't yell and betray that they were sick. Cold turkey was the only way they were going to kick, and if they had to kick it cold, it was better to do it where at least they could keep warm through the night of chills.

The jailer who took Cabiness in apparently thought he was hooked, because while he was manipulating the levers that opened the tank door, he gave him a smile of heavy superiority.

"It'll be rough about morning. But then you'll have lots of company. Take seventeen."

Far down the gray wall, watered by the wide-spaced night lights, a black rectangle appeared. He started for it, hearing the tank door close behind him. When he stepped into the cell, the door shuddered and closed, but not before he'd had time to see that three out of the four bunks were empty. A dark figure lay huddled in the lower right, and as the door slammed, it stirred and moaned.

The bunks were like carrot graters hung from the wall, solid slabs of metal except for the rows of holes, all uniform, the size of silver dollars. With the use of a mattress the holes would have tended to make the bunk more comfortable, a little yielding, but without a mattress they added to the torment of the hard surface.

He settled on the unoccupied lower and sat quietly while the stillness he'd dreaded rushed around him. But in the hard channels of his own mind he couldn't find much sympathy for himself. He'd understood the hazards of his environment, understood them well enough to caution Furg against them half a dozen times, and now the least he could do for himself was hang by his ankle in this square's trap and keep his mouth shut.

And just maybe, if some wild chance paid off and he could squeeze out of this, he'd blow the Beach. Blow so fast it would all seem like a foolish dream.

When he rolled over on the hard bunk and tried to sleep, it wasn't Clair he thought of, but Jean.

In the morning he found that he knew his cell partner, a short husky Negro called the Bear because of his enormous breadth of jowl and reddish eyes. Bear was a bootblack by day and a bass player by night, of large, if untrained, talent. But he had trouble getting gigs because he only showed up to play them when he felt like it.

Now Bear rolled over listlessly, still hugging his arms to his thick chest, and when he saw Cabiness he shook his head slowly.

"Cab. What they got you for?"

"Possession."

"Stuff?"

"No, just pot."

Bear blinked his deep-set eyes. "That still do it. They got you cold quack?"

"Cold enough."

"Whoo-eee... that rough. That mighty rough. I been sick. God, how I been sick."

Cabiness could see it. Bear's face, usually fat and shiny, was gray, and his eyelids were lined with an unhealthy-looking white substance. He struggled up, holding his side.

"Damn cramps so bad. They like to kill me in this jail, Cab. You know what that dirty mammy-jammer did to me? That Carvah? He told me I give him two dope fiends and he let me go. An' I give him two. I give him a couple of light-running nowhere dope fiends, an' I been layin' in this jail a week kickin' my black ass off."

He paused for a moment, then looked up, his eyes heavy and dull. "Cab, you think they gonna turn me go?"

"I don't know, Bear."

Cabiness stood up and stretched his stiff muscles. He used the toilet thrust out between the two bunks. The thing to do was decide whether you were pissing in the bedroom or sleeping in the can, and not think of Bear giving up two of his friends just on the desperate chance that he could stay free a while longer to poison himself. And even if Carver did street him, Bear would be eighty-six all over town, but Bear was too dull to realize that, too dull to comprehend anything but his immediate needs—

Cabiness winced at his own patronage... nice of you to forgive the Bear. Who the hell are you to forgive the Bear?

He turned back: "They'll probably let you out when they're sure you gave up straight drawings."

Bear smiled weakly. "You think that it?"

Cabiness nodded.

"Man, I sure hopes so."

The doors started rattling and pounding, and in a moment their door opened. A trustee shoved in two tin plates of farina and prunes. There were two prunes in each plate, like the eyes of a melted snowman. Bear looked at his plate but he didn't move to pick it up. "Cain't eat," he complained.

Cabiness emptied them into the toilet. A little later they were back with some bread and coffee. Cabiness ate all the bread and Bear sipped coffee, sitting hunched over, his head pulled into his shoulders, holding the cup in both hands. He snuffled continuously, and every few minutes he shook with chills. Cabiness looked away. He'd always liked the Bear for his honest and natural good-heartedness, as well as for the excitement he could create in a rhythm section with his big fat brown notes and pushing beat. He hoped Carver would keep his bargain, but it didn't seem likely.

The routine of the hype tank hadn't varied, and he found it easier to be fingerprinted and photographed with chilling impersonality, or to be walked out on the harshly-lit stage of the line-up, to hear himself described in the one-dimensional logic of the police—he found these things easier than thinking.

But it was all over before noon, and he knew the long wait had started. Bear was curled up in his bunk, sleeping or trying to sleep, and Cabiness, who already wanted a cigarette badly, knew the craving he felt wasn't a hundredth part of Bear's hunger.

A coverless magazine was spread open on the top bunk—part of some former prisoner's attempt at comfort—and he seized on it. He tried to read an article by someone who was describing how it felt to wrestle a giant squid, but his own mental accounting squeezed through the florid article... two years. Probably two years.

He threw the magazine aside and listened to an impersonal voice in his own head say, I'll do two years. With luck and management it could be shaded to eighteen months. But he didn't really believe in luck, and he knew his face and manner were antagonizing to authority types. So call it two and a half years, which would make him nearly thirty when he got out. That was painful arithmetic. Nearly thirty with no real trade, no background, nowhere to go except the Beach, and he wasn't simple enough to believe the Beach would remember him, or that it would even be the same place he'd left. Then he remembered the promise he'd made to whoever it was that listened to such promises, if anyone did, that he'd stay off the Beach.

After awhile the Bear came alive and they talked shop. Tunes, gigs, who was cooking and who wasn't. Bear said they had a good band in the joint, so at least they could blow if they made it over there, but Cabiness wasn't convinced too much could happen musically in the environment he imagined over there.

"This is a cold shot," he told Bear, and Bear shook his head gloomily.

"You right, Cab. It hard, but it fair. You know somethin'? That Carvah came at me out o' nowhere. I jus' score, and I'm makin' it back to the pad. And there he were."

"That's the same way he took me...." Cabiness paused, staring straight ahead. "Who'd you make the buy from?"

"That Sully. You know? Gray-hair dude, fools around that actin' group over on Union?"

"I know."

"I got a nice piece of stuff off him," Bear said. "Man, I could sho' stand a taste of it now."

The thought set the Bear off. He lay down with a fit of chills, shaking so his heels rattled against the metal of the bunk. "Lord, Lord," he moaned. "I got me some misery."

He sang it a little in a primitive cotton-darkie cadence, and Cabiness was fiercely certain that there should somehow be a better deal for Bear. Bear was being held to a mumbled and ambiguous bargain made behind his back by two people he didn't know or care about.

Cabiness wandered out into the tank, but he didn't see anyone else he knew. It was depressing. Everyone was sealed into the individual cells of their own discomfort and concern. He folded his jacket for a pillow and stretched out on his bunk. The jail was quiet, and he lay for a long time listening to the water drip in the sink like the beat of a very slow clock in a quiet week of a long year.

When his name was called on the loudspeaker, he assumed it was Carver. He stood up and put his jacket on without emotion but prepared for a disagreeable set in the Narco division.

The jailer on the door led him into the booking room and turned him over to the desk sergeant. A civilian, in a quiet gray suit, carrying a zipper brief case, looked him over with guarded curiosity. Probably a Narco he'd never run into.

The desk sergeant said, "This is him."

Surprisingly, he found himself shaking a soft dry hand and looking into mild brown eyes sheltered behind heavy-rimmed glasses.

"How do you do, Mr. Cabiness. I'm Ernest Acton—" He coughed gently and continued. "Miss Hubler has engaged me to represent you. Ah... we have arranged your bail."

"Sign here," the desk sergeant said routinely, pushing a form at him, dropping a ball-point beside it.

Cabiness continued to stare at the lawyer for a moment, not sure what he expected or was afraid he'd see—a pimp's veiled scorn?—but he met only a quiet formality, tempered by an alert conformation of eye that he'd missed at first.

"I didn't expect this," he offered as some explanation for his blunt appraisal. Acton nodded, a mannered gesture.

"What's this for?" Cabiness asked the sergeant.

"Your property. You want it, don't you?"

He signed and received his wallet, cigarettes, matches, twenty-three dollars, a handful of change and his saxophone. He lit a cigarette and asked the sergeant, "How much was my bail?"

"Five thousand."

Then he heard Acton saying, "Of course, you understand the money will be returned to Miss Hubler when this matter is concluded—"

And the sergeant broke in with rocklike humor, "providing you don't take it on the heel and toe."

Probably she felt responsible, Cabiness decided, but he knew instantly that was too generous an appraisal. She'd been balked in something she wanted, and she was going to get it. Well, Lee-Boy, he told himself mildly, this is a new dimension in a weird role. But he was irritated and uncomfortable in spite of himself.

In the elevator, Acton shifted his feet and coughed again, probably not too happy with what he conceived his own role to be. "Miss Hubler's waiting in the car," he said with a hint of embarrassed conspiracy.

chapter twelve

Clair's apartment was in one of the skyhigh-rent buildings a half block off Union Square. There was an impersonal modishness to it, and it didn't seem likely that she'd lived there long.

Very little had been said on the way over. Whatever partial fiction Clair had fed Acton, he played it resolutely, confining himself to general remarks, sitting gingerly between them on the broad front seat of Clair's car.

Once settled in her front room, on an oyster-white couch beneath a print of a long-necked girl with slanted green eyes that Cabiness recognized as a Modigliani, Acton said, looking up, "Of course, you realize, Mr. Cabiness, that I'm a civil attorney."

Cabiness didn't understand how he was supposed to have realized that, but he did understand the lawyer was gently rubbing out some implied onus.

He was still standing uncertainly just inside the door. It had occurred to him that he was, quite literally, dirty, but at the painful squareness of Acton's formal address, his sense of humor rescued him. He put his horn down and went to sit in the chair that matched the couch. Clair had gone to "freshen up"—whatever that meant.

"Don't worry," he told the lawyer. "If you were Fallon, you couldn't help me."

"Maybe," Acton agreed cautiously. "All I have is Miss Hubler's story that the two of you were arrested late last night in possession of some marijuana, and that you were charged but she wasn't. She feels herself to be equally involved, which is why she wants to move to your defense—"

Cabiness started to interrupt, but Acton held his hand up firmly. His eyes were steady, almost authoritative, and he realized the lawyer was trying to lay down the official basis on which future discussions could be held without embarrassment to him.

"She is determined that you shouldn't go to prison, and now that you are free on bail a great deal more is possible. As I said, I'm a civil attorney, but I'm not entirely naive as to criminal matters, and we're now in a position to stall through a number of postponements and, bluntly, try to make a deal."

Cabiness smiled faintly. He'd about decided to like Acton. "Do you think there's a chance?"

"There's always a chance," the lawyer said firmly with the same brisk professional optimism usually associated with doctors. "But I'm not in a position to estimate yet—"

He was going to say more, but at that moment Clair returned. She'd changed from a suit into a light-colored dress that dropped smoothly around the gentle weight of her stomach.

"Not now, Ernest," she said. "Let's talk it out tomorrow."

"Tomorrow's Saturday."

"Monday, then."

Acton stood up. "All right. Give me a ring before you come over so I won't be tied up."

When the door closed behind the lawyer, she just looked at Cabiness, chewing her lower lip. She reached up and removed one of her earrings.

"You don't mind giving him the idea you're in heat?" he asked with some irritation.

Her look changed to one of curiosity. "You don't really give a damn, do you? The wild tumescent beatnik?"

"Come off that beatnik kick."

"You dress like one." She took a few steps closer to him. "We'll have to get you some clothes," she said reflectively.

"I've got some clothes," he replied bitterly. "Yes, such as they are."

She stood waiting.

He closed on her, more in anger than anything else. Her head snapped back, and he felt her loose softness all along the length of his own body. Her legs sagged, and he was holding her up by the small of the back, while she said, not at all in a voice of complaint, "You need a shave."

Her eyes were closed, her small mouth slack, and she didn't seem to be breathing. He lowered her to the couch. Gathering a handful of the soft material of her dress, he pulled it up. She was naked underneath it, as he'd known she would be. Magic. She was trying to put everything back as it had been before Carver stepped out of the shadows. He started with her, but it wasn't the same.

Ten minutes later still unsatisfied, she was looking up at him out of brittle eyes, saying, "We need some tea."

He stifled an angry sarcasm because he knew it sparked from his vanity. Instead he said flatly, "I've had enough to last me for awhile."

Her dress was bunched under her chin, and, now, she tore at it seeking release from her frustration in some kind of action. The cloth parted with a thin snarl, and he raised it so she could free it from her arms. She tossed it aside and settled back with a weary sigh. Something in the set of her expression, the unhappy puzzlement in her unmasked blue eyes, released a trickle of sympathy in him. He took her face in his hands and kissed her.

After a while he felt a mild heat come on her, and, maintaining it carefully, he was rewarded with the faint tremor of her climax, like the muted impact of distant waves. She didn't say anything, make any sound—her face was to the side, lost in a faint introspective frown—and her only large reaction was to tighten her hands on his shoulders. Abruptly, before her tension had relaxed, he plunged on to his own climax, lit by a smoky color almost like anger.

That was a bad set, he told himself—hardly worth five thousand dollars. But she seemed content. Her eyes had taken on a freshness that was new to them, and she traced his hairline with the tips of her fingers—up around his ears, down his neck.

"I knew you were the right one," she said.

If I'm the right one, the wrong ones must have been real bums. Out loud he asked, "Didn't you ever make it before at all?"

She looked away. "Not with a man. Not like that, anyway."

"It would have been better last night."

"I felt that," she said eagerly. "It was like nothing could go wrong. The tea, I guess."

He was silent a moment while the crazy impulse strengthened. What the hell? He was going to make the joint. This was just a fancy vacation.

"There are other things," he told her. "There's lots of ways to get on."

Immediately she wanted to know all about it. She had a large share of that wistful urgency that caused people to gulp down unnumbered barrels of neutral chemicals in the hope of somehow changing the formula fate, or whatever, had compounded for them.

"We'll connect," he said. "Maybe tonight."

"Are you going to move in here?" she asked.

"Am I?"

She smiled: "Of course."

He thought of it as paying dues, the musician's expression for any debt or obligation. It covered the hours of practice and study required to perfect technique, or any tedious preliminary to a desired end. She wasn't hard to take; she was alert, she was soft and smooth and she smelt good, but he had an uneasy intuition into the complex tensions of her nature. Still, at the going rate, five thousand dollars bought a lot of his time.

She was growing cramped beneath him and he shifted so she could get up. She had no shame of body and paused to look at the clock before she walked to the door. She was small, the machinery of her waist and hips almost fragile, and her breasts rode without swaying, snubbed off rather bluntly with pinkish-brown nipples. Pure class, Furg would say. Cabiness felt a stir of excitement.

She paused in the doorway, and said over her shoulder, "We've still time to do your shopping."

She was gone before he could protest. In a moment he heard the rattle of a shower. He put on his pants. All right, he concluded, if it means that little to her, why should I be stiff about it?

He was lighting a cigarette when the doorbell sounded. "See who that is, will you, lover?" Clair called from the bathroom.

He slipped on his shirt. Carla was standing in the hall, her face tensely white above the collar of a plain blue suit. Her hostile eyes went over him and ended unerringly on his bare feet. He shrugged. She'd seen more than his feet.

"My things," she said stiffly, gesturing with her head.

For the first time he became aware of a set of matched luggage sitting in the hall. A cardboard box, neatly tied with white string, sat beside them. He noticed that the box had originally held White Star Tuna.

"Who is it?" Clair called.

Cabiness didn't answer.

"Lover?"

"It's me," Carla announced in a strained tone. "I just came for the rest of my things."

Clair was silent. Carla tried to manage the two suitcases with one arm, leaving the other arm free to carry the box. Automatically, Cabiness took the box and one of the suitcases from her. "I'll help you."

"I can manage."

"I said, I'd help you."

She shrugged, and he followed her down the hallway to the elevator, conscious of his bare feet. She pressed for the car and then turned to give him a level look.

"Do you know what you're getting into?" she asked.

She was probably backing toward forty. Her mouth was conventionally, if blandly, tinted, but otherwise she was without make-up, and the pores in the creases beside her nose were coarse. He was close enough to catch her scent, and it was the same one he associated with fresh laundry.

"I'm not getting into anything," he told her.

"Very well," she replied, and looked through the glass door, down the shaft, at the top of the moving car. Her head snapped back.

"She's utterly spoiled. She's no good to anyone, least of all to herself. She'll turn any affection you show her against you. It's her nature, and—"

She broke off. The elevator stopped, empty.

"I'm not easily damaged," Cabiness said quietly.

"Then you're fortunate."

In a gesture that was probably uncharacteristic, she stood aside while he opened the door and set her things inside.

"I can manage from here," she said firmly. "I have a cab waiting. The driver will help me."

Cabiness nodded politely.

Carla held up a dry-looking hand as if she were a teacher about to make an important point. Then the gesture wilted.

"Would you see that she doesn't hurt herself... with drugs, or anything like that? I don't mean to imply... I mean, I don't know what kind of a person you are really...."

She faltered.

"That's all right," Cabiness told her. "I don't know myself."

He pushed away the impulse to make an easy promise to look after Clair and stood watching while Carla inclined her head and closed the door. She kept her eyes turned away as the car sank.

Back in the apartment, Clair called to him, and he found her in the bedroom dressing for the street. A wall-sized mirrored door was slid partially back to reveal a deep closet choked with suits and dresses. Carla's things couldn't have been but a drop in that ocean of clothes.

Clair was at another mirror in a blue slip, vented with panels of lace. She was combing her hair, her face bland with the rhythm of her arm.

"What'd Carla have to say?"

"Nothing."

"Nothing! I'll bet. I could smell her spleen clear in the john. What'd she say? Come on, lover."

He sat down on the bed behind her, digging his toes into the fluffy white rug. "You want to know something?" he asked.

"Of course."

"Don't call me 'lover'—it makes you sound like too many other people."

The comb paused, and she turned to look at him. "What should I call you then?"

"My name's Lee," he suggested.

"All right. Lee." Then she smiled. "Does it make that much difference?"

"No, it's a minor point, but I thought I'd tell you."

She turned back to the mirror and inspected something about her right eye. Then, "While you're telling, why don't you tell me what the Iron Duke had to say?"

"She asked me to look after you."

Clair stared at him incredulously through the mirror; then she laughed. "Really?"

"Yes."

"I don't believe that. She probably asked you to look after me with a meat cleaver."

Cabiness lay back on the bed. "Is that how you think she feels?"

"You heard her last night. I'm glad she's gone. I couldn't have put up with her for another day."

She went on running Carla down, and he watched her making up her face. How quickly the nervous system adjusted even to compound shocks. A few hours ago he'd been in the hype tank, surrounded by the crumpled faces of sick and defeated men. Now this rich apartment, softness, even luxury, with a handsome girl moving around in her slip still carrying the glow of his energy—

He didn't feel anything because it wasn't real. A pot-dream to fade in the gray morning when some bailiff cuffed him and took him back into jail.

"You'd better shave," she said. "There's a razor and some new blades in the medicine chest."

She took him across Union Square to the Hastings, in the basement lobby of the Saint Francis Hotel—a rich, quiet store with deep rugs and without visual prices or advertising of any kind. The clerk was bland and very smooth. He led Cabiness down the rack toward the more expensive suits, and Clair acted wifely, sitting in a chair, calling him "dear," insisting that since it had been so long since he'd had a new suit, he should get two. Cabiness suspected that she was secretly amused at the clerk's successful, but still obvious, efforts to overlook the dirty and worn clothes he was wearing as he fingered the cloth of the hundred-and-fifty-dollar Hickey-Freeman's.

He bought shirts, links, shoes, even a topcoat, and when it was all totaled in the clerk's red book, Cabiness said, "She'll pay you."

The clerk's face didn't change in any way, but a flush of amusement went over it. "Of course, sir."

Clair wrote a check and arranged to have the suits delivered to her address when the alterations were completed.

Cabiness pretended to examine a silver-headed walking stick.

"Are you interested in that, sir?" the clerk asked be hind him.

"Hell, no."

They spent the rest of the afternoon moving his stuff out of the loft on top of the macaroni factory. It took two trips, and each time they passed under Jean Diamanto's windows. The second time, he glanced up and saw the blue ribbon Jean had tied to the shade to raise and lower it. He experienced the shock of seeing a familiar thing from a different viewpoint, then turned to catch Clair looking at him sharply. She remembered.

He was driving, so he pretended something on the street needed his attention, but he heard Clair asking lightly, "What do men see in a big girl like that?"

"I don't know. She's a swinging chick. Size hasn't anything to do with it. Anyway, she's not that big."

"She's enormous," Clair said bluntly. "Her breasts must weigh twenty pounds apiece."

He found that he didn't want to discuss Jean on that level, didn't want to discuss her with Clair at all. He changed the subject.

chapter thirteen

That night they spent feeling each other out under the surface. They ate in, opening cans, and Clair started talking about herself over the end of dinner—rediscovering some of herself through him.

Finally, she told him about the morning when she had calmly announced to her father that she was pregnant, and all he had wanted to know was "Who?"

She shrugged. "And I had to tell him I couldn't be sure. He howled. 'Can't be sure? Holy Mother of God, sixteen years old and you can't be sure!' So that about did it between us." She paused, staring past him.

"Did you have the kid?" he asked.

"Oh, no. He was efficient. He had me aborted the next day. But after that we were strangers to each other. If he was punishing me for the pleasure he thought I had from it, he was punishing me for nothing."

Cabiness didn't try to find anything to say to her; there wasn't much to say, and after a moment she grinned wryly and pushed her hair back from her forehead.

"I know this is old sad hat, but I had to spread for anyone who wanted me, because I had to find out what was going on with other people." She looked down. "Do you think it damages a girl to sleep around a lot?"

"No... well, it depends on how you feel about it. You know?"

"You do think so."

"No, I don't."

"Yes, you do," she said firmly. "Beneath that rhinoceros hide of yours, you're a rosy-eyed romantic. You believe those things you play on your horn, and everything else you say and do is part of a lie, and it's not even your own lie."

"You're just talking," Cabiness said. He picked up his coffee cup and set it in the center of his plate. "Let's do the dishes."

Clair winced humorously. "Let's not. Tomorrow I'm going to hire someone to come in and clean up every day—now that Carla's gone."

"It looks like you took something of a beating on her replacement."

"Oh, I don't know." She reached over and patted his cheek. "It has one dandy extra feature."

While they were stacking the dishes, the phone rang. Clair answered it and settled down to a long conversation with some woman. He started washing the dishes, recognizing it for a spiteful act. Well now, he thought, I'd like to stuff my dandy extra feature right where it would do the most good. And she should have bought me a little red velvet suit with brass buttons to wear while I was doing it. I only know one trick, but it seems I know that one pretty good.... Now you're getting corny, and sorry for yourself. True. But just suppose this Acton does pry me loose—it could happen—then I owe her for the use of her five thousand dollars as well as for whatever she's paying the lawyer, and they're not known to work for nothing. So it seems the only way I can be free of this dolly is by going to the joint.

For a moment he tinkered with the idea of turning himself back into city prison, refusing bail, but that was a negative, defeated choice. Still, how could he scrape together any loot? Deal dope like Sullivan and end up really buried? Almost smugly, he admitted he had no talent for money.

Stay loose, Lee-Boy, he advised himself. Drift with it. She's not the best by a long pull, but she's still good.

He chewed the lie for a moment and swallowed it. Finishing the dishes, he rinsed the sink out and went into the front room. Clair was curled in a chair, still talking. She made a face over the phone that said she was bored with the conversation. He sat down and picked up a copy of *The New Yorker,* flipping through for the cartoons. He came to one on beatniks: a dark, intense girl is telling a frowsy, bearded young man... *Armand, the trouble is that I just can't relate to you.*

He smiled dryly and put the magazine back.

Clair hung up in an effusion of promises to keep in touch and said to the now-dead receiver, "Like hell." Then she smiled at Cabiness. "Let's go over to North Beach."

"I think I've had the Beach. What's so terrifying about spending the night right here?"

"Nothing," she replied. "But you said you were going to... connect for us. Remember?"

"I will. But not tonight."

She thinned her lips and tapped impatiently on the arm of the chair, and he knew why he'd refused to go. Getting a little of his own back.

After a moment, she said, "Will you play for me then?"

He looked at her cautiously. "That wasn't a line?"

"That I like your music?"

"Yes."

She shook her head. "Not at all. I may not have any real right to the opinion, but I think you're very good."

She confused him, for she was obviously sincere. He unpacked his horn and played ballads for her. "You Stepped Out of a Dream," "Lush Life," "Angel Eyes" . . she nodded, heavy-eyed, keeping time with her head, and she sang a little of "Angel Eyes" in a small true voice. Usually singers bugged him, but he didn't mind.

Afterward she said, "I don't see how you've avoided making a lot of money."

"It wasn't easy," he replied lightly.

"I'm serious. You must have a genius for bad management."

She was going to persist. For some reason he had to find answers. "It's more complicated than you think," he told her. "Music is just music until you start trying to sell it; then it changes in a lot of ways. A lot of things change. You end up with a product."

"I still think you could succeed."

"Probably. But that's not the point. I'd have to be some other person. Change myself in some ways. You dig?"

"No, I don't. I don't think that's an attitude you can afford."

The flush of his anger didn't reach his face. He stared at her levelly for a moment, then said, "Well, I could afford it up to now."

That ended it. And he supposed he'd taken the round, for what pleasure he could get from it. They watched a movie on TV, and afterward, for lack of anything better to do, he made love to her again. She drew a blank, but she didn't seem to mind, although she was quick enough to let him know he'd failed with her, almost as if it were a continuation of their secret contest and this time she had won.

Later, when she was sleeping quietly beside him, he found himself thinking of what Clair had said—of what so many had said—that he really could make it with a horn. And he drifted from that into a game he often played—putting faces into a combo. He put in Furg firmly, and Kovin, if he could be donkeyed into it. He hesitated over BeeGee. She was even too far out. But she could blow, and he liked the idea of a broad piano-player who could swing. He couldn't see anyone sitting behind drums. Motion would do on bass, but Bear would be better, if he was streeted....

Who am I shucking? he wondered. I could never push that bunch of flip-tops and professional misfits into a working group.

But he went on thinking about it until he fell asleep.

The next night they ate out. Clair had spent most of the afternoon at her hairdressers, and her hair flowed over her forehead and down the sides of her cheeks in big smooth waves like honey. She wore a plain black dress with three-quarter sleeves and a deep collar that would have been daring if it hadn't been filled with a white pleated panel. A short cashmere coat and white gloves completed her costume. She looked very good.

Cabiness felt disguised in the new suit but not pushed out of shape about it. Clair had warmly approved the transformation. She had been warm all day, and it stretched into dinner, but there she drank too much and turned snippy. She waited until the last minute before she handed him the money for the check, and then it was too much again. Almost a hundred dollars.

They drove down to North Beach, parked on the boundary at Broadway, and started walking. Saturday night: The Beach was swollen with crowds, swarming from all over the city and the Peninsula, coming from as far away as San Jose, all drawn by the magnet of difference. There were college students by the hundreds in search of an offbeat identification; others, hungry for something they never quite defined, followed the self-important Judas goats, who claimed to know where everything was, winking solemnly over the "everything"; still others, led by professional tour leaders, penetrated the infected area in the sterile security of sight-seeing buses... "All right, folks, all out for drinks at the fabulous Red Beard... We'll be here ten minutes, then we're going to San Francisco's own Fisherman's Wharf for shrimp cocktails...."

They walked up Grant Avenue, and Cabiness found himself growing angry. North Beach had stolen the Zoo's thunder. Tourists were nothing new, but there seemed to be more all the time. What they didn't overrun, they altered. In a doorway, a bearded artist in a yellow beret was drawing sidewalk portraits for five dollars a subject. The drawings were as slick and pretty as the latest *Saturday Evening Post* cover. In the open shop behind him, above a counter display of bongos, flageolets and Spanish guitars, a line of pennants hung limply; hastily-cut strips of felt, they were lettered "Souvenir of North Beach." Cabiness felt like garroting the pennant maker with his product.

"Was anyone down here ever really serious?" Clair asked.

"I don't know. What do you care?"

"I don't. I'm just curious."

A group of men in conventional suits were coming along the sidewalk, their expressions a strange mixture of sullen disapproval and furtive eagerness. Cabiness indicated them with his eyes. "That's their trouble. They're just curious."

One of them caught his words and turned to stare at him with unblinking hostility. Cabiness stopped, but Clair tugged his arm. "Come on. I don't want to have to bail you out again."

Thanks, he thought dryly. And thanks again. Clair was looking around, probably trying to estimate her own effect. Liquor seemed to stiffen her up, pricking her composure with little angry lights.

At The Hoof, he pushed the door open, but Furg wasn't on the stand. A lackluster trio—piano, bass and drums—struggled along over the scattered, but noisy, crowd.

"I could've picked up a dime in there tonight," he told Clair, and she smiled as if he'd made a joke, but it wasn't that funny because Furg had blown the gig, too.

They pushed up the carnival street and checked the different clubs. A few people recognized him with amused surprise. Apparently they didn't know about the bust. Below the Bird's Nest, he spotted Ann's old Chevy. "We're getting warm," he said. Then he heard music and recognized Kovin's tone. "I wonder how come they're open?" he asked out loud. Clair shrugged.

Inside, the Bird's Nest was jammed, five and six people to a table. Candles made soft-orange light, gilding faces, and carving them with dense shadow. Two baby floods knifed into the area around the piano, and a bandstand had been improvised out of old risers. Furg and Kovin were blowing, backed by Motion and the regular piano player. The racket that was bugging the trio in The Hoof was missing. They had an intent crowd.

"No sit-ins," a dry voice said at his side, and he turned to see Dino gesturing at his horncase. "Be a couple a dollars for you and the lady."

Cabiness reached for the money, but asked, "What's the story? It's a session, isn't it?"

Dino smiled. "For crissake, man, I didn't recognize you in the fancy threads. What the...."

Then he looked at Clair again and his face closed into a bland Italian mask. "Sure you can play. Make it on over." He waved the money aside.

Cabiness asked, "How come you're open so early?"

"We weren't. They just came in to play for kicks—you know?—so they could use the piano, and the people started banging on the door. Looks like the place is going to move."

"Yeah. Good news for you."

Dino nodded briskly. "You keep trying, you're bound to make it sooner or later."

Cabiness smiled. "That's good enough to frame."

"Sure," Dino said sourly. "You like it, you frame it."

He considered hitting on Dino to hire the combo he was getting for nothing, but he decided to give it a little more time and talk to Furg and Kovin first. He knew one thing sure—people weren't in here to pay a dollar a throw for Dino's warm ginger ale and cold coffee.

On the way over to the stand, Clair took his arm again; her smile was fixed as they maneuvered through the tables. Eyes touched them and slipped away. Furg caught sight of him first and started grinning like a lunatic. Kovin was still soloing, but Furg dug him in the ribs and they both started laughing.

"Man, you're dazzlin'," Furg shouted. "Ain't he pretty?"

Kovin just nodded, but Motion switched his bass to stare around the neck. His left hand spider-walked along the strings. "Like the creature from Robert Hall," he said sarcastically. "You gone over to the enemy?"

Ann was sitting at the first table below the stand, playing a game with a small man in a wrinkled gray suit. They were playing on a squared board with what looked like small tiddly-winks. Ann wore an old black raincoat, but her hair was combed, and a hint of color graced her wide mouth. Blackened silver rings glowed somberly at her ears; snakes in square coils with tri-angular heads and green eyes.

She smiled. "Hi, Lee-Boy. Where've you been?"

"Holed up," he answered vaguely. "Ann, this is Clair. Ann's a teacher over at Marina Night School."

Clair's eyes widened. "Oh?" It wasn't clear what she meant, but she managed to put the wrong edge on it.

Ann's smile deepened. "You're very lovely," she said. "I envy you."

Cabiness pulled out a chair and Clair sat down, nonplused. Furg jumped off the stand and tapped Cabiness on the arm. "I'm sorry, sir," he said, "but this table is reserved for the musicians."

"I've got your musician," Cabiness told him. "I'll blow you off the stand."

"You're on. Get your whistle out."

"It's still your play," Ann said. Gray Suit hadn't once looked up from the counters. "This is John," she offered, and John ran his mild eyes swiftly around the table and went back to the game. "John's a writer."

"What're you playing?" Clair asked, with a show of interest.

"Go," Ann replied. "It's a war game."

"You finally get it figured out?" Cabiness asked.

"Not really. But someone's winning and someone's losing. What else has to happen?"

John placed a counter and looked sly. It was Ann's turn to stare at the board.

"I'm going to blow for awhile," Cabiness told Clair.

She paused, taking off her gloves. "Go ahead. I won't melt."

"Do you want anything? Coffee?"

"I don't think so. Not coffee."

When he took his place on the stand, the piano was meandering through a disjointed solo. Furg moved over and asked him, "What've you got into, old buddy?"

"The sugar bowl."

"You surely have." Furg looked down at Clair and nodded judiciously. Then he said, "Teddy, over at The Hoof, was mortally pissed when I told him we weren't going to make it."

"Screw him. He's a burglar anyway."

"His bread spent all right."

"I've got some money—"

"Well, now, that's dandy."

"When I've got money, you've got money. Now let me blow my horn."

The piano faltered and Cabiness came in, blowing right over him; the piano man shrugged and went back to chording. Cabiness played a bad solo and knew it. The next one was worse. Just not my night, he decided. He had too many other things going on in his head. They played for twenty minutes, blowing "Cherokee" every way it could be blown, and this time Kovin didn't challenge. They played together and it felt pretty good. But when the tune ended he knew he should pay some attention to Clair. She was smiling rather meaninglessly and looking around as if she might see someone she knew. He jumped off the stand.

"Drug?" he asked her.

"No. I'm having a fine time."

Dino had sold her a half-pint of some obscure brand of bourbon; she and Ann and John were drinking it in coffee cups. Ann and John were still deep in their game.

"Who's winning?" he asked.

"She is," John supplied.

Ann looked up to grin. "I'm the Clausewitz of North Beach."

"More like Genghis Khan," John added.

"What do you write?" Clair asked brightly.

John looked down. "Nothing special."

"Well, who have you written for?"

"Oh, I've never sold anything..." He smiled gently. "Unless you could count the jingle I wrote for Blue Jay Corn Plaster. I won five dollars."

Ann and Cabiness laughed. Clair colored and drank off the contents of her cup. She refilled it under the table and knocked it out again. She turned to find him watching her. "Want some?" she asked.

"I don't lush."

Ann made her play, and when she looked up Lee asked her if she had any pills. She shook her head. "No, we did in the last of them. But we're going to make the run pretty soon."

"Mind if we tag?"

Ann hesitated and glanced at Clair. Then she caught herself up quickly. "Sure. Why ask?"

"The heat... you know?"

Ann looked grave. "Yes, there's a righteous panic on. Kove's frantic half the time."

"He seems all right tonight."

"He's all right when he's playing. But other times...." She made a weary, defeated gesture. Cabiness looked up; Kovin was soloing again. His tenor was thrust fore, and like a golden phallus, but even in his pleasure he looked as if he were suffering. His eyes were shut, clenched knots in the shadow of his Fearless-Fosdick snapbrim, and his skin seemed like wax.

"It's too goddam bad," he told Ann. "The sonsabitches."

"Which ones?" Ann asked. "Who are you going to blame?"

"I don't know," Cabiness admitted. "But I'm going try to do something about it."

He called for a break and got Furg, Kovin and Motion back into the can, leaving the piano player to fill in. The can was a narrow, rank room lit by a bald overhead bulb. The club was too new to have collected the mass of pornographic inscription that usually decorated North Beach toilets. Motion lit a joint, and they passed it once before Cabiness hit them with his idea.

Kovin blinked at him. "Oh, man!" he said with heavy disgust.

"Crap," Motion added.

"What do you think, Furg?"

Furg leaned against the basin and scratched the side of his head. "I'm not prejudiced against loot, but I've heard likelier notions."

It was the reaction he'd expected—the callus they'd grown on hope—and he set himself to persuade them, as he knew they wanted him to, telling them what they knew already but needed to hear again. He directed it mostly at Kovin, because while Kovin had almost no personality away from his horn, with it he was the strongest of them all.

Kovin rubbed his eyes with his thumb and forefinger; then he looked down where he was hitting one shoe against the other in a steady drumming rhythm. When Cabiness paused, he asked tonelessly, "What'll we call the group?"

"I don't know. Some funny name. That's not important."

Kovin still didn't look up. "How about 'The Astrologers'?"

Cabiness smiled; Furg laughed out loud and said, "I kinda like 'The Buzzards.'"

"More like 'The Lames', " Motion put in. "It's still a punk idea."

Cabiness got hold of the roach and took a deep, scalp-tingling toke. "You know something, Motion? You can blow. But there are other bass men."

"Sure," Motion agreed. "You're not telling me anything. Don't get glued to that joint."

"Where can we rehearse?" Furg asked.

"What's the matter with right here. There's no action during the day."

"Cool. If Dino'll go for it."

"He'll go," Cabiness said. "Motion, you know a down drummer?"

Motion was holding his lungs full of smoke. He expelled it explosively. "You are going to put me in it, aren't you? All right. I'll stick for as long as it swings, but the minute it turns green, I'm splitting. Dig?"

"OK," Cabiness agreed. "You know a drummer?"

"How about Koehler?"

"Nutty! Can you bring him in?"

"Maybe. I'll hit on him."

"Lee-Boy," Furg said. "Something's turned you upside down, but you're all right, buddy."

Was he? he wondered. All he really wanted was the chance of working his way out of the trap he was in. No, it wasn't even that, because he wasn't foolish enough to think he could beat Carver in court. He wanted to make the effort. That was important.

Dino didn't make any problems, except to suggest they use his regular piano player for rehearsal, which was Dino's way of keeping his finger in it. The piano player was average, no real swinger, but all right. How Dino would take the demand for wages was something else. Time enough for that when they had something down.

When Cabiness returned to the table, he found Clair half drunk. "You're pushing the season," he told her. "We're going to pick up pretty soon."

She glanced sullenly at Ann and John, still engrossed in their game. "I had to do something to pass the time."

"I'm sorry. I guess this isn't much for you."

"I'm all right. I feel fine."

Ann looked up. "Well, I don't. I feel down." She turned to the stand. "Kove, let's go to Angel's."

chapter fourteen

Angel's place was on the far side of Telegraph Hill, the respectable side, where the rents nudged two hundred a month: no dogs, no children, no noise, no nothing... just sit cracking your knuckles in your nutty pad and be tickled crazy you could live in such a place. Cabiness smiled. I'm not that bitter.

He turned to look at Clair. Her face was shadowed in the corner of the back seat, and she watched the buildings as Ann's Chevy chewed determinedly up the hill. "What do you think?" he asked idly.

She looked up where Ann, Furg and Kovin were crowded together in the front seat. "Not much," she said dully.

He reached over and gripped her upper leg. "You'll feel better soon. That lush'll rot your gourd."

She put her hand over his for a moment; then lifted it off. "Like that?" he asked, but she didn't answer.

Kovin was parking, jittering the little black car in between two giants. The nice side of the hill was quiet. The yellow windows beat solemnly against the darkness, and the white apartment buildings rose like chilly virgins trying to deny the coyness of their red doors. For once, a few stars winked their ancient condition.

Angel's place was an anachronism, a small brown house almost lost beneath the smooth flanks of the new buildings. It sat, blurred and dissolute, in five hundred square yards of overgrown grass and atavistic flowerbeds. An angel cut from sheet metal was spotwelded to the pipe-and-chicken-wire gate.

As soon as they were inside the gate, a furious noise started—a hoarse honking like that produced by an old bulb-style auto horn. A round gray shape came flapping and hissing out of the shadows.

Clair grabbed his arm. "What's that?"

"A goose," he said. "Angel keeps two or three of them."

Kovin kicked out at the bird and it backed, beating its wings like a fighting cock. Furg went to barking like a dog. "Cut out, man," he told the goose. Across the yard the other birds started in.

"That's Angel's alarm system," Cabiness explained. "If the heat ever busts in here, he'll have plenty of warning."

Angel opened the door for them—a small, smooth gray-haired Mexican, who claimed forty. With color back, he could easily have passed for thirty, and was probably close to fifty. He smiled warmly, disclosing a gold tooth. The gold tooth was an ingenious fake, since Angel's teeth were false. His own teeth had rotted out years before in the wake of his numerous addictions. Cabiness knew that currently Angel wasn't hooked. He was on a peyote kick.

"What's the chit, guys?" Angel asked. His Pachuco accent changed the aspirate "sh" to "ch". His eyes were swollen and dreamy like ripe plums.

"We come to do a little light trading," Ann said.

"Very light," Angel said quickly. "Is all I handle."

"A few chemicals," Ann told him.

"OK. That's OK." He pulled the door open. "Come on in. We got a little party."

They stepped into the dim light and the soft beat of recorded music. The most noticeable, and the only Mexican, feature of the room they entered was a large photomural of Chichén Itzá—it covered the upper half of one wall, and a light shade was tilted to illuminate it. The ruins seemed to slumber in a frozen grayness. There were seven people lying around in the semi-darkness. Cabiness recognized Luth Grimes, Chet Datema, Karl Falkenberry; BeeGee was there—she raised her thin arm—as well as Didi Drachmann, Sandra McClure, and a large woman known simply as "Mac." All of them very beat.

Luth Grimes was sprawled out on the rattan matting, his head near the mouth of the record player. His glasses were pushed up on his forehead, and his beard was pressed down, fanned out on the front of his T-shirt. The T-shirt was lettered "YMCA" in faded red capitals.

"Hi, Cab," Luth said. "Where'd you get the hairy fiddle?"

Cabiness pulled at the front of his new suit coat. He made a model's half-turn, burlesquing. "You dig it? An admirer of mine bought it for me."

"Wow, isn't he beautiful," Didi said scornfully.

Luth was looking at Clair—she stood a little apart, examining the photomural with rigid attention. Luth whistled softly. "Some admirer. You get tired of these dirty chicks?"

He watched Angel take Kovin and Ann into the back; then he heard BeeGee say, "You really have gone funnystyle."

He turned to her and said, "I want to talk to you."

"You better talk fast," BeeGee said.

"Very fast," Luth added. "We're all cutting out."

"To New York," Datema finished it.

"Oh, yeah?" Furg asked. "Why?"

Luth shook his fingers in front of his chest, blowing his breath out through his teeth. "Heat. And crap. We're up to our ass in it here. In New York they're civilized. You could be purple with yellow stripes. No one would look twice."

"The Milkman gets his dreariest wish," BeeGee said. "He's finally run us off."

"The Milkman and Carver," Datema added.

"And all of Carver's little helpers," Luth said. "Snitchin' bastards. I don't mind cutting, but before I go I'd like to kick Sullivan's ass up around his neck—"

"Sullivan?" Cabiness asked.

"Sure, Sullivan! He's a real one. He works overtime."

"I've heard something like that before," Cabiness said quietly, "but I still wonder how you know. It's too easy to put out bum drawings. I know the idea shocks you, but some people lie and start false rumors just for kicks. I think you got bum drawings."

"I've got your bum drawings!" Luth was angry. He sat up and pulled his glasses down, and his face suddenly intensified. He flicked a finger out at Cabiness. "One, he was seen riding around the Beach with Carver. Two, he's still free and he's holding heavy. Three, last night Carver busted Fat Daddy ten minutes after he made a buy from Sullivan—"

Cabiness was shaking his head. "They wouldn't work it that open. He'd give Sullivan some cover."

"Not Carver. He doesn't give a crap what happens to Sullivan. In a word, man, he is insane. A fliptop cop. He's got war with the Beach, and we're not hanging around to see who wins."

There was a murmur of assent. Then the record ended, and in the moment of silence while the changer worked, Cabiness told himself, it's probably true. And if it is, what're you going to do about it. He knew the answer; probably nothing.

Kovin and Ann came back with Angel. They all seemed satisfied. Angel was telling Ann, "... two and you're gone, man. Chit!"

"I don't move easy any more," Ann said.

"You'll move," Angel replied confidently. The gold tooth flashed. "I back my stuff."

"Angel, are you going to make the Apple?" Cabiness asked.

"Me? Hell, no, man. I live right here all my life. My old man built this house."

The new record was starting. It was Cannonball blowing way, way up, so fast the sound was a continuous, multi-hued blur. Luth flopped back down, holding his arms straight up. He spread his fingers and waved them. "Oh, man," he shouted. "Birdland, here I come, baby. That is where they blow and blow."

"Tell the truth," Datema yelled at the record player. Mac had her arm around BeeGee's waist and BeeGee's eyes were closed. Her face looked blank, and the older woman stroked her carrot hair. Cabiness noticed Clair watching them. Her face was flushed, her lips parted. Sometime in the past hour her careful hairdo had come apart, but she hadn't repaired it. Nice mess, he thought. And within the thought and all around its edges he felt New York pulling at him. But it was no good.

Angel asked, "You guys staying?"

Cabiness turned to ask Clair what she wanted to do, but her face was frozen now, either with self-consciousness, or disapproval. Probably both. "Sure," he said easily. Ann, Kovin and Furg had already settled down together. He took Clair's arm, then turned to ask Luth, "When you cutting out?"

"Pretty soon... when it hits us just right."

They went to sit along a wall with the others—Angel had but two chairs and neither of them were in use—and Ann started shaking pills out of a small brown bottle. Kovin was complaining about how pills didn't do anything for him, and Ann told him what he already knew—that there was nothing else with the panic on, and that pills would keep him even.

Cabiness slipped Ann a ten-dollar bill. She looked at it and said, "This is too much."

"How many times have I freeloaded on you?"

"That doesn't signify."

"Oh shut up, Annie," he said, momentarily angry. "Just keep the stinking bread. I don't need it."

Ann said, "If you did need it, I'd like it better." But she folded the bill and put it away.

"Pass the goodies," Furg said.

Cabiness took six of the pills and handed two of them to Clair. She held them on her palm and looked at them. "What are they?" she asked.

"Just take them. They'll sober you up."

"I'm not drunk."

"Take them anyway," Ann said. "They might knock some of the stiff out of you."

"Is that what happened to you?" Clair asked with unexpected sharpness.

Ann's narrow gray eyes flickered with malice. "Girl, I never needed it. I was born flexible."

Ann turned away to talk to Furg before Clair could retort. She was left sitting with the pills in her hand. Angrily she pushed them at her mouth. Cabiness reached over and grabbed a bottle of wine. She washed them down, gulping with distaste. Then he took his own, going with all four.

Cannonball blew on through his album. The changer worked again, the records clicked, and then Miles was blowing his hoarse poetic horn. Cabiness sipped the wine, passing the bottle back and forth, and he felt the excitement pooling in his stomach, shivering in his scrotum, echoing down his legs. He pulled Clair into the crook of his arm, brushing her breast lightly. "How do you feel?" he asked.

"Strange," she murmured.

He pulled his hand tighter and she shivered. She spread her hand over his. Their fingers interlaced, and she moved her hand back and forth, pressing down. Her eyes were unfocused. No one was paying any attention to them. Kovin was sitting with his hat over his eyes. Ann had her head in Furg's lap. Angel was somewhere in back, and Luth was still by himself in front of the record player. The others were separate piles in the dark corners of the room.

Miles was blowing "It Never Entered My Mind." He went on and finally ended with one of his wistful codas, whispering off into silence and needle scratch. Luth sat up and said, "Now."

"Now?" Datema asked, pulling loose from Didi Drachmann.

"Now," Luth repeated, louder than before. "Now, man. Now."

He jumped up and grabbed his jacket, whacking Mac across the shoulders. "Come on, bull, let's split." He blew a kiss at the record player. "Miles, baby, next week we'll see you in your everloving black hide." He came and stood over Cabiness, his eyes blinking rapidly behind his thick lenses. "Cab, if this crazy bitch has slipped you any bread, you can win everlasting salvation right this minute." He struck a pose. "Help finance the exodus, boy. The chillun're leavin' Egypt. Ol' Milkman snappin' at our arses, and we scattin' to the land of plenty."

Cabiness divided the money he had in his pocket. He gave half to Luth, half to Furg. Clair watched smiling, Luth snapped his half against his fingers. "Good boy." He turned and yelled, "Angel, we're splitting."

Angel stuck his head back in the room. His face was covered with lather. "So split, man. I pick up on you later. All you guys."

They started out. At the door Luth paused and said, "Watch yourself, Cab. This town is full of trickeration."

You're a little late, Luth, Cabiness thought. But thanks anyway.

A moment later they heard the geese start up. Clair twisted to get closer to him. The knot of contention had dissolved from her face. She looked softer, younger. "So they just go to New York?"

"That's it," he answered. "They feel like it, so they go. Maybe they'll get there, maybe they won't."

"Well, I feel like going home," she whispered. "I'm not as uninhibited as these people."

"All right," he agreed. "Furg, we're going home. See that Kove makes it tomorrow, will you?"

"Surely."

Ann rolled over and smiled at him. "Stay loose," she advised.

He went in to say goodnight to Angel. Angel was still shaving, drawing the razor slowly down the left side of his face. The lather was dry and there was a red path on his cheek. He stared at himself in the mirror. Mechanically, the hand went up and pulled the razor down again. A fleck of blood glistened on the brown skin.

"Angel!"

Angel turned slowly. "What, man?"

"What do you call yourself doing?"

"Shaving." He pulled the razor down again. The fleck of blood widened into a trickle.

"You better snap," Cabiness told him. "You'll carve your face off."

He seemed to pull his attention back from an infinite distance. "You know, man... it's my face."

"OK, it's your face."

Clair was waiting by the door, and they ran through the yard ahead of the geese. When the gate was slammed behind them, Clair hung on his arm resettling her shoe. She was laughing. "Don't those things ever sleep?"

"Yes, but very lightly."

When she straightened, he slipped his hands inside her coat, and kissed her. She responded instantly. "I guess we better get you home," he said.

Walking down to the car she asked about Kovin, Furg and Ann. "Is that a *ménage à trois?*" she wanted to know.

"What?"

"Do they all live together?"

"Not all at the same time," he said lightly.

"Does she live with Furguson?"

"No, Furg's an afterthought. Or an extrathought. I don't know which. I thought there was going to be trouble there, but I guess I was wrong. They seem as compatible as the three bears."

It was one of those nights when even the ring of his heels on the pavement felt good, and when they reached the car, on a whim, he drove to the top of Russian Hill. They parked for a moment, looking down at the lights of the city. The grotesque square sign on the top of the Southern Pacific building turned like a child's toy in the wind, announcing "SP" to the indifferent stars. A ferry was halfway across the bay, a cluster of lights drifting purposefully on the darkness.

"I'll miss this town," he said.

"You're not going anywhere."

"Maybe. I suppose Acton's a good lawyer, but I don't think he knows the cold deck he's up against."

They were silent a moment, then she said, "He'll get you out of it."

"Yeah... well, anyway, I've got a couple of months left, no matter how it goes."

He started the car and drove back down the hill. In the apartment they went straight to the bedroom. He felt none of his former reluctance, no sense of paying dues. The stimulant had sharpened his appetite and, as he'd anticipated, it did the same for her.

They were successful enough and lucky enough to stun her a little, even afterwards, and she lay for a long while in the hollow of his arm, with her forearm pressed against her eyes.

Finally, she stirred and said quietly, "You're the first person in my life I ever felt grateful to. She paused, then added, "I'm not sure I like it."

chapter fifteen

The piano player was by himself in the empty club when Cabiness showed up. He was practicing, playing big block chords and whistling through his teeth. Cabiness remembered that Dino had called him Haley.

In the daylight the Bird's Nest was shabby, and, like all illusion, the letdown was solid and final. He looked around at the scuffed and soiled sawdust, the beat-up tables, the raw wood where the grocery fixtures had been torn out, and thought that Dino would be smart to use a little soap and paint before the Health Inspectors knocked him out.

He went over and talked to Haley for a while, telling him how he wanted some chords voiced. Haley listened, nodded, then played them wrong. So he sat down and showed him, playing several cycles. Haley was trying again when Furg came in.

Cabiness asked, "All right, where's Kovin?"

"He's coming. He's hung up in a bookstore down the street. And Carver's looking for you. He stopped me about an hour ago and asked me if I'd seen you around."

"What'd you tell him?"

"Huh?" Furg looked bland.

"Did you tell him you'd seen me?"

"Huh?" Furg asked again, managing to look almost idiotic.

Cabiness laughed. "I bet that went over big."

"Well, he stopped asking. What's he want with you?"

"Does he need a reason? He probably misses me."

Furg fingered the cloth of Lee's new suit and made a wryly humorous grimace. "You moved, huh?"

"Yes."

"I know. I was by your old place yesterday. Do you..." Furg paused. Then, "It's funny thinking of you someplace else. Long as you were in that old loft."

Kovin came in. He looked like a hood. He wore shades and his hat was pulled down to the rims. He had a book under his arm. An old musty work on demonology—full of spells and cabalistic designs. Kovin flipped through it, showing it to them, saying, "Dig that! Dig that!"

"What do you wanta waste bread on that for?" Furg asked.

Kovin looked sly. "I didn't waste no bread. I sloughed it." He thrust the book under his coat, and it appeared to disappear. "See?"

Kovin went looking for some chalk—he wanted to mark some of the signs on the bandstand—but all he found was a chewed-up pencil and one of

Dino's anonymous half-pints. They all had a drink and argued about which tunes to work on. Furg had half of an arrangement sketched out on a single piece of score paper—it was folded and smudged, and it was almost impossible to trace the individual lines through it, but it looked pretty good. They ran it down once or twice and it was good.

Motion came in an hour late—alone. Koehler was hung up in the Sunday afternoon session at The Blackhawk, but he was interested, and would make it next time.

They started rehearsing the tunes they'd decided on, building arrangements as they went, but it was hard to hold Kovin to it. He'd say, "I've got it, man, I've got it," but then he'd play something different, something good more often than not, but the effect was to destroy the agreement, and then they were just jamming again. When Cabiness re-explained the intention, the effect of discipline, Kove bobbed his head nervously, his shades as bland as the eyes of an empty gas mask. "I dig. I'm down with it."

Then he turned to Furg and started talking about *ju-ju*, rattling the keys of his horn like muffled castanets. "It's too much, man. They fix a hex and the cat cools it. He could be on the other side of the world. Nutty, huh?"

"If you wanted to cool someone," Furg answered tolerantly.

Kovin snapped his keys shut all at once and smiled up at Furg. "There's a half-dozen studs I wouldn't mind cooling, if it didn't put me to a whole lot of trouble."

"Let's run it down again," Cabiness said. "Come on, this is work. He counted off, "One-a, two-a, onetwothreefour."

They made some progress, and they were in an outchorus, blowing triple F, when John Randozza opened the front door and looked in. He started toward them, seeming half angry, half puzzled. Jean followed him, swaying on three-inch heels—witchshoes with long, pointed toes.

"What's happening?" Randozza asked.

"We're rehearsing," Cabiness said. His eyes were on Jean, noting her pallor, the nervous sketch of her mouth. He didn't remember the knit dress she was wearing. It molded her in a way that was poignant.

"I see," Randozza said. "But why here?"

"Is it something to you?" Cabiness asked pointedly.

"As a matter of fact, yes. I've got a piece of this place."

Cabiness was surprised, but he held his face under control. "In that case, you better quarrel with Dino. He gave us permission."

Randozza seemed satisfied. "There's no quarrel. I just wanted to know how you got in." He shot his cuff and ran a heavy hand along the side of his hair— a gesture subtly out of tune with his size and appearance. "It was strange to hear the joint jumping in the middle of the day. What are you doing? Putting a group together?"

"We're tinkering with the idea."

Randozza nodded heavily, very BTO, and looked again at Kovin, Motion and Furg. Then he asked Cabiness, "Think you'd like to work here?"

"We thought of it… if we can get anything down. But if you don't sell lush, how are you going to make the nut? We're not going to blow for peanuts."

Randozza looked vague. "A cup of coffee costs about a cent to make. When you're ready to make a deal, tell Dino. We can give you scale, anyway. OK?"

"Surely," Furg said quickly, and Cabiness nodded. Scale was seldom paid on the Beach, except in the name clubs along Broadway.

Cabiness turned to say something to Jean—he didn't know what, he just wanted to talk to her—but she had turned away. He walked over and looked into her face. With the heels her eyes were just a little below his. He noticed that the whites were not quite so clear as he remembered.

"How've you been?" he asked.

"Fine," she said brightly. "You look very nice."

"Yeah…" he murmured uncomfortably. "I fell into a thing."

"I heard that you had."

"You did? I guess it would make a story. Well… anything been happening?"

"No. Nothing."

Randozza was to the side, looking at the end of his thumb as if he were afraid he'd caught a sliver. He flicked his hand out at her. "Let's go, Jeanie," he said.

She moved towards the door—"See you, Lee"—her fine back held very straight. He noticed that she was wearing seamless nylons. Then the door swung closed.

"Is that straight?" Cabiness asked the piano player. "Does he have an interest in this place?"

"First I heard of it," Haley admitted. "I thought Dino was the whole show."

"I don't think I care too much for Mr. Randazzle," Cabiness said.

"He don't exactly move me either," Furg added. "But he's a sure enough handsome bastard."

Kovin was looking at his new book.

They played through the afternoon and again the next afternoon. This time with Koehler's rock beat and machine-gun left hand. Koehler was skinny, intensely nervous; the victim of a runaway thyroid, his eyes bulged and his hands shook, but he was a school drummer. He could have held a seat in the symphony if he'd leaned that way. After the first set, he pushed his hair out of his eyes and rubbed the back of his neck. They all watched him, waiting on his reaction.

"Might make it," he said. "Goddam! We might make it."

Koehler had a slim connection with the New Sounds record company in Berkeley, and they wasted half an hour talking about the album they might make. "We won't be ready for months," Cabiness said, but the enthusiasm was hard to resist... New Sounds from the Bird's Nest. He could hear it.

At one-thirty, Cabiness had to leave to keep an appointment with Acton.

Acton seemed more secure in his office, a modern, featureless room in one of the newer buildings on Montgomery Street. He ran through the clichés imposed on a man behind a desk: he straightened his blotter, fiddled with his desk set, examined his letter opener, rocked back in his swivel chair and clamped his hands behind his neck, but what he had to say was to the point.

Someone had the knife out for him.

Cabiness nodded. He explained Carver as well as he could and described the part Sullivan had played in it

"That's entrapment," Acton said quickly. "Did this Sullivan approach you?"

"No, I hit on him."

"Oh... then that's out. All we can do is delay, but there are three points at which we'll drag our heels." He stroked them off on the Formica top of his simulated-oak desk. "Arraignment, preliminary, and the actual trial itself. Any judge will give us at least two postponements before each action. Maybe the air will clear a little. And, incidentally, you have to appear in court next Tuesday for plea. We'll postpone, of course, but if we can't, I assume you'll plead not guilty?"

Cabiness nodded. He wasn't as interested as he thought he should be. He felt tired. Here in this formal room it didn't seem possible that he would beat it. He could close his eyes and see the scarred metal walls, the dust-furred electric lights smoldering in their little wire cages, the faces of hostility and defeat... it all seemed a permanent part of his consciousness. He wondered at his sudden lassitude, like a man out swimming in the sun who suddenly thinks it is possible to drown, and in the end of the thought finds himself sinking. The sun slips away like a tarnished penny....

Even talking to the lawyer, watching the white scalp glisten in Acton's severe brush cut, in another part of his mind he took off for Mexico, figuring Angel could tell him how to beat the border, and he ended up in Guadalajara; a swinging town he'd heard.... But with two Feds for every civilian American, it was nowhere.

Before he left he asked Acton how much all this was going to cost, but the lawyer demurred. When pressed, all he would say was that Miss Hubler retained him by the year to look after her investments, and that he couldn't estimate his fee at this time.

He thanked the lawyer and went home.

Clair was painting when he came in, but she quickly turned her canvas face to the easel. They didn't kiss. She curled up on the couch. Her face was pale, indefinite without make-up, and her eyes were shadowed.

"What'd Ernest say?" she asked.

"Soothing things mostly. Carver's coming hard against me, but he still thinks he can squeak me out."

"I'm sure he can."

He was tired of explaining that she didn't know anything about it, so her opinion was empty. He put a stack of his sides on her big hi-fi and sat down across from her to listen. The first side up was one of the Gillespie big bands: satiric, complex, but illuminated with a simple enthusiasm.

He went on to tell her about the recording possibility, forgetting how slender a possibility it was. His eyes lit, and the fit of pessimism he'd suffered in Acton's office was forgotten as well. The Gillespie brass started screaming.

"Could you turn that down a little?" Clair asked. Silently, he did as she asked. "Some of that music sounds so nervous," she explained.

"I thought you liked jazz?"

"Oh, I do—but I like to be there."

He changed the subject. "When'd you get up?" He'd left her in bed that morning, and she still wore a housecoat.

"I don't know. Sometime this afternoon. Those pills of yours turned me all around."

"You're not used to them."

"I'm not sure I want to get used to them—they're frightening in some ways."

"I thought you liked them?"

"Well, I did—I guess. I'm not sure."

She seemed querulous and edgy, but after a moment she forced a smile. "Let's go out somewheres and have a few cocktails before dinner."

"OK."

While she was dressing, he turned the painting around. It was a portrait of a doll, routinely, if competently, done. The doll had blue eyes, frizzled yellow hair and a saccharine smile. No guts, he thought. But then he looked again, realizing that somehow the painting was unwholesome, a parody of innocence. She couldn't have intended the effect, he decided—it had seeped in between her brush strokes.

They went to Otto's, drank gimlets, and watched some movies that had been made in the bar a few nights before. Mostly they were a succession of smiling faces raised to the camera, but the joke of it seemed to be to photograph women on their way to the can. Usually, they turned at the door, probably alerted by the laughter, to grin sheepishly back at the lens. It all seemed rather aimless, but presumably people would come back to watch themselves on the screen. Probably they would. Probably they'd break the door down.

After the second round, he told her he didn't have any more money. She flexed her mouth but didn't comment. She just reached for her purse.

Compulsively he explained, "I gave some to Furg."

"He doesn't work?"

"No—"

"Well, he should."

She handed him her wallet.

They passed the night as they had the two preceding. He played and she sat and listened. But this night she refused Ann's pills, and later when he reached for her in bed, she turned away. Perversely he wanted her then, but nothing he said or did had any effect.

"You can't arouse me if I don't want to be aroused," she said, and somehow it sounded like a boast. Pretty well loaded from a night's steady drinking, she rolled over and went to sleep.

The next day the Bird's Nest closed for a week of remodeling. They rehearsed day and night over the sounds of sawing and hammering. The club was being painted and a permanent stand constructed. In back, the old grocery storerooms were gutted and partitioned into smaller rooms. Randozza was in and out, talking to the carpentry foreman, directing the work. They were doing a quick, cheap job.

When they came into the Bird's Nest the night it reopened, they found more changes. Dino had another man on the door, a stout middle-aged man with a smooth heavy face and cynical eyes. Also, there were four waitresses. Jean was one of them.

"Tone the place up a little, don't they?" Dino said.

The girls wore cocktail dresses, each different, but all dark, and a tiny apron smaller than a handkerchief. Jean was in a sheath with her hair hovered around her white face like flames. The effect was striking. The added height of her heels made her seem slender—even so, he thought she'd lost some weight.

"Well, tonight it gets real," Dino said. Cabiness nodded. By the arrangement they'd made they were supposed to be paid every morning. Randozza had conceded that because most of the group were flat broke.

They set up on the new stand, and when the first people hit the door they started jamming one, waiting for the night to take form. Cabiness watched Jean moving through the tables, but she avoided his eyes. The girls functioned as cocktail waitresses, but he didn't see any reason to have so many. They were in each other's way. But they did look good, and they changed the tone of the club away from pure North Beach into a hybrid atmosphere.

Even though the bite at the door had gone up to two dollars, the place filled up early and stayed filled up. The crowd was mixed: a lot of them seemed to be there for the music, but others were partying. With the quiet crowd the arrangements clicked soundly, but the party crowd liked Kovin's wailing upper register. Whenever he went up there after the hoarse animal ecstasy, they shouted and stomped. Cabiness knew it was a trick, almost a conditioned response, but in his own solos he found himself straining his reed and riding high F. The atmosphere of the whole club thickened; it turned with a tinny sultriness.

Around three, Randozza came in with two other men. His teeth flashed at the stand, and he nodded congratulations. Cabiness nodded back and watched him work through to a table far in the rear. The three men were only shadows in the blue light, but in a moment cigars began to trace slow red paths.

During a break, when he passed the table on his way to the can, he noticed that Randozza was alone with Jean by his side. "You're doing great," Randozza called and then turned back to Jean, his voice going into a murmur, while she looked at him and nodded, her face mottled in the uneven light.

This is a weird scene, he thought. But bread doesn't make easy. If it did, everyone would be loaded. Remember that. And he did for a while, until Motion turned him on in the can with some grass he claimed was Cuban *moto,* and whether it was or not, it stoned him. He stood in the can for what seemed like a long time, breathing the smell of fresh paint, watching the light expand and contract....

After that the night separated itself into a series of vivid scenes—like the thrill tunnel at Playland—where he seemed to be moving in a warm salt darkness until lights flared in front of him and he was watching cardboard cannibals dance in the distance. . .

One of the waitresses looked very fine to him, and he kissed her in a warm haze somewhere in a long wooden hallway, but the second time she stopped his lips with her fingers and said, "That's good, honey, but this is no time for fun."

Then he was on the stand, fighting his horn for the last bit of mystery he could get out of it, the whole of it swirled in his brain like bright gas, and he wanted to tell it. He felt himself priest and leader while his people screamed with love down there in the darkness.

Then Furg and Kovin had a violent argument over a wrong chord Kovin claimed Furg had played, and Kovin, who didn't know one chord from another to talk about, but had ears like an elephant, was probably right. "I won't play with the no-blowin' sonofabitch," Kovin screamed. But somehow it was smoothed over. And after a while Dino was counting out money for them, telling them for crissake to be sure to come back, and then he was outside making it down Green Street with Furg. Between them they still had a stick and a half of Motion's pot.

"You're getting to be a regular stranger around here," Furg said.

"Yeah, I'm social climbing. I've got a big weakness that way."

"Your weakness got blonde hair," Furg said. "Blonde hair and a ball-bearing action. That's just right close to the best-looking stuff I've ever seen."

"Furg," Cabiness said, in an instructional voice, "I'm going to turn you on to a vital fact. You do not look at it. That isn't what you do at all."

"Do tell. You mean I've been missing out on something?"

"I doubt it. How's Annie?"

"Okay," Furg said.

"You still making it with her?"

"Yeah, whenever I catch Kovin on the nod, or talk her into coming over to my pad."

"You sound half pissed."

"It's getting to be a bad scene. Kovin's a good tenor player, real good, but as a human being he's the closest thing to nothing I ever ran across. I don't see how Ann can put up with him. It's about like shacking up with someone who's got sleeping sickness. I'm trying to talk her into getting a dog instead."

Cabiness laughed. "Poor Kovin. A saxophone playing vegetable. Well, when he wails, he really wails, he's got that much going for him. More than a lot of people, I'd imagine."

"I just get sick of seeing him laying around on that couch watching television all the time. If you want to communicate with him you have to wait until the commercial, and half the time he gets hung up in them, too. The other day he jumped up and broke his horn out like he'd been seized with the goddamdest inspiration ever since that chord got lost, and you know what he played?"

Cabiness shook his head.

"Ajax, the foaming cleanser..."

They cracked up, staggering down the street laughing, and Furg continued singing "Ajax, the foaming cleanser" as a riff.

> "Ajax, the foaming cleanser,
> The stuff that makes your hen purr...."

"Maybe Kovin has something after all," Cabiness suggested.

"He's unconscious," Furg said disgustedly. "Flat unconscious. Anything he does, he does without even knowing he's doing it. Believe me, he's out of it. I've got to try some of that stuff one of these days, see if I can ease up on that cloud-nine kick Kovin's always riding."

Cabiness shook his head. "You're just not going to be happy until you get yourself fixed, are you?"

Furg smiled. "Hell, I'm like some horny kid who ain't ever had any yet. That's just about all that kid thinks about, and he dreams on it like it was going to be the biggest turn-on ever. You know?"

"Sure. But it's hardly the same thing."

"Yeah? You mean to tell me you've never known anyone who was hooked on pussy? One particular one, or just in general."

"There's still no law against it," Cabiness said.

"The hell there ain't. They're just not enforced, but they've got them if they ever want to dig them up."

"Well, Furg, you're going to do what you want anyway. It's just that I've seen so many good heads, strung-out and ragged, behind smack. And a lot of them hit the deep-six. And damn few of them ever get back where they were when they started."

"Now, Lee-Boy, don't take it so seriously. I'm just talking about a little old light-running chippy fix—just to see—I'm not studying no oil-burner of a habit and a hundred-dollar nut every day."

Cabiness lit the half stick of pot, took a drag, and passed it to Furg. "Too bad you can't stay happy with good old Mary-Jane here. She's a lively little broad, but harmless."

"Well, I've had it," Furg said. "That's all, I've had it. I want to do everything once, I guess."

"Fine, I'll start making out a list for you. Tomorrow you can clean my john, you've never done that before, and then the next day—"

"Jam it, uncle, I do the picking."

"Well, if you do decide to make it, be careful what you're getting a hold of. There's a lot of bad stuff floating around. Lord knows what all it's cut with. Ask Kovin. He's an expert."

"I'll watch it," Furg agreed absently.

They walked in silence past the dark windows of the stores which sold everything from 25-cent flutes to fifteen-hundred-dollar abstractions constructed from flattened tin cans and Purex bottles, held together with strands of barbed wire. They stopped to look at the abstractions.

"I think I find the soup cans more interesting than the bean cans," Cabiness said. "Don't you agree?"

"No, I mostly get my kicks off them Purex bottles."

"Oh, the bottles are so blah, I mean they're so bottle-ly. You know? But the texture of the soup cans is really quite interesting, and their spatial relationship is one of charming impertinence. Don't you agree?"

"Hell, no," Furg returned. "If there's any one thing I can't bear it's an impertinent soup can. Fair causes my hackles to rise."

"Furg, your aesthetic sense is as numb as your impulse to take a bath."

"You implying that I'm funky?"

"I don't care if you're funky. I hardly ever feel like kissing you, and I always managed to control the impulse."

"Ann don't complain," Furg said.

"She's tender towards you. She bears your funk with a woman's compassion and goes to sleep dreaming of goats."

"You know something, Lee-Boy, I really dig that little chick. I really do. She's the greatest in my charts."

"Yes, she's real."

They came to a bus stop and Cabiness moved towards it. "I'm going to catch the Muni and make it on home."

Furg frowned, "I keep forgetting you don't live up here any more. Well, take it slow. I'll pick up on you tomorrow."

Cabiness stood watching Furg's tall narrow figure moving away on the street that would take him to Ann and Kovin's place. Maybe Kovin would be on the nod. Poor Furg. That must be a bad scene for him. A cab appeared in the street before the bus so he took the cab instead; he still had almost three-quarters of a joint left. Enough for Clair.

She was asleep in the front room. A magazine had slipped off her lap, and to his surprise, she had glasses on. He stood and watched her, marveling at how childlike she seemed. Her pajamas were open at the top, revealing the sharp delicate bones arched below her throat—a faint pulse flicked in the hollow between them.

Her eyes opened, and she yawned. When she really saw him, she snatched her glasses off and said, "I was trying to wait up."

"It's almost morning," he said.

"How'd it go?" she asked.

He was still a little high and he burst out, "Swinging! The best jazz crowd I've seen."

She nibbled at one of the heavy temple bars before she said slowly, "Good, I'm glad for you."

He picked up the magazine. It was *U.S. News and World Report*. He held it out and looked at her quizzically, just clowning because he felt good, but she took him seriously.

"Don't you care what's going on around you?" she asked defensively.

"No, and neither will you in a minute."

He lit the roach, taking the first toke, and then handed it to her. She held it for a moment, staring at it—almost until he was on the point of telling her not to waste it—before she put it to her lips. She took two small drags and held her breath until her face was pink. She tried to hand the joint back, but he brushed it aside.

"Get on," he told her. "I've had some."

She hit again. He sat down beside her chair, and while she smoked, he took her slipper off, separated her little toe and bit it.

"Don't do that," she said sharply.

But he didn't stop. He moved to her knee, and in a moment her eyes were closed. She dropped her glasses at the side of the chair and grabbed his head.

After a while they went into the bedroom, and it was like it had been the night on the ferry boat right up to the last moment. Then something swept out of some icy pocket in her mind and carried her almost out of it.

"That was fine," she said quietly.

He wasn't sure, but when he touched her he thought her eyes were wet.

chapter sixteen

Wednesday he went to court. It was on the third floor of the Hall of Justice, and while he sat waiting for the judge to appear he watched the pigeons strutting on the deep stone window ledges. He continued to watch the pigeons even after court was in session and while Acton, his lawyer, made his brief plea for a postponement. The judge granted the motion without comment, but he set the new date for the following Monday, only five days away. Acton immediately asked for more time, but the judge refused without comment.

Monday Carver was in the courtroom, sitting far in back, his hat held on his knee. The judge refused to hear further arguments for postponement. Cabiness entered a plea of Not Guilty, and the preliminary trial was set for Friday.

Carver stepped in front of him as Cabiness was on his way out, but he stepped to the side and continued walking. He heard the Narco behind him.

"I just wanted to let you know that it's not going to work, Cabiness. You'll get due process as fast as anyone ever got it."

He reached the apartment just as Clair was on the point of leaving. She wore a suit that was fashionable to the point of grotesqueness and green leather shoes, narrow as laths. The cleaning woman was running the vacuum in the front room, and he yelled to her over the roar of the machine.

"Ernest knows what he's doing," she said, after he told her the motion for continuance had been denied.

"Sure," he said. "And I know what he's *not* doing, and he's not working any miracle right at the present time."

"Do you want someone else?" she asked.

"No."

"Then what's the trouble?"

"The trouble is I've got a hunch I'm on my way to San Quentin. On rails, straight as a string—" he sketched a rapid line along the air and went, "Whoooosh!"

"Oh, you don't know. Nothing's decided yet. You haven't even been tried. Now stop brooding and find something to do, because I've got an appointment at the hairdressers."

He followed her into the hall and kissed her. Her jacket had a shawl collar that dipped deep in the back, and he got his hand inside it, his palm flat on the little ridges of her spine. Her lips were cool. He shrugged, watching her face as she moved back from the kiss.

"Blow hot, blow cold," he said.

"What do you mean by that?"

"Nothing. Something I heard."

"All right, I've got to go."

"Sure, I think I'll wander down to The Beach and see what's been happening."

"If you want to." She said, pausing again. "I suppose you miss that sort of thing."

He put on some of his old clothes and went over to North Beach. He stopped by Jean's room. Some of his feelings about the Bird's Nest had crystallized into a definite suspicion, and he wanted to talk to her. But she wasn't home.

He went looking for Furg and finally found him with Kovin and Ann at their pad on lower Columbus. It wasn't a shambles like most Beach pads. Ann had it clean and comfortable. He felt better just stepping inside it.

Kovin appeared to be asleep on the couch, Ann was sitting on the floor fooling with a guitar, and for the first time in days he saw her wearing Levis and a sweat shirt. Furg was in the can, but when he heard Cabiness' voice he came out. His hair was neatly combed, and he wore a white turtle-neck sweater instead of his usual suntans. Little by little the farm was wearing off him. But his grin was the same—his eyes squinched and his mouth stretched off toward the left side of his face.

"Damn, Lee-Boy, you look like yourself again—dirty, uncouth, and mad. What's buggin' you?"

"Lots—for a beginning, I think we're working in a cat house."

Ann started laughing. "So you finally snapped. I tumbled the other night when some lame hit on me to go in back—" She made a deprecatory gesture at her face. "I was so stunned, I almost went."

Furg said, "He wasn't so lame. He could pick good."

Ann waved it aside. "My charms aren't visible, but—"

"Dino must be out of his gourd," Cabiness said, "unless he's got giant juice."

"Not Dino. Randozza," Ann corrected. "And he probably has."

"I told you what he was, didn't I?" Furg reminded him.

Kovin stirred on the bed, and they fell silent watching him. He had his hat off, and the hairless head made him look old and tired.

"Is he fixing again?" Cabiness asked.

Ann nodded. "Some kid smashed into a drugstore, and he sold Kove a handful of dollies. He connected this morning, too. If there's stuff anywhere in town, he'll find it."

There was a large sheet of drawing paper pinned to the wall above Kovin's head—something was written on it in red pencil. Cabiness moved closer to read it. Behind him Ann said, "Kove wrote that this morning."

It was called "Kove's Blues."

> "Left foot say hungry
> Right foot say broke
> Mouth say nothing
> 'Cause I'm takin' a toke
>
> Of hay, hay, hay, and rain say
> weary, and cold say fever
> Heat say hope
> but head say cleaver
>
> And sharp—Oh, man!—the knife
> night, and the ol' forlorn
> stars say spike
> But heart say horn
>
> Of gold, gold, gold, and the bold
> sign of my sound—strong
> on the deadeye sky
> say I belong
>
> Say I belong"

"Was he high when he wrote that?" Cabiness asked.

"Yes."

"It sounds like it."

When he turned back, Ann was frowning, and so was Furg. "Let's make it out in the kitchen," Ann said. It was apparent that she didn't want to disturb Kovin.

The kitchen was an ordinary room, except for the massive table made out of a solid slab of scrubbed pine, anchored to the wall and supported by a single leg. It was sturdy as a bar and bare, except for a wooden bowl of grapes and a half-gallon of Vino Pastoso.

"He's coming unwound, isn't he?" Cabiness asked, gesturing back where Kovin lay.

Furg scowled. "Man, is he!"

But Ann turned on them sternly. "Leave him alone. You don't really know him. Kove's ..well, he's sweet. That's a stupid word, but he's sweet and uncomplicated, and things are too much for him. He needs help."

"All right," Furg said, "but why should it be you?" He was still standing, his head bent forward, his face pale and angry. Cabiness looked at him in surprise. Furg was never serious. It was hard to believe him in the role.

"It just happened that way," Ann told him, and she turned to fill a saucepan. "Who wants coffee?"

But Furg wouldn't turn. "I want you to come over and stay at my pad. I'm damn tired of making it with you while he's on the nod in the next room. Look, Annie ..I dig you. Maybe I love you. I don't know."

Ann set the saucepan on the stove carefully; the gas flame sizzled on the wet bottom. She looked up, her gray eyes soft. "This is my place," she explained quietly. "I've lived here for over five years."

"Then let's kick him out."

"No," she said firmly, "I couldn't do that."

Furg swiped angrily at something invisible in the air. "If you stopped giving him bread he'd cut out tomorrow."

"Maybe," she agreed. "But he's making money now—more than I do. So we'll see." She walked up to Furg, her head coming even with his knobby collar bones, and grabbed the side of his cheek hard. "I want *you* to live here," she said harshly. "But I won't kick him out. We'll have to wait."

Furg bent over her for a moment while Cabiness looked away. Then Ann was straightening her sweat shirt, saying, "Don't mind us."

"You know I don't," he said. "It's been so long since I saw someone with an honest yen, I'm ready to go down to the zoo and watch the monkeys make out."

Ann grinned, but not with much sympathy. "Is your gilded cage growing irksome?"

"More like frostbite."

"Oh, my—and everything *looks* so good."

"It's not really funny to me," he told her. "Any more than Kove is to you."

"I'm sorry," she said quickly.

Furg started back towards the bathroom. "Well, I'm still gonna turn on."

"What's he got?" Cabiness asked idly, watching Ann pour water for the instant coffee.

"Heroin," she said bleakly.

"Heroin?" He stood up.

"Kove gave it to him," she said, with a heat obviously left over from a former argument. "You try. I can't talk him out of it."

Cabiness rubbed his mouth, looking along the hallway to the door of the bathroom. "I've had that with him before," he said. Slowly he sat down again. "I guess he isn't going to be satisfied until he tries it."

Ann set a thick pottery cup in front of him and sat down on the other side of the table. "Then how come you don't have to try it? Why don't I?"

Cabiness picked his cup up and set it down again without drinking from it. "I don't know about you, but I'm scared." He gestured out towards Kovin.

"That scares me. I've seen a lot of it. Too much, I guess. Kove could be blowing with the best of them if he wasn't hooked."

Ann nodded soberly and fell silent. Then she said, "It won't take with Furg. He gets too much of a kick out of things. It's the sad nervous people who get sucked under."

He agreed with her, then changed the subject. "Did Randozza pitch at you once?"

She looked away. "Not hard. It was just an evening's notion with him. He described the beauties of laying around all day whether you were working or not while Big John looked after you. He's a pretty man, and I thought he wanted some action himself, and I was more than willing for that—but he never hit on me personally." Her eyes returned to his. Bluntly, "Don't think I wouldn't have turned out if I could have seen any future in it, but looking the way I do he'd have had me in some gook house in Fresno."

Cabiness shook his head angrily. "I don't like the setup. I don't like working there."

Ann smiled satirically. "Why? You don't have to turn tricks."

"Don't I? What do you think I'm doing out front with my horn. In the last four nights I've played every cheap trick I know at least a dozen times. That's pimping, too. Anyway, they can't handle action like that in San Francisco the way it is now—it's too obvious."

"I know clubs where they've been tricking in the back room for the last five years—and so do you."

That was true. As she mentioned it, he thought of several, so he had to shut up since he wasn't able to talk about the part of it that was really bothering him.

They heard a muffled sound from the bathroom. Ann called, "Furg?"

She waited a moment, then, "I'd better see."

Cabiness was sipping his coffee when he heard her gasp, a harsh wounded sound, and he turned to see her standing in the doorway with her knuckles crammed in her mouth. When he reached her side he saw Furg sitting on the toilet—the spike was still in his arm, his shoulders were hunched, but his head was thrown back as if someone were pulling his hair. His cornflower eyes were clear and utterly sightless. As they watched he slumped, shifted to the side, and fell to the floor.

"Oh, Jeezus," Ann said, cramped over as if she were going to vomit. "Sweet bloody Jeezus."

"Overjolt," Cabiness told her, "we've got to walk him," and as he turned Furg over, removing the spike with its trail of black blood, he said again, "We've got to walk him."

He was trying to hoist him up on his shoulders and Ann was crying, saying softly and bitterly, "Put him down. Put him down. Why can't you put him down? Don't you see he's dead?"

"Dead?" he repeated numbly, thinking, but an overjolt wouldn't ..not this fast.

But he was dead. Somehow he could sense it in the feel, and he lowered Furg back to the floor. The head jammed in a corner, the corners of his mouth turned up in a blind smile.

He stood dazed, listening to the ugly sound of Ann's crying; then he said, "Oh, Kovin ..Kovin you sonofabitch..."

He ran down the hall and snatched Kovin up and slapped him awake. Kovin threw his arm over his face and said, "What? What the hell?" He opened his pale eyes and closed them again.

Cabiness threw his arm aside and slapped him harder. Behind him Ann yelled, "Don't hurt him. It won't help to hurt him."

But he ignored her and shook Kovin until he opened his eyes again and smiled meaninglessly. "Leave me alone, Cab—it's not time to blow yet."

"What'd you give Furg?" he demand.

"What?" Kovin blinked up at him. Then he tried to look down where Cabiness' hand was twisted in his shirt front; finally, he wet his lips and said, "Stuff ..good stuff."

Cabiness hauled him off the couch and toe-walked him down the hall with his arm levered behind him. He forced him through the door and held him over Furg.

"That's what your *good* stuff did to him."

"Oh," Kovin breathed—then "Oh" again, a soft gasp of understanding and dismay. "Let me go, Lee. Let me out of here before I throw up... Please."

He released him and Kovin stumbled back into the living room and sank down on the couch. He sat with his hands pressed against the side of his legs—a stifled gesture as if he were on the verge of screaming.

"Hotshot," he said to himself, and his face collapsed. "Why would he give me a hotshot?"

His eyes came up to Cabiness, rational and frightened. He wasn't playing a part. He was terrified.

"Where'd you get that stuff?"

"Sullivan. Why would he hotshot me?"

"How do you know it was a hotshot?"

Kovin rubbed his forehead with the side of his fist so hard he left white streaks. Out in the hall, Ann was still crying. "Man, I've seen before. I was there when they hotshotted Rutherford. I was blowing with him. He went out the same way. . ." Kovin snapped his fingers and shook his head. "You've seen overjolts. That was no overjolt."

Cabiness had to know, and he made Kovin tell him just how he'd made the buy. But there wasn't much for Kovin to tell—he'd wanted to lay in a stash now that he had some bread, he'd heard Sullivan was still holding, and he'd made a buy off of him. When Furg had bummed him for some, he'd given him the new stuff instead of the dollaphine because he thought the stuff from Sullivan was cut pretty thin and wouldn't make Furg sick.

"I wouldn't louse up a swinger like Furg. Don't you know that, Cab?"

"Didn't you taste it?"

"Sure I tasted it before I bought it. What's that mean? They use strychnine. It's supposed to taste the same."

Ann came in. Her eyes were dry, but swollen and red. "Are you just going to leave him in there?" she asked.

Together they carried Furg into the front room and covered him with a blanket. Ann bent over him, lifted the blanket, and took something out of his pocket. Cabiness couldn't see what it was. Ann stood silently for several minutes. None of them said anything. Then she asked, "What are we going to do?"

Cabiness walked over to the window and twitched aside the burlap drape. It was late afternoon, still light. Across the street a girl was watering something in a yellow window box. "When it's dark," he said, still watching the girl, "we'll take him out and leave him... in the bushes around Coit Tower."

Ann made an angry sound of protest. He whirled on her. "What do you want? You want to call the heat? Will that help?"

Kovin said, "They left Rutherford on his own front lawn. His old lady found him in the morning."

Cabiness pointed at the blanket. "That's not Furg," he told Ann. "Furg's gone."

After that they sat silently for a long time, and even when it grew darker no one turned on a light, as if the darkness would fill the room and erase what lay there. Kovin began to sniffle, but he was either afraid to fix, or he withheld out of some kind of respect.

"Where's the rest of that stuff?" Cabiness asked him, and without answering Kovin went along the hall into the kitchen. In a moment he was back with a screwdriver, and, standing on a chair, he unscrewed the old-fashioned light fixture in the center of the ceiling. It came loose, swaying like a bowl, held up by two coarse wires, one red, the other white. He reached in and handed Cabiness an envelope. Cabiness examined it. It had been sealed and folded, and one of the corners had been torn off to make a pouring spout. The creases were dirty and worn, and when he opened it flat, he saw that "Empire Hotel" was printed in the corner, with an address on Turk Street.

"A gram," Kovin said without inflection. He hesitated, then screwed the fixture back in place. Cabiness felt the plumb bottom edge of the envelope where death lay so unobtrusively. He folded it back up and stuck it in his shirt pocket. Kovin put the screwdriver away.

At dusk Cabiness went out on the back porch and looked down the three flights of steps into the backyard. It was enclosed by a fence, but there was a gate and, beyond that, an alley. Over half the back windows around him were lit, and as he stood listening he heard the unmistakable sounds of someone fixing dinner nearby. He tiptoed down one flight to find the lights on in the kitchen below. If the layout was the same as Ann's, the window above the sink would overlook the stairs, and as he leaned against the wall beside it he heard a woman humming in a curious plaintive scale. If they made any noise she had only to glance out to see them. And they would make noise.

He went back and asked Ann, "Who lives below you?"

"A Chinese and Negro couple. I don't know them."

Cabiness stood still for a moment, rubbing his eyes with his thumb and forefinger. Then he said, "People like that are apt to mind their own business. I think we have to go ahead and do it. Do you want to wait until early this morning?"

"No," Kovin said quickly.

"How do you feel?"

"OK—"

"Why don't you fix? Then we'll get it over with."

"I'm OK. What do we have to do?"

He told Ann to get the car and park it in the alley—then he had another idea, and told her to come back after and ring the bell in the apartment below. That would draw the woman out of the kitchen and they'd move when they heard it. She put on the old black raincoat she always wore. Then she stopped to look over at the shadowy object where Furg lay along the baseboard. The silence grew thick and solemn, but all she said was that they should empty his pockets. Cabiness agreed, but he waited until she was gone before he did. Then they carried him into the kitchen, still in the blanket. They rolled him out. It was too dark to see features, but neither of them looked.

"If someone sees us—" Kovin said.

"He's drunk. Passed out."

"It's too early."

"Not around here.... Come on."

Kovin took the legs and he took the shoulders. They eased out on the porch, and, when they heard the bell below them, started down the stairs. Cabiness was aware of a radio going somewhere, playing a boisterous tune; he was aware of that and Kovin staggering back and forth in front of him, and the dull slumping sound the body made each time it sagged down and hit the stairs. In the yard it was easier.

They propped him up in the back seat of the car, leaning over in the corner. Ann came running back and slid behind the wheel. Kovin stood outside.

"I can't go," he said. His face was damp and he couldn't stop yawning.

"You've got to go. You've got to sit up front to make it look right."

"I can't, man. I just can't."

Ann reached over and snapped the door open. "Get in," she told him.

He looked around where the houses seemed to be looking back. He fought off another fit of yawning and wiped his nose with the back of his hand like a child. Then he obeyed her.

The drive up the hill was quiet. No one said anything. Cabiness remembered the night they'd ridden around with the lawnmower. Remembered Furg bellowing "Goodbye Blues" and making it with Ann the first time. Remembered him telling Ann that he had to have his cherry kicks and see for himself what the shouting was all about.

The lights were on around the base of Coit Tower, lighting the fluted column of white stone, but the bushes below it were shadowed like dark pubic fluff. The gravel lot was empty and the telescopes hung tilted in their metal stanchions. They drove along the stone guard rail until it broke for the mouth of a path.

The path twisted down the hill through the underbrush, and, while Ann waited beside the car, they took Furg down about thirty feet and laid him under a tree. When they came back they found Ann standing at the head of the path. Cabiness turned and looked out along the bay, where the piers stuck out like black teeth in the mouth of the water. He couldn't think of anything to say.

Kovin's tenor was in the back of the car. Lee took it out, fitted it together, and, while Ann and Kovin listened, he played "I'm Just a Lonesome Stranger." He wasn't used to the tenor mouthpiece, and he didn't play it very well. Some cold part of his mind said this is corny, but he went on playing.

Kovin took his hat off, looked at it, and put it back on. Ann's face was white in the shelter of her raincoat. She scuffed at the gravel.

A party of tourists drove up, and they stopped to listen, too, for a moment, before they got out and started putting dimes in the telescopes.

chapter seventeen

The Playhouse of the Masks was housed in an old burlesque theater. The marquee holders that once displayed stills full of rhinestone, feathers and flesh, now held low-key portraits of sensitive profiles and intense young women in tunics. The overhead marquee that had once announced Bubbles O'Dell and her sisters, now read simply:

THE DELICATE LION
a play by
Terence Sullivan

Inside the burlesque gaudiness had been replaced by combed plywood and ferns in hanging ceramic pots.

"Are you looking for someone?"

A girl in a black sweater was arranging a lobby display featuring a cartoon of an exquisite lion holding a sunflower. She was without make-up, and her eyes were severe.

"Is Sullivan around?" Cabiness asked.

"In the basement," she told him, indicating where a flight of steep red stairs disappeared abruptly.

The basement was confusion; flats stood around everywhere with parts of costumes draped over them, the floor was mottled with overlapping islands of spilled paint, a line of ladders leaned against the concrete wall like an abandoned attempt to scale it, and several old kitchen tables were littered with tin cans full of paint, nails, screws, as well as abandoned scripts and half-eaten sandwiches.

Standing quietly at the foot of the stairs, Cabiness heard someone typing and, following the sound, he came on Sullivan in a half-open room lined with books. He was sitting at a little table using an old typewriter. Beside him a metal bunk was made up with a gray army blanket. The floor at his feet was littered with candy wrappers and a carton that had held a strawberry milkshake.

Sullivan looked up. His eyes flickered and he wiped the back of his hand on his mustache. "Well, Lee...how'd you find your way down here?"

"The girl upstairs."

"Mara?"

"I don't know her name."

"That's Mara. Talented actress... dedicated, you know?" He coughed. "'She has the female lead in my new play. It's not much of a part, but she's putting a lot into it."

Cabiness sat down on the bunk behind Sullivan. The paper in the machine was heavy with X's. After a slow moment Sullivan said, "I'm just trying to sharpen up some of the stuff in the second act. We open Friday."

"What's it about?" Cabiness asked idly.

"Oscar Wilde—that's the title, you see? I meant it in the sense of a social lion..." He paused and swung around, his eyes milky, the pupils pinched almost shut. "What do you want, Lee?" he asked quietly.

"Nothing much. I was looking for someone with a 'fit, and I saw your name out there, so I thought I'd come in."

Sullivan nodded slowly. "So you finally hit the heavy?"

"I'm just chippying."

Sullivan didn't comment. He reached over and tapped the space bar a few times. "I heard you were in jail."

"Yeah? Where'd you hear that?"

"I don't know. Someone told me."

"I didn't think anyone knew. I was only in one night. I saw Bear in there— you know?—bass player. They busted him."

"Yeah?" Sullivan smoothed his hair. Not a vain gesture. "You want to fix?"

"That's the idea."

Sullivan leaned over and pulled one of the books from the lowest shelf. An old book—the gold stamping had mostly flaked away, leaving only indentations of the letters in the faded cloth: COLLECTED PLAYS of Richardson. He held it flat and opened it carefully. The middle pages had been cut to form a small box, and the dripper and spike were packed in old cottons.

Cabiness remained silent. He took the envelope out of his pocket, opened it flat, and placed it on Sullivan's table. "You cook up," he said.

Sullivan picked up a coffee cup, emptied a quarter of a cup into the wastepaper basket, and stepped over to an old-fashioned sink streaked with water colors. He rinsed the cup carefully, filled it, and returned, carrying a large tablespoon. He picked up the envelope, and when he saw the printing in the corner his mouth opened, closed, then smiled.

"Where'd you get this?" he asked.

"Kovin let me have it."

"Is Kovin dealing now?"

"No... he was doing me a favor. He made the buy for me."

Sullivan tapped the envelope. His smile had turned reflective. "You know, it's weird how this stuff travels around. Did you ever think of that? How many hands it goes through from the time they make it until someone finally shoots it. It's like a secret river under the earth...."

Sullivan paused, musing, and Cabiness said, "Cook for yourself too."

"Sure. Thanks, Lee."

He cooked the mixture quickly in the tablespoon, and reached a paint rag off the shelf. "Here, Lee, tie off."

"No, you go ahead."

Sullivan smiled nervously. "I can taste it already." He knotted the rag around his biceps and pumped his fist until the veins of the inner arm stood up like blue ropes. He sucked the fluid from the tablespoon, through a cotton, into the dripper, and laid the needle along a vein.

"That's my favorite," he murmured. "I could hit it with my eyes closed." The needle slid in and he tapped the glass barrel of the eye-dropper gently, watching for his blood to flow up into it.

Cabiness reached over and slapped his hand roughly. The dropper slipped out of the needle and broke on the cement floor. Its fatal charge made a small wet spot no bigger than a silver dollar.

Sullivan took three quick steps back, holding the inside of his arm. His eyes flared. "What the... what's wrong with you?"

"You don't know?" Cabiness asked carefully.

"Is this some kind of rib? I don't need your stuff."

Cabiness reached over and picked up the envelope. He held it out at Sullivan. "This is full of strychnine. If you'd taken that fix, you'd have been dead before you could get the needle out of your arm."

Sullivan put his hand out, a groping gesture. "But who...?" Then sharply, "How do you know?"

"Because Boyd Furguson is dead from it."

"Furg?"

"And this is the stuff you sold Kovin this morning."

Sullivan didn't seem to be able to say anything. His eyes were stricken. He sat down slowly and covered his face with his hands. "What're you up to, Sully? You didn't know that was a hotshot. I believe that. But something's rank."

"It was me he was after," Sullivan mumbled into his hands. He flung around and pulled another book off the shelf, dumping it open on the table. Two more envelopes slipped out of it. He threw them to the wall where they fell lightly to the floor. Then he began to shiver.

"In another hour I would have used some of that stuff."

"Maybe that would have been letting you out easy," Cabiness said grimly. "Where'd you get it?"

"From Carver."

"Carver?"

Piece by piece the story came out of Sullivan's gray lips. Maybe he felt he had to tell someone, erect some dam of justification against a hostile world. Cabiness didn't pursue it.

"And you snitched on me? And the Bear? Fat Daddy?"

"And others. He wanted someone set up every day or so. I had to. You know that? I had to. Now he's trying to kill me because I know he's hooked himself. He's got a giant habit."

Cabiness turned away. He didn't want to look at Sullivan any more. He stared over at a flat where some painted trees led along a painted country road. He started to ask Sullivan if anyone else knew where his stash was. But how would it help if he did assure himself that Carver had poisoned the heroin? Assuming that he could, how would that help Furg? What could he do to Sullivan, who felt he couldn't live without fixing, and now couldn't fix for fear of dying? Or if Luth Grimes, or some friend of Fat Daddy's, had found Sullivan's stash and done this thing, was he responsible for Furg's death? Someone had fired a bullet somewhere, and it had found Furg. Otherwise there was no relationship... except Carver.

The girl, Mara, called from the head of the stairs, "Terry, come and see what I've done." Sullivan lifted his head. That was all, "Terry?" she called again.

"In a minute," Sullivan called back weakly. "I'm busy."

Cabiness heard his chair scrape. Then, "What're you going to do, Lee?"

"I don't know."

"I'd better go see. She works hard, you know? Are you pissed at me, Lee? I couldn't help myself, but I guess you couldn't really understand that, could you?"

"No, I guess not."

He wanted to hit Sullivan until the snitch couldn't stand—just for the satisfaction of expressing his loss and anger on something that could feel pain, and not sense it draining away through all the weary channels of justification and uncertainty. But he just sat and watched Sullivan walk slowly to the stairs, heard his footsteps on the floor above. Again his thoughts turned to Carver.

Carver had set Sullivan like a trap, like a lighted bomb. The bomb wasn't responsible.

Then Sullivan was running back down the stairs, taking them two at a time. He stopped halfway down; his face was haggard. At his expression Cabiness automatically stood up.

"Jean..." Sullivan said. "I sold some of that stuff to Jean."

"When?"

"This afternoon."

Cabiness knocked Sullivan out of the way getting up the stairs.

chapter eighteen

The Bird's Nest was closed. He slammed the door with the flat of his hand and rattled the padlock, before he remembered it was Monday night—the off-night. He swore at himself. He was so rummy he'd misplaced the day.

He ran down Grant Avenue to Broadway, paying no attention to the people who stopped to stare after him. Jean's window was dark, but that didn't reassure him. He could almost see her slumped across the bed as evening crowded into the room—it was a terrible vision.

Her door was locked. He knocked once and then felt for the key on the ledge above it. It was missing. He put his shoulder to the door. The wood was flimsy and the tongue of the lock tore through it on his second lunge.

The bed was unmade, and he held his breath as he walked around it, but the narrow strip of carpet on the far side was empty. A book lay there, lit by the steady blue glow of the neon above the window. It was open on its face, discarded as she'd turned to sleep the night before. It recalled the many nights she had spent reading as he drowsed beside her. Then the book would thud to the floor, the light go off and maybe they'd make love again.

He looked behind the picture frame where she sometimes Scotch-taped her extra money, but there was nothing there. He went through the dresser and the wardrobe. Still nothing.

He didn't know what to do. He thought of waiting for her to come home, but knew his nerves wouldn't stand it. He even thought of going to the police, but they would know even less about how to find her than he did.

Somehow he was sure that if she were going to use the stuff, she'd do it in her room—alone—not as a party stunt signifying something thought to be smart and very hip. She would do it alone and for some different reason.

Thinking this, he wrote her a note of warning and thumb-tacked it to the door. Then he went down the street to the Bocche Ball where he'd so often seen Randozza in the past.

The Bocche Ball featured operatic entertainment, and as he came through the door a tenor in a ruffled silk shirt was struggling with *Il Mio Tesoro,* accompanied by piano and accordion. A feverish-looking soprano and a gloomy middle-aged baritone sat waiting their turns.

The light was all centered on the small stage, so he avoided an Italian in a black suit who tried to direct him to a table and went to stand in back where he could see the entire club. He looked for the theatrical crest of Randozza's head against the lights, the bold nose and heavy hair, but there was no one that even resembled him. He was on the point of leaving when he noticed a party of older Italians entering a door in back, and he remembered that the original courts, where they actually played bocche ball, were supposed to be in back.

The piano galloped into a ragged Polonaise by way of an intermission, and the soprano fumbled with her earrings and straightened her blouse, betraying that she was on next. Cabiness moved over to the back door, almost certain that whatever was back there was a private club or restricted by custom to Italians. As he turned the handle, he heard a muffled impact, followed by a series of clicks and a low murmur, and he stepped into a long, brilliantly-lit room with a hardwood floor laid out in courts. Men, and only men, were gathered at either end. Most of them wore hats and their suits were dark grays and browns. They were following a game that must have been similar to skittles. He never found out, because someone came over to tell him this was a private club. It was Dino.

"Where's Randozza?" he asked.

Dino's expression altered slightly. "Is it important?"

"Yes."

"Something to do with the club?"

"No, it's personal. Look, man if you know where he is tell me and don't screw around!"

Dino took a half step back and touched the knot in his tie. "All right... take it easy, fellow."

Cabiness was aware of his fingers tingling. He clenched his fist and jammed it against the side of his leg to keep from swinging on Dino. Someone on the courts made a score, and there was excited shouting in Italian that sounded like bets being laid.

He told Dino the story quickly, changing it around so Randozza had the hotshot. He couldn't be sure Dino was accepting it, but the other man nodded coldly and said Randozza lived out on the peninsula near Burlingame. He mentioned an address.

"Can we phone him?" Cabiness asked.

"He doesn't have a phone out there. He goes there to rest."

"Look! Drive me out there."

"Sorry. No wheels."

"Then loan me cab fare."

Dino shook his head slowly. "Your story's pretty odd, and even if it *is* true, Randozza and I are business partners—not friends. You dig?"

Cabiness didn't wait to answer. He caught a cab on the comer and told the driver, "Burlingame."

"That's a double-saw," the driver said without turning around. "In advance." Cabiness saw his cynical eyes in the rear-view mirror.

"Then go to "Nine-thirty Powell. And push it."

As the cab pulled out, he felt in his pocket to make sure he had a dollar, realizing that this was the night he should have worn the suit.

He found Clair sitting in the living room, smoking. As he came in she pushed an almost-fresh cigarette into an ashtray and stood up. She was angry.

"This *is* your night off?" she asked coldly.

"Yes, but—"

"Then I *did* have the right to expect you to take me somewhere?"

"Shut up, Clair. We'll talk about it later. Right now I need the car."

"Whatever for? And don't tell me to shut up, damn you! You look like a tramp again. What do you..."

She stopped and stared at him as he snatched her purse up and emptied it on the coffee table. He picked out the car keys and started for the door. She followed him, hitting at his back with her small fists. "Damn you! Damn you!" She ducked in front of him and spread herself against the door, but he threw her aside. In the hall he started to run, passing the elevator for the stairs.

"Lee? Please stop."

She turned her heel on the first flight and fell against the wall. He glanced back and saw her leaning there, breathing heavily, her face deadly white.

"I'll report it stolen," she yelled after him.

He opened the big green car up, racing out Valencia Street onto the Allemany freeway. He got through the speed-trap community of Daly City and out on to the El Camino Real. He made Burlingame in twenty minutes; he stopped at a filling station for directions, but then lost himself in the tree-lined circling streets that all looked the same. When he pulled up to question a couple of women walking on the sidewalk, they looked at his grim face and hurried on without answering. When he jumped out of the car they started running.

He found El Camino Real again and tried to re-orient himself. This time he spotted the almost hidden turning and drove out the right street. It wasn't even sub-divided; every several hundred yards there was a hermit house. Randozza's was a long low structure of redwood and fieldstone. His name was lettered on an iron plaque hung above the mail box. A light was on in the house.

Jean answered the door. For a moment he just stared at her feeling a great unwinding inside himself, while she smiled numbly and said, "Why, Lee..."

He grabbed her arm. "Jeanie, did you buy stuff from Sullivan?"

Her mouth tightened. She looked down and said with some difficulty, "That isn't any of your business, anymore."

"Then you did. Where is it? It's bad stuff. It's poisoned."

"What?" She looked up, comprehension slowly growing in her eyes. "Oh," she said, and covered her mouth with her hand. She swayed and he tried to steady her, but she pulled away from him. "I'm all right."

He followed her inside, into a low comfortable room with an upholstered leather bar studded with brass tacks. The furniture was oriented around a large TV. It was on, and the screen danced with color. She picked her purse up from a low table and took out her billfold. From the non-secret secret compartment she removed a small folded paper. She held it and looked at it a moment before he reached over and took it out of her hand.

He unfolded it. It was just white powder. He started to touch his tongue to it, but she said, "Don't!" He walked over and emptied the powder into the fireplace. He wadded the paper and tossed it in, too, watching as the tiny flames reached for it. The paper blackened and began to smoke. Finally he asked, "Why'd you want that?"

There was silence for a moment. Then he heard the springs in a chair adjust to her weight, and she was saying, "That isn't any of your business, either."

"Where's Randozza?"

"He'll be back in a minute. He went after some ice cream."

Ice cream! He turned to look at her, for the first time noticing how she looked, what she was wearing. He stared at her levelly, noting the liverish shadows under her eyes, the lipstick blistered on her dry mouth, the sharpness with which her black dress cut against the dull skin. He knew his eyes were cruel. She sat looking back at him, her arms stretched rigidly along the rests of the chair. Her hands tightened and her eyes slowly filled with tears.

"I made a terrible mess out of things," she said.

He felt a strong impulse to go to her, but it died in a clash of other emotions, and he walked over and switched the TV off. In the sudden silence he could hear her crying. He sat down.

"I know what's going on in the Bird's Nest," he said dryly, hating the stiffness he felt in himself, but unable to free it. "Is that why you wanted the stuff? To clear that out of your mind?"

She didn't answer, but her silence was clearly yes.

"Why?" he asked harshly. "Why did you have to go that route?"

She raised her head at the tone of his voice and rubbed her eye with the heel of her palm. "I never thought you'd talk to me like that. I never thought..." She paused and groped for something she was trying to say. "Do you think that what I did is any different from what you're doing with that girl?"

"It was a hell of a lot different!"

"How? In what way?"

Her question enraged him. He stood up and walked back to the fireplace— just to be moving—and stared down where some of the white powder was still strewn on the charred logs. Jean wasn't crying any more, and for some reason that made him angrier. He wanted to say that there was only one of Clair... only one! That was the difference.

Then the sound of a motor in the driveway gave him another and safer outlet for the dangerous pressure of his emotions. He turned to face the door, and Randozza came in, looking expectant, probably wondering who had driven the strange car parked in front. He was dressed casually, quietly, in light gray slacks and a blue sweater. He carried a paper bag in his left hand, and in his right he still held the car keys. His eyes widened when he recognized Cabiness. That was his only reaction.

"I got a thing with you," Cabiness said.

Randozza put his bag on the table beside the door. With a hand free he immediately sketched that curious smoothing motion along the side of his hair. His eyes were quiet.

"Yes?" he said politely.

"I don't like your action. It stinks. And so do you."

"Oh—" Randozza said mildly, "Well, in that case we can get another group."

"Not that. To hell with that. I'm talking about Jean."

Cabiness stepped closer. His shoulder dropped and he thought, Why talk? Why talk to the miserable bastard?

"Lee!" he heard Jean behind him. "He didn't force me to come out here. He didn't force me to do anything. What I did I wanted to do."

"That's right," Randozza said. He felt gently of his forehead, as if he were afraid it might be growing too thin to hold his brain, and then, as long as he had his hand up there, he smoothed his hair again. He walked toward Jean, while Cabiness pivoted to watch him.

"Have you any complaints?" he asked Jean.

She shifted uneasily, but shook her head.

Randozza turned back to Cabiness. "So what's your beef?" he asked.

"Don't put me on," Cabiness said hotly. "I know Jean, I know her good and she didn't come to you asking to be turned out. You worked on her case and you put a lot of crap in the game."

Randozza sat down abruptly. "Cool it," he said uneasily. "Jeezus, man you're no stiff. You know what's happening, and you know you can't turn out a broad that doesn't want to turn. They have to have the whore in them to begin with, and all you ever do is just show them what they really are. Jeezus, man, you know that."

"Talk won't help you," Cabiness said. "I don't like your action and nothing you say's going to change it. Now why don't you stand up?"

"Oh, man—" Randozza said wearily. "You really want to be that corny. You won't be satisfied until we black each other's eyes and break our noses and knock out our teeth? Is that the only thing that'll do it for you?"

"I said don't talk," Cabiness repeated. "You going to stand up, or am I going to have to pull you up?"

"Oh, shut up, Lee," Jean said, "you make everything worse than it is. You're not helping a bit. And anyway, I find your concern a little late. Even if this was worth a big scene, it's not your scene."

"Maybe," he said inconclusively. He felt faintly foolish. Then he shook it off. "Okay," he said. "You're right. It isn't my business. But one thing certain, I'm taking you back to the city tonight."

"What will *she* say?"

"That doesn't matter a whole lot. Get your stuff."

Jean shifted irresolutely in her chair. Randozza turned to her, "You're not going to cut out, are you, baby?"

She stared at him a moment; then said, "I'd better."

He moved his hands around vaguely. "Hell," he said softly. "You're my number-one girl. My real old lady. Don't I treat you good. Don't I make it good for you?"

"John, there's more to it than that. There's a whole lot more going on that's not happening between you and me. I'm sorry." Jean stood up. "I'll be ready in a few minutes," she told Cabiness as she left the room.

Immediately Randozza stood up. "Don't get the idea you can get hard with me," he said. "I know you're laying to go to my head the first chance you get, and you might just stomp me, but it wouldn't end there. I wouldn't want you telling it around that you kicked my ass; it would damage my position, give other studs the same kind of ideas. You know what I mean?"

Cabiness moved his hands indifferently. "Why not drop it," he said.

"Sure," Randozza agreed. "Why not? Why should I sweat the broad? She's built and her face is good, but she's a lemon. You couldn't make a hustling broad out of her in a hundred years. She's just not geared for it. You know what she said? She said, 'I wouldn't feel right profiting from the hungers and dreams of lonely men.' " Randozza laughed. "She wouldn't feel right! A bill a night I could get for that broad. More than most people make in a week. But she wouldn't feel right. Jeezus."

"Why don't you shut up?" Cabiness asked.

"This is my house—" Randozza began.

"Just shut up. Do me the favor."

They waited in silence until Jean came out with her suitcase. Randozza stood up.

"Are you really going, baby?" he asked.

Jean nodded.

"Well, take it easy," Randozza said. "You really were the greatest. That wasn't just a snow-job. And if you change your mind, you know, well give me a ring and I'll set you right up with some real good regulars. Old bastards who just want to feel a little. You know?"

Jean nodded again.

"Let's split," Cabiness said.

There was a strained silence between them as they started back to the city, but gradually, without either of them saying anything, it dissolved into something like their old ease.

"I'm sure glad you didn't turn out," Cabiness said. "I'd never be able to afford a bill a night."

They both laughed until they thought they'd go off the side of the road.

They left Clair's car parked in front of her building and took a bus up to Jean's room.

"What about your things?" Jean asked.

"I don't want them," he said.

"I saw you once in the dark blue suit going somewhere with that girl. You looked wonderful. I damn near cried."

"Come to think of it," Cabiness said, "I might be worth pretty close to a bill a night myself. In that case I'm willing to swap you even."

"You're on," Jean said.

chapter nineteen

Furg's room was in the Monkey Block—a decayed office building on the outskirts of the Beach. In better clays it had been called the Montgomery Block, but, as the neighborhood slid gradually downhill, the rents had slumped and slumped, until now only the bottom floors still held a few offices—one-lunged mail-order outfits specializing in palmistry, zodiac readings and mimeographed pornography—but most of the rooms had been converted to living quarters by the Beach people. The rents were within their reach; it was they who had dubbed it the Monkey Block.

Furg had lived on the fourth floor. He had two rooms. His folding cot was in one of them, a narrow windowless area, little larger than a closet, that must have originally been intended as a storage space. His hot plate, two pans, one saucepan and one frying pan, his three plates, and eleven pieces of mixed silverware were in the slightly larger room.

Cabiness closed the door and stood silently in a darkness relieved by the purple sky squared in the single window. He took a deep breath and felt the tips of his fingers tingle—his palms were cold and his stomach colder. Somewhere in the rooms around he heard excited shouting, and he remembered gratefully that anything went in the Monkey Block. You could parade through the halls naked—no one would care except to wonder why you had to go to all that trouble to attract attention.

After a moment he switched on the light. Nothing seemed to have changed in the hour he'd been gone. Furg's trombone still lay on the gate-leg table, and the light swirled on its oily curves. He noticed a dent in the bell that he'd never noticed before. That wasn't like Furg.

Compulsively, he checked the lock on the door leading into the small bedroom. It was a brass lock that turned by a knob on the outside of the door. There wasn't any knob on the inside. He closed the door, locked it, and threw his weight against it as hard as he could. One, two, three times. Then he stood back and wiped the sudden sweat from his forehead. He had been through the whole procedure several times before. The door was solid.

Dandy! The door was solid... as solid as his head. He should run as fast as he could down the stairs and melt into the dark streets and never show until he reached the Apple. Hubler could whistle for her five thousand. And what could Jean whistle for? If he was with Jean, he was with her. He couldn't turn it on and off like the water.

He walked over and switched the light off. The darkness bounced once, then the dim window settled into place, and he took up his post beside the door. Relentlessly his restless brain took it up again. It was a fool's gamble. There was no other way his common sense would permit him to call it, but there were many factors shading the gamble that allowed him to think he could win it. More than that, he had the idea that it was what should be done.

He lost his sense of time standing in the dark, and he had to control the impulse to turn the light on for just a moment to check Furg's clock. He could hear it ticking, with a solid impact, as if it turned half over each time. He took it to the window but he still couldn't read the dial.

Below him he saw the dark street where the International Settlement had once lit its tawdry fires. It was sad now with the lights off and decay setting in. The diagonal stickers were still pasted across each door: "Closed by the order of...." The McKales service station on the far corner was a glare of fluorescent light. A drunk ambled slowly across the asphalt apron and started down through the Settlement. He paused, looking at the dead neons, shook his head and started back.

Cabiness returned to his place by the door. Would he come? Yes. Would he be alone? Probably. Would he come? Yes. Would he... he tried to force himself to stop thinking about it, but he found there was nothing else he could think about.

When cautious footfalls sounded in the hallway, he straightened up and took the sock full of wet sand out of his jacket pocket. Someone knocked lightly on the door. There was a pause of ten heart beats; then the knocking again, a little louder. The next thing he heard was a scratching sound, followed by a muffled clicking. As the door opened, his vision was blocked, but he saw a thin shaft of light lick into the room and circle it slowly. Then the overhead light came on, and Carver stepped out in front of him.

His first blow was faulty. It took Carver squarely on top of his head, knocking him to his knees. His hands came up, and his head was turning. Cabiness threw his arm across the lower part of his own face to hide it and struck again—this time behind the ear. Carver toppled over.

Working quickly, he stripped the unconscious man to his underwear and carried him into Furg's bedroom. Carver didn't weigh a hundred and thirty. Stuff had done that—melting the flesh away. Again he locked the door and tested it. Carver was secure. In eight hours he would be miserable; in sixteen, violently sick.

Cabiness went through the suit, and, in spite of what Sullivan had made him believe, he was still surprised to find the outfit. It was in a leather cigarette case along with three caps. An emergency supply. An addict developed that kind of desperate craft—hiding stuff everywhere—and never felt secure unless it was where he could put his hands on it.

He emptied the caps into the sink and unloaded the small gun. Then he gathered the clothes up and put the gun on top of them, and took them into the bedroom, placing them alongside Carver.

He stared at the man sprawled on the bed and felt a momentary sympathy for the Narco. He looked like a broken doll: his ordinarily neat hair was crushed and pushed to the side, his eyelids twitched regularly with the beat of his heart, and the wasted white legs showed clearly the bluish-black tracks where needles had entered and re-entered until the veins were a mass of scar tissue.

Cabiness relocked the door and sat down in a canvas camp chair. Now all he had to do was wait. Sometime tomorrow he would call the police and tell them that there was an addict kicking his life out in the Monkey Block. They would hush it up, of course. Carver would probably be shipped off to Lex... hooked in the line of duty. Maybe eventually he'd even receive a certificate of rehabilitation and come back on the force, but one thing he wouldn't do— and that was testify against Cabiness.

With Carver out of it, the case against him would collapse of its own weight.

Lee shifted in the chair and took the envelope containing the hot stuff out of his pocket. He stared at it, thinking of the first moments when he'd conceived the plan of setting Sullivan to trap Carver. It had worked, because Sullivan was desperate to get out from under Carver and redeem himself, and because Carver played it alone so he'd be free to make his private haul of the stuff. If Carver had uncovered the mythical big stash that Sullivan had told him was in room 451 of the Monkey Block, he would probably have turned in only half of it—the other half would have gone for his own uses.

Now Carver was hung in his own web. That was enough. Cabiness knew he couldn't give the hotshot back to Carver. The energy, the anger, the outrage that had first flashed the idea into his mind had blended into a weary understanding. Now he only wanted to be out of it. That was enough.

He took the envelope over to the sink and slowly emptied it down the drain. Then in a sudden shock of rage and loss he crumpled the empty envelope and threw it against the wall. It bounced back at his feet, and he kicked at it savagely, sending it scratching across the floor.

He sat down to wait.

chapter twenty

Carver drifted uneasily toward the light. From the beginning he knew
something was wrong, and the sense of wrongness slowly increased. When
he gained true consciousness he had a sensation as if a spider web was laid
across his face, and he was aware of a familiar dull ache in all his large joints.

He sat up quickly, and a fit of dizziness forced him back down. Cascades of
painful light rained from the naked bulb above him. He closed his eyes,
momentarily grateful for the darkness. Then a violent wrench in his mind
said: sick! He was sick. A wave of cold misery crawled over him.

He sat up again, slowly this time, and blinked uncertainly around the small
room. Nothing happened inside his head; his brain was like frozen mud. He
didn't understand. It wasn't until he'd gone through his clothes and found the
cigarette case with the empty caps that he went over and tried the door. He
threw his weight against it once, then went back to the bed and lay their panting.

I... I'm the Law... I'm.... He still couldn't understand. With deliberate effort
he made himself remember what he'd been doing just before... he'd been hit!
Yes, he'd been hit from behind. He was following up on a tip when... he did-
n't have the energy to think about it. First he needed a fix.

Again he took the empty caps out and stared at them. He was unaware of
the noise he was making in his throat. Who would do this to him? He felt a
weak pity for himself. Who would want to make him hurt?

The inside of the caps were still glazed with the precious powder. A desperate notion formed, and he began to work up saliva in his dry mouth. Slowly,
with idiot concentration, he filled the three empty caps with his own spit.
When this was done, he found he didn't have anything to cook up in. He considered breaking the light bulb and using one of the fragments, but the
thought of darkness frightened him. He retained the idea of using glass, and
in a moment he noticed his wrist watch. Quickly, he dislodged the works—
the crystal and the frame formed a shallow vessel. Into this he emptied the
saliva, now mixed with whatever heroin had still clung to the inside of the
caps. He cooked the mixture with his cigarette lighter. When he fixed it he
didn't feel anything.

He worked knowing the amount was too small to hit him—it took three
caps at once to calm the storm of his habit—but he'd had to try it anyway.
He yawned compulsively, and the tears leaked out of his eyes and stood on
his cheeks. He began to sniffle. Every muscle in his body sent desperate signals.

Again he tried to consider the room. After a moment he grabbed up his empty gun and clicked it three times, pointing at the lock. He threw the gun aside and hit the door again, but it didn't even budge in its frame. He stared at it, trying to control his panic. He knew something about going through locked doors. This door would be protected against entry from the front; the builders couldn't have imagined that anyone would ever want to break out.

This time he went around the room with some idea as to what he was looking for. A broomstick had been toe-nailed across a corner to form a rack, and some clothes were hanging on it: a worn suit of khakis, a blue sleeveless sweater, a tan necktie and an army-surplus raincoat. The raincoat pockets were empty, and the wire hangers were too flimsy for what he had in mind. He inspected the folding cot. It was made of wood and canvas—the legs were in the shape of an X, and the juncture was reinforced with metal strips. Working with his fingernail clippers, Carver managed to unscrew one of the braces. When he was finished he had a thin piece of metal eight inches long.

He used this on the door, running it between the door and the frame until he found the resistance of the lock tongue. As he prodded it, the tongue shifted slightly. He was right. The tongue was beveled, and the bevel was on his side.

He stopped working to dress... the only vision in his mind was of the stash he had in his apartment, and in the ten minutes that he continued to work on the lock, he reached that stash a dozen times, opened it, and....

The metal strip finally caught under the lip of the bevel and slowly forced the tongue back. It clicked and he was out.

The room was full of daylight. He kicked a camp chair out of the way and headed for the door. But it was locked, too. There wasn't any night latch. The lock was the old-fashioned kind, where the key worked from either side, and the key was gone. Swearing weakly, he ran over to the window and looked down four stories. It occurred to him that he could break the window and shout for the police, but he couldn't be seen like this. Any harness bull would read his symptoms as easily as a doctor.

He went back to the door. The lock he faced now had a square tongue, so he couldn't use the method he'd employed on the other one. He'd have to dig into the door frame. He was looking around for something to use when he saw the wadded envelope. Something about the dirty creases and the torn corner snapped a train of associations for him. He picked it up and carefully unfolded it. Then he tore it open and touched his tongue to the dusty paper. Stuff!

There was a thin line of powder along the bottom crease, and trapped in the small pocket between the glued edge of the flap and the actual lip of the envelope there was a good fix.

He forgot all about the locked door. He put his outfit together again, and finding an old tablespoon in a cardboard box, he carefully scraped the white powder into it. A good fix. He cooked up, drew the liquid into the eye-dropper. Then he set the needle against one of the knotted veins in his ankle. Dimly he realized that these veins were almost shot, and that he would have to start moving up his leg. Where was it going to end? Where could it end?

For a moment he sat, tailor-fashion, on the floor, while waves of warm misery washed through him, a misery that bred tears and formless yearning; then he realized that he didn't have to be unhappy. He had the fix for that.

With a brooding smile of anticipation he slid the needle into the vein and pumped the fluid into his bloodstream. The gross muscles of his face never altered. It happened too quickly; his mouth was still smiling as he fell over, but his eyes had changed from surprise to terror.

chapter twenty-one

Cabiness watched Jean packing. She didn't know anything about what he'd tried to do to Carver, but she picked up his mood without understanding it. She paused, emptying a drawer, and turned to look searchingly at him. "Are you *sure* this is what you want to do? You're not just doing it to please me?"

"It's time," he said vaguely. "Don't worry. We'll make it."

"I'm not worried about that. It's you I'm worried about. I've been trying to picture you working at just some job, maybe in an office, and I can't see you doing it. Not for long. You'll start drifting back to your music."

He released his breath slowly. It was hard for him to concentrate on what Jean was saying, because part of his mind couldn't stop remembering Carver scratching at the walls of Furg's bedroom. It was the noises, particularly the grunting that was almost whining, and the scraping of fingernails that sounded like broken glass, that got him. He found he couldn't sit and listen. He left rather than back down completely and turn Carver loose. Now he found that he couldn't make the call he had planned to make to the police. He'd never imagined it would be difficult to step on a spider, but when the spider moaned and scuttled, broadcasting his pain, it was different. He couldn't do it.

"You know you will," Jean said.

"What?"

"Oh, Lee, you're not even listening to me. I said I can't see you giving up music."

"Hell, I'm not about to give up blowing. I'm just not going to try to make a living at it. That's where all the crap slips in. Trying to squeeze a few extra bucks out of your horn, playing what you know people like even though you're so drug with it you wouldn't care if you never played a horn again. Hell, that's just a job like any other job, and it doesn't even pay as well as a lot. I'll work at something else—anything—and play for kicks, but..."

He paused and looked at her carefully. He had to tell her before they went any further into this new intimacy, since each step carried with it the certain knowledge that it was going to be rough getting back out.

"Jeanie," he said. "Did you know that I was busted a few weeks ago?"

"I heard about it."

"Well, I might have to go to jail for a while behind that roust. I might even have to go to Q."

He told her most of it, and when he was finished, she said, "Help me pack. Let's move on and spend whatever time we have together in some square little house, near the park, with curtains and a backyard."

He joined her at the dresser and, taking her wrist, he shook the blouse out of her hand. It caught and hung down the side of the drawer. Jean twisted around, coming up against him. Her mouth tilted, opening.

Lieutenant Carver's death was sloughed off in a half-column on the *Examiner's* back pages, and an old photograph of the detective looked stern and responsible above the caption: VETERAN POLICE OFFICER VICTIM OF FATAL ACCIDENT.

Cabiness figured the fuzz must have had trouble organizing their own confusion, because while the *Examiner* was electrocuting Carver with some faulty wiring, the *Chronicle* was gassing him with a leaky heater. They agreed he was dead, and while Cabiness didn't doubt the fuzz knew how Carver had really gone out, he realized he was probably the only one who could guess that the Narco had picked up his own hotshot.

With the loss of Carver's testimony, the case against Lee faltered. Clair looked him up to tell him she was going to volunteer as a State's witness and that she'd see him behind bars where he belonged, but the case never came to trial. A week before the date set for trial, the DA called him downtown and offered him the chance to plead guilty to a reduced sentence. Cabiness understood that the DA was telling him he wasn't sure of a conviction but was nevertheless convinced of Cabiness' guilt. He took the lesser plea and got off with six months in the county jail.

It was a rough six, without a day's good time, but it finished the clearing that had started in his mind the night Furg had died, and when he was streeted and had a job, he asked Jean to marry him.

"Baby," she told him, "there's no good reason why we have to make that scene."

"Sure," he agreed, "but there's no *good* reason why we shouldn't, either."

But they didn't get around to the actual ceremony until eight months later when Jean discovered she was pregnant. Lee stared at her when she told him. "Isn't that a gasser," he said. "Isn't that a goddam gasser!" Then he smiled and asked, "How do you suppose that happened?"

"I can't imagine," Jean said.

THE END

It's Cold Out There

BY MALCOLM BRALY

IT BEGAN...

...with JD Bing, a large, a very large man, who didn't show the desperation he felt. His broad, pale face was set phlegmatically, and it appeared hard, not with the hardness of rock but with the dense, smooth solidity of fungus. His big arms and shoulders strained the shape of his cheap coat. His hat rode his head like some vandal's debasement of a colossal statue.

The '50 Ford he drove was smeared with oil and dirt and marred with evidence of hard and frequent use. The seat stuffing spilled in gray, visceral wads, the head liner hung in tatters, and the door on the driver's side was smashed shut where someone had calmly made a left turn into it. JD, though clearly in the right, had sped away, half-sick with anxiety. His anxiety was chronic. He was in a line of work saturated with desperation and the sour sweats of failure, and he sensed that door-to-door selling might be little more than a training period where he would first learn to accept the humiliations that would become the routine exchanges of everyday life when he finally found himself on skid row.

Success at door-to-door selling depended almost entirely on a special knack, a kind of kitchen magic similar to "card sense" or a "green thumb," and unless you had it, you could depend on a hungry and hard way to go. JD didn't have it. He could sometimes anger his prospects, but he couldn't frighten them. He couldn't hook surely into the vital and galvanic nerve of their guilts, and more often than not it was JD who finished an interview feeling lousy and no good, his courage for the day exhausted.

But there was nothing else he could turn his hand to. At thirty-seven he found himself completely inexperienced, untrained, and unconnected because of the thirty-seven years he had lived he had spent twenty of them in prison and now, discharged into this alien world he had been told was the real world, he was almost as bewildered and helpless as an aged nun cast from her convent.

What had he done? It was sometimes almost impossible to recall, and he had to force his memory to rebuild that night, pulling the hard bone of fact from the sickened flesh of regret and self-justification until he had reassembled the skeleton of the original monster that had eaten his life.

He had just turned seventeen when he and his buddies, armed with .22 rifles, had attempted to rob a filling station, and while they didn't get a dime, they had proven the effectiveness of their weapons before they were through by killing a police officer. Since there was no way to determine who had fired the fatal shot, though each of them blamed the others, they were all held to be equally guilty of murder under the law, and JD's friends, both older, were sentenced to death; while JD, too young to be executed, was given life. After twenty years, years that often found JD wondering if his long-dead partners weren't after all the lucky ones, he walked out into the awful freedom of a world as alien as the bottom of the ocean.

JD found himself to be nonexistent. No past employer had ever seen him, and no one he asked for work was willing to make the effort to see him. Their eyes focused beyond him as if he were inhabiting a vacuum, and they were "very sorry, but...." No store had ever extended him credit, no bank had ever held his money, and even scrutiny as all-seeing as that of the computers recording Social Security data had never glimpsed him. He stood unshaded by reference or recommendation, a man trying to begin his life at an age already beyond the age where many employers hesitate to train and many more will not hire as a matter of set policy. More than that—he was an enemy alien in his own country.

After a month of free-world scuffling, JD couldn't have told himself whether he thought he was going to make it or not. He had been hustling Universal Encyclopedias for a week without a sale and now he was down to nickels and dimes. Today he had to sell a set of books. That was as much as he allowed himself to realize. It was—as he put it to himself—root, hog, or die!

He was doing a cautious forty-five miles per hour in the slow lane of the Santa Ana Freeway when he saw the large overhead signs beginning to signal the off-ramp leading to the suburb assigned to him. He braked abruptly and winced when a horn began to complain directly behind him. A moment later a long white convertible sliced up alongside, and he was aware of some kid's exasperated face. "If you can't drive it, park it," the kid shouted. A girl rode close beside him, and as they passed and pulled ahead, her long blonde hair streamed back toward JD. The numb mass of his resentment stirred slowly. Goddamn punk! he thought.

JD eased down the off-ramp into the community of Bellflower and drove at random until he spotted a large, square apartment court. In the past week he had made his way, door by door, through a dozen such courts with names like Le Sabre, The Cavalier, The Pink Pussy Cat, The Flamingo—this one was The Bali Hai. The name swooped across the front in large cutout letters, but the lime-green paint was faded and sun blistered, and the white stucco just below the sign was rust-streaked where the rain had leaked past the hidden nails. The rust streaks faded down toward the tops of some painted palms that had been dashed on the wall so as to appear as if they were growing from the small plots of baked earth bordering the entrance, but they were crudely rendered and resembled tattered green umbrellas somehow taken root.

JD parked and set the hand brake. He rested his big hand on the sample case Universal Encyclopedias had provided him and looked up at the sky, depthless as some enameled surface. The sun rode toward noon. Already half a day gone, used in repetitious (Think Positive!) pep talk by the regional manager, then a two-hour drive, and still JD didn't move. How did you Think Positive! when the water was around your knees and rising fast. You thought about getting out and going to work on a farm, someplace quiet and uncomplicated, where they rang the chow bell at the same time every day. He was listening for the chow bell in the calm evening of a fairyland farm when he noticed an old man peering around the edge of the apartment court with the leery craft of a wild animal; his features, except for the pale blue eyes, were lost in a wild tangle of beard and dirty white hair.

JD leaned forward to watch, fascinated as the old man padded toward him. He wore bib-overalls, faded almost white, and under the overalls a ragged coat sweater. He was barefoot, his feet brown and gnarled as roots, and he carried a croaker sack slung over his shoulder. Pinned with a slender finishing nail to the bib of his overalls was a torn piece of gray cardboard, and printed there in what looked like red crayon was: THE CROSS IS THE MARK OF THE BEAST.

The derelict shuffled swiftly across the street and began sorting, with an attitude of thoroughness and system, through a garbage can. JD was finding this free world full of things that caused him to pause in amazement, and most of them filled him with a gnawing sense of loss, but he had yet to root in the garbage. He felt better.

He stepped out with his sample case, stretched, and looked up at the clear blue sky. Then he walked briskly over to examine the names above the mailboxes in the entrance court of the Bali Hai.

There were ten apartments in two wings of five each, all facing on a central walk, and each apartment had been provided with a small area of fretful grass. Apartment A: Sanjit Parnahuma. Apartment B: Grover Alexander. Apartment C: Mr. and Mrs. Hugo Haas. Apartment D: Kristie Olson. The names didn't mean anything to JD. The Haases might have children, so he started down to Apartment C. He twisted a knob in the center of the door and heard a two-note chime sounding inside.

The door opened six inches, and JD looked down at a broad, thick man in a blue cotton bathrobe. He had a bent nose and swollen pouches under his hard green eyes and was bald except for a thin fringe of ginger hair brushed straight across from the side. His scalp, looking hard as marble, glistened.

"Yeah?" he said.

JD began, "Well, I got this *free* twenty-five-dollar gift certificate for you—"

"Shit," Hugo Haas said bleakly. JD was aware of a woman's face, round and pleased, coming up behind the man.

"What is it, honey?"

"Nothing." Haas began to close the door.

"Wait," JD said, beginning to fumble with his sample case. "Your free gift certificate—"

"Jam it!"

JD slammed his hand against the door, throwing it half open. He leaned over Haas. "Listen, sucker," he began. He had started to pour a week's accumulated frustration and anger at Haas when he realized that the woman he had dimly seen was naked. She stood with a startled expression, her hands reaching to cover herself. Suddenly the room seemed to heave, and something like heat lightning flashed in front of JD's eyes. His lips parted. He stared speechless and made no resistance as Haas shoved the door closed.

Jesus! he thought. He closed his eyes, and the woman was as vivid in his mind as she had been in the flesh. He walked back to his car and sat down to roll a cigarette. His hands trembled, and his fingertips seemed hypersensitive. Except for one night in a burlesque theater two weeks ago, this was the first naked woman he had ever seen.

He smoked, tapping his ash out the window, and after a while he was calm enough to go back to work. Rechecking the mailboxes, he decided to try Kristie Olson in Apartment D.

KRISTIE...

...was dreaming when she heard the muffled clicking of her mutilated chime. She had deliberately broken the chime, using a pair of pliers, because it frightened her when it sounded in the night, reminding her of that anonymous voice on the telephone.

She was dreaming but not truly asleep, and she was directing her dream, turning it into one of her favorites, where a pirate captain, who looked like Yul Brynner wearing a hairpiece, carried her—blonde, fragile, in a half-swoon—down into the silken and purple-shadowed cave of his cabin....

She sighed deeply, shifted her hips, and was suddenly fully awake. It was a moment before she realized she had heard someone at the door, and she suppressed a twinge of apprehension. Her covers were tangled, half on the floor, and again she wondered what it was she did in her sleep to tear her bed up so. She sat up, stretched, wrist pressed hard against her small teeth, and quickly stood up. She was slender, almost tall in heels, with the breasts of a fourteen-year-old and legs, hips and bottom all considerably more mature. Her ordinary brown hair was bleached and tinted to a rich reddish-gold and even now it fell in slow waves around her face. She was described in terms varying from "exquisite" to "that miserable bitch."

Someone knocked briskly, and she hurried into the living room to open the door a few inches. "Yes?" She looked up to meet the eyes of the man standing on her porch, and she was less aware of what he was saying than of his bulk, his harsh black hair, and heavy eyes.

She said, "I'm sorry, but I'm not dressed," watching the effect of this information spread through the broad white face above her.

"I'd be happy to wait on you."

"Excuse me for a moment."

She went back to her bedroom where she rapidly applied some lipstick, brushed her hair, and put on a light-blue dressing gown, tied at the throat with a large looped bow. She went back to the door.

"Now you can come in," she said pleasantly.

"Thanks. I'm JD Bing for Universal Encyclopedias."

She nodded an acknowledgement, smiling gravely. She was already play-acting. This handsome man had come to show her a collection of jewels she was considering buying, and when she saw him looking around uncertainly, holding his hat and his sample case, she said, "Use the coffee table. Here, just push that stuff aside." She cleared away a litter of magazines, newspapers—folded open to the want-ad section—and novels checked out of the Bellflower Public Library. "There," she said and went to sit on the end of the couch. She crossed her legs and watched JD opening his sample case. He seemed acutely aware of her, and she took it as natural—a customer's man calling on a young and beautiful baroness. She began to feel a warmth of almost fearful excitement, the same kind of excitement she felt when that man called her on the telephone, but she didn't want to think about that. She wanted to enjoy this, but at the same time she assured herself she didn't intend to allow this common Don Juan the slightest liberty. She wanted him to be aware of the tension, to smell it, taste it, to sweat with it in the privacy of his tight suit, but remain too uncertain of his reception to attempt one of the doubtless clumsy moves with which he would open a seduction.

JD settled on the other end of the couch, talking steadily, handing her one pamphlet after another. She took them, allowing her hand to brush his. His voice became an even drone, never quite separating into individual words, and the printed material under her unfocused eyes appeared a multicolored blur. She must remember to ask Nathan whether diamonds or sapphires suited her better—sapphires perhaps, to match her eyes. She was aware of the bare fact of JD's physical presence, his anonymous maleness, a satisfyingly large and solid mass blurred on the edge of her vision but sharply recorded in her nerves—

"You're not much interested in this encyclopedia, are you?" JD asked.

She didn't quite grasp the sense of what he had said, but on another level of her mind she noted his change of tone and understood well enough. She shot him a brief glance, stopping short of his level stare. She sensed a blunt power in his face, colored by—colored by what? Amusement? Amusement!

"Yes?" she asked coolly.

"I don't think you give a rat's ass about this phony encyclopedia. If I was selling brushes, polka-dot paint, or frozen dog turds, it'd be all the same to you."

"What? I'm sure I don't—"

"You got any idea how many of you teases I've run into in the past week?"

Kristie sensed the heat rising in her face, knew her cheeks would be hectic, and tried to summon a feeling of disgust, but her rising excitement wiped it away. The customer's man with the jewel collection vanished, and in his place a bandit leader stood watching her with lustful and contemptuous eyes. She shivered around the hard core of a rejection so casual, so degrading. Her hips shifted forward. Her eyelids beat with her pulse.

"I fail to see—" she began breathlessly.

"Listen!" JD said, taking her arm in his big hand. "I've got to sell some of these phony books."

"—completely fail to see what your vulgar experiences have to do with me."

"No, listen." JD persisted. "You're different. You're real class. Do you think you could take these books on a thirty-day trial basis?"

She had taken his arm to loosen his grip on her, and his arm felt like warm rock. "You're so big," she whispered.

"I lift weights," he said. "I did a lot of time—in the army. I put in a long hitch and I lifted weights to pass the time." He pulled her closer and rocked her gently. "A broad like you. A broad like you. If you take these books, you only pay twenty-five bucks today."

In her dream, which she knew wasn't real, she had the bandit captain tell her that her ransom would be $25,000; $25,000 American, he stipulated, will save your life. Anything else is between you and me as man and woman. My father will pay, she said, for my life, and if you get pleasure from taking a defenseless woman, I can't stop you....

She felt herself being kissed, kissed hard, her teeth grating against his, and she let herself go completely limp, rolling her head from side to side and murmuring "No, no, no, no, no..." denying any responsibility for what was happening. It is rape, she told herself, and behind her closed eyes she seemed to look up into the intense blue of a Mediterranean sky, feeling the intricate irritation of the knotted grass beneath her back and the wind on her bare legs. She gasped and sobbed at the savageness of this attack. Then she was being pounded with furious energy, literally to the edge of her senses. She heard her own voice, her real voice, screaming with pleasure.

When it was over, her eyes snapped open, and she was lying crushed beneath a door-to-door salesman who had neglected to shave that morning. They both were quiet for a moment. Then Kristie said, "Let me up."

JD drew back and looked into her face, and she was amazed to see tears in his eyes. He was sucking air in ragged breaths, the tears standing on his broad cheeks, his eyes straining with some emotion she immediately took for weakness.

"Get off me," she said sharply.

"Lay still, baby," he said hoarsely, and she could feel that he was ready again. "Get off! Get off!"

He sat up, and instantly she was up too, pulling her robe closed. She hurried into the bathroom. How did that happen? she asked herself. How is it possible for me to feel like that? When she dreamed of sex, it was gentle, romantic, a man stroking her hair and saying lovely things while she lay in a warm glow; but when she got it, it was savage. *She* was savage, and if the man were truly gentle, she despised him for it. She wanted it—the only word that would come to her was "dirty"—she wanted it fierce and dirty, and this just now was the best or the worst she had ever had. She prepared to forget how much she had enjoyed it.

When she returned to the living room, JD was dressed except for his tie, which still hung askew. He held an order form and a ball-point pen. "If you'll just give me your name—" he began.

"Jesus H. Christ!" She flared indignantly. "Do you really imagine I'd buy those cheap books?"

"But you said—"

"If you were *any* kind of a man, you'd offer them to me."

"Any kind of a man? I was all the man you could handle a few minutes ago."

"Oh, take a bow, hero," Kristie taunted fiercely. "Take a big bow. You were like an ape, a slobbering ape."

"Yeah?" JD said unhappily. "Maybe you'd like an ape. An ape ought to just suit you."

"An ape doesn't talk. An ape doesn't sell encyclopedias."

JD dropped the order blank and grabbed her by the arms. He pulled her tight against him. "Listen, girl," he said, "I don't know why you got the needle out for me all of a sudden. There's a whole lot of things I don't know, but one thing I do know—you liked what I done to you, and I could do it again right now, and you'd like it again. Isn't that right?"

She tried to control her reaction, but her knees were suddenly giving way, and she sagged against him.

"That's right, isn't it?" he demanded.

But she wouldn't answer. She just hung in his arms, wondering what he was going to do to her.

"If you really want these books, I'll try to get you a set. I can probably get them cheap. You want them?"

"All right," she said faintly.

He kissed her again, then held her off and looked at her. "I've got to go. I've got to work. But I'll be back, you understand?"

Again she wouldn't answer. She watched him gather up his printed material, some of it creased and wrinkled where they had lain on it, and stack it back into his case. He moved toward her, and she quickly turned her head, so his lips brushed her cheek this time.

"I'll be back."

She didn't watch him leave. When she heard the door close, she made an angry face. Let him come back. She'd have the police on him. He had raped her. He could go to jail for that. For years.

She went to the kitchen and took her journal from the utility drawer, where she kept her pliers, screwdriver, hammer, her bills, and rare personal letters. Her journal was entered in a thick ledger intended for some form of accounting, and she seldom wrote in it anymore except to add to the list on the back page. It was to this list she turned now, glancing automatically at the name where the burden of her love still smoldered. She made her seventeenth entry, writing *Encyclopedia Salesman,* since she didn't remember JD's name.

She wrote it just below *Nathan Holleran,* the most influential and important vice-president of the management company where Kristie had recently worked and, even more recently, been fired. Nathan had allowed it and just stood by and let them get her.

Oh, you rat, she said over *Nathan Holleran. You* beautiful, lousy rat.

She tried to call the General, but learned he was in the East. She left a message for him to call her on his return. The General would not only see her safely into a new job, but he would be the instrument of her loving revenge. The General she had handled very well.

Restless now, she sat down to figure out how long her money would last and decided it would last another two weeks, which she knew meant ten days at the most. But, like Scarlett O'Hara, she decided to think about it tomorrow. She was confident that if she ever fell into a river, someone on a yacht would pull her out. It would never be a garbage scow.

The phone rang, and she picked up the receiver uneasily.

You dirty bitch, a sick greasy voice began like an armless and legless ball of prurient flesh moaning into the telephone, and it told her in the grossest possible terms what she had just had done to her and how she had felt about it. How does he know? she asked herself in real terror as her mind skittered wildly around the court registering the male faces to whom this voice might belong. He must watch her door day and night. Sweet Jesus, she prayed, who is it?

JD...

...was stunned. He had turned a corner in his empty life and stumbled into a Chinese carnival. He was in love with Kristie Olson, whose name he knew only from her mailbox, and this is how he had known it would happen. How many times, sitting in the darkened prison mess hall, temporarily a theater, had he watched similar situations unfold between the huge gray figures on the screen above. In this primer he had studied women and had studied life. He knew the roles, and for his part he must sell.

After copying Kristie's name from her mailbox, he decided to try Arnold Courtney Howe. Two women were standing talking, blocking the walk, and he recognized the larger one—Mrs. Haas, dressed now, and her face, girlish in comparison to her body, freshly made up. Her eyes met JD's, and she blushed. The other woman, years younger, was pretty and small, with a boyish shape, and she stood, arms folded beneath her breasts, the toe of one bright sandal behind the heel of the other.

JD nodded and skirted around them, and he heard Mrs. Haas saying behind him, "It was just awful, Kathleen," and for a moment JD thought she was talking about his staring in at her, but then she continued, "and I don't know what I would have done without your help."

The younger woman said, "That was nothing, Gloria." She laughed. "Someday you might find me in the same shape."

"No, you're much too nice."

"I'm not sure what niceness has to do with it."

JD continued up the walk to twist the bell at Apartment H.

"No one's home there."

He turned and found Mrs. Haas watching him with an anxious expression. He nodded to thank her for the information, and at that moment the door opened. JD turned back and looked down into a wrinkled and yellowed face, the face of an old man whose eyes were somehow still boyish in sharp contrast to the thick white mustache, richly tarnished with amber nicotine stain, and the work-worn hand holding the half-open door. He wore a blue denim apron.

"Can I help you, sir?" he asked.

JD threw a puzzled glance at Mrs. Haas, then turned and began working this prospect. He managed to hand him the "free" gift certificate and mention the encyclopedias.

Mr. Howe nodded with massive solemnity. "Yes, sir, fine books. Wonderful books. The storehouse of all knowledge."

"Dad"—JD heard Mrs. Haas behind him—"whatever it is, you don't need any."

The old man squinted spitefully. "Gloria, I didn't raise you up to have you turn around and start treating *me* like a child. I'm still the best judge of what I need, and you and that man of yours should realize just how it is your bread gets buttered."

"Yes, Dad," the woman said reluctantly.

Mr. Howe turned back to JD, his face brightening, and JD found himself remembering the men in jail who had been so lonely they had been willing to talk to anyone from the outside world, even ministers and social workers—and even policemen. He felt a trickle of hope beginning in the parched springs of his optimism. Damn, he thought, this old mother might actually buy these books just because he's been told not to.

"I'm Arnold Courtney Howe." He introduced himself. "Arnold Courtney Howe the Second," he added lovingly. "Won't you come in?"

JD entered and found an apartment laid out something like Kristie's, but the furniture was all dark and cold. The shades were drawn, and the light was deeply stained with an amber glow, but the light was good enough for him to make out the unframed prints that crowded every foot of wall space. The subjects were boats, and even JD was able to see they were poorly drawn. In some the boats drifted eerily a few feet above the water, and in others, through some cosmic warp, they appeared to be merging with the sun, which was itself setting with furious banality.

"You like them?" Arnold Courtney asked, eyes eager.

"Yeah, they're great," JD lied.

"Let me give you one. Pick one, any one, and it's yours."

JD made a choice at random, and while Arnold Courtney removed it from the wall, JD looked around with some vague idea left over from his indoctrination that he was determining whether Arnold Courtney could afford the books he had to sell. He noticed a heavy table against the wall, where something was covered with a sheet. The sheet was thrown carelessly, obviously quickly, perhaps to hide what was on the table. At one point the sheet had hitched up in a large fold to disclose a stack of paper, bill-sized and green, but of a green too pale to be that of money.

"Here you are," Arnold Courtney said, and JD stared at the print, wondering what he would find to do with it. He stood holding it.

"Thank you," he said at last.

"It's nothing. Just an old man's way of amusing himself." But the pride in Arnold Courtney's voice undermined this expression of modesty, and he went on to tell how he made the prints on his own press in his garage, and how ...

JD tried to switch the conversation to encyclopedias, but he quickly learned that Arnold Courtney loved to talk. He was swiftly and tangentially led from encyclopedias to education, from education to British schools, from British schools to Arnold Courtney's own school, and JD hadn't read enough as a boy to recognize that this was also the same improbable school attended by Tom Brown and other fictional English schoolboys. Then for fifteen minutes they planted rubber in Malaya and stalked a particularly large tiger who had had the effrontery to eat Arnold Courtney's dog.

"Look," JD interrupted, "I've got to try to sell these books."

Arnold Courtney looked at him reproachfully. "I was going to buy them."

JD swallowed heavily. "You were?" He yawned with nervous pleasure and realized that his armpits were wet. "I can have them delivered to you tomorrow, and all you pay down today is twenty-five dollars."

"Twenty-five dollars," Arnold Courtney repeated and made a tentative gesture at his hip pocket. JD's heart sank. "I'm not sure—" Arnold Courtney began, and this time he got his wallet out and, holding it so JD couldn't see, he peeked into it. "I'm not sure I have that much cash."

"Well," JD said and stopped. The two men sat looking at each other.

"How much is this set in all?" Arnold Courtney asked.

"One hundred and twenty-five dollars if you pay cash," JD recited dully.

"Good. Excellent. I just happen to have a check close to that amount. Took it in on a debt and haven't got around to cashing it. You don't mind?"

"Hell no."

Arnold Courtney hurried over to the table with the sheet on it and came back snapping a check in his hands. He seemed proud of it and passed it to JD with a small flourish.

"There you are, sir."

The check was made out to a J. F. Byrnes in the amount of $127.50 by the Weber Insulation Company. JD turned it over. The back was blank.

"Well," Arnold Courtney said mildly, "Jim neglected to endorse it." He pulled a pen from the narrow pocket in the bib of his apron and, taking the check, signed J. F. Byrnes in an elaborate and old-fashioned hand. "There. And no one the wiser."

"Shouldn't you endorse it too?" JD asked, remembering a particularly grim section of his indoctrination entitled "Dealing with the Check."

"Oh, no—well, I hardly could now, could I? I shouldn't imagine it would make any difference to the bank."

"No, maybe not, but—I don't have any change on me. I owe you two-fifty. Can I bring it by tomorrow?"

"No need, no need at all. Please accept that as a small tip."

JD frowned. "A tip?"

"Just add it to your commission."

"Okay." JD folded the check and put it away. Then he placed the print in his sample case, and Arnold Courtney, seeing the preparations for departure, started talking again. He offered to show JD his shop, but JD refused. "I have to work," he said.

"Yes"—Arnold Courtney nodded to approve the value of work—"a man's reflected in his work, isn't he?" His face emptied, and with his bright liveliness gone, Arnold Courtney looked very old and used up.

"Thank you," JD said sincerely, thinking of his commission.

"Oh, I should thank you," Arnold Courtney said absently. "Wonderful books. A privilege to own them." He brightened a little. "You might try Grover Alexander across the way. In Apartment B. He's an artist, too."

"Thanks. I will." They shook hands gravely.

As JD was going down the walk he passed Hugo Haas. The man seemed familiar to JD in a way he couldn't understand. He was certain he had never seen him before this morning. Haas looked even angrier than he had when he had tried to slam the door in JD's face.

GROVE...

...like Kristie, slept on toward noon. Unlike Kristie he wasn't out of work but fortunate enough to be able to work when he felt like it. He had never, not once in his life, felt like working in the morning. The intensity of his reluctance to get up had forged a hard core of ambition in an otherwise relaxed and amiable man.

Now his doorbell dingdonged him into resentful consciousness and sounded again to roll him reluctantly out of bed and send him shuffling, canted like a veteran lush, until he stumbled against the front door and eased it open. Leaning on the jamb, he shaded his eyes against the hearty and somehow simpleminded glow of the noonday sun and took in enough of JD's appearance to realize that it wasn't anyone he knew. He blinked resentfully.

"Yeah?" he asked, and didn't really listen until he heard "free gift certificate." Then he winced with a coward's instant reflex. The last "free gift certificate" he had been so hapless as to accept had cost him over ninety dollars for merchandise he hadn't wanted, couldn't use, and hated the sight of.

Grove squinted out at JD, recognizing him, now too late, as the enemy. He was in grave danger of ending up with several of whatever it was this big idiot sold, even if it were funeral lots or vibrator chairs.

"Yes... Yes..." he murmured, wondering why it was so difficult for him to say "No." A firm "No," close the door, and that would be the end of it, but it was too easy for Grove to put himself in the sweating shoes of the people who came to stand outside his door.

Numbly he put his hand out and felt the "free gift certificate" slipped into his unresisting fingers. Now, I've gone and done it. Now, I've taken the lousy thing. Then he heard with great clarity "...the Universal Encyclopedia in twenty-four volumes."

"I've got the Britannica," he said, grinning with relief.

"What?"

"I've already got the Encyclopedia Britannica. I'm sorry."

But JD wouldn't give up. "The Universal Encyclopedia is supposed to be much better than all those other sets, and besides—"

"Really, no thanks. I'm sure your set's a good one."

"The best on the market."

"I'm sure it is."

JD stared glumly for a moment, then shrugged and said, "It's probably mickey-mouse. Thanks anyway for listening to me." He turned on his heel.

Grove watched after him, vaguely offended by the salesman's disloyalty, offended that all the hawkers who so glibly wasted his time didn't even believe in what they had to sell. JD had reached the central walk and was standing there, looking both ways like a baffled animal. That one, Grove thought, had better hit back for the farm.

He closed the door and walked flat-footed, no longer on a slant, into the bathroom. He leaned on the washbasin, and after a brief glance at his face he studied his tongue in the mirror. He took no pleasure from his face. It was round and bland, still slightly swollen with sleep. A tongue, he decided, was a silly and grotesque thing to be carrying around in his mouth, and he resolved to be rid of it so he could install something useful like an ashtray or a change holder.

The chill and hostile blue of the fluorescent tube above the mirror depressed him. Surgery light, morgue light, cop-and-social-worker light—it made his face look as if it should be attached to a case history. A man trapped and isolated in one of society's barren and clinical deserts. Why was he alone? The blunt truth, which he could sometimes admit, was that when people thought of other people, they somehow forgot him. He was, in most senses, an extra man, a spare part. To be used in case of emergency.

He thought fleetingly but vividly of Kristie and then turned his mind firmly to other things. While he was shaving he found a cartoon idea in his mind, and it was the first he had thought up entirely on his own in several weeks. The drawing would show a father attaching a jug of bottled water and a Dixie cup dispenser to the headboard of a baby's crib. Mild, very mild, but it would stand without a caption. He grinned and shuffled a little in what he imagined was a dance step.

After breakfast he began to rough out the idea. He drew plump, short-necked people with big, soft-looking noses and round eyes and eyebrows that angled up to suggest a chronic uneasiness. One character had come to seem the essence of the type, and Grove's best work centered around this living malaprop, who always stood, bland and faintly puzzled, pinned by his wife's incredulous scorn in the middle of some surrealistic goof. His chronic state was one of innocent perversity—he put the milk outside and the cat in the icebox, pulled flowers and left weeds, and appeared among his wife's bridge guests in his underwear, looking for the glasses he was already wearing. He was instantly victimized by dogs of any size. Small children regarded him with wary hostility, larger children with good-natured contempt.

Grove was fully aware of the element of self-portraiture in his creation. He finished the "rough," viewed it without either approval or satisfaction, and slipped it into a manila envelope already addressed to a magazine likely to buy family humor of so gentle a stripe. He decided to drive to the shopping center. There were several magazines he wanted to buy.

He stepped outside and found Kristie lying in the sun. She was on her stomach, arms folded beneath her head. Her eyes were closed, and the straps of her halter were unfastened to leave her back bare to the sun. Grove experienced an immediate flicker of lust. It was the second time in recent days he had noticed Kristie home when she would have ordinarily been working. He went to stand over her.

"You trying to crash the leisure class?"

Kristie started, her eyes snapping open. "Oh," she said, "it's you."

"Yes," Grove answered mockingly, "only me."

Kristie smiled. "You needn't put it like that. It's a pleasure to see someone nice."

"You mean harmless."

"Maybe. I wonder if anyone's really harmless. Anyway, I'm not at leisure. I'm unemployed."

"No kidding? I thought you were the fair-haired girl over there at Trans-Western?"

"There's no such things as a fair-haired girl in a man's business. I found that out. They thought I was worth eighty-five dollars a week; I thought I was worth a great deal more and I pushed too hard. Then someone I'd depended on let me down, and everything began to come apart. As a woman I was disturbing to have around, since I was doing the work of three supervisors. So why should they have me around?" Kristie smiled bitterly. "Technically I was discharged for coming in late over three times in one month. Three times! That was the biggest joke. I was late one hundred and seven mornings in the last five months. It was virtually my privilege by custom. Suddenly they discover I come in late. Just when they need something to hang me with."

Grove remembered Kristie's boasting that she had one of Trans-Western's vice-presidents in her pocket—her expression had been "my little vice-president"—but he didn't suggest that this man could easily have had her fired once he tired of her. He smiled sympathetically and asked, "What are you going to do now?"

"Find something better."

"Such as?"

"I know what I can do. There are bound to be people who care more for how the job is done than they do for their own vanities."

"Well," Grove said soberly, "they would be few in number, but probably there are some—around somewhere."

"There are. You'll see. It's not healthy to be as cynical as you are." Kristie thrust her arms out straight in front of her, stretching and arching her back. Grove watched the shadowed curve of her breast, pulled taut and briefly visible. A well-made girl. He knew he was a fool to want her, but who could help wanting her? Thinking this, he asked, "Does your friend still call?" He smiled.

Kristie nearly snarled at him. "It's not funny!" Her face had gone flat and tense. "It's not a goddam bit funny!"

"I'm sorry," he murmured. "Did you call the police?"

"Yes, I called them, for all the good it did. They acted as if they thought I was imagining the whole thing. As if I could imagine something like that." She shivered.

"Didn't they make an investigation?"

"A detective came by to see me. He suggested I change my telephone number."

"And did you?"

"Not yet. I'm behind on my phone bill and I don't want to bring myself to their attention right now. Maybe they'll turn the damn thing off and solve my problem."

"I don't suppose it's much fun," Grove said reflectively. "Like listening to someone screaming with pain."

Kristie frowned. "I'm not sure I understand that."

"Just a notion." Grove shrugged. "You know I get notional sometimes. Did you hear the Haases last night? They pitched their best one to date."

Kristie tried to look uninterested. "No, I wasn't home."

"Hugo made his load and threw Gloria out of the house bare-ass naked. And you think that isn't an awesome spectacle? Teeming abundance."

"And what did you do besides stare at her?"

"That's all. I leered and minded my own business, since I couldn't whip either one of those Haases, Gloria or Hugo. Kathleen brought her a blanket, and after Hugo passed out, she crawled in through the kitchen window."

"Sweet Kathleen," Kristie said acidly. "When did she join the Girl Scouts?"

"She's a pretty nice person," Grove said. But Kristie wasn't listening.

"I can't see why the Haases haven't been asked to move," she said. "I hear them through the walls sometimes, and they sound like wild animals."

"Hippos," Grove said. "But then I imagine hippo to hippo is sweetly harmonious."

Kristie snorted delicately. "Hugo Haas is little better than a wild man and a very annoying person on top of that. I had him tapping on my bedroom window for a month before he finally got the idea I wasn't interested, and now I'm sure he tells everyone I'm frigid, since he can't tell them anything else."

Grove flushed. He'd heard just that from Hugo and had agreed with him, since most of the winds that blew from Kristie seemed cool, cautious, and contained.

"And?" he asked curiously.

"And what?"

"Nothing."

Kristie smiled faintly. "I'm not."

"Oh?"

They fell into a silence that for Grove quickly grew uncomfortable. He sensed that an opening had been made and he wanted to respond, but he didn't know what to say. He seldom did when it was important to him. He stood feeling round-faced and foolish, while Kristie looked up at him with an expression he imagined concealed amusement.

The opportunity was lost when the book salesman stepped out of the apartment across the way. After a short, hard look at Grove he stared at Kristie. He seemed about to come over, then, appearing to change his mind, he jammed his hat on and went to ring Kathleen's bell.

"I see you've made another instant conquest," Grove said dryly.

Kristie shrugged indifferently. "He's going to bring me a set of encyclopedias."

"Really? As hard as those things must be to sell, I wouldn't imagine he could afford to give them away."

"He can sell them," Kristie said smugly. "He just sold a set to Mr. Howe."

"What? Old Arnold Courtney is lucky when he gets money for pipe tobacco. Haas supports him, you know."

"No, I didn't know, but I don't see how Haas could support anyone. Does he work?"

Grove shook his head. "He's supposed to have some investments. That's all I know." He slapped his envelope against his leg. "Well, I've got to consign this to the morass of editorial apathy. You need anything from the shopping center?"

"Yes, you can get me some tea. Lipton's."

"I remember. Lipton's tea, Hunt's tomato juice—do you drink anything else?"

Kristie smiled. "Sometimes."

"That's something I'd like to see."

Kristie closed her eyes, and her face immediately seemed vacant. She's waiting for me to make some move, Grove told himself, and he decided to ask her out when he returned with the tea. It was a question he had been postponing for weeks, so it was easy to put it off a few minutes longer. At the same time he was aware that if he never asked, she could never say No.

"I'll be back," he said and started off. Kathleen was standing in her doorway listening to the book salesman. Kathleen was sensitive. The lost quality of the man would come through to her, and she would stand quietly and hear out his whole crummy pitch.

Grove walked out to the back alley where his Volks was parked and stood for a moment with his hand on the door, watching an old man in bib-overalls sorting through the garbage and nodding vigorously with a dense mass of white and apostolic hair. He darted brief and wary side glances at Grove.

Like a gull, Grove thought. The same shallow eye, the same restless and apparently mindless picking and gathering.

Then Grove saw the badge—THE CROSS IS THE MARK OF THE BEAST—and he experienced a flicker of uneasiness that quickly turned to curiosity. The Scavenger, as Grove immediately thought of him, betrayed insight. Wasn't the cross, that tool of slow, unnatural, and unimaginably painful death, a fitting symbol of all that was bestial in man? How would this garbage-eater come on such an intuition?

The Scavenger was now moving away, walking on his toes in a light, shuffling gait like that of a punch-drunk fighter. He held a gunny sack, over half full, in one hand, and the other hand opened and closed emptily as if still busy in the garbage.

"Hey," Grove said.

The Scavenger jerked half around, eyes wild, and broke into a run.

"Hey, I'm not going to hurt you."

But the Scavenger was gone around the end of the garages. Grove smiled to himself. You might call that a failure of communications, he thought. He tried to place himself in the Scavenger's alien mind, but he couldn't begin to make the transfer. How would such a creature live and how would he comfort himself? Was he bound to some strange and self-imposed vow like a holy hermit, or did he crouch in a burrow like an animal, shivering and snarling at every footstep? Did he even think of himself as a man?

The distance was too great for Grove to cross, but he sensed that as it became easier and easier for him to spend the nights alone in his own apartment, he would grow closer to understanding; for even this Scavenger, traced back in time, would become a little boy. A little boy who might have wanted to grow up to become a fireman.

When Grove returned from the shopping center, he found the book salesman sitting on his heels beside Kristie. He had his hand on her back, and, by contrast, her back appeared breathtakingly fragile. In spite of this familiarity, however, they seemed to be arguing.

As Grove approached they fell silent, and it was into an air of constraint that he handed the tea and accepted Kristie's brief thanks with a nod. Before he was ten feet away, he heard the deep drone of the man's voice, and Kristie's voice, flute-like, beneath it. They were arguing, but deep in the center of their argument Grove's inner ear detected some basic understanding.

JD...

...knew what he wanted. He wanted to live. He wasn't able to say clearly all he meant by this, but he knew well enough. He had dreamed it all so many times after 10 P.M., when the lights went out but sleep would not come.

Now, driving the freeway with greater confidence, he saw a way to live. A road map, he thought, with his route marked in bold red strokes. He was headed toward the company's downtown office to turn in his sale. Afterward he could expect to have $37.50 in his pocket, and that was $37.50 he had made if he never hit another lick. But if he had hit one, even if he had lucked on it, he could hit another. And another. It was hard-earned money—his sore feet and frayed nerves testified to that—but he could do it.

He had a lot to drive him. Add to his first sale Kristie, his first woman, and this was easily the best day of his life. Within his huge frame and behind his heavy face his enjoyment of it was as pure and childlike as that day when, after months of watching, he had finally eaten his way into a Popsicle stick marked with the magical purple star that entitled him to a free Popsicle. He had long since forgotten that finding this valuable stick had first involved him in a bloody fight with his older brother, who had wanted to share this fortune, and, second, after a long walk to the store he had been told that the Popsicle company no longer honored their "free" offer. Finding the stick had won him only a black eye, but he still remembered his joy when the faint purple star began to emerge from the sweetened red ice. He felt like that now. He was beginning to glimpse a life so rich it had been beyond his power to imagine it.

The first flaw in this paradise was exposed to him by his regional manager Mr. Smeed, a narrow, thin-lipped man who reminded JD of a chaplain. Smeed glanced at the order JD had written authorizing shipment, initialed it, and dropped it in a tray designated "Hold." JD made a vague gesture of protest—he had promised delivery—but Smeed was already studying the check he had taken in payment.

"This is a large check," Smeed observed with a prim doubtfulness. "Did you see any identification?"

"No—well, I didn't think to ask."

"You should always see some identification, preferably a driver's license. Try to remember that in the future. I'll have to hold your commission on this pending clearance of the check. Try to get an early start in the morning."

JD stood numbly.

Smeed looked up, his eyes a pale, brittle gray. "Yes?"

"How long will that be?"

"What do you mean?"

"How long for the check to clear?"

Smeed smiled thinly. "You wouldn't know, would you? Well, it depends. A day or two—maybe three."

"Thanks."

"That's all right." Smeed examined him briefly. "Do you think you're going to be able to move our product?"

"I'm doing my best."

"Yes, well, it's difficult for many men to sell in this way, but those who can, do very well at it. That's all. Try to get an early start."

But JD couldn't get a start, early or late, because by the next morning he was out of gas and penniless. His few remaining cents had been spent for dinner. He had to eat, so he had taken a loaf of day-old bread, which he paid for, and a can of sardines, which he didn't pay for. He slipped the sardines into his inside coat pocket and carried them past the check stand. They hung against his chest as if they were enormous, smoking with guilt, and obvious to anyone who glanced at him. He counted out pennies for the loaf of bread, watching his fingers fumbling the coins from his palm into the impatient hand of the checker, humiliated that he should be put to this. Twenty years of free food had not prepared him to face the true value of it. He took the bread, feeling the weight of the sardines as he moved his arms, and hurried for the street. Outside he paused to take a deep breath and when he felt the cold air on his face, he realized he had been sweating. Well, I got to eat, he told himself and started off.

"Hey! Big Britches!"

JD turned and saw a red-haired kid in a green smock coming toward him. "Whatever you got, you better put it back," the kid said.

"I ain't got nothing. Nothing I didn't pay for."

"Now, that's a crock," the kid said, cocking his head insolently. "I seen you take something. What if I was to search you?"

JD leaned over until his face was inches from the kid's. "You search if you want, but you better find something."

The kid drew back, uncertain. "I seen you take something," he repeated, but his voice lacked conviction now.

"You're crazy. You're seeing things. You better stick to stacking cans and stop playing cop."

JD turned and walked away. Just before he reached the corner, he heard the kid yelling, "I still seen you take something, you big slob." JD broke into a run, ducked around the corner, and ran the three blocks to his hotel and up four flights to his room, where he dropped on his cot, gasping more from apprehension than the exertion. Lousy punk, he thought. Lousy little punk.

He was deeply humiliated. It was an hour before he felt like eating, and then he ate without appetite or pleasure, washing the oily fish and stale bread down with glass after glass of water. He put half the loaf away for morning and went down to the lobby to watch television. An old man with bad eyes sat nearly on top of the picture, with the sound correspondingly low, and JD was forced to sit to the side and strain his ears. The set was old, the picture grained and flickering, and JD couldn't avoid contrasting it to the new model—a donation from a fraternal order—he had watched for years in the honor dorm. He shrugged heavily and looked around. The lobby looked is if it had once been filled with muddy water that had drained away to leave everything faded and stained with dusty shades of brown. The potted elephant ears were dying of some plant disease, and the desk clerk sat hunched almost below the level of the counter, working crossword puzzles and nursing a smoldering grudge against the world. JD had already had words with him over his bill, and now JD could sense that bill, as if it were scored in his mind, rising like the level of fire danger in a dry forest. He had never owed a bill before. He had never promised to pay without being able to pay.

I've got to get out of here, he thought, before I suffocate in his crummy joint, and he began to dream of a small apartment he might rent near Kristie, and then, though he hardly knew how to imagine it or how he might bring it about, of an apartment with Kristie. She was probably a little nuts, he admitted, but, God, she was sweet. He recalled the feel of her and of her rapid breath beating against his shoulder, and he closed his eyes.

He felt a hand on his arm and heard a whispering voice. "Well, Big One, you still pushing iron?" He turned to find a man he knew only as Seldom Seen Slim standing above him.

JD grinned, glad to see a familiar face. "Ain't no iron out here in the free world."

Seldom Seen had skin like translucent wax and eyes that slid as smoothly as mercury. In the prison it had been said of him that no one knew he had been around until he was gone, and he did move in an emotional vacuum so complete that, while no man called him friend, no man bad-mouthed him either. His true name had been known only to the record clerk.

"You better keep working out," he told JD with ironical gravity, "or you'll turn into a barrel of jelly."

"Not as much walking as I get in. I'm hustling books. Anyway, I'm off that muscle kick. Pushing iron was just a way to do time."

"Yeah? You thinking about putting all that muscle to use? I know hustling books don't buy too many biscuits."

"Where you drifting to?" JD asked uneasily.

Seldom Seen ignored the question, staring reflectively at JD. "So they finally cut you loose?"

"Yeah—finally."

"And how you making it, Big One?"

"I ain't. Not really."

"Too much for you?"

"I can't seem to get started. I can't get a hold anywhere. I've been on nickels and dimes for weeks."

Seldom Seen produced an aluminum tube, from which he took a large, greenish cigar. "It's rough," he murmured in agreement. "Rough as a cob. 'Specially for you—many calendars as you pulled." He lit the cigar, turning the tip in the flame.

"How *you* making out?" JD asked.

"Pretty good. Pretty good." Seldom Seen answered soberly.

"You been out awhile?"

"Going on six months. I'm getting a nice taste of it, you know what I mean?"

JD studied Seldom Seen's neat gray clothes, colorless as everything else about him, and the bright tips of his tiny shoes. "What you doing in this flea bag?" he asked.

"I live quiet." Seldom Seen gravely closed one eye. "Very quiet. You probably wouldn't be wise to it, but that's a mistake many a guy makes—they take off a few touches, get a little gold in the oscar hock, and right off they start studying a Cadillac automobile, expensive broads, and a trip to Vegas. There's finks in Vegas just waiting for those fools to roll up. They wind up in the slammer and never know what happened to them. Me, I live quiet."

JD nodded uneasily. "You telling me you're rooting?"

"Does a bear crap in the woods?"

"Then as far as I'm concerned, you're fixing to get your ass sent back."

Seldom Seen took his cigar out of his mouth and looked at it. It seemed to please him. He smiled gently. "Big One, what you don't know would fill a goddam library, and you're square as a churchhouse brick. What else could you be? Much big time as you pulled? And some of what you don't know is that there's many a way to cash out a little velvet without going rawjaw, and—" Seldom Seen paused and looked JD straight in the eye for the first time. "I wouldn't mind having you standing behind me. Just for window dressing. Jesus, would you shake the apples. They'd think they were up against King Kong."

An electric tingle of apprehension went through JD. "I'm working," he said shortly. "And lighten up on that King Kong crap. You should know I don't play."

Seldom Seen stared at him levelly for a moment; then his eyes slid away. "So you're working." He pointed with his cigar at JD's coat. "And still wearing the threads they handed you at the gate?"

JD shrugged. "It's a coat. I didn't ever think it was going to be easy out here. But there's things worth scuffling for. There's things worth getting—and keeping."

"Okay." Seldom Seen nodded reflectively. "Okay, if you want to apple it up, I'm not going to try to pull you off it. You never were no true thief. You never had no chance to be. But you were one of the reg'lars up there—you didn't take no crap and you didn't put none out either. You might make it, Big One. But if you don't, don't sit around picking glass out of your ass. Come up and see me. I'm in three-twelve."

JD wanted to ask Seldom Seen for a loan, but he couldn't get the words out. His pride stopped him as much as his reluctance to become further involved with a man he knew was going wrong. He watched as Seldom Seen, with a dry wink, slipped quietly past the desk clerk and on upstairs. The desk clerk didn't look up from his puzzle.

So I'm square, JD told himself resentfully. An apple. Briefly he wondered if Kristie thought of him as square, but his good sense told him she couldn't have formed any real opinion of him. Anyway, the world seemed to be full of squares who made out, but probably they wouldn't want to hear it, either. He began to wonder what it was that Seldom Seen was pulling and how much risk it would involve to back him just one time. For two bills he could get out of this rat's nest for good, but he realized that it wasn't a question of risk but one of principle. He sensed that a short cut, once taken, was far more difficult to decide against the second time around. He had his commission coming, he told himself. He could wait. He turned back to the television.

The next afternoon he switched on the ignition in his car and watched the needle tremble on empty. He couldn't risk running out of gas in the middle of the street, so he set out to walk the five miles to the downtown office. He was hungry. He had awakened in the night, ravenous, and bolted down the half loaf of bread. Now he had missed breakfast and lunch—he wasn't used to missing meals. He wasn't used to walking either. In spite of his abnormal strength, he tired quickly because he had never had to walk more than a hundred yards in any direction to exhaust all the places he was allowed to go. The last blocks were difficult.

He arrived at the office in time to make it appear as if he had just driven in from his district, and he stood in line with the other salesmen, most of them much younger than he. He watched several of them walk away with cash vouchers. It seemed so easy, but he knew as a fundamental condition of his life that nothing ever went easy for him.

When his turn came, he asked Smeed if the check had cleared.

"No, not yet. No paper at all today, Bing?"

"No, I had a bad day."

"Well, try to do better tomorrow."

"Yes, sir."

Outside again he stood on the sidewalk and watched the cars passing. Everybody rode while he walked. Where was the fairness in that? Where were the clothes, the car, the girl he might have had if he hadn't wasted his life? Or had it wasted for him? The sense of waste choked him for a moment. Then he deliberately turned his mind over. Because all his time up until now had been wasted was not good cause to set about wasting the rest of it, however long that might be. It was his—or was it? He started back toward his hotel.

That night he sat again in the lobby, trying to forget his blistered feet and his growing hunger. He felt useless, and it oppressed him. He found himself watching for Seldom Seen. If he told Seldom Seen he was hungry, it would most likely lead to dinner, but it would probably also lead to a repetition of Seldom Seen's suggestions, and JD was afraid to hear them. The more he knew, the more he would be swayed.

But Seldom Seen didn't appear, and later in the evening JD allowed himself to be approached by another person, one he thought he understood immediately, an old man with bright blue eyes and thin red lips pulled away from a set of oversized, glistening, and patently false teeth. He was dressed in a gray flannel suit, several sizes too large, and he wore sandals and maroon hose. He must have been close to seventy, and he began to call JD "Dear Boy" in that round, savoring, and—to JD—unmistakable tone. He said his name was Everett.

JD forced himself to talk to Everett. Like a little boy, he thought, hoping for a candy bar from a suspicious stranger, hoping he can get the candy bar without obligation, knowing that surely this is not the way it will work. After a while Everett asked if he had eaten, and he quickly said, "no."

"Well," Everett said. "Well, well, neither, as it happens, have I."

They went around the corner to the Ideal Cafeteria, and Everett bought him an order of macaroni and cheese. JD selected it thinking it would be filling, but it was poorly prepared and watery, and JD couldn't help contrasting it to the mac-and-cheese served every Thursday night on the main line, the big dippers banged in his tray by the long progression of different cooks, who always dug deep when they saw him coming and saluted him with "How's it going, Big One?"

Everett picked at a cottage cheese salad, sucked noisily at a cup of tea, and nodded with undisguised pleasure as he watched JD's big hands moving over his food.

"You're certainly a well set up young man," Everett said.

"Yeah," JD mumbled.

When they left the cafeteria, JD, unable to think of an easier out, broke into a run. He turned down a dark side street, lit only by cautious night-lights burning in the rear of small stores, and for a while be heard the slap of Everett's sandals on the pavement behind him.

"Please, dear boy, please wait for Everett "

Then it was quiet, but JD, in spite of his aching feet, walked the streets for several hours because he could picture Everett sitting in the lobby waiting for him. Several times women turned to look after him, but he kept walking. He paused for a long time, studying the stills stapled on the marquee of a cheap theater where four old features were being shown on a single bill. During his first weeks of freedom he had spent nearly every night at the movies—they were all new to him. And now the quiet darkness sucked at him like a drug. If he could just go in there and sit, sit and watch. Up on the screen nothing was ever so bad it couldn't be fixed. He knew Everett would have taken him to the movies, but he had a horror of what Everett represented to him, of what he imagined Everett might require as they sat there in the dark. He pictured Everett's hands crawling over him like pale old spiders, and he grimaced with disgust.

Late that night he returned to his hotel only to find his room locked against him. So Everett had buddies. For a moment JD stood trembling, teeth locked against the explosion he felt swelling inside him. He wanted to run wild, break up the lobby, throw the night clerk through the plate glass window, and empty the till. He wanted to break the cage tightening around him with bold, free anger.

Then the habits learned through twenty years of walking small took control, and he slipped fearfully from the hotel. It wasn't until he was walking the streets again that he remembered that his rent was several days overdue, and this might be why his door was locked, rather than anything Everett had done. And finally it occurred to him that possibly Everett had only been lonely, lonely as he was himself, and looking for common company, and that everything he had thought he saw in the old man had only been a reflection of his own mind. He winced. Could he ever hope to be like other people?

The corner streetlights cast his shadow, grotesquely elongated, against the pavement in front of him, and he studied his height and bulk with sour scorn. You're harmless, he told himself. If someone doesn't hand-feed you, you're a mortal cinch to starve to death.

A black and white police car passed slowly in the street, and JD automatically increased his pace, trying to look as if he were going somewhere, but the car drifted to the curb twenty feet ahead of him. "You live around here?"

JD looked into the young face under the uniform cap. "Yes, at the Imperial Hotel." He gestured in the direction of the hotel.

The young cop exchanged glances with his partner, then asked, "What's the address there?"

"It's over on Hill Street."

"Where on Hill Street?"

"I don't know exactly."

"You live there and don't know the address?"

"I never paid no attention to the address. I know how to get there."

"You carrying any identification?"

JD obediently reached for his wallet and started to hand it to the cop.

"Just show it to me."

He opened his wallet. His Social Security card was enclosed in a clear plastic envelope; a second envelope held only a picture of a starlet placed there by the manufacturer.

The policeman studied the Social Security card. "Is this all the ID you have?" he asked. His voice carried a harder edge, and his partner stepped out of the car on the far side and stood watching JD over the roof.

"I'm just going home," JD said. "What's the beef?"

"Where's your driver's license?"

"I don't have one. I don't drive."

"A man your age?"

"I don't have a car."

The policeman stared at him as if he were reading some message of guilt in JD's face, and JD bitterly resented the necessity for thrift that had caused him to postpone paying the three-dollar license fee.

"I've got rent receipts," JD said.

"Let's see them."

He unfolded a stock receipt for two weeks' rent, a square of lined yellow paper with the name of the hotel written in at the head. It seemed to satisfy the officer. He nodded to his partner, who stepped back into the car, sighing like a soldier momentarily relieved from duty.

"You should get some better ID," the young policeman instructed, a hint of primness in his voice. "Particularly if you're going to wander the streets at night. In this area you're subject to be stopped at any time, and another time you might find yourself down at the station answering questions. You understand?"

JD nodded and turned away. He heard the motor start and he had to restrain the impulse to look back and make sure the police car was pulling away.

He tried to sleep in the back of his car, but the car was too small, and he spent the rest of the night in cramped discomfort drifting between waking and sleeping, never losing in either state the awareness of how cold he was.

When he came awake the last time, it was as if he were struggling up through foul gray water, his lung crying for air and his mouth strained open in a silent scream. He lay instinctively gulping for breath, his mind stained with weariness and a sense of helplessness as the gray light of morning seemed to blend into the water he had fought against in his dream.

He managed to steal a quart of milk and a carton of yogurt from the hallway of an apartment house and, while the yogurt nearly nauseated him, he managed to force it down. He made an effort to take hold of himself. As difficult as it was, the only thing he could do at this point was wait. One thing, he wasn't going to spend the day walking. He remembered a dingy block-square park where idle men sat throughout the day, and he determined to spend the morning there.

He quickly recognized that the park was near the end of the line—the drinking fountains were plugged up, and over half the benches were on the point of collapsing. The cops walked through in pairs, swinging their billies, followed furtively by the dim and fearful eyes of the men who made this place their final sanctuary. They sat crowded together on those benches that would still hold their weight and around the stained cement lip of an empty fish pond. They talked quietly, without interest or enthusiasm, without hope or anger. A few passed sections of an old newspaper back and forth.

JD realized that these men had abandoned all pretense and embraced failure. They were sick with it but no longer had to fear it. They could fear cold and hunger without having to fear what these conditions might mean. JD avoided them as if they were afflicted with a virulent contagion. He still had some hold on the real world. Surely the check would clear today, and with the money he had coming he could begin to fight his way back.

Shortly after noon he started out. Each step was painful, and he was aware that he was limping.

He arrived late, dirty and unshaven. The last of the other salesmen were checking in and out, and Smeed looked up to say, "Would you wait until I clear this up, Bing? I have something I wanted to talk to you about."

JD nodded uneasily and went to sit down. He would have liked to take his shoes off, to slump wearily, but he sat up as alertly as a bailiff. Now what? Now what? he asked himself.

The last of the other salesmen left, looking as defeated as JD felt, and Smeed gestured for JD to follow him into a small office, the same office in which he had received his hiring interview. Smeed settled behind a metal desk and looked up at him with brittle distaste.

"Sit down, Bing." Smeed handed him a narrow sheaf of papers.

"What's this?" JD asked automatically.

"Can you explain it?"

He leafed through the papers—his order authorizing shipment to Arnold Courtney Howe, a bank form, the original check stamped FICTITIOUS in red ink. "What does it mean?" he asked.

"It means, Bing, that it's no good. There is no such company, no such account, and I wonder if there is any such Arnold Courtney Howe, whose name, you'll note, doesn't appear on the check."

"He endorsed it."

"A.J.F. Byrnes endorsed it."

"Howe endorsed it for Byrnes."

"What? Are you aware that that's a forgery?"

"Jesus, I don't know—the man gave me a check, and I took it. I need this commission. I need it."

Smeed drew back. "Surely you realize there is no commission." He studied JD as he might study a potentially dangerous animal. "I hired you, Bing, because I felt sorry for you—"

"I don't need you to feel sorry for me!"

"Because I felt you had been harshly used. Now I wonder. I think I'm going to have to turn this whole matter over to the police."

"Now wait a minute. Would I just walk in here and give you a bad check?"

"You might. I don't know, and it's not my business to decide."

Smeed reached for the phone, and, without thinking, JD slapped his hand away. The control in Smeed's eyes faltered, and JD saw his fear.

"You lousy fink. You don't have to call a cop. You ain't lost a dime, and if it was any other salesman, you'd let him go out and see if he couldn't straighten it out."

A muscle ticked in Smeed's cheek. "But you're *not* any other salesman, Bing, and that's not my fault. And I can't take the responsibility. Don't you understand that?"

"No, I don't."

"If you haven't done anything, the police aren't going to bother you."

"You believe that?"

Smeed stared at him uneasily. He looked at the phone, then back at JD.

"I can't stop you from calling them, but when they get here, I'll be long gone." JD stood up. "And you won't have anything to show them." He stuffed the bad check and the other papers into his pocket. "Go ahead and call," he said.

As he reached the outer office, he looked back to see Smeed with the phone, and he broke into a run.

KRISTIE...

... was frightened, but it was a major part of her pride that no one would ever guess it, that her fear was hidden as deeply and securely inside her as her crimes. She knew now, standing in her doorway talking to Grove Alexander, that he saw her as serene and unobtainable. She was in her robe, but she took care to shield herself with the half-open door.

Grove was "nice," she had long ago decided, by which she meant quiet and harmless—but how could she be sure? How could she ever be sure? Someone in this court was torturing her, and it could only be this mild-looking young man standing in front of her. Or Hugo Haas, but he was too direct, too pure an animal. Or the Indian, Parnahuma, or old Arnold Courtney. One of the four had to be behind the telephone calls, and she couldn't eliminate any of them. It might well be Grove.

She watched him, knowing he was working up to something in his indirect manner, and she didn't like the way his hands moved. His face didn't appear strong, but his hands obviously were. They flexed together, the veins rising on the backs like blue cords; then, as if aware of what they might be revealing, they sought cover in his pockets.

Briefly she recalled the time only a few years back when she had been unaware that the world was full of wildness and danger, and, most frightening, illogic.

Then she might have taken this boy-man for a sweetheart and held his head between her hands while sweetly and gravely he—stabbed at her! Her teeth grated, and her eyes snapped shut over this treacherous vision.

"What's the matter?" she heard Grove asking.

"Nothing," she said in a tight voice.

"Are you worried about finding work?"

"No, not at all."

He stared at her soberly for a moment. "If you are, I know a few people. I can't promise anything, but I know some magazine people. That's interesting work."

"It's nice of you, but I have contacts of my own."

She watched Grove smile wryly. "The General?" he asked.

"Yes, the General."

"Is he active?"

She frowned. "What do you mean?"

"He's retired, isn't he?"

"Yes," she admitted.

"An old ex-general. Can he help?"

"Yes, of course. He went directly from the army into private management. His prestige, both official and private, is enormous. Why just last week—"

And as Kristie was telling of the crisis the General had been called to cope with, she was, briefly, a beautiful countess explaining to a young poet why she, to her regret, must reserve herself for one of the emperor's most powerful ministers, a man whose shadow darkened all Europe. And the poet urged her, in glorious language, that the young belonged to the young, that security and power were the pathetic props of those who had lost everything else. Perhaps, the countess agreed, my heart persuades me, and here she touched the upper swell of one small breast—

Grove had her by the arm. She could feel the strength of his fingers, and that treacherous swimming feeling was coming on her.

"Do you have to do that?" he demanded.

"Do what? Do what?" she asked in confusion.

"You know—this general?"

She laughed breathlessly. "I'm sure his intentions are strictly dishonorable, but his intentions"—she continued with deliberate vulgarity—"have left his pants and gone to his head."

Grove tightened his grip on her arm, and she sensed her breath beginning to quicken, but she could read in his face that he was, fortunately for her, unaware of how he was affecting her. What is the matter with you? she demanded of herself. She felt as if her face must be swollen and pulsing with her wanton blood, giving off a scent like a bitch in heat. She started to tell herself still another story—Grove was a burglar who had broken into her house, but no common burglar, a great jewel thief who stole for excitement—

"Kristie?" he asked.

And she felt an immediate Yes in her throat, melting there like warm syrup, but she forced herself to remain silent, and she watched his expression falter and grow mild.

"Will you have dinner with me tonight?"

"Yes," she said quickly.

"Good. Around seven-thirty?"

"Whenever you like."

"Maybe we could go dancing after?"

She pretended to consider this, then smiled. "Maybe," she said.

She closed the door on Grove and leaned against it with her eyes closed. With their wary light shuttered, her face became soft and girlish. Her lips parted softly. Grove could be an exciting man, she decided, if only he would gather himself together and throw himself into something with all his strength. She could have been a man, she thought. She would have known how to be a man, but since the thought came dangerously close to an admission that she didn't know how to be a woman, she let it drift away.

She must do something! Anything, even if it's wrong. She called the General and was put right through to him. She smiled with satisfaction when she heard the eagerness in his voice, and when she agreed to have lunch with him, his bass rumble grew sleek and fat like the purring of a lion. She hung up and thought, Now, he *is* a man.

She took a bath and, with soap creamed around her delicate shoulders like a froth of lace and the constant guarding tension of her stomach, legs, and hips melted into the warm, scented water, she was as close to relaxing as she could ever allow herself to be. It seemed to her she really was the warm, generous, and honest person she had always hoped to be. She must throw a party for all her friends. Soon, she decided, tomorrow or the next day. And if she gave her friends pleasure, could she help it if her enemies grew sour—all those who had envied her, who had been glad to see her fired and were now waiting for her to go down?

She dressed quickly but with care and drove to Trans-Western, where she teased the security officer into letting her use one of the executive parking places. She deliberately left her ten-year-old Chevy next to Nathan Holleran's white Mercedes.

For a moment, aware that the security officer was still watching her out of the corner of his eye, she paused to turn slowly and look over the impressive buildings of Trans-Western, recalling the deep thrill she had always experienced coming to work here, where some of the country's most important projects were managed. She had watched NASA projects slide across the PERT charts toward completion and had glibly repeated the executive remark that "building the damn things was nothing" once the smooth flow of logistics had been successfully ordered. She had felt such a strong sense of participation, of belonging, as if the company were her family and she were one of a rich and powerful clan. Now they were working on the M.M.F.T., the job of the century, and she was out of it! Amazed to feel the sting of tears, she whirled and glared at the security officer, who coughed and pretended to be studying his feet. He still thinks I'm Executive Tail, she decided savagely.

As she walked through the halls toward her old section, she noted avidly how everyone still watched her, and she thought she could sense them wondering what it was she was up to now. There was a hushed, wary quality to their regard, as if they were near a bomb they were almost sure was a dud and would be quick to dismiss with grateful contempt once they had seen it officially disarmed, but were still uncertain—such was the quality of Kristie's presence.

Irene Pappas, at Kristie's own desk, looked up questioningly. "Hello, Kristie. Are you authorized to be here?"

Kristie studied the vulgar and falsely emphasized swell of Irene's large breasts and smiled thinly. "I believe I left a few things in my desk, and while I was here I thought I might cut and run off a stencil."

"A stencil?" Irene repeated warily.

"Yes, an invitation to a party I'm giving."

"A party—" Irene began, then caught herself and said coolly, "You left nothing in this desk, not even dust, as you well know, and I can't allow you to use company equipment for personal work. Not even if you were still employed here, which you are not."

"If I were still employed here," Kristie said in a flat, hard voice, "you'd still be offering your fat ass to get out of the file section!"

"Well, honey," Irene returned in a poisoned whisper, "I'm *out* of the file section, and you're *out* of a job. Now you draw your own conclusions."

"That you were available, and I wasn't."

Irene flushed with anger. She opened her mouth to continue, but Kristie, catching a glimpse of Mel Sirclum, one of the supervisors, moving toward them, turned away and smiled warmly.

"Mel! How are you?"

Sirclum was a roundheaded hobgoblin of six and a half feet, youngest of the supervisors and still uncertain what attitude to take toward his own rapid advancement. He seized Kristin's hand and smiled down at her.

"How are *you?*"

"Fine."

"Are you coming back to work?"

"Just visiting."

"Too bad. Things are dull since you left."

Kristie smiled delightedly. "What a wonderful compliment."

"It's true. Do you have something lined up?"

"Some prospects," said Kristie in a manner that implied that several large concerns were bidding for her services.

"When you're settled in, send for me."

"I might just do that," Kristie said. She waved her hand around. "May I use one of the typewriters?"

"Take your pick."

"And a mimeo stencil?"

"I don't think it'll break the company."

Kristie resisted the temptation to smile triumphantly at Irene Pappas—real winners never bothered to underscore their victories. She typed out her invitation and handed the stencil to the mimeograph girl, who ran it off without question, automatically assuming Kristie to be someone of importance.

She passed a few of the copies around the office, to Sirclum and one or two others, and folded another into a U-Save-Em envelope, addressed it to

Nathan Holleran, and marked it *Personal,* which she knew to be a futile gesture, since Nathan had a staff of three for whom nothing was too personal. As it happened, she was able to deliver it personally.

On her way out, passing through the corridor that connected the executive offices, she met Nathan. The sight of him affected her far more than she had imagined it would, and she handed him the invitation like one member of a relay team passing the baton to another.

"Hello, Kristie," Nathan said evenly. "What's this?"

"Read it and see."

She studied Holleran intently as he read her invitation, admiring his blunt male face, his coarse, rust-colored hair, and the solid way he held himself. His hair must have been red once and his face freckled (she could always imagine this high school face set with determination beneath a football helmet, or over a physics text), and then the hair had dulled and the freckles faded as these frivolous characteristics were sloughed off along with youthful wonder to be replaced with great drive and relentless ambition.

She recalled, in a vivid shuffling of impressions, their first night together. She had been able to persuade herself that what she was going to do she was doing for the company, her foster parents, and for the good of the project. Nathan was overworked and worn down carrying the responsibilities of a dozen mediocre men in addition to his own. His wife was demanding and inadequate, unable to appreciate or properly respond to a man of Nathan's caliber. Kristie had told herself that only she could give him pleasure and release, but actually in the motel she had been bloodless, unable to respond, and too perversely proud of her coolness to fake an excitement she didn't feel. It had been a failure, a disaster. But then in the car, as Nathan had leaned over to kiss her good night, she had come suddenly and violently to life, and there in the cramped discomfort of the small Mercedes, with her legs hanging out the open door, they had made love again, and it was as if they were held aloft in the hand of a giant while the whole dull and unfeeling world plodded beneath them. Afterward she had clung to Nathan as if he were the container of everything she had ever thought precious.

Then the dismal ending with Nathan, in spite of the grim finality of his tone and expression, actually pleading with her to understand while he told her perhaps he loved her, he didn't know, but he did know she was too difficult, too complicated. He couldn't understand her and he didn't have the time or the emotional energy to make the effort.

Oh, Nathan! she thought, watching his hard white hands holding her invitation. Nathan, let's try again.

Holleran looked up. "This sounds like fun—" His eyes were careful, but for an instant they betrayed something she read as hesitation. She reached out to him.

"You will come?"

"I'm sorry, Kristie, I can't make it."

"But you want to, don't you?" Kristie demanded with sudden fierceness. "But you're afraid. Afraid of your wife, afraid of your job."

"Damn it, Kristie, we've talked and talked. What am I supposed to say? Why won't you just let me say I can't make it? Yes, I'd like to come, but I can't make it."

"As you wanted to stop them from firing me, but just couldn't?" Again Kristie was fighting tears. "Do you know what this job meant to me?"

Holleran shook his head like a large, sturdy animal worried by a hornet. "When my bosses want you out, what can I do? It would have endangered my own position, and in all fairness, Kristie, my job was far more important than yours. I could have threatened to resign, but I'm certain even that couldn't have saved you, and they may well have accepted my resignation."

"You could have made the gesture."

"Kristie, I don't make gestures. Haven't we talked about this enough?"

"Yes. Yes, quite enough."

She snatched her invitation and turned on her heel. This was the man of whom she had written in her journal: *He is an eagle! A woman must either love him or hate him. There is no in-between with this man.*

Now she felt nothing but contempt. Nothing but contempt. She tried to forget the electric shock that had passed up her arm when her hand had brushed his.

Ex-General Irving sat behind the wheel of his late model Cadillac flipping through a magazine called Pan. A tall, thick old man, he wore a conservatively cut gray suit. His bald head was covered with a narrow-brim hat, and his hands were well cared for. He paused, staring at a photo spread, nudes and semi-nudes, of a young girl, titled: Those Virgin Islands. The photographer had made use of a single prop, a white sheet, which by turns became a cowl, a crumpled bed, a child's dress, and Delphic robes.

Kristie opened the door on the far side and slid in, handing Irving one of her invitations. She had deliberately calmed herself and now smoothed her skirt with a practiced hand. "I'm late," she said.

"Not that late." He handed her the magazine. "How old would you say she was?"

Kristie studied the girl briefly and thought her thin legged and cheap-looking. She shot a quick side glance at Irving and found herself looking into his hard, yellow and humorous eyes. Take the intelligence from Irving's eyes and you would have the eyes of a turtle. Take the humor as well and you would end with the eyes of a barracuda.

"She's made up to look younger than she is."

"Even so?"

"Fifteen, possibly sixteen."

"What an improbable age for anyone to be," Irving mused. "I'll be sixty-nine in a few months. One more turn of the wheel and I'm seventy."

"You don't look it," Kristie assured him automatically.

Irving snorted. "I look like the old man of the sea." He put his hand on her thigh. "Unfortunately I don't feel that way."

Kristie slid away. "What do you think of my invitation?"

Irving turned it in his hands. "Am I to admire it or am I invited?"

"Of course, you're invited, but you won't come and you know it."

Irving stared at her hard. "Invite me to a party where you only make *one* invitation."

"To *that* party you must invite me."

"I have—several times."

"Well"—she reached over and patted him lightly on the cheek—"keep asking. Who knows?"

Irving laughed and took her hand. "I don't know why I put up with you, Kristie."

"Because I'm pretty and smart, and you tire of those dumb little girls you buy, and because there's enough of the hunter in you to despise sitting game. In short, because you're a man."

Irving released her hand. "Where would you like to have lunch?"

"Some place quiet."

"Asmund's?"

"That sounds nice."

When Irving had the car in motion, Kristie asked, "Is Trans-Western in trouble on the M.M.F.T.?"

"They're a long way from clear sky, but I wouldn't say trouble."

"The word is that all the tech stuff is coming in first-rate, but that management's falling apart. Too much pressure."

"You know Holleran, don't you?"

"I knew him."

"Top man," Irving said sternly. "He was with me in Texas. A goddam bear. Point him, and he'd keep going until he came out where you said he would. And talk! That boy could charm a hornet out of biting him—"

"And charm it into biting someone else."

"Yes, that too."

They rode in silence for a block. Then Kristie said, "If he blows this project, he's through in aerospace, and he will blow it if—"

"He won't blow it. It's important to too many people to see that he doesn't. This is a vital matter, young lady, not a question of spiting someone's chances of becoming student body president."

"I see," said Kristie dryly.

"No, I don't think you do see. The future defense of this country may well depend on what Nathan's trying to do, and he's in that spot because he's the best man for the job. It's a man-breaker, but it won't break Nathan!"

"Yes, yes, yes, I understand—wonderful Nathan!"

Irving smiled grimly. "Easy, Kristie. Something, somewhere, will get Nathan. Something always does. Life will, even if it only turns him into an empty-hearted, hot-handed old man like me. No one rides free."

"I can't wait that long."

"I'm afraid you'll have to. You can't hurt Nathan professionally, and it's obvious you've lost the power to damage him emotionally. What else could you do? Try to be sensible."

"All right, all right." She nodded, trying to smile, but in her thoughts she fiercely assured herself that there would be something she could do. No one could enter her life to ruin it and then leave her to suffer alone. Not even Nathan.

Asmund's featured a fashion show for the luncheon trade, but a show more reminiscent of burlesque than of the salon. A handful of models dressed in playsuits, bathing suits, and shorty nightgowns walked up and down in front of the booths, pausing at each table to execute a series of model's maneuvers, turning slowly while they held out what little fabric they might be covered with for inspection, while their cynical eyes reflected the sure knowledge that it was not cloth that was being inspected. Theoretically the items they modeled were on sale somewhere in the restaurant.

Irving watched closely, to the point of ignoring his lunch. He looked directly into the girls' eyes, and they stared blandly back.

"You're always working, aren't you?" Kristie asked sharply.

"Why not? At my age one expects a high percentage of rejection, so it's necessary to increase the rate of incidence in order to keep favorable returns at anything like the same level. When I was young, I could have any woman I asked, so I only asked the ones I wanted. Now I ask them all."

"I've learned one thing," he continued after a moment. "Pleasure depends on the desire for it, depends on appetites and the means by which to satisfy them. If my hungers falter, I'll not be far behind them. If I'm afraid of anything, that's it. That my desires will fade away as if someone had shut off the gas and lights in a decaying house. It's probably much better to be whipped by needs one can't satisfy than to sit empty waiting to die. Anyway"—he crossed his knife and fork on his plate and took out a thin, dark cigar—"I'm well off and not entirely powerless."

"I'm sure you do very well," Kristie said. "Perhaps you should have a social secretary."

"Hardly." Irving's eyes glimmered with amusement. Kristie knew anxiety, and it made her awkward. "Anyway," Irving continued, "you'd be wasted as a secretary of any kind."

"If you really think that, why aren't I working for AVCO?"

"No, no, honey, not in my company. It's a nice, quiet plant. I enjoy watching you operate, but those dull, dependable boys of mine wouldn't know what hit them."

"So," she said mildly, "poor Kristie starved to death. She was cheerful to the last—"

Irving indicated the large piece of steak she had left uneaten. "You don't appear to be in any immediate danger of starving to death," he said.

"I'll freeze then. They're going to turn off the gas."

"Perhaps that's just fate. You're handy with the freeze yourself."

"I knew your generous and impulsive nature would get the best of you."

Irving chuckled. "You must have a theory that if you want something, demand it. Well, I have a few favors coming from General Electronics. They're working up the components for the Neptune-Three—"

"That's an important project!" Kristie exclaimed.

"Very. Perhaps as important as Nathan's project."

"Could you get me on that? Could you?"

"Maybe."

"How do I know you'll keep your word if I—if I give you what you want?"

"You don't. But we don't need to discuss this as if we were negotiating a ransom payment. I'll talk to Ross over there, and I'll do it because I think you'll do a good job for them. Not for any other reasons. When I pay, I pay cash. It saves complications."

Kristie reached over and covered one of his hands with both of hers. "Would you? Would you do that for me?"

"Yes, Kristie, I will. You're a strange girl in many ways, but you're not ordinary, thank God, and I like you. That's one of the few advantages of my age—one finds it possible to simply like a woman."

"You talk too much about your age, Bill." She tightened her hands over his. "It isn't that important. Maybe—" She lowered her eyes. "Would you like to come over this evening?"

"Yes, I'd like that very much."

"Oh, damn! I just remembered. I've a date for dinner."

"With whom?" Irving asked, betraying disappointment.

"No one important. The kid who lives' across from me. A cartoonist. He's not a kid, really, but he acts like one. Why don't you come by later. Around eleven?" Kristie grinned. "I'll eat fast."

After lunch, Irving drove her back to the Trans-Western parking lot to pick up her own car. The security officer was red-faced. "Jesus Christ, Miss Olson.

You said ten minutes. You've been gone two hours and that old sled of yours cluttering up executive country like a dead horse."

"Did Mr. Holleran mention it?"

"He sure as hell did. He sure as hell did."

"Tell him to bring it before the grievance committee."

"Grievance committee? Hell, it could mean my job," the security officer was saying as Kristie jammed her car in gear and drove off. He stared after her. "Why, you miserable bitch. Just you come trying to park in here again."

Kristie drove into the alley behind the Bali Hai and left her car next to Grove's Volks. She cast one disgusted glance at the dairy across the alley from the court. A small herd of black-and-white cows lay on the baked mud, seemingly dazed by the heat. What business did they have allowing a dairy right in the middle of a residential neighborhood? That the neighborhood had grown out and encircled the dairy never occurred to her. The sight and smell of cows recalled too vividly the dreary countrysides of her girlhood, and she dreamed of living in Beverly Hills where she need never see a cow or hear a chicken.

She noticed Kathleen in her garage, loading the dryer with another of her endless washes. She decided that Kathleen's kids would have to spend the best part of each day rolling in the mud and smear themselves with jam the rest of the time to account for the amount of dirty clothes they produced. Wendy Ann was sitting on the pavement in the entrance to the garage, stabbing at the concrete with a broken screwdriver. Kristie knelt and took the tool away from the little girl, who immediately burst into tears.

"Oh, that's all right," Kathleen said. "Let her have it."

"She's liable to hurt herself."

"Babies can hurt themselves with anything if they put their minds to it." Kristie stood blank-faced with disapproval. "You can't be serious!"

"In a way. I don't believe in hovering over them twenty-four hours a day."

"They're *your* children."

"Yes."

Kristie had heard Kathleen described as "pretty"—she didn't share the impression. Kathleen was too thin and flat, her face was too open, and she walked with a brisk, purposeful stride like a female marine. Small wonder her husband had left her. To hear Kathleen tell the story, she had run him off herself with a ball bat, but Kristie dismissed this as an obvious fiction. Still she supposed that some men might find Kathleen attractive, and she invited Kathleen to her party mostly because she needed her to help with the arrangements. Kathleen accepted, saying that it was fortunate for her that Kristie had decided to give the party on one of her evenings off.

At this point Kristie saw Mr. Howe crossing the backyard. He wore the apron he worked in, and his cheek was smeared with ink. He studied some papers he was carrying, smiling to himself.

Kristie turned to Kathleen and asked impulsively, "Does he ever give you any trouble?"

"Mr. Howe? He's an old dear. What do you mean by trouble?"

"You know what I mean."

Kathleen grinned. "He must be close to eighty. The only thing he's ever given me is a picture of a sailboat and an ear-bending. He's lonely. But that son-in-law"—Kathleen frowned—"Haas, he gives me the willies. The way he treats Gloria."

"She asks for it. Living with an animal like that."

"I know what it can be. It's not as easy to break away as you might imagine, Kristie."

"There's a mystery there," Kristie said thoughtfully. "None of them work. How do they live?"

"Gloria told me Haas has some stock. Telephone stock, I believe she said it was."

"I've heard that story, and that's just what I think it is—a story."

"What are you suggesting?"

"I don't know. You're too trusting, Kathleen."

"Fiddlesticks."

"You are, though. Well, I have to wash my hair."

In the backyard in the warm sunlight Mr. Howe was pinning his papers on the clothesline. Kristie saw now that they were prints.

"Miss Olson," he called.

"Yes."

He came toward her. "Forgive the intrusion, but did you happen to purchase a set of encyclopedias when that young man was through here selling them?"

"No. Why do you ask?"

"I merely wondered. I bought a set myself, but they haven't been delivered. They were promised for the next day, and I thought perhaps if you had bought a set—"

"I don't know anything about it." Kristie hurried away. She recalled JD vividly. A big man, broad and as hard to her touch as bone. A man like that could handle Nathan, hurt and humiliate him as he had hurt and humiliated her. He could deal with Nathan as easily as an adult dealt with a child. She wondered if JD would come back to see her again, and she smiled with sudden purpose. He would come back.

JD...

...hunched and miserable, shifted his weight on his smoldering feet. His socks felt as if they had been soaked in molasses, coated with dust, and now kept moist with his own sweat. He thought of the Sock Man passing the cells every night, dragging his bag behind him, calling: "Oscar Hocks, Oscar Hocks." Clean socks every night. Clean clothes three times a week. Now he stood hungry and filthy in a mission, cynically dubbed The Last Resort, waiting to be fed.

A pale, earnest young man at a lectern was praying over JD and over the winos, the stumblebums, and the broken-down rubber tramps crowded around him, praying in a voice that sobbed in his narrow nose while his thin white hands fluttered above them, and his glasses flashed with a light his tired eyes could never equal.

JD felt someone twitch his sleeve, and he looked down at Doc, the bitter old man who had led him to this mission. "Ain't this a noble assemblage?" Doc whispered.

JD looked around. As dirty as he was, he was still the cleanest man here, and most of the others looked more than half sick. They shuffled feebly, as if their minds were drifting in the heats of fever, seeking sleep but fearful of delirium.

"Cured in wine," Doc continued. "But don't knock it. It makes as much sense as anything else."

JD smiled faintly. He figured Doc's heart pumped acid and port wine in equal parts. And his face was as intricately shriveled and soured as the face of a shrunken head. Except for his eyes—they burned a hot and disgusted black. He had approached JD to put the bum on him, asking for a quarter in a voice that plainly said he didn't give a damn whether he got it or not, and would like to spit on the donor whether he gave or not. He stayed to lecture JD on the evils that were "turning the world into a ball of crap," obviously relishing the bitter taste of his own scorn.

The young minister ended his prayer, and instantly the bums, suddenly full of energy, struggled toward a tarnished steam table, where they bunched together at the opening. "Stop shoving, you crud-sucking slobs!" Doc snarled while the minister pleaded with them to form a line. Reluctantly, still jockeying for position, they did. JD took a tray and as he walked down the steam table he was given a dipper of thin stew, black-eyed peas, two slices of bread, and a cup of tea. The feeding process reminded him so vividly of institution life that he found himself shivering. He didn't kid himself; he was an inch

away from it. In deep, dark water, sinking fast. But he was even less frightened of his situation than he was of an impulse he sensed in himself—an
impulse to relax and let go, to give himself up to the peace of drowning.

He found a seat next to Doc at a long wooden table, and a man with a fes-
tering purple scab along his temple sat down across from them. He was tooth-
less and had a ragged island of hair in a sea of baldness, and the cuffs of his cast-
off coat were crusted with the remains of former meals. He nodded familiar-
ly at Doc and eyed JD with the leery hostility of a mongrel dog. Then he studied his tray, grunted sourly, and took a sip of tea. He spit it back in his cup.

"Tastes like horse piss," he told Doc.

"Now how'd you know that?" Doc asked. "You drank much horse piss?"

"You're funny. You know that? How'd you get so funny?"

Doc scratched his hairy, sunken cheeks. "It come natural to me, Bogus
Eddie, like my good looks."

Bogus Eddie was rapidly spooning his stew, still staring resentfully at the
tea. "You know what's a hell of a drink in them 'sclusive hotels?"

"I don't spend too much time in hotels," Doc said.

"Ice coffee. Those people drink ice coffee. They make hot coffee then put
ice in it. How do you like that?" He directed his question at JD.

"It's all right, I suppose."

"Bet it tastes like horse piss," Doc said.

"One of these times someone's gonna cure you of your funniness."

"It won't be you, Bogus. You'd do better to tackle a wild tiger with a toothpick than to mess with me."

Bogus Eddie glared, then glanced sideways at JD. "Who's your big buddy?"
he asked mildly.

"Ask him."

"He looks like he's holding."

"He's not," Doc said flatly.

"Maybe he's got something we can pawn. A watch, maybe?"

"We? Where you get 'we'? You got a mouse in your pocket?"

"I just asked. I got nowhere to flop and nothing to get wet with."

"Join the club."

"You gonna stem tonight?"

"Maybe."

"You wanta go in on a bottle?"

"Not tonight."

"Yeah? Well, that's no big thing."

JD found himself wishing Bogus Eddie would take his scab and his big flapping mouth somewhere else. He'd been watching faces and listening to talk
like Bogus Eddie's all his adult life, but time hadn't eased the impression. He
mopped his tray with the last of his bread, and discovered that someone had

scratched an obscene word across the bottom. He hadn't noticed it when he had picked the tray up and had eaten down to it like a child discovering Mickey Mouse in the bottom of its bowl. He stared at the ragged letters with a feeling of dull anger. It seemed that all his expectations of freedom, now come to reality, could be scored with the same word. He showed it to Doc.

"No-class slobs," Doc said.

Bogus Eddie finished his tray and moved off. JD and Doc sat on, rolling smokes from what was left of the Golden Grain JD carried.

"Where'd you take up smoking dust?" Doc asked.

"In the joint."

"You pull much time?"

"Some."

"Just get out?"

For some reason JD said, "No, I been out awhile."

Doc studied him for a moment. "You're too big and too healthy to stem. How you figure on making it?"

"I don't know. Everything I touch turns sour. But I don't plan on laying down to die. I got something working for me. All I need is some gas to get to it."

"You got a car?" Doc asked quickly.

"Yeah. Fifty dollars worth of junk, but it runs okay—when I put gas in it."

"How much gas?"

"Two, three gallons—five to be safe."

Doc looked up, figuring. "A buck-fifty. That buys a lot of wine."

"If you could come up with it, I'd give it back double."

"I don't doubt you. I don't doubt you. But every time I rack up a little jingle, I race myself to the store. I wonder often what the vintners buy, one-half so precious as the stuff they sell. You know that?"

"No."

"It's a poem."

"I figured that."

"This guy says wine has robbed him of his robe of honor, but he doesn't much give a damn. But you do?"

JD frowned. He wasn't ready for this kind of talk. "My feet hurt. I've been walking for days. I just ate and I'm still hungry—"

"You must try to live. That was another poet, a Frog poet. Well, I'll try to help you, but you ain't making no loan shark out of me. If I get the buck-fifty, and if you make this touch, and if you come back, and if I'm not in jail or dead—well, then you can buy me a good drunk. Deal?"

"That's a deal." JD held out his hand. Doc stared scornfully for a moment, then slipped his own hand, dark and wrinkled as a monkey's paw, into JD's. They shook solemnly.

"Don't go making no slob out of me, JD. I ain't no goddam eagle scout and don't claim to be, but you act bewildered as some kid just got kicked in the head by his own ma. And you ain't all that simple, now, are you?"

Walking toward one of the districts where Doc did his begging, JD asked, "How come they call you Doc?"

"How come they call you JD?"

"That's my name. My given name."

"You folks had a lively sense of humor."

"No, we had such names in my family—where I came from." He smiled. "You didn't think I was from California, did you?"

"Well, I ain't no doctor, neither. The reason these slobs on Five Street call me Doc ain't got nothing to do with me. It's because they all had such great lives they walked out on—they were rich, with two Cadillac automobiles, and beautiful broads flopped for them. Ask anyone of them, they'll tell you. Don't ask, they'll tell you, anyway. And since every slobbering wino down here was formerly a man of great importance, I have to be too. And since I ain't completely forgot the English language, they call me Doc, but, truth to tell, I been a tramp and a crossroader and a nothing-minus-nothing since the day I slipped out of the barn. And it's even money my folks didn't even know I was gone for two weeks. Anything I know from books, I know because it's warm in public libraries."

As Doc talked on, they moved out of skid row into a commercial district. They passed a Volkswagen garage, a trade school, and a printing firm, where the presses were running on into the evening. Across the street a truck loaded with pipe was maneuvering toward the curb, and blocks ahead a movie marquee lashed with multicolored neon gained brightness against the darkening sky.

"The trick to stemming," Doc was saying, "is to pick middle ground. A poor neighborhood, no one's got nothing; a class neighborhood, the bottles bust you on sight. And here in L.A. the farther you get from Five Street, the better, because the slobs are too beat or too lazy to walk more'n three, four blocks in any direction. I like to work a street by myself. They give because they're afraid. Me, and slobs like me, they pay to go away. They bribe us not to exist because we remind them of where they can fall, where they will fall if they ever let go—or get knocked loose. Me, I'm worse'n a ghost and twice as ugly." Doc laughed, a dry rustle high in his throat. "How old you think I am?"

JD shrugged. The figure 60 jumped to mind, and he was starting to say 50 when Doc cut him off.

"Don't you tell that lie, JD. I know you think I'm old enough to have been a waiter at the Last Supper, but, truth to tell, I'll be forty-two the fifth of next month, so don't ever let anyone tell you outdoor living's good for you. I got eight teeth in my head—three lowers and five uppers—and only two of them come anywheres near matching up. It would take me a week to eat a steak, like a termite gnawing through a bowling ball. I figure I got something coming for looking like I do. There's lots of bastards never knew how well off they were till they copped a gander at me."

A block below the theater they turned into a congestion of lights and activity, where the cars waited at the intersections nose to tail like elephants, and the people milled around each other without interest. "This'll do," Doc said. "You better wait for me."

JD nodded and stepped into the doorway of a paint store that was closed for the evening. "This shouldn't take long," Doc said, and he was off down the sidewalk, turning from side to side, bobbing like a chip of wood carried on a stream. JD saw him turned down three times before he was out of sight. JD pulled the brim of his hat lower and watched the street. A group of high school girls passed, talking in musical voices, and to JD they seemed like a float of exotic flowers. They made him think of Kristie Olson, and he looked away. He shifted from foot to foot, like a restless horse in its stall. An hour passed.

I might have known, he told himself. He waited another fifteen minutes, then started in the direction Doc had gone. In this neighborhood people were beginning to stare at him. He knew he looked rough. He was unshaven, and his coat was turned up around the crumpled collar of his dirty shirt. He was beginning to limp. The large blister on his left heel was infected. Still, he bore their eyes with resentment, a resentment that grew as it became apparent Doc had hung him up.

He remembered Doc reaching over to shake his hand, and his anger grew hot. He didn't have to promise me nothing. I wasn't holding no gun to his head. If he done me like this, and I caught him on the Big Yard—but he was beginning to realize that bad faith didn't prosper on the Big Yard only because there was no place to hide with a broken promise. Here in the free world a lie could safely vanish.

But Doc hadn't vanished. JD found him in the next block leaning in an empty doorway. Above the sidewalk a few doors down the single word LIQUOR, traced in urgent neon, pulsed regularly like a beacon. Doc was staring out over the street. In his hand he held a bottle as if he were about to throw it as hard as he could.

Two empties lay by his feet. He looked up at JD without dismay, his mouth crimped in a wry, despairing smile.

"Have a drink, kid."

"I don't drink," JD said bitterly. Doc's nervousness and tension were gone. He shambled like a broken doll, and, like some dolls, he had wet himself—his crotch and the inside of his pants legs were dark with urine.

"You don't drink—and you don't do much of anything else, either."

"I didn't ask you for nothing."

"That's right. That's right. You think I enjoy sucking up to these scum?"

"I still didn't ask you for nothing."

"You better have a drink."

JD threw his hand in a gesture of dismissal and started off. He became aware that Doc was wavering along behind him. "Listen, kid, I meant to come back, and that's what God loves. I had a buck and I was on my way back when I saw that goddam sign. Hey, slow down, you longlegged clown!"

JD slowed his pace, and Doc came up beside him. "I figured I'd have a belt or two and then I'd go out and stem some more. I figured—hell, you got no idea how I really feel."

"It's all right," JD said.

"Sure you don't want a drink?"

JD noticed a middle-aged woman, her face round and white as an unbaked pie, staring with disgust. He grabbed Doc's bottle and raised it to his lips. The wine was warm and sour, and he didn't like it any better than he had liked home brew, but in a moment he felt warmer and less frightened. From a loudspeaker above the door of a record store a saxophone sang with a high, throbbing vibrato like a nanny goat.

"We better get out of this neighborhood," Doc warned. "Or we'll find ourselves with thirty days D and D."

JD shrugged. "Looks like we got our choice of being locked in or locked out. Some selection. This is a city of closed doors."

"They're better closed than open. There's nothing behind most of them."

"Maybe."

"Where you heading?" Doc asked.

"To see a friend."

He left Doc across the street from the Imperial Hotel. Doc settled on the curb, half-hidden between two cars. "Good luck," he called.

Through the hotel window JD saw that the night clerk was working a crossword puzzle, and he eased the door open and headed for the stairs. Halfway up, a step groaned under his weight, and he froze there until he heard paper rustling, then bolted to the third floor. Three-twelve. The number had turned in his mind since the night Seldom Seen had hit on him in the lobby, turned like a charm or the combination to a vault.

He rapped lightly with one knuckle and held his hand poised above the door to knock again. The corridor smelt of steam heat and ancient dust, and nearby a radio was playing a nameless waltz. He heard a muffled voice.

"Yeah?"

"It's JD."

"Who?"

"JD. You know, Big One."

The bolt creaked, the door cracked six inches, and JD was looking down at mild blue eyes in a worn face. "Where's Seldom Seen?" he asked.

"Never heard of him."

"He told me he lived here."

"Maybe he did, but he don't now. I moved in today."

"You got any idea where he might have gone?"

"None at all. I rented a room, and they put me in here."

"Okay, okay."

JD stared at the silver numerals 312 on the closed door. He raised his big fist as if he were going to smash the plywood panel, then crammed his hands in his pockets and started downstairs. He didn't try to slip past the clerk.

"Hey, Bing!"

"Yeah, you got some mail for me?"

"No, I got a bill."

"Tell me something new."

"You'll pay it if you want your gear. That new enough for you?"

JD leaned over the desk. "A shoe box full of dirty laundry and a worn-out toothbrush? I'll pay it *when* I pay it, because I pay my bills."

"Just pay it. We're not interested in your reasons."

"I said I'd pay. Now what happened to—" He found he had no name for Seldom Seen that would mean anything to the clerk. "Where's the guy who was in three-twelve?"

The clerk smiled peculiarly and turned back to his puzzle. "Gone," he said.

"Gone? You got any idea where he went. I got to see him."

"You can see him any afternoon between two and four. Those, as you probably know, are the visiting hours at the county jail."

Involuntarily JD grunted as an icy shiver went over him. "What'd they bust him for?"

"Bunco. He was trying to lay the note. He picked a cashier whose boyfriend was the beat cop."

"Yeah," JD said uneasily. This particular hustle had been described to him, a complicated routine with the change from a twenty-dollar bill, but he had never been able to keep it straight in his mind. Lucky, he thought, since he had understood it to be foolproof. He also realized that had Seldom Seen been arrested a week later, he might well have been arrested with him. But this no longer seemed the worst thing that could happen to him. He studied briefly how easy it would be to yoke the clerk, this soft, bad-mouthing city man. Yoke him up tight and empty the till. But with the line showing plain in front of him, he found he wasn't yet ready to cross it.

Doc had slipped to the side. His head rested on the grill of a new Lincoln; his reflection stretched away in the bright chrome like a rubber mask pulled into a grotesque caricature of its former shape. The bottle, almost empty now, was propped between his feet, and for the first time JD noticed that his shoes weren't mates. One was darker and maybe a size larger. Both shoes were laced with white string.

Doc opened his eyes. "Any luck?"

"No, he's busted."

"Busted? What for?"

"Laying the note."

Doc made a dry noise. "That's a burnt-out hustle. Laying the note went out with gold bricks." He got to his feet, holding on the hood of the Lincoln for support. "Your friend was a rumpkin."

"Maybe. Maybe he just got left behind and didn't know it." JD rubbed his face wearily. He thought of one of those hairy elephants, saw it frozen, huge, and gray in the ice while the years pass. The world changes, but the elephant can't change. Finally the ice melts, freeing it into a world that has never heard of hairy elephants.

"Any ideas?" JD asked Doc.

Doc leaned over to scissor the neck of the bottle between two fingers. He lifted it to JD. "Have a drink."

"You drink it. It don't do much for me."

Doc grinned wryly. "It's my heart's blood." He emptied the bottle, stared at it a moment, and then smashed it in the gutter. "Come on, let's find some place to flop. Tomorrow I'll scrounge up—" He broke off, snapping his fingers soundlessly. "I'll be damned. JD, if brains was dynamite, I couldn't blow my nose. You sold any blood yet?"

"What do you mean?"

"There's your gas money. There's an outfit on Fourth and L.A. that'll pay for a pint of your blood. And it's open 'til nine."

JD swallowed uneasily, his throat suddenly dry. Selling blood wasn't new to him. Several drives a year, for one cause or another, were promoted in the institution, and still other inmates volunteered to be inoculated with whooping cough vaccine and were then permitted to sell their blood to be made into serum. JD had never volunteered for any of it. The thought of a needle tearing into his veins was enough to make him nauseated.

"It makes me sick," he told Doc.

Doc shrugged without much sympathy. "Well, how bad do you want this gas?"

JD didn't answer.

"I can't do it. They mark you." Doc held up his hand. "You can't see it, but they stamp the back of your hand with some kind of fluorescent crap. You're supposed to wait six weeks. No one does, but it takes awhile for their mark to wear off." Doc smiled. "Even if you wash reg'lar."

"Where's this place at?"

The clinic was housed in a gutted store, painted white now, a white already beginning to yellow in the sour air of Fourth Street. The bottom half of the triple window was painted black, and on the top half was crudely lettered: MERCY BLOOD BANK. HOURS: 12:00 Noon to 9:00 P.M.

"Mercy." Doc sneered briefly. "I'd better wait out here. They'll think I'm getting ready to play some game on you."

"Okay." JD nodded. He took time to roll a cigarette, passing the bag to Doc. He made a sloppy roll, something he seldom did, but he fired it up anyway and drew the raw, hot smoke into his lungs. He looked up but couldn't see a single star. A scattering of yellow lights marked the rim of a distant hill.

His cigarette fell apart; he dropped it to the sidewalk and stepped on it. "Stick around," he told Doc.

Inside the clinic JD found little more than a row of cots covered with green sheets and small, hard-looking pillows. A corner was closed off with several white folding screens, and two people, a woman in a nurse's uniform and a man in a white jacket with a stethoscope around his neck, sat by a desk talking idly. JD wondered if the man was a doctor and decided he would have to be. His shoes rang on the concrete floor, but neither the nurse nor the doctor paid any attention until he was standing directly over them. He noticed some rusty brown spots on the doctor's sleeve and swallowed uneasily. The air was heavy with a hospital smell.

The nurse looked up, her eyes brittle. "Yes?" she asked.

"You buy blood?"

"That's what we're here for," the doctor said in a friendly but cheerless voice. His eyes were morose, his face worn and colorless. "Have you been here before?"

"No."

"You haven't—ah—been a donor lately?"

"No, I've never sold any blood before."

"And why should you need to sell it now?"

JD drew a deep breath of resentment. The nurse, a huge woman with a small, neat head, watched him with idle curiosity, her little pink mouth twisted in a reflex of habitual distaste. "I need money," JD said bluntly.

"Yes—ah—some physicians recommend it for high blood pressure." The doctor's tone implied that such physicians were quacks. "But you need money." He paused, studying JD with weary sympathy. "All right."

He switched on a lamplike machine. "Hold your hand here," he said, demonstrating briefly. JD obeyed. The back of his hand glowed with a cold, silvery light. The doctor sighed. "You haven't been here recently."

"I told you I've never done this before."

"Yes, of course. Take off your coat and roll up your sleeve, I'll have to test your blood pressure."

With the apparatus tightened around his bicep, JD could feel his heart. It seemed to pound throughout his whole body. The doctor, stethoscope in place, frowned gravely. "You heart's working overtime. Have you ever had any trouble with it?"

"No."

"You've never had a diagnosis of tachycardia?"

"No, nothing."

The doctor settled back and shook his head. "I don' know—"

"I'm nervous, Doc. Needles bother me, and that's the whole story."

The doctor reached out quickly and took JD's hand, sliding his thumb along the palm. It was hot and wet.

"I *need* the money," JD insisted.

The doctor turned to the nurse. "What do you think?"

She said, "He looks strong enough to give a gallon."

"Looks are deceiving," the doctor said solemnly, as if coining an original observation. "But—ah—all right. Go over and lay down on one of those cots."

JD settled himself, turned his head away, and closed eyes. He tried to keep his mind empty, but he heard the nurse moving around, then felt her cold hands on his arm. He held his breath while the needle was forced into his distended vein. It didn't hurt; the pain was nothing—but the idea was somehow horrible. He lay quietly, pumping his fist as the nurse had told him, and just once he sneaked a look and saw his blood foaming into a bottle, pink as a strawberry milkshake. He nearly fainted.

"Blood into wine," he heard the doctor say from somewhere behind him. "A shabby miracle. They're like sheep who come obediently to be drained, and wine is their shepherd who maketh them to lay down in gutters—"

"You talk too much," the nurse said coldly.

"I always have," the doctor agreed.

When it was over and JD was able to sit up, the nurse brought him a paper cup full of lukewarm coffee and a stale donut. She stamped his hand. After a moment the doctor came over to hand him a worn five-dollar bill and a small booklet.

"You might look this over—when you have time."

JD read the title—*The Twelve Steps*—and recognized it for an Alcoholic's Anonymous tract. He started to tell the doctor he didn't drink, but why should he bother?

"Thanks, I will," he said.

"It helps some people."

Outside, JD handed the booklet to Doc, who glanced at it, grinned scornfully, and tossed it in the gutter.

JD started off. "Come on," he said.

"Hey"—Doc hurried to catch up—"now that you're holding heavy, why don't you spring for another jug?"

"After we get back."

It wasn't until he heard the "we" that he realized he intended to take Doc with him. He wasn't sure why except maybe he didn't want to go it alone. He began to tell Doc about Arnold Courtney Howe.

GROVE...

...decided to share his speculations concerning the Scavenger with Kristie. He had watched the old man sorting through the garbage again today and decided that their bins were part of a route the Scavenger grazed along. He felt like a naturalist uncovering the life secrets of some rare, wild thing, and he stood motionless as the Scavenger passed within six feet of him, watching him with the bright, nervous, and alien awareness of a bird torn between its feeding and its sense of danger. The old man wore a different badge; it had been cut from glossy white cardboard and striped with a fine gold line like the lid of a gift box. The motto on this one read: WE ARE HIS TROUBLED SLEEP.

The phrase came back to him as he watched Kristie, who was daintily but methodically sectioning her meat, and he seized on it as something that might interest her, because the evening was collapsing into her polite, vaguely sweet disinterest. First she had rejected the drive to Hollywood because it wasn't sensible to spend two hours on the Freeway when they could get good food right here in Bellflower, and now she was paying as much attention to her wristwatch as she was to anything else, including him and her dinner. It was covert; she wasn't rude, but he couldn't help watching her closely, trying to read the intent of her every motion. She fascinated him. He saw her secretive eyes as mysterious and read the wary tension of her bearing as a mark of poise. It came to him with real pain that he must be boring her.

He launched into an animated account of his encounters with the Scavenger and tried to convey his sense of the eerie import of the notices he wore pinned to the bib of his overalls. He was amazed to see Kristie's composure falter.

"In back of *our* court?" she asked in a high voice.

"Yes, by the garbage bins."

"Have you notified the police?"

"No, they'd lock him up."

"Where he belongs."

"How can you say that? I wouldn't want to make such a decision, even if it were my job to make them, which it isn't, nor is it yours."

Kristie put her fork down. It clattered briefly against her plate. Her face looked stiff. "Everyone is responsible. Someone has to report degenerates. Why must they do it as a victim?"

"There's no reason to think this harmless old bastard's a degenerate. In fact—"

"Where does he spend the night?"

"Where does anyone? Why jump to the conclusion he's a sex maniac? There's better reason to think he might be a saint."

"A saint digging in garbage cans?"

"One man's garbage is another man's dinner. And I think the less one has to do with this can of worms we've made of ourselves, the better chance he has of pleasing heaven. Which would put that old man high on the list."

He smiled, but Kristie couldn't return it. She swallowed several times with difficulty, and her face seemed suddenly worn, as if it were being eroded from within by the trouble in her mind. A waiter passed carrying two wet, green salads, his virile face firm with purpose, the white surfaces of his starched jacket bright as armor.

"Do you know," Kristie asked, "do you have any conception of what it might be like to lay alone in the dark and think about something like that sneaking in the night, wondering if it's just outside your window waiting for you to go to sleep?"

Kristie's words sketched for Grove a vivid picture of her curled in bed, frightened and lonely. His face grew hot, and at the same time a warm tenderness worked at his throat. "Kristie, don't worry about this. I'm sorry I told you. If I hadn't, you wouldn't even be aware of him. Can you pretend I made it up to interest you? If you go on building it up in your mind, you could hurt a harmless old man."

"I don't know where you get the right to regard anyone that strange, that far from the norm, as harmless. It's far more reasonable to assume he's harmful and let people who know decide. Or are you more concerned for him than you are for me? Even if you are, can you honestly say this creature of yours wouldn't be better off in an institution?"

Grove sighed, looked in Kristie's frightened gray eyes, where she was making her true plea, and surrendered. "Call the police if it really bothers you. Anyone who conceives of us as the bad dream of God can probably find some way to tolerate the comparatively mild fantasies of the fuzz."

After dinner they went to a bar that was drenched in tropical atmosphere. Their table was thick plastic, with the ocean encased within it, with tiny rubber starfish and Celluloid seahorses. A slumbering hulk was set in a mound of sand and rigged with stiff white thread. Living fish wove their colorful patterns in a thirty-foot aquarium behind the bar. It was Kathleen, in a brief sarong, who came to take their order.

"You two slumming?" she asked with a smile.

Grove stared briefly at her legs. "We came in on the copra boat. We're missionaries."

Kathleen indicated a small stage. "The natives will be on in a few minutes, but from the way they go at it, you missionaries have your work cut out for you."

"Natives?" Grove asked.

"Tahitian dancers. They're pretty wild."

They ordered, and Kathleen moved away through the tables, her white legs flashing in the blue light. "I didn't know she worked here," Grove said.

"You sure?" Kristie asked tartly.

"I wanted to go to Hollywood—remember?"

"I can't imagine someone wearing something like that to work in."

"She looks pretty good in it."

"She looks cheap."

"I don't suppose she has much choice—with two kids."

Kristie shook her head. "Everyone has a choice. I'm tired of hearing that excuse. People become what they choose to become. Kathleen may persuade herself she can make more money here, but basically she likes running around half-dressed."

Grove tapped the table top. "I'd rather watch her than these plastic fish."

"That was obvious."

"Kristie, we don't know each other well enough to begin this sort of quarrel."

"You're out with me."

"And glad of it."

Kathleen brought their drinks and began a mild joke—"Me Kathleen. Me good girl."—but broke it off when she sensed their tension. She refused Grove's tip and left quickly.

Kristie sipped her drink, a mai-tai. "I can't handle many of these."

"What are you trying to tell me?"

"That I won't drink many."

The lights dimmed, and a spot came on to pick out the stage. A blind Hawaiian, his sightless eyes sheltered behind large, round sunglasses, was led to the microphone. Costumed in an aloha shirt and ice-cream pants, with his bush of thick white hair tinted violet in the lights, he sang with a high desolate throb in his voice, as if the sugary island songs might really mean something to him, as if he could cut through all the encrusted layers of commercial Hawaii to the heartland of his birth and see it all unchanged in the vision of his blindness. He sang for fifteen minutes.

Grove was moved and he saw that Kristie was, too. Their glasses were empty. He signaled for refills, and another girl answered the call. She took his tip and glanced at it as if he'd handed her a wet rock.

When the singer finished, the lights lowered still further, almost to darkness, the main illumination coming now from the small bulbs set in the corners of the aquarium, where the tropical fish continued their unceasing and mindless ballet.

A deep gong sounded, filling the air with a metallic shimmer. A brown man, carrying a torch and wearing only a blue *lava-lava,* vaulted to the stage and lit, knees bent, then strained up on his toes until his feet formed tense arches. He scowled and suddenly thrust his pelvis at the audience. It was delivered with great vigor and punctuated with deep, hollow drumbeat, heard less with the ear than with the pit of the stomach, and with it Grove was sure he heard Kristie gasp. He looked at her closely. The drum was continuing, taking that first beat as the beginning of its pattern, and now the Tahitian was beginning to dance, pelvis still pounding in the rhythm of love, but hammering with an intensity that, were it really love, Grove imagined it would prove unbearable. Kristie's lips were parted, her eyes shining, and Grove experienced a moment of intense envy for the absolute male authority of the native's hips. And probably he wasn't even a native. Probably he drove a red T-Bird, wore white tennis shoes, belonged to a hospital plan, and at two o'clock, when the bars closed, he reaped some of the harvest he was sowing now.

Two girls joined the man on the stage, their hips pumping as fiercely as his, their small, hard breasts rising and falling against the red cloth of their sarongs; their faces expressed only the electric tensions of their bodies. There wasn't a shred of coyness or fake seductiveness. The man raped the empty air with greedy possession, and the girls matched stroke for stroke, rising to meet their phantom lovers.

When they finished, Kristie said, "Well!" She had finished her second mai-tai. With a degree of calculation, Grove ordered another. She looked at it, smiled, and said, "I don't dare." But as the Tahitians made their finale, with whirling torches and leaping brown bodies, she began to drink it.

When the stage cleared for intermission, Grove said, "I wonder what those girls are really like."

Kristie stared down into the table top at the miniature wreck and said slowly, "It's so—animal. They were like small brown animals—in heat."

"And the man?"

"Oh"—she put her hands up and touched her cheekbones with the tips of her fingers, looking somewhere above Grove's shoulder—"I don't know exactly."

"He was a noble savage?" Grove asked, smiling.

"He was very handsome." Her eyes met his briefly. "And it's a man's dance. The hula seems more a woman's dance—soft, rounded, graceful."

He caught sparks from her eyes. His legs tingled with it and he reached for her hand, but she drew it away and in the same motion glanced at her watch. "I must go home," she said quickly.

He looked at his own watch. It was a few minutes after ten. "This early?" he asked, not bothering to conceal his disappointment, and his suspicion of her earlier concern for the time came back on him.

"I have to get up bright and early. Accent on bright. I have an appointment to be interviewed for a new job. I'm sorry."

"Ten o'clock?"

"Well, I've things to do. I have to set my hair."

"It looks lovely."

"It won't after I've slept on it for eight hours." She touched his wrist lightly. "Grove, I do have to get home."

"All right. Want a nightcap?"

"God, no. My head's spinning now."

On the way out, they passed Kathleen. "You guys leaving already?" she asked.

"Yes," Grove said, "I'm afraid we have to."

He felt Kristie take his arm. She leaned against him as she said, "You have a nice place here, Kathleen."

Kathleen's expression sharpened, but she answered agreeably, "I don't own it, Kristie. I just work here. What did you think of the natives?" she asked Grove.

"They were wild."

During the short drive home Kristie leaned, legs crossed, into the narrow corner of the Volkswagen seat, and whenever Grove shifted his foot to brake, their knees touched briefly. It seemed to him that a vivid current flickered across these encounters like the meeting of two charged wires. Kristie swung a slender foot and hummed one of the songs the Hawaiian had sung, singing the last few phrases herself in a light, true voice, her eyes idling over the homely neighborhood faces of the streets they were passing along. She pointed at a corner bakery and murmured, "They make wonderful jelly donuts."

Too soon they were behind the court. He let the car drift to a stop and cut the motor. In the sudden silence he thought he could hear her breathing, a light, even stirring of the air that, as the moment lengthened, seemed to quicken. He put his hand on her hair. It was cool and soft, and her head fell toward him like a flower before the wind. It was all the encouragement he needed. Despite the awkward confinement of the small car, he gathered her into his arms so that she came to him half-lying across his chest, her legs folding upon the seat. Their mouths met, and her lips seemed to swell. Below his thickening senses he experienced a reflex of amazement. He wondered if during all these weeks of hungry watching, all he had ever had to do was simply reach for her?

In five minutes her dress was rucked up above her underwear. She offered nothing, but whatever he did, she allowed, and now his hand, wrist strained, was cupped over the warm center of her. But his legs were going to sleep, the circulation cut off by her weight, and the knob of the gearshift was boring against his thigh.

"This is the wrong place," he said.

"Mmmmm."

"Let's go inside."

She remained silent, her open mouth quiet against his cheek.

"Come on."

He got her out of the car and pulled her toward the court. She didn't resist—she was heavy and slow, as if dazed. But when he started toward his apartment, she set her feet and with a sudden reverse was leading him toward her door. All right, he thought with the same practical sense of campaign that had caused him to continue ordering drinks. She probably had things in her apartment she would need to use. He didn't dwell on what these things would be, anymore than a music lover dwells on the resin, catgut, and calluses of a violinist. And he wasn't deceiving himself about his campaign. He had approached it with all the craft of a Boy Scout planning an overnight hike—he wasn't getting anything she didn't intend for him to have.

And he found that she intended him to have a great deal less than he expected. At her door she straightened and gave him a look that was kindly, tender, and sober. "Thank you for a lovely evening."

"What?" Her intent was clear, and a throb of anguish hit him where his legs joined. "Kristie, you can't do this, it's not—" He was going to say "fair," but it seemed so childish he bit if off. "It's not adult."

"I told you before you started anything that I had some things to do, didn't I?" She reached out—he was sure it was to pat his cheek—and he grabbed her wrist and pulled her back into his arms. She hung passively, accepting his kiss, and when he lifted his mouth, she said, "There's tomorrow."

He gulped, furious in his disappointment and frustration. He sensed that if he had her inside, he could take her, that she wouldn't or couldn't resist him. He released her, watching her take the door key from her purse. When she opened the door, he intended to step in behind her, but again she frustrated him. "Grove, I'm sorry," she said with obvious sincerity. "I want to ask you in, but you'll have to believe me when I say I just can't." She pecked him swiftly on the mouth. "Now, good night. I'll see you tomorrow—at my party, if not before."

Her door closed and seemed to quiver in the frame with a bland rejection. "Jesus," he swore softly. He turned her bell, but it clicked like a child's broken cricket.

He walked over to his own apartment and checked Kristie's number in the phone book. He dialed and listened as her phone rang once, twice, three times. Then the connection opened, and he heard her breathing, but she didn't say anything.

"Hello? Kristie?"

"Who is this?"

"It's Grove. I just wanted—"

"Goddam you! Don't you ever phone me at night."

Her receiver slammed down, and Grove cradled his own phone, rubbing his ear as if he'd been slapped. It was a moment before he remembered the anonymous calls she had been receiving and he attached her reaction to that cause. He smiled with relief.

Knowing he couldn't sleep and reluctant to stare at the dull face of his own apartment, he went for a walk along the quiet back streets. When he returned, he passed along the alley where they parked and paused to lean against the fence that marked off the neighboring dairy. The dairy remained floodlit throughout the night, and the cows, tricked by the light, didn't have sense enough to go to sleep, but continued eating. Light, eat: dark, sleep. Their ancient rhythms were now perverted in the name of increased milk production. But one thing had always lived on another, and if the only difference was the degree of sophistication, it wasn't worth his pensive indignation. The words of an old song came to him: "Money, money, you got lots of friends..."

He wondered where the Scavenger was holed up. Or was he, as Kristie so vividly assumed, prowling? Or had he, a bargain Judas, sold a holy man to a woman's anxiety?

A heavy black car glided down the alley, washed Grove with its headlights, and stopped soundlessly a few feet past him. A large man stepped out, glanced briefly at Grove, and started into the court. A quick suspicion shook Grove with the strength of intuition. He recalled the face as it had been briefly lit in the dairy's floodlights—an old man's face, but still as rough and hard-looking as Carborundum.

Swiftly Grove entered the court through an open garage. He was in time to see Kristie's door closing, and he knew it was the General he had seen. She had late-dated him. He shook with anger and humiliation, but, worse, he was sickened, as if at some grotesque perversion, to think of that hardened old pirate plundering the sweet treasure he had found.

Someone walked by him, and he looked up to recognize the book salesman who had worked the court a few days before. Ah, Grove thought with savage humor, all of Kristie's ugly birds are coming to roost—at the same time. But the book salesman passed Kristie's door and started up the walk to Mr. Howe's apartment.

JD...

...was surprised to see Arnold Courtney smile. His expectations had been less than clear, but he could have never pictured this childish and genial face. Was it just that? The old man was too childish to know exactly what he had done. Or was JD himself dead wrong?

"Good evening, sir," Arnold Courtney said, looking around to see if JD had brought anything with him. "This is a pleasure—"

JD stepped inside and closed the door behind him. Except for a green eye-shade, the old man appeared the same. His apartment was unchanged. A light was on in another room, probably the kitchen, and the boats still sailed their awkward courses along the walls.

"I don't know if it's going to be much of a pleasure," JD said.

"You haven't brought the books?"

"This is what I brought." JD took the fictitious check from his pocket and held it up.

Arnold Courtney stared at it, blinking uncertainly. "There must be some mistake," he said.

"Yes, and I'm afraid you made it. This is worthless."

"I certainly don't understand how a thing like this could have happened"—Arnold Courtney reached for the check—"but I'll be happy to make it good." His fingers closed on air as JD flicked the check away and returned it to his pocket.

JD put more edge to his voice. "You'll make it good and you'll do better than that. This isn't the first piece of bogus paper you've laid. You've probably got this town plastered with it, as free as you put it out, and more."

JD glanced at the table, where he had thought something might be hidden the first time he was in this room. The table was bare now.

"You've got more stashed or I'm no guesser. You've got plates too. You print these, don't you?"

Arnold Courtney had been slowly shaking his head, more in dismay than from any spirit of conviction. His eyes appeared to have shriveled. "You're mistaken, sir, very mistaken. It's difficult to imagine that"—he paused, mouth still open, eyelids fluttering with uncertainty—"that an old friend would do such a thing to me. What are you going to do? I'd like to protect—this old friend."

JD was certain now. Arnold Courtney couldn't remember the name on the face of the check. "Don't try to con me, old man. I've been conned by experts. I don't want to turn you in to the police, but that's what I'll do unless you give me five hundred dollars. Here, right now. Tonight. And that's the way it has to be."

Arnold Courtney shuffled a half step in retreat. "But I don't have that kind of money. Where would I get that kind of money?"

JD forced himself to snarl. "That's not my problem. That's *your* problem."

"But I don't have any money. Can't you accept that? I just can't—" He broke off and stood silent, his face wavering with despair. Then he began to call, "Hugo! *Hugo!*"

JD instantly recognized the balding head and the hard green eyes as Hugo Haas stepped out of the kitchen, and in the same instant he realized what it was he had sensed in this man—the smell of thief. Here was his thief, not the old man. JD squared himself, senses tingling with disaster.

"You goddam tramp," Haas said, advancing as smoothly as a short, thick cat. "You think you look pretty good leaning on an old man? You think you're some hardrock? Give me that check and get out of here before I tear your head off."

Hugo stopped three feet from JD, rocking easily on the balls of his feet. Arnold Courtney had shrunk to the side, his face half covered with his yellowed hands, his eyes shifting back and forth between JD and Hugo as if he couldn't decide which of them frightened him the most.

JD took a half-step back and, reaching behind himself, took hold of the doorknob. It felt icy against the heat of his hand. "You don't scare me, Tiger," he said slowly, "and you can't take me. You might mark me, even shake me some, but I'll be the one who walks, and when I walk, I'll call cops. I've got you, and you know it. You'd better get off the five bills and save yourself some jail. If you don't know already, that can be a cold way to live. Now, make your selection."

Haas looked JD over, measuring his size. "I could fix you so you wouldn't walk away from here."

"Get started, then."

Haas stood for a moment, hands opening and closing at his sides, while he seemed to lean toward JD as if restrained by an invisible leash. Then he settled back and looked at the floor. "Much pleasure as I'd take in it, it wouldn't cure nothing." He feel silent again and then, after a moment, asked in reasonable tones, "Five hundred this week, five hundred next week, and five hundred every week from now on?"

"No, this ain't my game. I'm just looking for a stake. That's all. I'm drove to my knees and need a stake. One time around and we're quits."

"Maybe you'd better give him the money," Arnold Courtney said.

"You shut up!" Haas turned back to JD. "Give me the check. I'll go get the money."

"Don't try to play with me. Just get the money."

"All right, all right, but I don't have that much on me. I'll have to go over to my place and get it."

JD nodded and cautiously circled away from the door, taking care to face Haas and keep the same distance between them. He stopped where he could reach the phone. Then his stomach sagged as he realized he'd trapped himself inside the apartment. He should have stepped outside. But Haas had apparently given up and he contented himself with a gesture as feeble as slamming the door.

JD took a deep breath and blew it out in a slow, fat whistle. He felt his pocket to assure himself the check was still there, although he didn't know what he thought could possibly have happened to it. He turned to Arnold Courtney. "What'd you have to give me that phony check for?" He was ashamed of what he was doing and angry with the old man for having made it possible.

Arnold Courtney gestured vaguely. "He never lets me have enough of the money. He gives me an allowance as if I were a child, and where would he be if I didn't do the printing for him? Working with his back. Working with his back like the animal he is. A fine craftsman, an artist, doing the filthy chores of an animal like that because my little girl says she loves him, and because—because I'm old."

Arnold Courtney went to sit on the sofa. He put his face in his hands. JD was sure he was beginning to cry and he was surprised at the intense shame the old man's tears caused him. I got to live, he told himself fiercely. Jesus, ain't I got a right to live? What about the hundreds of people this old fool has helped rob? JD asked this of himself righteously, invoking an imaginary crowd of widows and orphans, each holding one of the worthless checks. But the picture collapsed from the weight of its own unlikeliness to be replaced by row on row of insurance clerks in neat gray suits, noting the checks and adjusting actuarial tables to compensate for them.

I got to live, JD thought dully. Arnold Courtney's sobs were now audible.

Haas came back briskly. He'd put on a jacket and as he closed the door he dipped in the pocket and came out with a .32 revolver. He aimed for the middle of JD's chest.

"Give me that check."

JD didn't move. He couldn't. He stared at the bright silver eye and thought that twenty years had gone full circle, from one gun to another. This time he was in front of it. In a moment he found his voice.

"Go ahead," he said thickly. His tongue seemed to have swollen to twice its normal size. "Go ahead. I don't give a damn. I got nowhere to go and no way to get there. Shoot. Do me a favor. I'm spread so thin I don't give a damn."

He fell silent, watching Haas with something akin to patience. Slowly it came to him that Haas wasn't going to fire. Then the immensity of his relief tore his lips into the shape of a smile. "I would make one big pile of cold meat, wouldn't I? And the old man here—he'd never hold his mud if anyone came around leaning on him."

Haas nodded slowly and put the gun away. He brought out a wad of bills and threw them at JD's feet. "Give me the check. I'm tired of looking at you. But don't you *ever* come back looking for more. I'll use this on you no matter what happens to me."

JD picked up the money. He stopped counting when he passed two hundred with over half the bills still left. "You've seen the last of me. I don't like this any better than you do."

"Just get out."

JD pocketed the money and laid the check on the phone table. He waited until Hugo moved away from the door into the center of the room, still moving warily like one large animal skirting another. JD stepped to the door and threw it open. He paused to say, "Why don't you take it easy on the old man?"

Haas stared at him until he shrugged and closed the door. He stood for a moment on the porch listening—he didn't know what for. He stared hungrily at Kristie's windows. Only one soft light was glowing. He rubbed his jaw, feeling the sharp drag of his heavy beard. I'm crummy, he thought. But he wouldn't be crummy tomorrow. He had another thought and he sorted through the bills until he found five dollars to give to Doc. It wouldn't be smart to let Doc know just how heavy he'd hit.

He started down the walk, his eyes fixed on the single lighted window in Kristie's apartment. That would have to be her bedroom. He tried to imagine her in there, and he could see her most clearly, lying in bed reading. After a while the print would begin to blur, and she would drop the book, close the light, and turn to sleep.

KRISTIE

...lay rigid on her back, her legs held straight and tense, her small hands made into fists. The glow of the mai-tais had faded, and the unexpected pleasure she had found in Grove was gone. Now she waited in her best night-gown for the wrong man. She opened her eyes to watch Irving loosen his tie and hang it neatly over the back of a chair. He sat down to remove his shoes. For the first time she noticed that he wore high-tops, an old man's shoe of wrinkled black leather. Aware of her eyes, Irving smiled ruefully and slapped the shoe with his palm.

"I have to wear these. I broke both ankles when we jumped into Nor-mandy. Fool stunt. It finished me as a line officer. I went staff then." He held up one shoe and looked at it distastefully. "Frequently the aftermath of a man's heroism is neither very heroic nor very manly."

He stood up, removed his shirt, and loosened his pants. He was wearing some type of support underwear, and his heavy belly rolled beneath it. Why doesn't he turn out the light? Kristie wondered, but she thought she under-stood that his pride wouldn't allow it. She turned her head to the side so she wouldn't have to look. She wasn't so disturbed now that she could think of this man, not young man even then, stepping out into the empty darkness a mile above France. Surely that one positive act, out of so many in the years when he and men like him had saved the nation, entitled him to any woman he wanted—Kristie smiled here—in perpetuity.

She felt his hand on her bare arm, and her eyes flew to the window to make certain the shade was secure. She saw four inches of dark glass beneath the end of the blind and she was about to ask Irving to adjust it when something seemed to come into focus out there in the darkness.

She cried out, pointing rigidly at the window where the vague conforma-tion of a face, the eyes glinting in deep shadow, stared back at her. "Some-one's out there."

Irving stepped quickly to the window, unlatched it, and threw it open to lean out and crane his head both ways. He turned back to Kristie. "I don't see anything."

"There was someone there!"

"What's out here?" Irving indicated the area beyond the window.

"Nothing," Kristie said. "It's an areaway between this court and the next one. It's walled at both ends. No one's supposed to be out there."

Irving leaned out the window again. "Do you have a flashlight?"

"Yes, in the kitchen."

She was up in a flash of white legs and pale blue silk, her bare feet soundless on the wooden floor. When she returned with a small red plastic flashlight, Irving had his pants on and was lacing his shoes.

"I'll take a look around," he offered, and it was apparent he was going because he thought he should, because it was part of his role, not because he thought there was any real danger.

"Thank you," Kristie said.

He gestured toward the window. "This is the only way in?"

"Unless you climb one of the walls."

He nodded and started out the window, grunting softly as the sill dug into his body. Kristie watched him move off, stepping high to clear the weeds, the beam of the flashlight swaying in front of him like a radiant feeler. With a sudden apprehension she ran to check the night latch on her front door. It was secure. She walked slowly back to the bedroom, the floor cool to her feet, and stood for a moment in the doorway watching her reflection in the mirror above her vanity. She moved forward to meet the girl in the mirror and lifted her hand to touch the cool, silver cheek of this girl who would always be so much lovelier than she.

When Irving returned, she had to help him through the window. He was panting, and she waited impatiently until his breathing slowed.

"There's no one out there, but they could have easily gone over one of the walls or back through another window. There's a packing box shack. You don't remember when people lived in Hoovervilles, do you? During the Depression many of those who had lost their homes were forced to live in huts made from cardboard, scrap metal, and discarded crates. This is something like that, only even more primitive, and it's most likely some boy's clubhouse."

Kristie shook her head rapidly and told him about the old man Grove had described, and she told him of the phone calls, but she didn't elaborate on the calls, particularly not on the details that were so frighteningly accurate. She called them "awful" and left Irving to wonder what she meant.

And he looked at her with something that might have been amusement in his eyes. "You think this is all one and the same person?"

She threw out her hands. "What am I to think?"

"Kristie, there wasn't any telephone in that shack, and I suggest that this ragpicker your friend describes would hardly be likely to make calls from a pay phone. Your calls, no matter how distasteful, are most likely harmless. They could be from any crank, someone who calls any number of single women—possibly even from the other side of town."

Kristie's eyes flashed with an odd mixture of fear and exasperation. She couldn't tell Irving why she was certain the caller was someone close by, someone who spied on her, because she couldn't admit that the incidents she

heard reported back to her, strained through the diseased mind of her tor-
mentor, had really happened in any version. She lowered her head and began
to cry softly.

She felt Irving's hand on her shoulder. "Here, here," he murmured in a
hushed voice, seemingly dismayed at her tears. "I'll get someone on this.
We'll have this oddball picked up and your phone number changed. If you
have the new number unlisted, this can't happen again. All right?"

She nodded, trying to stop her tears. She laid her cheek against Irving's
hand, and through the mist of her eyes his big yellow diamond burned like a
miniature sun. She felt herself being drawn gently backward, down onto the
bed. She closed her eyes, and against the velvet shadow on her inner vision
the diamond dazzle grew and grew. She didn't have to dream. A General was
a General already.

Irving failed with her. After his big show of still hearty male vigor he had
proved to be feeble, a creeping old man. And when, as a substitute, he had attempted something she couldn't bear, she had been quick to let him see her
revulsion. Any gratitude and friendship he might have felt for her was burned
away in the fire of his humiliation. He stood briefly at the edge of the bed
looking down at her, a slumped, rounded old man, and she remembered
what he had said over lunch—desire fading away as if someone were shut-
ting off the gas and lights in a decaying house.

He left without another word, and she knew she had seen him for the last
time. The job, his help and sponsorship—all lost. How could she have been
so foolish? she asked herself bitterly. She should have known Irving was bluff-
ing and she despised her own generous impulse that had forced him to
expose himself. Once she had held her door open, he was bound in his pride
to make a show of entering, but if she had had sense enough to keep it
closed, Irving could have continued banging lustily for as long as the game
lasted, content with the form, since it obviously helped him forget that the
spirit was lost. Lost—how awful that must be for him.

But she could think no more of Irving. She had to realize she was in trouble and bring herself to a sense of urgency. But it was such nonsense when
she knew with deep conviction that wonderful things were waiting for her,
had always been waiting for her, and she had always known—even when she
stood in the dusty fields where her father pitched his tent with her head
thrown back to watch the airplanes crossing the sky, marveling as they
seemed to burn as they passed the sun, and staring after them until they
became tiny specks that blurred to nothing against the horizon. She dreamed
of the great capitals of the world to which she imagined these glittering
machines were bound, and came to love the airplanes for their promise of
escape from the dreary and humiliating life she knew as the daughter of a

traveling Evangelist, who was, she realized, though her love argued with her good sense, a small-time fraud. Soon after her eighteenth birthday she joined the WAF's and had worked near, even if only on paper, flying things ever since. She couldn't bear the thought of an ordinary job. It would be the end of the most magical part of her life.

She heard the phone. Listening intently, she let it ring four times before she rose and, walking like a dutiful child approaching a deserved punishment, went to answer it.

JD...

...drove back toward L.A. on an expanding glow of self-confidence. It seemed as if his old Ford was propelled as much by his renewed vigor as by its laboring motor. Now, he thought, now—it was clear his moment had started to arrive. The five hundred dollars stretched out in a plain of prosperity the end of which he couldn't see, or, as yet, imagine.

"Slow down."

"What?"

"I said slow down, you big asshole. You'll kill us both."

Doc was staring at him nervously, a fresh bottle harbored between his legs. JD lifted his foot from the accelerator and glanced at the speedometer to see the needle drift away from eighty miles per hour.

"I feel good," he said.

"You won't feel so good if you shake this shivering pile of tin to pieces. I want to live—at least until I drink up this Finski."

JD nodded to this, smiling broadly. "I got a few things I want to do myself," he said.

"You going hack to hustling books?"

"No chance."

"Anywhere someone needed something heavy lifted, they could use you."

"I don't know what I'm going to do except not get broke again. That'll do for a place to start."

"Well—" Doc consulted his bottle, the Port rushing in his throat like grape soda. "Brokeness draws at some. They're bound to find it at the end of everything they do, but maybe you ain't in that class. Twenty other guys could have gone down thirty miles of road chasing an outside chance and come back empty. You didn't. Maybe that means something. Least you can get cleaned up some so you don't look like Charcoal Bill just down from the hill. Maybe you can get some old hay bag to pick up your tabs."

JD smiled again. "More the other way around."

"I take it all back. I thought you had good sense."

He laughed out loud and began to maneuver toward the right lane so he would be in position to take the Fifth Street off-ramp. He eased from the Freeway, which was so featureless it could be anywhere, down a curving concrete chute into the cramped street with its strong sense of particular place, and started down Fifth past Broadway into the underbelly of the city.

"Back to the mission?" he asked Doc.

"You can't flop there. I'm flush. I'll rent a sack when I get around to it."

He didn't want to leave Doc—he thought of him as "good people"—but he had business to take care of now and he couldn't see Doc doing any of the things he had it in mind to do. He was impatient to begin. Still, nothing had taught him to make a break. In an institution breaks were made for you, whether you wanted them or not, by an isolated authority officially unaware of the friendships between prisoners. Transfers, cell moves, job changes, paroles—these were most often the levers that had engaged or disengaged JD's former affections; these were the marriages, the deaths, the business successes or failures of another society.

He drove idly, stitching through the dim streets of skid row, until Doc eased the hook. Doc rapped on the side window. "There's one of those chumps I hustle with." JD slowed, turned his head, and saw a man leaning against a building. He wore a khaki overcoat, sizes too large, and his appearance of apathy was relieved by an edge of curiosity.

"You want out?" JD asked Doc.

"Yeah. Might as well, since you ain't going to do no serious drinking."

JD pulled to the curb and stopped. "Well, Doc," he began, feeling awkward. "I don't know if I'll be back down here."

"You ain't gaited for it. That free State food didn't soften you up enough. But if you can't cut it and find yourself drifting back, I'll be around here somewhere."

"Okay, Doc."

"Take it easy."

JD drove off, feeling cheap. He'd given Doc such a small taste of the grab he'd made, and Doc had marked it so high that it made JD ashamed of his caution and calculation. Some things he knew well, and many others he could only guess at. Doc really was good people.

He stopped again at the Imperial Hotel, and the desk clerk, apparently sensing that something was different, put down his puzzle, rose, and stood warily behind the counter.

"How much I owe you?"

"You going to pay?"

"Why would I be asking?"

The clerk's face was wooden, but something behind his eyes was busy. He turned and took a slip from a pigeonhole—it wasn't a formal bill, just a scrap of paper with some figure on it. He glanced at it and said, "Thirty dollars. That's two weeks' rent."

JD reached for his pocket.

The clerk continued with a hard alertness. "Fifteen a week and five dollars extra charges."

JD had separated fifty dollars from his stake before he entered the hotel and held this now in his hand. "What extra charges?"

"Cleaning your stuff out of your room and storing it."

"Uh-huh." JD counted out thirty dollars and slid it across the counter. "I didn't ask you to do none of that other."

"We have rules here."

"They got rules everywhere. You could of trusted me. I told you I'd pay you. Now you say I got to pay you more for not trusting me."

The clerk stared up at him, and his expression grew openly mean. "Some fuzz was around here a few days ago. They wanted to talk to you."

"What about?" JD managed to keep his voice firm.

"They didn't say. They don't. But I'm supposed to let them know if you show up."

JD dropped another five dollars on the counter. "Give me my stuff."

The clerk looked at the remaining bills in JD's hand. "There's also a ten-dollar cleaning charge. That room was a mess."

"That room was twice as clean as when I moved into it." He reached out quickly and grabbed the bills he had already placed in front of the clerk. "Don't outsmart yourself. I know what the police want, and it's nothing, but if I have to sit in their jail answering questions, you can sue me for what I owe you."

"You can't stand many questions, farm boy. A couple of hours ago you're in here dirty and broke, looking for a real wrong number, and now you're back waving a handful of loot. This is the wrong time of day to go out broke and come back flush. The banks are closed."

"You're a bad guesser. I'll pay five to avoid a roust. You want it?"

The clerk tried staring at him for a while longer, then nodded stiffly and held out his hand. "Get my stuff first," JD said.

He followed the clerk into a back hall and watched him unlock the door to a storage room. His gear was dumped into a cardboard box with his name grease-penciled on the side. JD picked the box up and handed the clerk the money.

"I was going to go on staying here until you got cute."

"Who needs you? There are a hundred like you through here every month—without the fuzz following them around."

JD drove to another hotel, a better hotel where the desk clerk wore a coat and a necktie and stared vaguely at his cardboard box and unshaven face until he offered to pay a week in advance. The register was turned quickly for his signature.

He had asked for a room with a bath and as soon as the door closed behind the bellhop he threw his box on the bed and began to strip. With hot water pouring over him, his nostrils full of the fresh, neutral odor of hotel soap and his feet feeling as if he had just pulled them free from a pair of iron boots, JD's joy spurted to a new peak.

The next day he bought a suit, paying extra to have the alterations rushed through in a few hours, and the salesman began to press other things on him: new shoes, shorts, socks, handkerchiefs, shirts. The salesman asked; "French cuffs, sir?" And of course he wanted them, since he wasn't going to ask what they were. He left the store with twice what he had planned to buy. He spent an hour and a half in a barber shop and after that he went looking for a set of encyclopedias. The irony wasn't lost on him, but his smile was becoming grim by the time two companies had refused him. Eager as they were—a shark's joy was in their blunted eyes—to take his deposit, his demand for immediate delivery and his transient address put them off. It was late afternoon before he located a set in a secondhand bookstore priced at a figure he felt he could pay.

"Nice?" the proprietor said hopefully behind him.

"They're old."

"But well cared for. See?" He had a volume out and open on his hand.

"Probably not used."

"So? It is the same thing. You will use them."

"No, I want them as a gift."

"Excellent. How could you do better?"

The price, $75, was printed in black marking ink on a small tent of cardboard that sat on top of the heavy books. "I'll give you fifty dollars," JD said.

"And I will take sixty."

JD smiled and ran his hand over the face of the books. "I used to sell these damn things myself. I know what they're really worth."

"Sixty is a fair price."

"It's near enough. Can you put them in a box?"

"Naturally."

While he waited JD found time to wonder why he would let the cool, disdainful voice of a clothing salesman goad him into buying more than he had wanted and then turn right around and con this courteous old man out of fifteen dollars.

He had dinner, the best dinner in a cheap restaurant, and then walked back to his hotel to shower and change into his new clothes. He found he hadn't wanted French cuffs. His lingering irritation at the salesman grew stronger. He looked at the cuffs hanging over his hands and wondered why the hell he couldn't have asked just what it was he was paying for. He folded the cuffs back and determined that they were made to be fastened with a separate fitting that it was probably too late to buy. His old shirts were all dirty. After some thought he went down to the desk and asked for a couple of paper clips. The desk clerk started to look vague again, and something in his expression reminded JD of the clothing salesman.

"I use them to dig the wax out of my ears," he said heavily.

"Certainly, sir."

It was after nine before, dressed in his new suit, his cuffs paper-clipped together and the encyclopedias loaded on the back seat, he was once again on the Freeway headed toward Bellflower. He felt as if he were wearing a disguise.

GROVE...

...was one of the first to arrive at Kristie's party. He had spent the day telling himself he wasn't going, that this fly was sharp enough to stay out of Venus's flytrap, no matter how sweet the smell of the soft, deadly petals, but by evening he assured himself he was misreading Kristie through the myopia of his own pride. He had asked her to dinner, she had gone to dinner. Certainly she saw this general as a necessity, nothing more, a harsh necessity, and that she should be put to such a shift melted his resolve with an acid pity.

Kathleen, slender in a simple white dress, let him in, but he passed quickly from her friendly smile to the dim orange light. The living room was lit entirely by candles, some in holders, some sealed to saucers.

"Atmosphere?" he said quizzically.

She was quick to read his tone. "I think it's nice."

"Yes." He was going to say that it seemed a little corny, but something odd in Kathleen's face stopped him. She looked very nice. Yes, nice. He realized he had seldom seen her with her face made up. "How are you tonight?" he asked.

"Fine."

Low dance music was coming from a small portable phonograph, a trombone choir playing a long, sweet, almost delayed line while a tight Latin beat built slow fire beneath it, and the record, dead to its own message, turned slowly like a disc of frozen oil. The candles licked gently at the walls, stirring the shadows over a trio of paintings: a matched set of Mexican pastorals. Grove had once painted such pictures. They were mass-produced, factory style. He had been a cactus man—stroke, stroke, round and stroke with a large flat and a small sable in darker green to dash on the spikes. It was dull and hungry work, and he was disappointed to see the products of it on Kristie's wall, but the furniture was in keeping: stained wood covered in a heavy blue fabric, woven with strands of metallic silver like a plaster figurine flocked with glitter.

"Where's Kristie?"

"Dressing. We've been getting ready all afternoon." She trailed her hand over the bowls of dip and plates of party treats: white onions and red-eyed olives impaled on multi-colored toothpicks, small triangular sandwiches and plates of chips and crackers. "How about a drink?" she asked.

"You bet." He handed over a bottle of Scotch he'd bought that afternoon in the shopping center.

"She should have enough unless this is a very thirsty party. She bought what seemed like gallons."

"From my limited experience there is never enough." He followed Kathleen into the kitchen, wondering how Kristie could afford to supply all the liquor. There were three more candles in the kitchen, and a tall young man in his late twenties was standing stiffly against the drainboard. Kathleen introduced him as Mr. Sirclum.

"Mel," he said, sticking out a large smooth hand. "Haven't I heard your name somewhere?"

"Maybe. I draw cartoons."

"That's it. You draw those poor-slob cartoons."

"He's very good," Kathleen said. "You want this?" She still held the Scotch. "With water."

Sirclum was looking at Grove with polite curiosity. "I always thought I'd like one of those off-beat jobs."

He smiled. "Charter boat captain, professional tennis player, cartoonist, you know?"

"The disadvantages eat up the advantages, and you end up about like everyone else, speaking as a cartoonist, that is." Kathleen brought him his drink, and he thanked her. "Mailman's holiday," he said. "I should make your drinks so you'll be sure you're not working."

"I'm sure I'm not working when no one's trying to pinch my butt."

Both men smiled, Sirclum a little owlishly. Grove said, "You looked good in that sarong."

"I've been told that."

"I guess you have."

"I wait cocktails," Kathleen explained to Sirclum. "In a little more than my underwear."

"Is there any other way?" Sirclum asked.

Kathleen raised her drink to her lips, and Grove's eye was caught by a bit of adhesive tape she had used to anchor her bra strap so it wouldn't slip below the narrow shoulder of her dress. This homely detail seemed to bring her into focus.

Kristie made an entrance. She was dressed casually in black-and-white checked slacks, and a black sweater, which made her hair glow vividly. An authentic beauty, Grove thought, and he followed her face.

"Grove," she said with a merely pleasant smile. "And Mel!" The smile increased. "I'm glad you could come."

"You couldn't have kept me away," Sirclum said, catching one of her hands. They fell automatically into company talk, Kristie listening eagerly. Like a young girl, Grove thought, listening to a description of some glamorous life she aspired to. He understood and resented Kristie's passion for airplanes.

He turned to Kathleen and found her studying him. "Say something," he said rudely.

Kathleen frowned and walked into the living room. Grove tried unsuccessfully to enter the conversation and make it general. But Kristie immediately returned to the industry. She was questioning Sirclum in detail about a company in Pasadena.

After listening awhile, Grove followed Kathleen into the living room. He found her sitting on the couch, eating a sandwich and swinging her foot in time to the music.

"Those any good?" he asked.

"Try one."

He picked up a sandwich and bit into it, but he wasn't aware of the taste. Kristie was laughing in the kitchen.

"Look," Kathleen said, "it's none of my business—" She broke off and leaned forward to take a cigarette from a ceramic dish on the coffee table. "It's none of my business," she ended firmly.

He held his lighter for her. "Miss Fix-it?"

"I have that tendency. You seem like such a nice person."

"Don't embalm me in that word. There's part of me that yearns to jump out of trees and slither up the drainpipes of girls' seminaries to ravish entire dormitories."

"Fiddlesticks," she said with a sensible flick of her head. "Why should you go to all that trouble?"

"Why did Michelangelo go to all the trouble to paint the ceiling of the Sistine Chapel? It's the expression of an art form."

She looked at him steadily for a moment, then smiled. "And you're full of it."

Kristie and Sirclum came out of the kitchen, and Kristie began to try to play hostess. She set the needle of her phonograph back to the beginning of the record. "I love this," she said, and now Grove recognized the orchestra as Henry Mancini's. She saw that everyone had fresh drinks, and they settled down to talk about recent movies, but Grove was aware of a growing strain. It centered in Kristie, and they were catching it from her. Her animation grew increasingly forced, and she glanced repeatedly at the door, then at her wristwatch.

Her concern was obvious—she expected more people and as it grew later she was beginning to be afraid they weren't going to come. Grove wanted to tell her not to worry. Many thought it smart to come late. If you were early, you betrayed eagerness, and this was somehow a failing.

During his first trip to the bathroom he discovered why Kathleen had seemed defensive about the candles. The bathroom was also lit by candlelight, one on the flush tank and another on a small vanity, and Grove, impatient with the motif, flipped the light switch. There were no lights. That didn't make sense. For some reason his mind refused the obvious explanation, and then he remembered the music. Back in the living room he knelt by the phonograph pretending to be interested in the records, and he saw that it was battery-powered. He walked into the kitchen and drew a glass of water. While he drank it he tried the gas. It was off, too.

She had lights last night, he thought, so it had happened today, too late to cancel the party. But the pretense couldn't possibly succeed. He looked along the row of bottles she had provided. They represented enough money to satisfy several light bills. What was the matter with her? Why hadn't she said she was in trouble? Pride. The same reason she had tried to bluff her way through with the candles.

His thoughts were interrupted by a loud knock on the door, and he returned to the living room and saw Kristie answering it. Her smile faltered, then recovered, and it was a moment before Grove recognized the large man who had entered and was getting his hat off with one hand while he handed Kristie something with the other. It was the book salesman, but now turned out so smoothly that Grove jumped to the conclusion that his former appearance of farmerishness was a deliberate device he employed, a psychological selling aid. Again he marveled at the control some people were able to exercise over themselves.

"Why, this is wonderful," Kristie was saying. "The rest of the set's in my car. I'll bring them in."

"Yes, please do."

Kristie turned, sparkling with animation, to show them a large red book. Her eyes found Grove's. *See?* they seemed to say. "He's brought me the whole set," she confided to Sirclum. She handed him the single volume, and he studied it glumly.

"These are neither as complete or as accurate as they claim," Sirclum said.

Kristie was in no mood to hear anything negative. She frowned. "I'm very glad to have them."

The salesman came back carrying the books stacked on his arms and steadied with his chin like cordwood. Kristie helped him to line them along one wall. Grove thought of the massive authority and tradition mustered within the books and what a curious intrusion they made into this apartment.

When she came to introduce the salesman, he had to supply his name—JD Bing. Grove shook a hand as hard as mahogany and watched Sirclum stand to shake. The two men were about the same height, but Bing was twice as broad. Sirclum asked him how he made out selling the encyclopedias, and he said, "Lousy," in a deep baritone. He seemed at ease until Kristie asked him what he would like to drink. For a moment he looked confused; then he shrugged and said, "Whatever's handy." When she handed him a drink, he stared at it a moment, then sipped tentatively. His heavy white face puckered.

"Come sit down," Kristie told him, patting the couch beside her. Now she had Sirclum on one side, JD on the other.

The evening began to seem unreal to Grove: the candles burning bravely in the lightless apartment, the guests who were not coming, the big, quiet man with his expensive present, and all of them—Bing, Sirclum, and himself—enthralled by Kristie, who continued to stare at the door apparently hoping for the appearance of still another man, whose importance, if it could be measured in the clues of her hidden anxiety, made fools of them all.

Grove smiled bitterly and, in a conscious effort to get off the hook, turned to Kathleen, who was, when he came to think of it, the one element of sanity in the evening. "Would you like to try dancing?" he asked.

She smiled. "I've tried it."

"Why not risk it again?"

"All right."

Kathleen proved to be a much better dancer than he was, so good that it was a while before he even realized it. He shuffled one-two, one-two in a pleasant haze and was surprised to discover he was enjoying himself.

Gloria Haas appeared at the door. She wanted to borrow some black thread. "Your baby-sitter said you were here," she explained to Kathleen, looking eagerly around the room.

Kristie invited her to stay. "We have a lot to drink up," Kristie said in what Grove took for a gallant tone. Gloria fluttered like an overweight butterfly—she wasn't dressed, she looked a mess—but she allowed herself to be drawn in, and Grove made her a drink.

"A hairy one," he told her, "so you can catch up." He made drinks for everyone. JD took his and murmured a heavy-eyed "Thanks." For a moment Grove thought the man might be bored, as well he might be, but when he went to lift his glass, his hand wavered uncertainly.

Gloria was big but not fat. Her waist was exceptionally small, and her body soared out from this emphasis. Only her eyes were girlish, but they lit with an easy happiness. She exclaimed over the candles, "Kristie, you're so clever," then turned to Bing. "Don't you think Kristie's wonderful?"

JD nodded.

"Say, don't you sell something?" Gloria asked.

"Yeah, books."

"Oh! I remember you." She grinned. "You come around at the damnedest times."

"Eleven o'clock in the morning?"

"You sure look different."

"I combed my hair."

"You did more than that."

"Where's Hugo?" Kristie asked, an edge buried in her voice.

Gloria waved her hand as if to shoo her husband's name away. "Out somewhere. He's always out somewhere. Big, frosty deal."

"I imagine he has to work sometime," Kristie said sternly.

Gloria ignored this. For a while she sat quietly, sipping her drink, watching Grove and Kathleen dance. Every once in a while her eyes went to JD. Finally she asked, "You dance?"

"No, I never learned."

"It's easy."

"I wouldn't know how to start."

"Come on, I'll show you."

JD was less awkward than inert. He moved with a plodding slowness, and his eyes lingered on Kristie with a baffled determination. Gloria, unaware, was telling him, "Dancing with you makes me feel like a little girl."

Grove danced Kathleen into the kitchen and said, "I know why we've got candlelight."

"You're very clever."

"I'm wondering if I should try to do something."

"If you're thinking of helping Kristie," Kathleen said dryly, "you may have to stand in line."

"You say that, but if it were really true, would her lights and gas be off?"

"I know. It was a miserable thing to say."

"It was understandable."

"No, I don't mind Kristie's beauty. Or I haven't up to now."

Grove drew back. "Are you trying to tell me something?"

She released herself from his arms and turned to the drainboard Kristie was using for a bar. "Let's get lit. This party's a funeral. I can see confused and uncomfortable people any night of the week."

"What do you think of the big salesman?"

Kathleen shrugged. "He's joined Kristie's legions. But he's lucky—she's interested in him."

"How do you know?"

"By the way she looked at him, as if she were considering him for a role in one of her plays."

"I don't think I get that."

"I've known Kristie a lot longer than you have."

He was going to try to dig out what Kathleen wasn't saying, but at that moment Kristie screamed.

It was more a scream of outrage than of anguish, and right through it came a hoarse exclamation and the pounding thump of furniture hitting a wall. Grove ran toward the living room.

Two figures struggled in the center of the floor. The coffee table was over, sandwiches were mashed on the rug like scraps of dirty paper, and only two of the candles were still burning. As Grove tried to grasp what was happening one of these was knocked down. Until he saw Sirclum, he had the crazy idea it was JD and Sirclum fighting, but Sirclum was standing with his arms protective around Kristie, whose expression was furious with dismay. Then he saw the front door standing open, and as the two locked figures bucked and heaved against a wall he recognized Hugo Haas. His bald head shone briefly in the light of the remaining candle, then disappeared under the shadow of JD's arm.

This is crazy, Grove thought. Kristie was demanding that someone stop them before they ruined her apartment. Grove snatched the phonograph and put it in a safe place. Kristie was shouting, and Sirclum didn't move from behind her, so Grove reluctantly stepped in to try to break the two men apart. He got someone's arm and yelled, "Break it up! Break it up!" Gloria rushed out of the shadows to kick at Hugo and call him "Pig." Haas scissored her legs and sent her sprawling. Grove took a stunning blow to the throat from someone's elbow and sat back with both hands clutched to his windpipe, breathing in short labored gasps. When the fight moved toward him again, he scrambled out of the way. He couldn't help. But then he was aware that JD had mastered the situation and pinned Haas in some manner. JD, not even breathing hard, asked quietly, "You ready to quit this foolishness?"

Hugo swore at him. "You want that bitch, too? You want everything?"

"I don't want nothing you got. Now you going to be quiet if I let you go?"

Hugo didn't answer, and in the silence Kristie said, "Get out of here, Hugo Haas. Just get out."

"You're going to have to let me go sometime," Haas said to JD, "and when you do, I'm going to finish you.

"You talk like a fool," JD said. "I'll let you go if you'll behave yourself until we get outside. Then we can really get it on if that's what you want."

Again Haas didn't answer.

A beam of light spurted through the open front door, coursed the room, and homed on the two men locked together on the floor. JD had Hugo in a traverse pin, one arm scissored between his legs and the other held with both hands. Both stared blinking into the light.

"What's going on here?" someone asked behind the flash, and the voice carried an almost physical weight of authority.

"Police?" Kristie asked quickly.

"Yes." A short, heavyset man stepped into the room and asked in milder tones, "Will someone turn on the lights?" A younger man moved behind him.

No one answered for a moment, so Grove spoke up, "The lights are off. I mean, there is no electricity."

"Why is that?"

"I don't know."

"Nelson, will you get a couple of floods?"

"Yes, sir."

"I asked what's going on here."

The policeman was in civilian clothes, and appeared to be well into his middle years. When no one answered him, he unbuttoned his coat and moved the flash over JD and Haas as if he were stirring them with the beam. "Are you going to stand up? Come on—*up.*"

Slowly, mistrustfully, JD released Haas, and they both stood. Grove was reminded of the ominous reluctance with which large cats obeyed their trainer, appearing to yield only to the whip, the gun, and the unmistakable habit of command. And if they were large cats, JD was the lion humiliated in a paper ruff, for both his French cuffs had pulled loose and hung down over his hands like the floppy sleeves of a clown. His shirt was torn open, and his tie sagged in a forked tangle. Haas, in a knit shirt and sweater, seemed hardly mussed, though he was breathing hard with either exhaustion or fury.

The second policeman came running back with two floodlights, almost as large as headlights, mounted on square red battery cases. He set the lights on the floor and directed the beams at the ceiling, and the room was fully lit. Immediately Kathleen began to pick things up, but the older officer said, "Let that go a minute, will you, please? Are you Miss Olson?"

Kristie stepped forward. "No, I am."

He turned to appraise Kristie. Then he looked back to his partner and nodded at JD and Haas. "Nelson," he said, and Nelson squared himself to watch the two men.

"I'm Detective-Sergeant Strickland, Miss Olson. Perhaps you can tell me what's been going on here?"

"They were fighting."

"Yes, I got that. What about?"

"One of them was dancing with the other man's wife. What difference does it make? They've ruined my party, my furniture."

"You'll probably be able to make a claim for damages." He paused to study Kristie, pinching his lips vertically between his thumb and his knuckle. His paunch jutted frankly. "You're the same Miss Olson who reported the anonymous telephone calls a few weeks back, and today a peeping tom, and now tonight, this?"

"Yes." Kristie still appeared angry. "What are you suggesting?"

"Nothing. We learn to look for patterns."

He turned back to JD and Haas to ask, "Whose wife?"

"Mine," Haas volunteered quickly. "I was out—taking care of some business. When I came back, she wasn't home. So I started to look for her. We live right next door. I heard music in here, so I glanced in the window, and she's in this—" He bit off a word and jerked his thumb at JD. "In his arms with all that lousy candlelight. He was loving her up. So I got hot and came through the door."

Strickland asked, "You look in windows much?"

"Hell, no. She comes over here sometimes."

"Which one of these women is your wife?"

Gloria was up, standing to favor one ankle. Her eyes were no longer girlish. Haas indicated her with his head.

"Is this true?" Strickland asked her.

She nodded.

"She was only teaching me to dance. All of a sudden this clown comes busting through the door. I was trying to hold him until he cooled off, but he wasn't all that easy to handle, and I'm afraid we messed things up some." He directed this last at Kristie, but her face didn't soften.

Strickland turned slowly, taking in the entire room, his eyes resting briefly on each face in turn. "If this is a neighborhood brawl," he observed dryly, "it's a strange one, or"—he looked at Haas—"you're a great deal more jealous than most men. Unless this has been going on for a while."

JD said, "I just met her tonight."

Strickland appeared to consider this as he took a small black notebook and a yellow plastic mechanical pencil from his coat pocket. "I'll have to ask you for your names and addresses."

After they had each complied he continued, "I'm not going to run anyone in because none of you seems that drunk, but another time it will be different. Now I have to talk to you, Miss Olson. That was my original purpose in coming here. If you want to continue your—your party, perhaps we could talk in another room?"

"I can go?" Haas broke in.

"You live next door?"

"Yes."

"You're free to go."

Hugo gestured at Gloria and walked out without a backward glance. Gloria limped reluctantly after him. She paused at the door to look around the room, her gaze vague and still fearful. No one met her eyes but the police.

"Mel, I can't tell you how sorry I am," Kristie said. "I'm afraid my party, such as it was, is over, but if you'd like to wait—"

"I should go, Kristie. I still have to work tomorrow—" He shut his mouth, and his open face grew troubled. "That was a stupid thing to say."

Kristie reached out for his hand with the unstudied quickness of someone grabbing for support. "Call me? Ask me to lunch? Will you?"

"Of course, I will," Sirclum said, but without conviction. He nodded at Kathleen, Grove, JD. "Well," he said feebly, "It was fun while it lasted. I hope I meet some of you again."

"Where can we talk, Miss Olson?" Strickland asked, and Kristie led him into the kitchen, where they sat down facing each other at the small breakfast table.

Kathleen began to clean up the spilled sandwiches, crackers, and broken candles. Grove and JD moved to help her. The detective, Nelson, watched, his face as bland as a paper plate. JD, hampered by his hanging cuffs, took his coat off and rolled up his sleeves, and when they had things picked up and the furniture back in place, he took off his tie as well and sat down on the couch. It was apparent he intended to stay.

Strickland stepped out of the kitchen. "Nelson, there's some sort of alley-way behind this building." His hand sketched the length of the rear wall. "Take a look. You'll probably have to climb in. Use the windows here."

Nelson nodded briskly. "Yes, sir," he said.

"And watch yourself."

Grove looked tentatively at Kathleen, and she lifted her shoulders slightly. "Do you want to go?" Grove asked.

"Yes, let's."

On impulse Grove turned to JD. "Haas is a creep."

"He doesn't bother me."

"Good night," Kathleen said.

JD hesitated, then stood halfway up. "Take it easy."

Outside they paused where the walk divided. Kathleen looked back at Kristie's door. "I can't help worrying about her," she said.

"Would you like a cup of coffee?" Grove asked.

"Yes, but I'd like to look in on the kids. I won't be a minute."

"I'll leave the door ajar."

"Thanks," Kathleen said when Grove handed her a cup.

"It's just instant."

"I don't drink anything else myself. Too lazy, I guess." Kathleen looked around his front room and indicated the large inclined drawing board where he had tacked a fresh sheet of white paper. "Do you work here?"

"No, that's a ski slope I put in for the mice."

Kathleen threw her head back to laugh, and Grove's eye was caught by the clean line of her throat. "All right," she said. "You know, I've been hoping to meet you ever since you moved in here and I recognized your name. I knew anyone who could draw those ridiculous people would have to be as funny in real life." She paused, studying his face, and nodded, seeming to agree with something she saw there. "I'm frank, you see?"

"I don't have an easy time meeting people."

"You didn't have much trouble with Kristie."

"That's what you think." At the mention of her name Grove automatical-ly looked in the direction of Kristie's apartment.

Kathleen followed his eyes. "Would you rather be over there?"

"I don't think so. No, she's living in the eye of a storm."

"She's frightened."

"She doesn't act like it."

"You wouldn't see it—the things that frighten her the most are the things she wants the most."

"And she doesn't want me? That's not news."

"She should, but she—" Kathleen broke off as someone knocked at the door.

It was Strickland. "I hate to keep bothering you, Mr. Alexander, but I understand you're the only one who's actually seen this vagrant Miss Olson is upset about."

"Yes, I'm afraid I told her. Look, can you, I mean, would you like a cup of coffee. The water's still hot."

Strickland smiled. "Thank you. Black and not too strong. I drink too much of it and I think it's gnawing the lining out of my stomach." He took his hat off and with it he seemed to remove his official identity to become a pleasant, middle-aged man with thinning silver hair and clever gray eyes.

When Grove brought his coffee, he asked, "What's your impression of this old fellow?"

"I told Kristie I thought he was harmless, like a religious hermit or a pillar saint." He began to describe the mottoes, and Strickland listened with apparent interest.

When Grove finished, Strickland said, "Yes, aside from the religious angle there are dozens of similar derelicts in any large city, particularly a Southern city like this, where the weather's mild enough to permit them to live outside. And, as you say, most of them are harmless. They're morons, idiots, getting by the best way they can, not from choice, but necessity. We don't go out of our way to cause them still more trouble, but they inspire women like Miss Olson with, well, xenophobia, fear of the stranger, and when that happens, we have to consider the interests of a productive citizen over those of a rootless stray. And, of course, not all of them are harmless.

"There was a similar character in a nearby resort town. He lived on the beach and ate mussels and seaweed. Almost every day he would station himself on the highway and point at people in the passing cars, particularly at children. Just point, nothing more. He did this for years and became well-known. They sold postcards and statues of him, and artistic young females walked with him on the beach, communing with his mysterious silences into which they read great meaning. He was a Jesus figure, who stood on the road saluting humanity, particularly the children, and what few people ever noticed was that each time he pointed, he cocked his thumb as you cock a revolver.

"He died a few years back of exposure, and no one ever knew what was in his mind. If he stood there day after day slaughtering people with a phantom gun, at least it shot phantom bullets."

"I remember him," Kathleen said. "He had a huge gray beard and looked like the healthiest old man in the world. His eyes actually glittered."

"Indeed they did," Strickland said. He finished his coffee, and put his hat back on. "Now, one other matter. Miss Olson has been receiving anonymous telephone calls, and from what I gather, they're of a pretty disagreeable nature. She's convinced they're being made by someone close by, possibly someone right in this court." He watched Grove calmly.

Grove felt himself tightening and he smiled quickly. "Whenever I make a dirty phone call, they always hang up before I can get anything out."

Strickland's eyes turned severe. "It's not really funny."

"No, it's not. I don't know what else to tell you. I certainly don't make them."

"What about this Haas?"

"He's a disagreeable man—we've all had trouble with him—but I can't imagine him making those kind of calls."

"There's no type, unfortunately," Strickland said. "A few months ago we had one that was leaving notes. This was in a large office, and the notes were left in the girl's desk, usually during the lunch hour. The products of a desperately sick person. Rank stuff, and I'm far from prudish. When we caught the fellow, it turned out to be the most popular young man in the office. He looked like the face in a necktie ad." Strickland held out his hands, palms up. "How do you figure these things?"

"I guess I'm glad I don't have to," Grove said slowly.

Strickland turned to Kathleen. "You've never been bothered?" he asked.

"No, nothing like that, ever."

"You have a telephone with a listed number?"

"Yes."

"I wonder why this pervert would call Miss Olson but not call you?"

Kathleen looked at the floor. "I'm not—like she is."

Strickland smiled graciously. "You're a very attractive young woman."

The door sounded again, and it was the younger detective, "When you're through here, Sarge, I ran into something you'd better see."

"I'm through. Was there someone back there?"

"I'm not sure, but—you'd better come and take a look."

"If you hear anything, see anything, let me know," Strickland said to Grove and Kathleen. "You can reach me at the Bellflower Station. Detective-Sergeant Strickland."

When the door closed behind the two officers, Grove said, "He's no fool, that man."

"I think that's reassuring."

"Yes, I suppose it is."

"Grove, there's something weird about those calls of Kristie's, and I don't mean to be bitchy, either, but—well, I came over to borrow something from her, and she was on the phone. She looked sick, just sick. She motioned for me to listen, but when I did, there wasn't anything but dial tone, not an open connection, just dial tone. There was no one at the other end."

"They probably hung up."

"Yes, I thought of that, but there's another thing. You had something in that crack of yours—why doesn't *she* hang up? If the moment she recognized this creep's voice she hung up, wouldn't he quit? I mean, he wouldn't be getting whatever kicks it is he gets when he knows she's listening."

Grove was frowning. "Did it occur to you that she might be afraid to offend this lunatic? That if he could no longer reach her on the phone, he might come knocking on her door?"

"But wouldn't a person who uses the phone like that be too much of a sneak to ever come out in the open?"

"How's Kristie supposed to know that? You heard Strickland. There's no type."

Kathleen sighed. "I didn't mean to make you angry."

"I'm not angry."

"Well, then, stop yelling at me. Anyway, here we are talking about Kristie. She has that gift. She's noticed." Kathleen took a cigarette from her purse, and Grove moved quickly to hold his lighter for her, watching the flame flush her cheeks and light a somber glow in her eyes.

"You have no reason to envy Kristie," he said quietly.

"Oh, I don't really."

He waited until she took the cigarette from her mouth, then lowered his head to kiss her. She returned his kiss frankly, but after a moment she raised her hands to his face and gently pushed him back. She left her hands in place, against his cheeks, and said, "Don't think I'm not interested. I'm probably more interested than you are, but can we let this jell a while—until sometime when I wouldn't feel like a substitute for Kristie?"

"Kristie again?"

"I know it's silly, but that's the way I feel."

He looked down at her a moment. Her eyes were very clear, and her lashes seemed spun from smoke. He stood up and walked across the room.

"You're still angry," she said behind him.

"It's not silly, and I'm not angry." He moved to his drawing board and took up a soft-lead pencil. "Imagine there's something interesting in that corner and watch it for five minutes." He began to sketch her in swift positive lines.

JD...

...watched Kristie relight several of the broken candles. She did it with a precise deliberation, as if instinctively understanding how even such an idle chore might be accomplished most efficiently. Finished, she gave the last saucer an approving touch, admiring her own performance, and turned to look at JD. The candles laid a wavering haze of warm light along her cheek, the ridgeline of her nose, and soft underchin, but her eyes were left in shadow. Their hidden expression could be sketched only from the implications of her forehead, which was smooth and blank.

"What do you want?" she asked.

The bluntness of her question slowed his mind for a moment. He flushed and said, "You're in trouble, aren't you?"

"I don't know what could have given you that idea." On the surface her voice seemed as precise as her hands, but JD thought he could sense something desperate beating deep within it. He stood up and moved toward her.

"Don't shuck me."

"What?"

"Don't lie to me. I know you're in trouble. Do I look simple? When I was here before, you had the want ads out and marked. I've been in the want ads myself. I know what they mean. Now your lights are sloughed. You've got some sex nut after you. You need a man."

Kristie threw her head back so she could follow his face. "If I needed a man, I'd have one."

He paused for a moment, wondering at the apparent truth of this. Why didn't she have a man? But he was too moved to think clearly, and he pulled her into his arms, pressing her face against his chest. He heard her voice, muffled now, saying, "And you almost wrecked my apartment."

"That wasn't any fault of mine, and you know it."

He put his lips against her neck, and she didn't resist. In a moment, to his amazement, she began to cry. A low wretched sobbing, as if the act of crying hurt her far more than the deeper cause of it. He stroked her hair awkwardly, whispering, "Hey, it ain't that bad. Believe me, I know. You have no idea how bad things can get."

And when she calmed down and hung in his arms, her wet face looking up at him like a ruined flower, she said tonelessly, "It won't work. I haven't the strength to fight you off, but it won't work."

He shook his head heavily. How many times, through countless novels, had he traced the tortured path of love as it moved to conquer all obstacles. He lowered his mouth to hers, but she turned aside. "I'm trying to be honest with you," she said.

He didn't hear. He caught her mouth with his own and tasted her tears. Her lips pressed to the side under the force of his kiss, and then loosened and opened like something warm and moist growing into his mouth. Everywhere his hands touched her, they found heat and softness, and his throat thickened until he gulped at the air as his mind grew enflamed with the sense of feminine mystery so long denied to him. He struggled with her clothes.

She drew back to ask, "Can you have the lights turned on?" And her eyes were vaguely unfocused. She was looking straight at him, but he had the feeling she was not precisely seeing him. It was a moment, a beat of doubt, but it bothered him more than any of the things she had found to say.

"Yeah, sure." He pulled his money clip from his pocket. "You do it. In the morning."

She took the clip, and it vanished into her clothes in a gesture as old as money. Then he picked her up and heard her breath move in a sighing moan as he headed into the dim tunnel leading to her bedroom. He pushed the door open with his foot and edged into the dark room. Lowering her to the floor, he began to pull at her sweater.

"Let me," she said.

In the darkness their differences vanished as if they were all products of the light. JD began to undress. The narrow plane of her bed was just visible in the twice reflected starlight, and when the surface shifted and grew lighter, he understood that she had pulled the covers down to expose the white sheet. He found her and felt her fingers spreading on his arms as he lifted her and lowered her to the bed. He fell on her awkwardly, but she was ready for him, and when they came together, she cried out softly. Her cries never stopped. They came repeatedly and rhythmically, as if he were pushing them up through her to bloom in her throat, and as they grew louder and more urgent they came to seem the only thing he had ever wanted to hear.

"Where were you?" he asked.

"In the bathroom."

"I didn't hear you leave."

"You were asleep."

Kristie sat down on the edge of the bed, and when he put his hand on her back, he found she was wearing a robe. He could feel her renewed tension and he rubbed her back gently. Probably he shouldn't have copped out about his time. It had poured out of him in a burst of emotion. He had wanted to make her a part of his past so that they could celebrate the future together. She hadn't seemed dismayed by what he was telling her. She had asked a few questions and then, drowsy and tender, had fallen asleep in his arms.

"Come to bed," he said.

"This bed's not large enough for both of us."

"It was awhile ago."

"I'll sleep on the couch."

"I'm not going to take your bed."

She didn't answer, and he pulled her down beside him.

"Don't."

He shook his head, forgetting she couldn't see him in the dark. "I don't understand why a broad that likes it as much as you do fights it so hard."

"I'm not a broad," she said dully.

"That's a word I don't mean nothing by—you're the best thing in every way I ever came across." It was the simple truth, and he didn't add to it.

"Thank you," she said.

"Thank you? You've given me more than I've given you. Why can't you relax and enjoy yourself? I'm asking because I want to know."

"There are other things," she said with a hint of primness. "And after we have—done that, then what do we do?"

"I think you want it both ways."

"I'm going to sleep on the couch."

"The hell you are."

He sat up, swollen with stubbornness and, fishing in the dark, found his pants. When he lit a match to recover his socks, he saw her huddled with her knees up in the center of the bed.

"You can come back in the morning."

"All right."

"It's not the kind of neighborhood where you can stay all night. People would notice."

"Are you afraid of me?" he asked.

"No, not really."

"I swear to God I don't mean you nothing but good. It might be I ain't got nothing you've got any use for, but that don't change how I mean it."

"You come back in the morning."

"Okay."

The court was silent and the windows were lightless when he stepped from Kristie's door. He paused for a moment to stare at Haas's windows, then across to where Arnold Courtney lived alone, an old man who had moved through a lifetime to become once again a little boy who was boarded out. The liquor had left JD with an uneasy ringing in his head, and his mouth tasted foul.

The street where he had parked was shadowed and empty. Far down it a single car sped quickly across an intersection, and as he started off he passed a *Times* truck plodding along, laying newspapers as a giant turtle lays eggs. The Freeway, too, was empty, and its even, slow curves were frozen in the cold light of the tall, hooded lamps, stretched off seemingly forever like the landscape of a dream.

The bed was too small. There was no sense chewing that—he would have to do something about it. But when he was back in the neutral calm of his hotel room, he discovered he had less than a hundred dollars left. He stood dumbfounded, holding the thin sheaf of bills he had hidden in his room, trying to figure out where the money could have gone. Four hundred dollars in a little over twenty-four hours. It wasn't possible. Carefully he worked his way back. The clip he'd handed to Kristie had held about a hundred dollars. Then sixty dollars for the encyclopedias, one hundred for the suit, thirty-five for shoes, shirts, and socks. He didn't know what else—a new belt, maybe, thirty dollars in all. Fifty dollars for rent here, thirty-five to that punk at the other hotel, five to Doc, five for gas—he couldn't think of anything more. He found a pencil and added these amounts. He stared at the sum. Four hundred and twenty, with maybe another six or seven burnt up by food and taxes.

He was stunned. In a day he'd managed to piss off more money than he'd been able to earn in the entire time he had been free. And what did he have. A new suit, roughed up now by that bastard Haas, a pair of sharp-toed ones-and-twos that hurt his feet, and a couple of shirts with trick sleeves. And he'd got himself laid.

When he'd big-handed the clip to Kristie, he'd somehow thought he still had several hundred in reserve. You big clown, he told himself, you can't even count.

His eyes fell on a hair brush, the only object on top of his bureau. He'd had the brush for over ten years, ever since Bob Platkey, his lifting partner, had passed it on the morning he was due to hit the bricks. They had called him Iron Bob because he could military press three hundred ten pounds, a joint record and a good lift anywhere, although JD eventually bested it. "Well, kid," Iron Bob had said, "this ain't a whole lot to leave you, but it's the best I got. Maybe if you use it, you won't blow your wig."

JD had carved his initials in the wooden handle with a razor blade, and for many years the brush was literally the only thing he owned. But that hadn't meant anything to him because no one around him had owned anything either, and a few had even envied him the brush, while many had envied him the body he had worked out of the iron pile. If his shoes wore out, he exchanged them. If he tore his pants, he asked for a pass to the tailor shop. Everywhere he stood in a line and waited until he got his issue. Now there were no lines, no issue, and the hair brush he had treasured so long seemed shabby and useless.

He wondered where Platkey was now—he had never heard of him again. When it came JD's time to go, his friends had come to shake his hand and to caution him "to walk slow and drink lots of water," and they had snapped his picture as he went down the wide front steps, taking from the rear so as not to embarrass any chance he might have to begin a new life. By the time the papers had hit the streets, JD had bought his Ford and started his trip a thousand miles to the West.

He drove dreaming of white beaches and palm trees and wondering if twenty years in jail entitled a man to his picture in the paper, even if it were only above the caption: Cop Killer Freed.

Now he rubbed his hand over his thick hair and thought that whether it had been the brush or not he hadn't blown his wig, and at the end of all those lines and all his issues there had never been anything remotely like Kristie or even the pleasure he felt just driving his car through the city streets. If he had never been allowed to leave, he could have found ways to bear it, as the blind adjust to darkness, but to go back now would be like dying, or worse, a form of death where the mind continued to live on while the body decayed.

In bed he began to consider Hugo Haas. Any reluctance he had felt originally was gone because whatever grief the old man might have to take from Haas, he was now taking, and, while a shakedown didn't leave the sweetest taste, it had worked once. But he couldn't persuade himself that Haas would sit quietly on a smoldering bomb. It was lock cinch that however clean Haas could get in 24 hours, that's how clean he was now. But that still left Arnold Courtney, and the old man was an indelible soft spot. Any cop with sense enough to spit would turn the old man inside out in fifteen minutes, and that cool gray bird tonight, Strickland, would read the story like a billboard. The question was, would Haas believe this? And if he could be made to believe it, then what would he do to the old man?

It was all a much poorer notion than it had been originally—the trap was damaged, the man warned and now humiliated for a kicker, because no matter what the others might have seen and thought of their brief fight, Haas knew that he had been easily handled, and that's hard to take for a man who thinks of himself as bad news.

No, JD thought, he'd better take another turn around the "no employment" bureaus, and maybe the new suit would give him enough front to pick up a decent job. Still, another five hundred would set sweet.

He did go to the unemployment bureaus, but the best chance he could turn was a berth on a farm labor gang they were recruiting to ship to one of the valleys. A week ago he would have taken it. Two days ago he would have taken it. Now he didn't consider it. Fruit tramp! It he were cut to a measure no larger than that, he might as well lay down and let a truck run over him. And that was pretty much what he set out to do next.

He found Haas before he'd made up his mind he was going to see him at all. He parked this time in the back of the court and walked along the alley, automatically looking into those garages that were standing open, and there was Haas in a tee shirt, khakis, and bedroom slippers, thumbing through a stack of paper. The garage was fitted out like a shop. A small, handfed press stood on ink-stained 6x6s, and a green shaded lamp was lowered over it from a drop cord. The walls were covered with Arnold Courtney's prints, in various stages of completion, held by paper clamps. A jerry-built bench ran along one wall; cans of ink with bright labels and open packages of stock were stacked upon it. There was an irregular circle of soot on the concrete floor where something had been burned.

Haas looked up and saw JD. His face paled, then turned red, as if he'd been scalded, as if JD had paused in the door of the garage to dash a bucket of boiling water in his face.

"You better move out," Haas said hoarsely.

"I got other business here than you."

"That slut! You better find someplace else to get your ass. It hurts me to even look at you."

"You better learn to keep your ugly mouth shut and keep cleaning house."

"You better believe I'm cleaning house. You could have cops through here in droves—they wouldn't get a smell."

"You got some sense, anyway."

JD turned and started off, but Haas came out into the alley behind him. "I ain't gonna tell you again. The next time I catch you around her, I'm gonna kill you." His voice shook with fury. "You hear me? *You hear me?*"

Haas's voice followed JD around the corner of the garages and stayed with him as he crossed the backyard and knocked on Kristie's door. He knocked louder than necessary. As he waited he stared at a fat robin, and the robin stared back, its yellow bill half-open, closed on some still unswallowed bit of forage, and its breast feathers were not red at all but a dull brownish orange. The bird swallowed and defecated in the same motion.

Kristie opened the door, her blue robe held at the neck with one hand, her face still slow with sleep. As he stepped in she glanced at him, then looked harder.

"What's wrong with you?" she asked.

"Nothing."

He grabbed her, but she tensed and turned her face aside. He contented himself with kissing her cheek. "Are you going to start that again this morning?" he asked.

"I'm not covered with buttons for you to push."

"No?"

"No."

"You liked me well enough last night."

She didn't answer.

"Now this morning you start bad-mouthing me."

"Bad-mouthing you?"

"You know what I mean."

"I tried to warn you last night, didn't I? I said it wouldn't work. But you wouldn't listen."

"All I got from that is you like to say one thing and do another, and if that's the price, I guess I can pay it. Did you get the lights straightened out yet?"

"If you want to talk to me, you'll have to come in the kitchen. I haven't had breakfast."

He followed her into the kitchen, and even when she was making trouble, he enjoyed watching her. He could have sat in a chair and just watched her walk back and forth—she had him up that tight. It wasn't until she put a pan of water on a hot plate that he thought to wonder how she intended to cook. Then he saw that the hot plate was plugged into an extension cord that ran out through the kitchen window. She plugged a toaster into a second outlet.

"Would you like something?" she asked, and her voice had softened.

"No, I ate. Some coffee, maybe."

"All I have is tea."

"That's all right." He took off his coat and hung it on the back of the kitchen chair. He sat down and asked, "Did you pay the lights?"

"No, not yet."

"Give me the money. I'll go do it."

She stared at him blandly. "I banked the money."

He returned her stare for a moment, his face hot. "Honest to God, Kristie, do I look that simple? Tell me, do I have a fool's face? How the hell would you have banked that money? You just got up."

She shrugged delicately. "One can bank by mail."

"And you're asking me to believe you got up last night after I left and mailed that money to some bank?"

"That's exactly what I did. I don't like to keep money in the house. It makes me nervous."

"It makes you nervous," he repeated flatly. "There was three times what you'd need for your light bill."

She smiled: "You have more money, don't you?"

"Some."

"Can't you get more?"

He blew his lips out in a mirthless snort. "Not where I got that. That little playhouse is shot up."

"What are you talking about?"

"Never mind. You didn't think I made anything offing them lousy books, did you?"

"I never thought about it."

"I'll bet that's the truth."

"It is." She looked at him steadily, and it was as frank a gaze as he'd ever had from her. "No matter what we do to each other in this apartment, that's as far as it can go. When you step out that door, you don't exist until you come back." The toast popped up, and she turned to butter it.

"That doesn't make sense," JD said slowly.

"It's the only way that does make sense. People smother each other."

She served him his tea, then brought her own breakfast of toast and marmalade. Before she sat down, she put her hand on his hair and kissed him lightly on the cheek. "Don't scowl so," she said. He started to get up, but she pressed down on his shoulder.

"Sit still." She laughed. "You're always ready, aren't you?"

"With you I have to be."

"I'm not so difficult when I know someone." She stirred sugar into her tea. "When I feel safe with them. You're very strong." She put her spoon down and rubbed her upper arm. "Even if I didn't know that directly, I could have seen it in the way you handled that brute Haas."

JD couldn't find any ready answer. He looked into his teacup where the leaves hung above the bottom in clusters and a stem floated like a tiny log. When he was a child, his grandmother had told him that such a stem in his teacup meant he was going to have an accident.

"I used to lift weights," he said, "when I was doing my time. It was mostly just a way to burn up energy." He slapped his chest. "I'll probably lose some of this bulk now that I've laid off."

"That would be a shame," she said obliquely.

"Come off it. I didn't just step out of a comic book."

"Would you like it if I started losing—the things I've got?"

It was a moment before he realized she was teasing him. Then he experienced a mingling of surprise and warm pleasure. "I wouldn't like it." Impulsively he reached out and laid his hand over her breast.

He saw her lips whiten, and her face grew bleak as she started to draw away from him. Then in a flicker she changed and was smiling a heavy, sleepy smile, pressing herself against his hand, but again, for just a moment, he had the eerie impression that her eyes were focused somewhere through him and just beyond him, as if he were transparent. Then he accepted his pleasure and leaned over to kiss her.

"Let me drink my tea."

He nodded, willing to wait. They had all day, all night. He couldn't quite conceive of it.

She said, "You did handle Haas as if he were a child." She seemed to be establishing a fact.

"He's nothing."

"Perhaps to you." She spread marmalade on her second piece of toast, watching her knife closely, as if this, too, was something it was important she do well. "Most men would seem like boys compared to you."

Not if they had guns, JD thought. He knew one thing surely—it was a mistake to push any man too far. As a boy he had watched a squirrel back off a large dog and send it howling in retreat with a torn and bleeding nose. Abstracted in his own concern, he almost missed what she was saying.

"What?"

"I think I know where you can get some money—for us."

Her voice had an odd edge to it, and her smile was glassy.

"Yeah?" he asked cautiously. "Where?"

"From a man. A man I used to know."

"And how do I get it?"

"Take it away from him."

"Steal it, you mean?"

"Does that bother you?"

"Yes and no. It would depend on how I was going to go about doing it."

"Just take it." Her eyes flashed. "You might have to beat him up."

He shook his head slowly. "I wouldn't want to do nothing like that."

"Are you afraid?"

"No. If you want a reason, it doesn't sound right."

"*Right?* This is a man who cares nothing for what is right. He'd do the same thing to you if it were to his advantage. This man, ordinary rules don't apply to him. He doesn't abide by them. Why should they protect him?"

"That's not exactly what I meant by right. Who's this guy?"

"Is that important?"

"Who's he to you that you're so hot at him?"

"I'm not—hot at him. We were talking about money."

"You were talking about money, and I'm not sure that's what you were talking about at all."

"Listen to me." Kristie put her hand over his. "He carries a great deal of money with him. He likes to display it. That's the kind of man he is. What you take from him won't hurt anything but his vanity, but think what we can do with it." She smiled. "We could go away—to Hawaii, to Mexico. Wouldn't you love to see Mexico?"

JD nodded, but still doubtfully. He'd heard stories of those who flashed huge bankrolls and those who only pretended to flash them. Like the Minnesota bankroll, a large wad of ones with a single twenty showing. That was all he knew—stories—but he remembered handing his own money clip to Kristie and he understood the urge well enough.

"That sounds great, Kristie," he said earnestly. "But if I get caught at this stunt or anything like it, I'll take a trip all right, but it won't be to Mexico and it won't be with you. If you see me at all, it will be through six inches of screen."

"That's something you shouldn't even think about."

"But I *do* think about it, and it would just about kill me to find my sorry ass back in blues. You don't have the least notion what you're asking me to risk."

"I know what we could do with that money," she said urgently. "Couldn't you try to get it? You're a man, aren't you?"

"You don't have to challenge me like that. I'd like to put this kind of thing behind me."

"I know," she said scornfully. "It's wrong."

"More than that, but I don't think you understand."

"I understand you're afraid."

"I'm not afraid!" He grabbed her soft arm, squeezing so hard that she winced and snapped at him.

"*Damn you!*"

He snatched her to her feet in a single motion that sent the chair tumbling and held her tight against his chest while he stared down into her small white face.

"Stop damning me," he said fiercely. "And stop needling me. I don't need it from you."

His words appeared to have no effect on her. Her face remained pale and still. He could mark her pulse clearly where it stirred her eyelids, and against his chest he sensed the light, rapid action of her heart. Then her hips shifted up and in, and her stomach was warm.

"Couldn't you just go out there and see?" she asked softly.

Jesus. He shivered against her. "Where is it?" he asked reluctantly.

She began to tell him about a man named Nathan Holleran, where he lived, his habits and appearance, and her voice was eager and caressing. "You may have to watch the house for several nights until his wife goes out. Nathan's never home early. He has—many things to do and he seldom leaves his office much before seven. He and his wife lead more or less separate lives, and it won't be at all unusual for her to go out by herself."

"You know this guy pretty well, don't you?"

She looked briefly impatient. "I used to. Now I'm only interested in the money. I'm sick and tired of it here. I want to get away." She looked up and added, "With you."

"All right, all right. I'll look, but that's all I'm promising. This kind of thing ain't my game, and, strictly speaking, I ain't got no game. Maybe I need one."

Her eyes had grown dreamy. "Where will we go?" she asked.

"Christ, I don't know. You'll have to decide."

"Mmmmmmm, that's half the fun."

JD smiled faintly. He had an uneasy feeling they were play-acting, that nothing that had happened between them had been quite real, that it was growing progressively more unreal. His thoughts were broken by a knock on the door. Instantly Kristie was out of his arms, looking alarmed.

"I'd rather no one saw you here," she said.

"You ashamed of me?"

"Keep your voice down. Please, won't you wait in the bedroom?"

"All right." He kissed her swiftly to seal his ownership and started toward the bedroom.

"Close the door," she whispered after him.

He sat on the bed and in a moment he heard a man's voice, but he couldn't make out what was being said. He experienced a twinge of anxiety that took him a moment to recognize as jealousy. Face it, he told himself, you're hooked.

He stood up and walked to the window. Pulling the curtain aside, he stared across at a dull cement wall, the back of another building only five feet away. The ground below him was spotted with irregular clumps of coarse grass and a few weathered, cement-splattered boards. Farther along, a puddle of spilled tar had soaked into the earth, and the whole area was strewn with odd bits of paper almost disintegrated by the rain, alternately soaked, then bleached by the sun. The wall itself was densely scrawled with the crayoned marks of children. One massive legend dominated the others, chalked in jumbled, foot-high capitals. It read: FANNIE BROWN STINKS.

STRICKLAND...

...studied the cool blonde woman across from him and wondered what it would do to her apparent composure if she were able to guess the true reason they were here to see her. That she was, at best, an afterthought. Thirty minutes ago he had had no intention of making any further contact with the Olson woman. He had been studying the material Nelson's sharp eye had picked out, studying it with the growing feeling that it was significant and at the same time marveling at the underground continuity of human experience, how one event was subtly linked to another, to where it was impossible to mark—here!—any point where one thing ended and another began. An hysterical woman calls in to report a night creeper, and in a nest, which may or may not be the night creeper's, Nelson finds a jay's treasure of bright paper and cardboard, and among them the evidence before him.

The two prints were clearly rejects. One showed a double image where the press had struck twice; the second was smeared. The art was crude to the point of childishness, but the reproduction seemed expert. The third sheet, which he could only by association connect with the first two, was a good grade of bank paper, difficult but not impossible for a private person to purchase. In the upper right-hand corner, entering the paper at a sharp angle, was a fragment of what was obviously a larger body of type. If the paper were rotated until the outer border of the printed matter ran straight up and down, it could be seen as the left-hand side of a rectangular form, bound by an elaborately engraved border. In the upper corner there were the numerals 306844, underlined with a hairline, and beneath that, 109. The capitals PANY, the P broken at the edge of the page, indicated where some title ended, and under that—and most significant—was a short line broken by the numerals 19.

Nelson was tilted against the wall in a straight-back chair, his feet on the rungs and his balance maintained by the pressure of his head against the wall. He was eating a bag of peanuts, shaking the peanuts in his band to knock off some of the salt before he threw them, two or three at a time, into his mouth.

Strickland asked him, "What do you make of this?"

Nelson dropped his chair to the floor and leaned forward. "I think it's a check. The paper slipped in the press until only a small part of the type form hit it, and then, quite possibly, it fell through the press to the floor, where it was forgotten and picked up and thrown out with this other stuff."

"You think if we find the person who made these prints, we'll find someone printing checks?"

"I do, sir." Nelson smiled. "The prints are so crude that it's hard to imagine they're anything more than a blind."

"Yes. I think these may be the checks they've been killing us with. The lab can tell us." Strickland began to put the spoiled prints and the bank paper into large plastic envelopes. "Maybe we should go make some kind of report to Miss Olson and, while we're at it, ask a few questions of our own."

Nelson paused, peanuts halfway to his mouth, and grinned.

"You like her?" Strickland asked.

Nelson whistled soundlessly and shook one hand, fingers limp, at his side.

The older man smiled dryly. "Your admiration is a monument to your inexperience."

Now, watching Kristie, he saw what Nelson saw, but he also saw other things—the constant posing, the intense self-consciousness, the role playing; she was handling this situation like the lady of the manor taking a report from her private guards. But the coat hanging over the kitchen chair didn't belong to the lord of the manor. It belonged to—his memory supplied the name—Bing, JD Bing. Did the two brown paper cigarette butts in an otherwise virginal ashtray also belong to Bing? The brown paper interested Strickland.

"I'm sorry I can't bring you more reassuring news," he was telling Kristie, his eyes still lingering on the butts, "but if this was the man the officers chased, he's most likely thoroughly frightened and he may keep low or leave this neighborhood."

"I don't understand," Kristie said. "Your men chased this creature and couldn't catch him?"

"That's what I gather from the report. They sighted him and got a light on him, but he went right up the side of a building and over the roofs."

"They should have caught him."

"Well, Miss Olson, they only have to catch him once and they will. The patrol through this neighborhood has been doubled. Meanwhile, have you considered having your phone number changed?"

She nodded.

"It's removing the symptom, not the cause, but it might give you some peace of mind. But then you're having trouble with the light company, aren't you?"

"I told you last night that was an oversight. I intend to correct it today."

"And you'll have the number changed?"

"Yes, of course."

"May I smoke?"

"Please do."

He lit his pipe with one of the kitchen matches he carried loose in his pocket, and when he shook it out, the aromatic tobacco sweet and thick on his tongue, he began to tell Kristie that she should refer the phone company to him if they were reluctant to make a change, and at the same time he prodded one of the butts with the dead match. It opened and spilled a few grains of ordinary tobacco. He had decided that Bing was in the bathroom or in the bedroom and that he was likely to stay there. Probably the woman had insisted—there was nothing in that. Still, the big man tugged at his curiosity; he had been too tractable the night before.

Strickland asked idly, "Does anyone in this court or in the neighborhood that you know of make etchings?"

"Why do you ask?"

"We found some etching equipment out in back and we think possibly this vagrant may have stolen it and hidden it for some strange reason of his own. We'd like to get it back in the hands of the rightful owner if we can locate him."

"That would be Mr. Howe. He lives across the way in apartment H."

"Thank you." Strickland stood up. "We'll be in touch with you. Meanwhile, I hope you rest easier."

Kristie nodded curtly, turning his gesture of dismissal around. "I will when I know this neighborhood is safe."

Strickland wondered if she thought any neighborhood was really safe, but he said nothing further beyond a brief good-bye.

Outside, Nelson said, "She's still a wild-looking broad."

Strickland smiled fondly at his young partner. "Yes, and she has her troubles. More than most, I imagine." He pointed with his pipe stem across the court at apartment H. "And there's your printmaker."

"Should we get a warrant?" Nelson asked.

"Let's take a look at him first."

The door opened, and Strickland gazed down into the old man's face and saw his loneliness and his eagerness, and when he watched it wash away into a gray anxiety at the sight of his badge, Strickland felt a shadow cross his mind. He saw himself, for a moment, as a garbage collector looking down on the body of an aborted child. The things he had to do.

JD...

...drove toward Mesa Verde and the ocean he had traveled a thousand miles to see. It was evening. Lights were coming on, and the streets were still clogged with end-of-day traffic. Mesa Verde, his street map had shown him, was between L.A. and Long Beach just off the Pacific Coast Highway, a labyrinthian complex of avenues stretching over the hills to the edge of the Pacific.

He'd already glimpsed the water ahead of him, small patches of a darkening and placid blue framed in cutouts of narrow white buildings, massed trees, and a sky already marked by night. Even now the water seemed to hold the secret of freedom, the freedom he still had not found, and another time he would have parked and stared out over the ocean, watching darkness take it. Now he noted it mostly as an indication that he was nearing his destination.

Waiting on a red light, he watched a boy carrying lawn furniture from an outdoor display into a long pink stucco store designated along its entire length as Hurricane Harry's. Across the street an auto dealer signaled his location with an actual car welded to the top of a thirty-foot pole. Streamers of plastic pennants—red, yellow, and blue—stirred heavily, and a bored salesman, thumbs hooked in his back pockets, stood just off the sidewalk. As JD watched he removed a half-smoked cigar from the center of his mouth, looked around, and spit carefully between his feet.

The entrance to Mesa Verde was marked by a concrete arch spanning the street, the Spanish name following the curve of the vault in wrought iron letters, and beyond the arch there was a parklike expanse of grass. JD slowed, tensing with a sudden anxiety. His notion of Mesa Verde had been vague at best. A nice neighborhood, he had thought. But he found himself entering a district of a type he hadn't imagined really existed outside the fantasy world of television. His eyes grew crowded and uncertain.

The wide, white streets were lined with tidy palms, trees that clearly demonstrated the amount of work spent in making them appear identical. The houses were distant from the street, each set jewel-like in its own grounds. Hedges and shrubbery lined the buildings in neat dark patterns broken now in the gathering dusk by the warm light of windows. It was lucky he hadn't arrived earlier in full light because his old Ford would have appeared as out of place on these streets as a tractor. Twice he was aware of it when passing motorists turned to stare after him.

He found the address Kristie had given him and parked across from it. The house was low, spread out, and an enormous window poured a flush of light

down a sloping lawn. The driveway was empty, but the garage was closed—
it was large enough for four cars.

JD sat staring up at the house. He didn't have any clear idea what he was
looking for or waiting for. His hands opened and closed on the steering
wheel. Once he switched on the ignition, but he didn't press the starter. He
had said he would look and he would do that much.

A colored woman came down the driveway carrying a shopping bag, and
as she neared the sidewalk he could see she was middle-aged, wearing narrow glasses and a frivolous hat. As she got into a small, dark coupe he sensed
her eyes on him. For a long moment they both sat in their separate cars, staring across the street at each other. Then she started up and drove away.

When her taillights were out of sight, he stepped from his car, hurried
across the street, and ducked into the bushes. He paused, wondering if anyone had noticed him, and if they had, how would he know it? Only when the
neighborhood was crawling with the heat. But he was committed now. His
nerves steadied into a hum of not unpleasant tension, and he moved toward
the house, crouching to diminish his height. He could handle most anything
he met.

He circled the house and discovered a patio in the rear with tubular lawn
furniture and the square bulk of a barbecue. Then he found a window in the
back of the garage through which he saw the ghostly white top of a convertible. Along the side of the house he came on a vantage from which,
through the slats of a carelessly adjusted Venetian blind, he could see into the
living room.

He found himself watching a beautifully dressed woman in her early thir-
ties. She sat in a white leather chair, a magazine open on her lap, and just on
the edge of his vision JD could make out the television screen she was view-
ing with an expression of bored discontent. The picture was in color, something JD had never seen before, and for a moment he stared fascinated.
When he returned to the woman, it was with a feeling of resentment. How
could she watch something so marvelous with such a disagreeable expression? He noted that while she was not beautiful, nothing that could help to
make her appear beautiful had been spared. Her hair, sculptured around her
face, could have been fashioned from gleaming plastic, and it was almost
impossible to connect it with the hair that might have grown in her armpits
had she allowed it and most probably did grow at her crotch, though it was
difficult to think of her being anything there but smooth and pink and neutral as a doll. Her eyes were doll eyes, large, round, thickly lashed, and somehow aimless, not quite sharing the discontent of her thin pink mouth.

She lifted a glass from a table beside her, and her rings flashed. Kristie was
right. This house was full of money like thick cream.

The woman heard the particular motor even before JD, probably because she had been listening for it alone, and she began to pat her already flawless hair and adjust her clothes. JD became aware of light boring up the driveway, and he crouched lower still, listening to the sound of the garage doors opening, and closing, then the firm sound of leather heels on concrete. Another door sounded.

JD saw that the woman was up, mixing a drink at a portable bar, and then a heavyset man moved in behind her. She turned, flashed a bright smile, and handed him the drink. Her mouth moved, but it was impossible to catch anything of what she was saying.

The man—JD identified him as Holleran—leaned over to kiss his wife, brushing her forehead with his lips. Then he toasted her with the glass and drank deeply. He was a large man with a pale, heavy-jawed face and sharp eyes. His hair had yielded reluctantly to the discipline of the brush, and a clump of it had pushed out of the ranks of his military haircut and fallen over his forehead. He brushed at it absently with the back of his hand while he talked with his wife. She was leaning against the bar, her body posed in a seductiveness that seemed far more urgent than the comfortable habit of marriage.

JD instinctively recognized Holleran for a strong man and an important one, who had caused this house to be built and furnished with white leather and color television. And this haughty-looking broad jumped for him, and if he had nodded, she would fall on the floor, even though it was obvious she suspected him of two-timing her, just as he must have once two-timed her with Kristie and crapped on Kristie in the shuffle.

Against the cool of the evening JD felt his face growing hot at the hurt he imagined Kristie must have suffered from this man, but at the same time he was aware of a feeling of envy and, stranger still, admiration.

He started back around the house. He could do nothing tonight unless he was willing to try to handle both the man and the woman, and while it was probable that he could, he had no heart for forcing a woman with his hands or the threat of them. Women—all of them—seemed too precious. He followed the driveway back to the street.

Two men were by his car. One was peering in the window to look at the registration with a flashlight, while the other stood off noting his license number. One had on a uniform cap, the same cap worn by mailmen, gas station attendants, and street car conductors, and the other sported an oversized Stetson. They were clearly not the police though they were armed. A dark sedan, its lights illuminating JD's Ford, sat with the motor idling.

JD hesitated and was wondering whether to slip back into the shadows or to face it out when the man who had been taking his plate number turned to look over at him.

JD stepped forward firmly. "What's this?" he asked.

"Mesa Verde Patrol. May I ask what you're doing here?"

"Minding my own business. What're you doing?"

The one with the flashlight and the large hat turned and deliberately put the beam in JD's face. JD blinked rapidly and instinctively pawed at the light. He heard a nasal voice. "You're our business, old buddy."

JD took a quick side step, out of the beam of the flash, and looked down into a narrow, ridged face. The brown eyes beneath the hat brim were hard and direct. JD noted the leather gloves with the ridged seams and the heavy boots. He tried to control his growing uneasiness. He knew that the patrolman's suspicion was based on the battered appearance of his car; he would have automatically Yessirred a new Lincoln Continental.

"I'm no business of yours," JD said with a false easiness. "I'm a salesman."

The patrolman with the flash put the light at JD's feet and raised it slowly in deliberate inspection. He didn't seem impressed and he was apparently the one in charge.

"What you sell? Other people's stuff?"

"Encyclopedias."

"En-cyclo-pee-dee-uhs," the patrolman repeated with an exaggeration that was both doubting and faintly scornful. "Not that I question your word, old buddy, but you got a few of them around?"

"In my car."

The patrolman stepped aside and directed him with the light. "Let's see them."

JD brought out his sample case and opened it under the flash. The patrolman picked up one of the promotion booklets, glanced at it, and dropped it back in the case. He looked at his partner and shrugged.

The partner asked, "How come you didn't take this up with you?"

JD tried to grin. "A neighborhood like this, they see you coming with a sample case, they turn the dogs on you."

The patrolman had been tightening his gloves over his fingers. Now he reached up and tapped JD on the chest. "A neighborhood like this, you don't sell nothing, you or no one like you. This is a class neighborhood. You understand class? They pay to keep tramps like you out."

"Who'd you see up there?" the quiet one asked. "The Windners? The Hollerans?"

"I didn't see anyone." JD spread his hands. "I lost my nerve. You're right. This neighborhood has too much class for me."

The patrolman stared up at him scornfully, apparently unwilling to accept or credit anything JD said, even when it was to agree with him. He turned to spit off to the side, then pulled the brim of his hat still lower. "Get in the wind," he told JD. When JD was behind the wheel of his Ford, he added, "Don't come around here again."

JD nodded grimly. He started off, watching the two patrolmen in the rearview mirror. They stood looking after him. Then the one in the Stetson squared his shoulders, and said something, and they both laughed.

In an hour JD was parked in the alley behind Kristie's apartment, waiting for her. He didn't have any idea where she was or even that she had been planning to go out.

The garage where he had encountered Haas was locked, and the alley was dark and quiet except at the upper end, where it let out onto the parking lot of a drive-in, Tio Poncho's Taco Stand, and the lot was crowded with old model cars full of teen-agers. They were shouting nonsense jokes in a language of their own, and their laughter drifted back to him with a crystal purity, and, as he thought about it, he couldn't remember ever laughing like that. It was reasonable that once he must have, but that time was lost to him.

To his side he saw the cows moving in the glare of the cold bluish lights that burned above their feeding troughs, and he assumed that the lights had been placed to prevent people from stealing the animals. A half-grown boy rode by on a bicycle and a little later came back drinking a Coke with one hand while he steered with the other.

JD rolled a smoke, brushed the spilled grains from his pants, and lit up. He watched a police car come gliding down the alley, and returned the officer's appraising look as he flicked ash out his window. Cops, he thought. The city crawled with them. He wet his forefinger with his tongue and repaired the seam of his cigarette. So far he was just another lump of humanity strewn along their path—if he didn't count the hummer over in L.A., and he didn't. That was a meatball beef, and the only thing that would gall him about answering those questions was that he would have to protect a crud-sucking creep like Haas.

Every fifteen minutes or so he walked into the court to see if Kristie was home, but her windows were always dark. Her door remained silent, and each time he stood there hoping this time she would answer, the flesh between his shoulder blades began to crawl with the thought of Haas. He whirled, half expecting to find the other man standing sheltered in the darkness, his gun leveled.

He ain't going to shoot me off the sidewalk, JD assured himself, but he knew that if no one was ever shot out in the open, there were a lot of people who were dead for no reason, and he hurried back to his car to sit with the motor idling.

Once he glimpsed the old bastard he'd seen rooting in the garbage. When the old man saw JD, he started like a frightened animal and, with surprising agility, wheeled and vaulted a fence.

You don't have to be ascared of me, old man, JD thought. I ain't but about two jumps behind you, only I ain't going to eat out of no garbage can or sleep in a tree.

The prowl car came through again, and this time they slowed down to just a few miles an hour and stared at him with that hard look they put on when they're trying to worry someone into exposing himself. JD stared back calmly, but it took effort, and when they were past and turning slowly in the lights of the taco stand, he knew he would have to leave. If they came through again and found him still sitting here, they were going to stop, and he didn't want to talk to them. L.A. wasn't that far away.

He drove for a while without going anywhere, just back and forth through the streets of the immediate neighborhood. Then he stopped in front, slipped in, and knocked at Kristie's door. The silence mocked him. Reluctantly he realized he had better give up.

He hit the Freeway, once again kicking the old car along until it began to shudder. Minutes later he pulled off the ramp into downtown L.A. He headed toward his hotel, but the thought of going up to his empty room was suffocating, and he drove around looking at the marquees of all-night shows. Nothing he saw appealed to him enough to start him looking for a parking place. He didn't want to sit alone in a theater, either. He didn't want to be alone.

He stopped at a small grocery store and bought half a gallon of Port wine from a Chinese clerk; then he cruised the streets of skid row until he spotted Doc.

Doc was standing with two other men under a feeble blue sign offering Rooms—75¢. None of them seemed to be saying anything or looking at anything in particular. They were just standing like tired old horses when the graze is gone. JD rapped his horn, and Doc glanced up. He smiled, showing his bitter teeth, and started forward. The other two men moved with him as if they were tied to him. He turned, scowling. "Mope," he told them. One of them said something plaintive, but Doc shook his head in dismissal, and they held back like ragged children refused a party.

"This is a goddam jungle," Doc said, getting in. He spotted the Port. "Hey!" he exclaimed softly. Then, glancing back at the other two, he said, "These lice'll crawl all over you if you let them."

JD started off, and Doc told him, "Well, you look different."

"I don't feel too different."

"Yeah?"

"Nothing. I'm chasing a broad."

"Broads!" Doc was unscrewing the top from the half gallon. "That's a problem I've always been immune from." He tilted the bottle and drank off a quarter of it, then sighed and lowered it to rest between his legs. He pulled his fingers across his lips and wiped them on the car seat. "Broads," he said, "are the biggest gaff on the midway."

JD parked on a quiet dark street lit only by a single light over the back door of a store to discourage burglars. JD took the bottle and drank. The wine tasted warmer and less sour, and they passed the bottle back and forth in a slow, reflective rhythm.

"How you making out otherwise?" Doc asked.

JD shook his head wearily. He didn't have to play the part for Doc. "I don't know. It's worried money either way, whether I catch hold of something or fall on my ass. But I'm scuffling."

"Scuffle, don't scuffle. Either way you end up boxed and tagged."

"Maybe, but while I'm alive I'm going to live."

"Who wants more?" Doc held up his empty hands, the palms grained with dirt, and slowly turned them over. "But the minute you start to do anything, you're in some kind of trouble."

JD smiled. "That don't keep you out of that bottle."

"This bottle ain't easy to get into. I ain't got friends who hold heavy drinking up every night."

"You empty again?"

"When you showed, I had two cents, a dry throat, and a good start on the whips and jingles."

JD took the change from his pocket and poured it into Doc's hand. "It ain't much."

"You didn't take me to raise, JD." Doc rattled the coins in his fist. "This is a lot of mileage for me."

JD waved his hand vaguely. He was getting drunk, and it seemed he was growing smaller and smaller inside his own head while the world outside him loomed progressively larger. "It's nothing," he said. He felt warm friendship for Doc. Doc was his own kind of people. And he felt guilty, a betrayer, because Kristie was going to turn him into a stranger, and he was going to allow it. "You ever pull any big time?" he asked Doc.

"No, but I done enough thirty days and ninety days and six months to wear out a murder beef, but I never went behind the walls."

"It's a different world. As far away from this—" JD waved his hand vaguely at the dark street beyond the windshield. His lips worked briefly, and he seemed to be trying to find the point of what he'd been saying. Then he swung around to stare at Doc, his eyes blinking slowly. "As the moon," he said. "As far away as the moon."

"I could tell you stories myself," Doc said. "Maybe anybody could."

JD nodded to this, uncertain just what it was he was agreeing with but willing to agree to anything. His face felt numb and it was a yard away from his usual sense of it. He was dwindling. He flopped a hand over to squeeze Doc's shoulder, then clumsily grasped the bottle. He drank deeply, unaware that a thin stream of wine was leaking down his chin and into his collar. He paused briefly when he needed air, then drank again.

There was something he wanted to say, something shivering in his mind like the flame of a match cupped against the wind, but his tongue was rubbery, and he couldn't feel his lips at all. He stared through the windshield at the night-light down the block and tried to read the narrow, foreshortened lettering beneath it. The lettering rippled gently, and his eyes slowly closed.

Doc watched him for a while, raising the bottle at regular intervals, and when JD began to breathe deeply and evenly, Doc's gaze grew speculative. "Hey, JD," he said softly. Then louder. "You asleep?"

JD didn't stir. He sprawled behind the wheel, his chin lowered to his chest, and in the shadows the wine stain seemed to carry the line of his mouth down into his throat like the scrolled lips of a sad clown. His eyes were closed. Doc drank the last of the Port and shouted, "Wake up, JD!"

And when JD still didn't stir, Doc, with great caution, began to go through his pockets. Scissoring with two fingers, he removed a few folded bills from the right-hand pocket. He flipped through them, counting rapidly, and grunted with pleasure as the total mounted to sixty dollars. He opened the door and eased out of the car. He paused, still bent over, looking at JD and shaking his head, half in disgust, half in reluctant sympathy. He detached a five from the bills and reached over to slip it into JD's coat pocket. He said quietly, "You better learn, it's a taker's world."

He pushed the door shut and melted into the darkness.

KRISTIE...

...drove home in a mood bordering on desperation. She'd had dinner and a vague, inconclusive interview with an executive of a small aircraft company in Burbank. The executive, a man of fifty, had watched her with an obvious sly speculation in a manner she could only think of as "greasy." He avoided any firm commitment through an evening of labored dancing—his hands were always edging where they shouldn't—and forced drinking. She came away with the feeling that Holleran had marked her lousy throughout the entire industry.

She imagined she could hear Holleran's blunt male confidences: *She's efficient, a good thinker, and* (here he would smile) *she puts out, but she's trouble, serious trouble.*

She drove with controlled recklessness, shaving disaster at several intersections, her face white and impassive, her mouth grim as she reaffirmed her confidence here at the wheel of her car, but at the same time she sensed the cords that had once bound her life fraying and parting. The strings she had once pulled so deftly now broke in her hands.

Where would she end? This was a question she couldn't face. She literally couldn't consider it. When she tried, her mind would go as blank as a screen after the film has run out and left only a panel of faintly pulsing, empty light.

She half-expected JD to be waiting for her. He now seemed to be a rock in the formless sea where she struggled on the verge of drowning, but she refused to acknowledge disappointment when it became apparent he had not returned or had not waited, just as she refused to acknowledge to herself the use to which she was attempting to put him. She now almost automatically saw JD in the person of the pirate or the bandit chieftain, a man of swift and ruthless action, an ardent lover, yet a man familiar with fine things, as well as a man who was the confidant and secret advisor of kings and presidents. She knew JD was none of these and at the same time she believed it was all true.

She locked her door, tested all the windows, and made the shades secure with bits of masking tape. Then she undressed swiftly and put on an old flannel nightgown she had worn as a girl. She brewed a cup of tea and carried it into her bedroom to watch the mirror-girl drink it. The mirror-girl looked distraught, and Kristie consciously smoothed the brow because the mirror-girl had to be always pale and shining, glimpsed in brief perfection as she moved from one episode to another in her wonderful life.

When she couldn't sleep, she began to read a novel, one she had read before, where the heroine was a spectacularly beautiful girl whose father dies, leaving her in control of a vast financial network, which she, through a series of masterful manipulations, expands until she is virtually a modern-day empress with armies to command, heads of state at her call.

She woke to a heavy pounding on the door that was now familiar to her. The pounding was token of the ease with which he could break the door down, and she hurried out, neglecting her robe in her haste to get her arms around him. But JD shoved through as soon as she got the door open, and went directly to the window, and pulled the blind aside to peer out.

"What is the matter with you?" she asked.

He turned to her, and his face was grim. "You spend all your time in bed?"

"I fail to see—"

"It's no goddam wonder you're out of a job and broke. It's afternoon. Where were you last night?"

"I don't know what's bothering you, but I won't let you take it out on me. I had an interview last night, and it was miserable, and then I couldn't sleep."

His face softened. "You're right, I'm bugged. The one friend I had burned me."

"What happened?"

He shook his head. "It's not worth talking about. I just can't get used to the idea. These free-world people would crawl over their dying mammies to whip you out of two bucks."

"And convicts are all noblemen?" Kristie asked dryly.

"I don't know—no, Christ, no. I just thought it would be different." He studied her now, taking in the nightgown. "You look like a little girl," he said and came over to kiss her. Her hands sought his back, greedy for the strength of it, and then she asked, whispering along his ear, "Did you find the house?"

"Yes. There was a woman home—"

"His wife," Kristie said dully.

"He came along later, and it looked like they were both in for the night."

"You'll have to go back this evening."

"He looks hard to handle."

Kristie snorted. "Don't be deceived by how he looks. I've had him crying, literally crying, on my shoulder. His job was too difficult, his bosses were angling to replace him, his wife was barren—everything was wrong. There's no strength in him."

"I mean to handle without hurting him. I think he'll fight. But that ain't all—I ran into some kind of patrol in there. They took my license number. So I don't see how I'm going to get back. They'll recognize my car the minute they lay eyes on it. It was the reason they checked me out in the first place."

Kristie hugged him tighter. "Please. You have to go back."

"Don't you hear what I'm trying to tell you? If they catch me, those guys are going to give me all the trouble they can. That might not be much going in, but coming out? They could bury me."

She freed herself and stepped back. She refused to see his caution as reasonable. She read it for fear, and he couldn't be afraid. "If I'm going to have a man around here, he has to he a *man*."

"And you think that's a man's work—delivering your trouble?"

"If he's *my* man and *I* ask him. And it's not trouble I want you to deliver, as you put it. We simply need that money and we have a right to it."

He was staring at her with an open wonder. "Kristie, do you really want me around here? I mean, to stay here with you?"

She looked up at him blindly. "Do you have to ask?"

"I don't know."

"You should know. You should know."

He walked over and sat down on her couch. Methodically he rolled a cigarette, tamping the ends firm with a match before he lit it. "It'll be slim business," he said thoughtfully, "but I'll find some way to manage it. It's not too far. Maybe I could walk it."

"And you could drive one of their cars out," Kristie said, bringing the practical side of her mind to bear for the first time. "They have two, both new."

"Yeah. What's GTA on top of robbery."

"Robbery?"

"That's what it's called, honey."

She hadn't thought of it like that at all. The word suggested something so ordinary, and she dismissed it from her mind. "Have you eaten?" she asked.

"No, but I'm not hungry."

"You should eat."

He smiled slowly. "You're the damnedest broad. Half the time I'd give odds you didn't care whether I lived or died."

"I care," she said in a small compressed voice, but it was the Bandit Chieftain to whom she spoke.

She made him soft-boiled eggs, playing at this homely task she had so seldom performed, and fixed her own unvarying breakfast of toast, marmalade, and tea. "Are you still having trouble with Hugo Haas?" she asked as she served him.

"What makes you ask that?"

"The way you've been acting."

"He's got a sore head and a toy gun, and he can soak the one because I don't think he'll use the other. But I'd just as soon he doesn't see me around here. It just rubs it into him, and if he does snap a few caps, we'll all spend time answering questions. We don't need that right now."

"A gun," Kristie repeated, as if that were all she heard of what he had been saying.

"A little thirty-two. It's big enough."

Kristie shivered, her eyes dark. "That man with a gun." She dropped her head as if it were being forced down by a hand on her neck.

"Easy, honey," he soothed her. "It's me he'd like to shoot. But he's got better sense than that. There's a whole lot of people getting by on jawbone. To them there's no big difference between what they really do and what they only say they're going to do. They can con themselves through a lifetime like that. Believe me, Haas is a kind of man I understand, and I'm telling you not to worry."

She tried to accept his confidence, but for the rest of the afternoon she had the persistent feeling they were under siege, and this theme became part of the fantasy she began to weave when they went to her bedroom... a cabin high in the mountain fastnesses of Sicily. While sheltered in the ravines, in the sparse cover of the timberland, the *carabinieri* waited for darkness to rush the cabin. It was the end; their best hope was for a quick death, and she would die with him. This was their last time together, a moment of life stolen from their mountain death. She put her whole self into it, and in that curious double vision where she both dreamed and didn't dream she sensed herself being genuinely moved in another way, separate from the rising climax of her nerves, and this strange emotion shocked her back to full reality.

JD was breathing heavily through his open mouth, and his tongue pulsed like a separate and rudimentary animal trapped there in the murderous vise of his large yellow teeth. *Ugly, Ugly, Ugly,* she chanted to herself, summoning a charm against this dangerous beauty she felt. But he was not ugly. Not ugly. He was simple and vital—and not for her!

"What's the matter?" he asked.

"Nothing. Don't stop."

"It felt like you closed a door somewhere."

How could he know that? "Please," she urged him, "don't leave me like this."

"Now you are talking foolishness."

When he began to move over her again, she surrendered greedily to him, JD Bing, and everything he was making her feel for him, but in a dim reflex of childhood, without willing it, her fingers moved to form King's X.

Later she told him, "You can take my car. The patrol won't recognize it."

He accepted her keys with pleased gratitude, and she watched him shrug into his coat and settle his hat. She moved to volunteer her kiss and tried for lightness. "Hurry back."

He looked at her soberly. "I'll be back. Don't worry about that."

As soon as he was gone, she began to feel uneasy, and the feeling grew. She curled tensely on the couch and when the phone rang, she knew she had been expecting it, and her hand went automatically to lift the receiver.

"Rotten slut," the voice said and shrilled on in the same relentless tautology while she accepted it in a shivering crouch like a cowering dog until the voice began to tell her she could never love anyone, that her rotten blood was all she felt, not love, never love, and she began to cry. She didn't know she was crying until she sensed the tears working over her face, and then absurdly she thought, I never cry. And with this she began to sob.

"Please, please leave me alone. Please, God, please leave me alone."

She began to jerk the phone back and forth in a tense arc. The voice rose and fell in her ear. Once more she heard "bitch," and she screamed and threw the phone from her, slipping off the couch to her knees. She lowered her forehead to the harsh nap of the carpet and cried, "But I didn't want to be this way. I didn't *want* to be like this." An overwhelming sense of her girlhood dreams came back to her just as she had recorded them in her innocence, and how sweet and wonderful she was going to become, how lovely and loving, how—

Nathan, what am I doing? She was suddenly horrified to have set those two men, strangers to each other and both decent men, on a collision course. What could she have been thinking?

She crawled to where the phone lay, closed the connection, and dialed Nathan's office. But she couldn't get through. A cool female voice competently blocked her. "I'm sorry, Miss Olson, but Mr. Holleran isn't in." But she guessed from the sharp point of the "Miss Olson" and the cold relish of the bitch's voice that Nathan had left instructions he would never be "in" to her, and the senseless cruelty of this precaution caused her so much pain she was literally sick with it.

"Tell him I called," she said with difficulty and hung up. There, she thought. When it is too late, he will realize why I called, and he will understand how miserable he has been to me and how little I deserved it.

When she was calm again, she locked her door, checking it with extra care, and made the rounds of the windows. When she raised the blinds to check the latches, she noticed it was beginning to rain. The drops appeared on her windowpanes almost without force, as if they had condensed there to hang heavily a moment before they began to roll down the glass, each with a captured glint of light.

She settled down to read and wait, but again and again her mind rolled and bobbed to the surface of the book, and she found herself staring blindly at the wall as she tried to picture all the things that might be happening in Mesa Verde. The rain drummed softly at her window.

THE SCAVENGER...

...was pinned down by the rain, as if by shrapnel. Rain terrified him—most things did—and at the first hint of it he had been driven back to his old place for the cover and the powerful security he had created here.

Too frightened to come out into the growing darkness to hunt for food, which he needed badly, he huddled on the floor of the packing crate, his head covered by a loosely woven cloth sack that had once held onions. The tart scent of their particular decay still lingered, and through the open weave his eyes throbbed with the beating terror of a cornered squirrel.

He lived entirely on refuse, and the single characteristic, other than to cover himself, that distinguished him from any other foraging animal was his rudimentary sense of religion. Though he had, years before, gradually abandoned the painful struggle to communicate with anyone, he still retained a magical apprehension of the power of language, and among his gleanings of bread crusts, bones, and vegetable trimmings, he included pencil stubs, nearly exhausted ball-points, broken crayons, and odds and ends of paper and cardboard.

Often in the mornings and the early part of the evening before the light failed, crouched in the security of his burrow, he wrote, covering the salvaged paper. Often he wrote along the sides of larger cardboard boxes, turning the box around and around, so that sometimes an enormous sentence would spiral down from the top left-hand corner, filling all four faces, cutting through such bland communications as BAB-O CLEANSER, Disinfects and Deodorizes, 2 Doz. 14 oz. Cans.

These boxes, like everything he wrote, became charms, charms against evils he could no longer formulate, and when their power was exhausted, he destroyed them so they couldn't be reanimated and used against him. Like all charms, sometimes they worked and sometimes they didn't, but this was a condition he never questioned because it was his faith that he could not survive without them. His charms had failed when they allowed the police to chase him, and he had been close to panic since then. In his sense of time it had been many years since anyone had tried to molest him. Children shouted at him, dogs barked—these things he could bear—but for someone to lay hands on him .. . he shuddered now with the echo of his revulsion. This anxiety was so great that it had schooled him into a mechanism of exclusion where he was seldom, except in the harsh focus of terror, aware of other people as anything more than objects, no different than the bright, noisy things that moved swiftly in the streets. Both were equally incomprehensible, equally dangerous.

During the day, now fading, he had created a dozen charms and wards and had placed them around himself in a perimeter of defense like supernatural cannon, and the strongest of all was pinned to his person. This great charm frightened him almost as much as it reassured him, and he used it only when his anxieties had grown unbearable.

A light went on thirty feet away, one of the small lights that came on in such numbers during the early part of the darkness. He moaned and drew his knees tighter to his chest. Beyond the symbolic cover of the onion sack he watched the rain slanting down into the large tin can he had placed to catch it. As always, throughout his life, he hoped only to survive. He didn't question why.

JD...

...took his hat off before entering Mesa Verde. Even in Kristie's car there was a chance the two private patrolmen might recognize him, but without his hat, and if he slouched down in the seat to disguise his height, he could improve his chances. The rain reassured him.

The closer he had driven to the ocean, the harder the rain had fallen, until it seemed that he was moving into the heart of a storm. Here in Mesa Verde the white streets were awash, and the passing motorists remained anonymous behind the shuttering windshield wipers; their headlights flared over the wet pavements and flickered along the pale trunks of the bending palms like sticks pulled across a picket fence.

He parked in the same spot. The charm dangling from Kristie's key ring tapped against the dashboard as he switched off the ignition. He freed the key and stared briefly at the charm, a miniature gold book set with brilliants, before he dropped the ring into his coat pocket. He watched the house, as he had twenty-four hours before, but now the large front window was shaded, and he had been sitting for only a few minutes before it went out.

He rolled a cigarette, holding his legs widespread, so the excess tobacco fell between them. He searched his pockets for matches, found a book, and as he lit up he saw the maid hurrying down the driveway. She wore a hooded plastic raincoat, and he saw her dark face moving in the hood as she was attracted by the flare of his match. She stopped, peering over at him.

JD dropped the dead match to the floor and looked away, pulling at his cigarette, but from the corner of his eye he saw the woman start across the street. He opened the ashtray and tapped his roll against it, though no ash had yet formed. When she rapped on the window, he turned with simulated surprise to roll it down and look out questioningly into her dark severe and disapproving face, barred across by the narrow glasses that were speckled now with fine beads of moisture.

"What you want 'round here?" she asked.

JD tried to sound pleasant. "I'm waiting for someone."

"You been waitin' since last night?"

"Don't that come under the heading of my business?"

"Ain't your business to be waitin' 'round here. No folks 'round here has your kind waitin' on them."

"It is my business. I sell books and I'm sitting here trying to work up enough nerve to go knock on some of these high-tone doors."

She was studying him closely, and JD could see that now she believed him.

She continued with a condescension that was almost kindly. "You ain't goin' do *no* selling 'round here. These folks buys they books special made. Now you best to move along and save yourself some trouble. I'm tellin' you fo' you own good."

JD nodded agreeably. "Okay. Thanks for the tip."

"You just mind what I say."

She dipped her head in an abrupt dismissal and hurried across the street to where her own car was parked. JD rolled up the window, started the motor, and moved out slowly, watching her taillights come on and diminish up the streets before they winked away. Then he threw Kristie's car into reverse and eased back. He switched off the motor, pocketed the keys, and stepped out into the rain.

In the shelter of the nearest bushes he paused to turn up his collar and then continued rapidly up the hill to circle the house. He looked into each of the windows—they were all lightless—and ended at the garage. It was empty. The woman was gone.

The garage would make a good place to wait, but though he saw no obvious lock, he couldn't find any way to get the door open. He had given up and was walking down the driveway when he heard a sudden whir of machinery. He spun around, heart catching, and saw the garage door lifting.

Christ! He jumped to the side, instinctively seeking shelter, and dropped on his hands and knees behind a low hedge. The door folded up into the garage and stopped. A light went on, but no one stepped out. It was obvious from his vantage that no one was inside the garage. He shook his head, baffled, then slowly smiled at his own panic. He remembered reading of such automatic systems in one of the many ragged and coverless magazines that had passed through his hands, and he realized he had probably tripped some sort of switch.

He stood up, slapping his muddy palms together, and walked into the dry stillness of the garage. The concrete floor was stained with oil, the smeared gray of old stains, and the hard bright black of fresh droppings. On one side a metal bench supported a neat row of bottles and cans; tools were racked above it: two saws, a set of wrenches, a hammer, a brace and bit. At the other end a small gym had been fitted out. He walked over to examine it. Indian clubs, a pulley setup with adjustable weights, a bicycle-type exerciser—this caused JD to smile tolerantly—and on an oak platform there was a small set of dumbbells. He checked the brand. Healthways, a make he'd never heard of, and with every ounce of iron loaded on, counting the bar, it wouldn't weigh three hundred and fifty pounds. He stared at the weights thoughtfully, then found a rag and wiped his hands.

He went back to the tool rack and took up the largest wrench, hefting it and slapping it into his palm. He laid it down and tried the hammer. Sudden death, he thought, and he picked up the wrench again. He stared at the slender silver shank and heavy tool-steel jaws, turned once to look out the door down the driveway, washed with rain, and then returned the wrench to its place. He'd never had any use for someone who picked up a piece of pipe, a shank, or packed any kind of steel.

He decided that the overhead light had come on automatically with the opening door and, pulling the exerciser underneath it, he climbed up, balancing carefully to unscrew the bulb. Then he found the switch that controlled the door and watched the aluminum panels as they lowered and shut him into the darkness. He squatted down to wait.

He waited for an hour, the chill of the concrete seeping through his pants, while a constant churn of vague apprehension worked at him. He wasn't afraid, only uneasy, but several times he found himself thinking he should get out and make it back to his hotel room.

To put your head under your pillow? he asked himself scornfully. You blew whatever chance you had to be a spooky kid. Now you can be a man, some kind of man, or you'll be nothing.

The distant murmur of car motors rose and fell in the street below, and finally one continued to rise until with a sharp click the machinery that opened the door began to work. JD stood up quickly and placed himself flat to the wall. The rising door let in the glare of headlights, and JD saw the tips of his shoes shining in them and turned his feet to the side. The lights flared up as the car rolled forward, growing brighter until they were muffled against the far wall, leaving the large, round taillights glaring back like the eyes of a demon. He saw the silhouette of a man in the driver's seat. Then all the lights went out.

JD moved as swiftly as he could, tiptoeing toward the sound of the opening car door. He hoped his vision would sharpen. One shoe scraped against something. Then he saw Holleran's back rising up directly ahead and, aiming where he sensed the neck should be, he delivered a sidearm rabbit punch. Pain leaped in his own hand, and he realized he landed high on the head. He swung again, chopping down. Holleran, with a startled shout, tried to sidestep but landed against the car. Immediately he tried to butt JD, but JD, locking both hands together into one large fist, delivered a savage uppercut. Holleran went down, but as JD moved in he lashed out with his feet to foul JD's ankles, and both men were down. JD had time to realize that Holleran was fast and hard to hurt. Then the other man was on him, searching for his throat. JD tried to use his strength, but could find no leverage—Holleran slid through his hands—and when he tried to reach Holleran with a finishing blow, the other man went under it, and JD hit the car door. After that he couldn't feel his right hand.

They rolled back and forth in a fumbling melee, trapped in the narrow space between the metal bench and the side of the automobile—all to JD's disadvantage. He could use neither his size nor his strength and it was this very size and strength that had made it seldom necessary for JD to fight at all. He was discovering that he didn't know how. Holleran had him outmatched, but even knowing this, he wasn't able to make a break and run for it.

It didn't end until both men were at the point of exhaustion. Then Holleran managed to clamp his forearm across JD's windpipe and hung on grimly no matter how JD bucked and twisted until the larger man blacked out and went limp.

Holleran got up slowly and stood, legs spread, chest heaving as he sucked at the air. He explored the side of his head with gentle fingers and swore softly as he fumbled for the car door. The door opened eight inches and jammed against JD, who shifted and groaned. Holleran went around the front of the car, holding onto it for support, opened the far door, and took a gun from the glove compartment.

When JD opened his eyes, the first thing he saw was the gun. Holleran was leaning against the metal bench pointing it down at him, and a shock of dismay went through him. He started to sit up.

"Easy," Holleran said, still breathing hard. "Get up, but get up easy."

JD was looking at his right hand, wondering if it was broken. Already it was beginning to swell. After the first shaft of dismay a dullness was beginning to set in. He turned and stared up at Holleran.

"Get up." Holleran prodded him.

He stood. Other than his hand he didn't seem to be hurt, but his fight was spent. Holleran had backed away carefully and now he used the gun to indicate a side door. "We'll go in the house. You first."

Mechanically, as he had so often obeyed the voice of authority, JD moved to obey. They went along a short walk, and he stood aside while Holleran unlocked the back door with one hand, the gun steadied on him with the other. They moved through a large kitchen into the living room, and it seemed different than it had appeared through the window, even larger and more luxurious. A winner's house, JD thought.

"What was that all about?" Holleran asked him.

"I needed money."

"You needed money." Holleran stared at him angrily. "Everyone needs money." In the full light JD could see that Holleran was marked. A purple bruise was forming at his temple; one eye was swelling. "Sit over there on that couch and keep your hands locked behind your head."

JD held out his damaged hand, and Holleran leaned forward to look. "You do that on my head?"

"No, your car."

"Keep your hands on your knees then. Keep them where I can see them."

JD sat down, and Holleran moved to the phone. He consulted an Autodex, dialed a number, and said, "Send a car to 113 Haversham Drive. Tell them to come right in. The door will be open... No, but I'm holding a prowler here... Yes, everything's under control."

He walked over and unlocked the front door, then went to the bar, where he poured a drink and downed it. He looked at JD and poured another, which he brought over and left on a table at the end of the couch. Then he sat down in a chair facing JD and indicated the glass. "Better drink that."

"I don't want it."

"Suit yourself."

They sat in silence for a while; then Holleran asked, "What made you pick me?"

JD shrugged. "No particular reason. You looked like you had money."

Holleran smiled grimly. "How'd you get that idea?"

"I don't know. I was desperate."

Holleran shook his head. He seemed disturbed and he walked over and downed the whiskey JD had refused. There was a rush of steps on the front porch, and two private patrolmen, guns drawn, came through the door. JD recognized them. The little one was in front, toeing almost daintily in his high-heeled boots, the large hat pushed back off his forehead.

"Well!" The patrolman turned rapidly between Holleran and JD, his eyes bright. "We ran this same punk off last night. I thought I told you to stay away from here?"

"I'm turning him over to you," Holleran said, "and you can handle it with the police. He attacked me in my garage when I came home tonight. I believe his object was robbery."

"It was robbery all right. I told Fred last night, that big punk's looking for someone to jump. Ain't that right, Fred?"

The quiet partner, his hat under his arm, nodded.

The patrolman holstered his gun, leaving the flap open. He smoothed his gloves over his fingers, bouncing on his heels as if he were getting ready to hit JD, but he only reached for the cuffs fastened to his belt. "On your feet."

"Better search him before you cuff him," the partner said.

"Yeah. Take everything out of your pockets. Put it here." He indicated a low coffee table. JD stood up and began to go through his pockets. He could use only his left hand and he dug awkwardly into his right-hand pocket for a few coins, his keys, and Kristie's keys. He laid them on the table and added his wallet, a comb, and his sack of tobacco.

"That's it."

The patrolman picked the sack of Golden Grain up by the string. "You're a regular sport, aren't you?" He cracked the billfold to disclose a few dollars and nodded knowingly. "And moving on very short dough."

Holleran had walked over to look at JD's things. Now he reached down to touch Kristie's car keys, tapping them lightly with one finger like a man attempting to determine whether some small and possibly dangerous thing is alive or dead.

"Where'd you get these?" he asked.

"They're mine," JD said.

"With a jeweled charm?"

"A girl friend loaned me her car."

"What's her name?"

JD hesitated and the patrolman said, "Answer the question."

"Ann—" He gave his mother's name, but he wasn't quick enough to supply a last name.

"Ann who?"

"Just Ann. I'm not bringing her into this."

Holleran picked the keys up and, holding the little jeweled book between two fingers, he fanned some cards out of it. JD stared. He hadn't examined the charm closely. Now he saw that it was a miniature address book, and he watched Holleran's expression turn troubled as the other man read through a few of the addresses. Holleran looked up at JD and he appeared to be trying to see something in JD's face. Then he turned to the patrolmen, and asked quietly, "Would you mind waiting over there by the door for a moment? I have something I want to say to this man."

The little patrolman hesitated. "He's our prisoner now."

"Just wait over there."

JD noted grimly that he wasn't the only one broken to authority. The patrolman backed off resentfully, and his neutral partner followed him. They stood by the front door, both guns pointed at the floor.

"Did you steal these?" Holleran asked quietly so his voice wouldn't carry.

"No."

"Then Kristie gave them to you?"

JD remained silent.

"I know these are Kristie Olson's keys. Look, my own address is here."

JD read the entry. "She had nothing to do with it."

"You can't expect me to believe that. At the very least, she told you about me. And I'll tell you something else. She tried to call me earlier this evening. I didn't receive the call, but I was informed of it." Holleran paused, studying him closely, his pale eyes steady and alert. Something enormous was trying to tear loose inside JD, but he kept his mouth shut and his eyes indifferent. "Well," Holleran said, "I intend to find out."

He walked to the phone. The patrolmen started forward, but Holleran waved them back impatiently. He dialed quickly a number he knew well.

"Kristie? This is Nathan... Take it easy. I just learned you were trying to reach me earlier in the evening... Yes, I'm home." He listened for what seemed a long time, then said, "Kristie, that's an incredible story... No... No, that's not possible. You should know it's not possible... Yes, I'm sorry too... Good-bye." He hung up quickly and turned back to JD, his face impassive.

"She says you stole her car. That you were coming here to rob me and that she had tried to stop you."

JD sat down, and it seemed he was pushed down by a great weight. He rubbed his eyes with the back of his good hand. "That lousy bitch."

"What really happened?" Holleran asked.

"Does it make any difference."

"It could—to me. I think I have a right to know."

"Maybe you do, but I'm telling *you*, no one else. If you repeat me, I'll deny it." With a bitter foretaste of the memories that would come to haunt him during these new years in prison he began to sketch his brief experience with Kristie. He left nothing out. The patrolmen shuffled restlessly in the background, but Holleran listened intently, shaking his head at intervals.

When JD finished, Holleran asked, "How long were you in for?"

"A while."

"And then you got out and met Kristie?"

"Yes."

"You could have run into a hundred different women, but it had to be Kristie, and she used you for everything but a man."

"She saw me as a man."

"Did she? She didn't see me as a man or even as a person, but only as something she was making up. I've been there and I know." He stretched out his hands to look at them, perhaps picturing them as they had held Kristie. The backs were still lightly freckled. "I ached for her, and I kept thinking if she were only a little different, what a wonderful woman she would be. I don't know if she could have sent me on her dirty errands—" JD winced and Holleran went on quickly. "Perhaps she could have. I came close to ruining my career over her, not to mention my home. So I know how it is with you. In her narrow way she's a lot of woman, but it isn't enough, and she's poisoning herself and those around her. This should show you."

Holleran took his billfold from his pocket and held it open so JD could see that it held a five and three ones. "There might be twenty more around the house, and Kristie knows I pay for almost everything by either check or credit card. At the most, you might have caught me with fifty dollars. Do you see?"

"Yeah." JD didn't understand why Holleran was bothering to point out to him how badly he'd been had. "I never thought the money was the whole story, but I thought you'd screwed her over and deserved to lose something for it."

Holleran looked uncomfortable. "I was married, but she knew that. I don't know—she took it hard when we broke up. Maybe..." He trailed off and sat for a moment staring at something inside himself. Then he stood up and walked over to the patrolmen.

"I was mistaken," he told them. "This turns out to be a private matter. I'm sorry I got you up here for nothing."

Holleran held the door open, but the patrolman balked. "Now wait just a minute," he said. "There's been a complaint made, and it will have to be heard by a judge. That's law."

"A complaint made to whom?"

"To me. I'm a special officer."

"Boy"—Holleran's voice cut with the word like an axe—"you're here to keep kids from breaking the streetlamps and to prevent strange dogs from pissing on our lawns. Now, get out of here, and if any word of this gets to the real police, you're out of a job. And the next time you come in this house, take your goddam hat off."

The patrolman took a step back, his face pinched, and made an abortive grab for his hat, which he checked halfway up, and spun on his heel to walk out stiffly. His partner followed him, giving Holleran a careful and respectful nod in passing.

JD sat up alertly now, looking at the gun Holleran had left lying on the arm of the chair across from him.

He had no plan to make a grab for it—the implication of the gun was one of trust.

"It's not loaded," Holleran said behind him.

"You could have fooled me."

"That was the idea. I fooled you a second time. Kristie didn't say you had stolen her car. She told pretty much the same story, but I wanted to hear it from you."

"That takes a little weight off her."

"Very little. Tomorrow it will all seem different to her, and the next day still another way. If I went back to her, as she seems to want so badly, I'd be her 'hero' for two weeks. Then one day she'd look at me and see an ordinary man approaching middle age, who spends his time making sure other people are building a rocket. No, once is enough. You better put your things back in your pockets."

Holleran watched, rubbing the bruise at his temple, as JD redistributed his belongings. "You pack a godawful wallop," he said.

"Not good enough," JD said. "You cutting me loose?"

"Yes."

"Why?"

"I like to handle my own trouble when I can. Look, would some kind of decent job help you get straightened out?"

"I like to think it would, but no one will hire me."

"I'll hire you." Holleran took a card from his billfold and handed it to JD. "Call me tomorrow. I'll find something for you. Maybe not too much, but something to give you a toehold, at least."

"Why are you doing this?"

"Two reasons, I suppose. First, you could have left me for dead if you'd bothered to hit me with anything. You came at me like a bear, but all you used were your own hands. You gave me that chance, and it beat you, but I think it means something about the kind of man you are. And, second"—Holleran smiled wryly—"we're both veterans of the same war."

KRISTIE

...shivered and rubbed the goose flesh on her arms. Her apartment was cold, but she didn't get up to turn on the heat. What would be the use? She felt as if she were exposed in the middle of a giant hand that would presently close on her.

Why had she tried to punish Nathan? She didn't want him. She compared him to JD. She didn't want JD either. She no longer knew who or what she did want—if she had ever known. Peace, she thought, and folded her hands in her lap to wait.

When the pounding started, she thought, I'm not afraid, and as the word "afraid" formed in her mind she realized she was terrified. She tiptoed to the window and made a small crack at the edge of the curtain. JD was standing on her porch, pounding with his left hand, his right hand stuck in his coat, resting on the support of a fastened button. He's hurt, she thought. Nathan hurt him. She felt a brief contempt, but then she saw his face.

She gasped and ran into the bedroom, then threw herself on the bed with her hands over her ears. The pounding only seemed to grow louder. Please stop. I'm sorry I can't let you in. Then above the sound of JD's persistent knocking came the shriller tones of the telephone, and Kristie's eyes grew blind. They would break in. They would all break in. She thought she heard the door splintering and she ran to the bedroom window and opened it. The rain had died off to a light sprinkle, and the night was like cold hands on her face. The raw, unfinished cement scratched her knees and forearms when she lowered herself from the window, and the weeds brushed her bare legs with wet fingers as she ran down the narrow alley, stumbling in the darkness, until she came to a high fence of wooden palings and jumped futilely, inches short, trying to reach the top. A car started up on the other side, and she called out, but the motor ground into gear, and the sound of it diminished up the street.

She turned to run back, past her own windows, toward the other end. She tripped over something that boomed hollowly between her feet, and when she threw her hand out blindly for support, her fingers scraped down the side of the building until a large cardboard box broke her fall. The shock cleared her mind for a moment, and as she lay trying to get her breath she realized that it was another box she had tripped over. They were all around her. Then she was suddenly, with an icy shock, aware of something moving near her. Instinctively she screamed, jerking her head around trying to locate the source of the motion. Then she saw a large crate with something half out of it like a bear emerging from the mouth of a cave.

She screamed again until she thought the sound would tear her throat. A huge, bearded figure was crouched over her, waving its hands, making a grunting noise low in its throat as if its vocal cords were paralyzed. Panic beat in Kristie's mind like a thousand bright metal wings. She screamed on every breath until she felt her mouth covered by a hard hand and her nostrils filled with the smell of earth. She began to struggle.

GROVE...

...was at Kathleen's when the screaming started. They had spent the day together, taking the kids down to the Long Beach Pike to ride the battered little airplanes, horses, and cars that to kids weren't battered at all, but bright as the young eyes that yearned for them. They rode on the lazy circles of the Ferris wheel and the eternal gallop of the merry-go-round, and walked along the asphalted lip of the beach while the kids flirted, shrieking with excitement, along the edge of the waves. Then the threat of rain drove them home. Kathleen fixed dinner and afterward put the kids to bed.

"Beer or wine?" she asked.

"Both."

"In what order?"

"Just mix them."

She smiled and brought him a glass of wine, and sat down with her own at the other end of the couch. He looked at her until she said lightly, "Relax, I'm not trying to marry you."

"What you see is not fear—it's calculation."

"Well, I lied. I am trying to marry you. But not in any final way. It's an awful expression, but 'trial basis' seems to fit what I mean."

"Is there anything that isn't on a trial basis?"

She sipped her wine thoughtfully, a little of the deep red tinting her cheek in reflection. "I'm a married woman who has no husband. Not the most rewarding way to live. So I date, and sometimes it goes further but it's not the same thing. You seem more than a date, yet less than a husband. Does that bother you?"

"Not at all. Of course, I'd like a little time to consider your—ah—proposal."

Kathleen started laughing, and he put his wine on the table in front of them, took her glass, and placed it beside his. She slid into his arms. Her back was slender, her mouth sweet and warm. She drew back and made a curving gesture above her hip. "I'm not built like Kristie," she said.

"Forget Kristie."

"I will if you will."

"I already have."

Then their eyes caught, and the lightness went out of their faces. It was a few minutes later when they heard the first scream. Grove said, "That sounds close."

"It sounds like Kristie."

At the second scream, they both jumped up. Grove headed for the front door, but Kathleen said, "It's back here." She ran toward the kitchen, Grove behind her, and when she opened the window, the screams, vivid as lightning, were right below them. Grove leaned out to see Kristie's pale hair and someone over her.

He vaulted the sill, grabbed a handful of cloth, and found himself looking down into a bearded face, the eyes like oil, the mouth a torn black hole rimmed with grayish teeth. He drove his fist into the face. The Scavenger reared up, making a sobbing noise, and the way he threw Grove's arm off was vivid with animal strength, but he didn't stand to fight. He turned and ran.

Grove dropped to his knees beside Kristie. Her face was as pale as paper in the darkness, and when he touched her, she screamed again with a harsh, broken sound. He looked up to see the Scavenger scrambling over the top of the concrete wall that led to the backyard. Then he was aware of Kathleen beside him. "Take care of her," he ordered.

When he topped the wall himself, Grove caught a brief glimpse of the old man heading around the garages toward the alley. Grove jumped, but one ankle turned when he lit, and he fell face down in the grass. He scrambled up. His ankle twinged, but he started off. As he passed the opening to the center of the court someone shouted at him. He turned and saw Haas running toward him in that light-footed way so incongruous in heavy men.

"What's going on?" Haas demanded.

"That lunatic attacked Kristie."

"Who?"

But Grove turned and started running, aware now that Haas was following him. There was nothing moving up and down the alley, and, making a quick guess, he ran across the asphalt and began to climb the fence into the dairy.

"I heard all the ruckus," Haas said behind him.

Grove waved him silent, trying to concentrate on the darkness ahead of him. The center buildings were illuminated by the feeding lights, and the reflections in the mud puddles made them look like ice floes stretching out across the yard.

"*Who* we after?" Haas asked.

"An old man. He has to be caught before he hurts someone."

Haas grunted and looked away. But when Grove began to range across the wet earth of the cattle run, Haas came with him. The cows milled restlessly. Several lifted their muzzles to bawl at the sky, their round eyes glittering with apprehension, and as the two men passed through the herd they scattered and started running wildly until they piled up against the fence in a heaving jumble of brown-and-white bodies.

"There goes someone," Haas shouted, and Grove followed the thrust of his arm and saw the Scavenger running from a small shed toward the barn.

"That's him."

Then he realized he'd seen a gun in Haas's hand. *"Don't"* he shouted, but his voice was lost in the crack of a shot. The Scavenger swerved as if hit by a sudden and powerful gust of wind, but he didn't stop, and Grove lost sight of him around a corner.

"Haas, put that goddam gun away."

But Haas was off, running hard, eager as a bull who has seen a man, and Grove, trying to follow, slipped on a cow pat and nearly lost his footing. When he hit his stride again, Haas was fifteen feet ahead of him and turning the corner. When Grove rounded the corner, he saw Haas standing in front of the large double doors that led into the barn. The gun was up, and Haas appeared to be aiming deliberately. Grove launched himself into a long, desperate dive. As he hit Haas at the knees he heard the gun fire, and then both men were rolling in the mud.

"What the hell?" Haas exclaimed.

Through the barn door Grove saw the Scavenger halfway up the ladder that led to the haymow, still climbing slowly. He reached the top and tumbled into the shadows.

"You bloody bastard," Grove told Haas. "You want him to get away?"

"He can't get away. You just feel like shooting someone."

"Smart punk."

"Shut up and give me that gun."

Haas drew back the gun to cover Grove. His eyes seemed to twitch. "All you smart punks," he said hoarsely. "I'm going up after that old mother and—

He broke off. A searchlight was probing from the alley, and coming through the beam, a uniformed officer was running toward them. Haas quickly put the gun in his pocket. "Keep your mouth shut," he told Grove.

"You damn fool."

A dairyman reached them before the policeman.

"What was that shooting?" he demanded. "You trying to scare my cows to death?"

"There's a molester up there," Haas said, pointing up in the haymow. "He raped a woman in the court over there."

The policeman came up in time to hear the last of this. He was a young man, his face wary beneath his helmet. "What's going on here?" he asked, directing his question at Grove. Grove told him, leaving the gun out.

But the dairyman said, "There was shooting."

The officer nodded. "We heard it."

His partner came up, and the first officer nodded at the barn. "They got someone treed in there. He was either shooting at them or they were shooting at him."

"I like them shooting at him," the partner said. "Stand free of each other." He patted them down swiftly and pulled the gun from Haas's pocket. He sniffed the barrel. "It's been working."

"I got a right to protect my neighborhood," Haas said.

"We have nothing but your word there's anyone in that barn."

Grove said, "He's in there and he may be wounded. Call Detective-Sergeant Strickland at the Bellflower Station. He knows about this."

The two officers spoke together briefly, then one of them headed back to the car, and the other shifted to guard both Haas and Grove.

They lowered the Scavenger out of the loft. He had been bleeding into the hay from a wound in his thigh. Grove moved closer to watch as they applied an emergency tourniquet. The old man's eyes were closed and, lying there on the ground, he looked like a dime-store Santa taking a nap on his coffee break. The card pinned to his overalls read: THE GRASSHOPPER SHALL BE A BURDEN.

Detective-Sergeant Strickland knelt beside him and unpinned the card, and as he did the Scavenger's eyes opened and his lips began to tremble. Then he appeared to faint. Strickland turned the card in his hand. There was some printing on the back. Grove couldn't make it out clearly, but it looked like part of a breakfast cereal box. Strickland looked up at Grove to say, "He collected bright bits of paper like a magpie."

"What will you do with him?"

"What *can* we do?"

Grove walked with Strickland back to the court. Haas was sitting in back of one of the police cars, an officer guarded him and an ember caution light beat methodically in the rear window.

"What about this fellow with the gun?" Strickland asked.

"That's my fault," Grove said quickly. "I was excited and feeling guilty because I had tried to persuade Kristie that the old man was harmless. Anything Haas felt, he caught from me. That and the chase. I'd hate to think I was responsible for his arrest."

"You're not. He was due to be arrested on another matter. Not quite this soon, but it was coming. He's Arnold Howe's son-in-law, isn't he?"

"Yes."

Strickland nodded. "We had to talk to him anyway. Your old ragpicker must have had a curious view of humanity. Did you ever consider how much you can read of people in their garbage?"

"No, I don't suppose I did."

Strickland smiled, his face weary for a moment. "We see a lot of garbage."

Kathleen had Kristie inside, stretched out on the couch and a young intern worked over her. She no longer screamed and struggled when anyone touched her, but her face became drawn, and her teeth grated against each other. Looking down on her, Grove realized how much of Kristie's beauty had been art, a demand she had imposed upon herself as well as on others. Now her skin was slack and gray; her wet hair, lifeless. The calf of one leg was smeared with mud, and her knees were bloody. It was as if he had come on the scene of an accident and walked up to look down on an injured stranger lying on the sidewalk.

"This has been much harder on her that it would have been for someone else," Kathleen said softly.

"What was she doing out there?" Grove asked.

"I don't know. She isn't able to tell me."

"Kristie," he said, but nothing changed in her face.

"Shock," the intern said. "I don't think it's physical. She's scratched up, but otherwise all right. In my opinion she should be under observation for a day or two."

Strickland agreed. "I'll sign her in."

The intern shot her with a sedative, and they loaded her on a stretcher. When Kathleen knelt down to squeeze her hand in reassurance, Kristie gave no indication she was aware of the gesture.

"Withdrawal," the intern murmured.

Strickland said, "A shame. She had enough trouble."

"She'll be all right," Kathleen said.

"We'll hope so."

When they were gone, Grove sat down and put his face in his hands. "What a miserable mess."

"It's not your fault, darling."

"Isn't it?"

"No, and don't start thinking like that." She started toward the door. "I'd better make sure Kristie's apartment is locked up."

Grove stood up. "No, I'll do it."

He found the door locked, but in the center of the small porch he discovered Kristie's car keys. He picked them up and put them in his pocket to keep for her. When he returned to Kathleen's, he found her looking in on the children. He stood behind her while she adjusted the covers over the little girl and picked up a fuzzy purple monkey discarded in sleep. The boy, in his own bed, lay on his back with one arm over his eyes.

"They slept through everything," Kathleen whispered.

Grove felt a sudden rush of warmth. He put his hands on Kathleen's shoulders and turned her to him.

IT ENDED...

...when Kristie regained consciousness and found herself in a bare white room. For a moment, as she was coming awake, it was as if time had not passed, and she still struggled hopelessly, the smell of the Scavenger burning in her nostrils, and she thrashed wildly on the bed and screamed once before she realized she was alone—and safe.

She stared at the empty walls and took in the large white door, vented at eye level by a narrow window of pale green glass patterned with octagons of reinforcing wire. There was something else wrong with the door, but it was a moment before she realized that it had no knob. She looked with growing wonder at the larger windows on the opposite side of the room—she saw a distant lawn and the tops of some trees, shimmering in the midday sun, all sliced into neat vertical sections by the bars on the windows.

Bars? She sat up to discover she was wearing a rough white nightgown, open in the back like a smock, and on the table beside her bed sat a plastic pitcher, half full of water, and a stack of paper cups. Her inventory was interrupted when she became aware that someone was watching her through the window in the doors. She saw a narrow slice of face, young eyes, and part of the striped cap of a nurse's aide. The eyes crinkled as if the hidden mouth might be creasing into a reassuring smile. Kristie stiffened with resentment.

"Come here," she called, but her observer was already gone. Kristie jumped out of bed, but the door—as she had known it would be—was locked.

"Damn!" She struck at the door with her fist. How did they dare? She put her mouth to the crack and shouted, "Open this door." She peered through the observation window, craning her neck trying to see something more than the bland white walls of an anonymous corridor. She shouted again.

She was still calling when the phone rang. She turned, looking for the instrument, and found it on the nightstand where she hadn't noticed it before. Don't answer, she told herself, but she always answered. It might be something important.

It was with no sense of surprise that she recognized the voice. *Were you trying to get away from me?* he asked in the same tones of greasy insinuation. He began to tell her what she wanted done to her and what she would do with any man who put his hands on her, and she listened, hardly breathing, until the voice finally stopped, and she continued to sit, her teeth locked, her fists pressed into her thighs. She didn't remember hanging up the receiver.

After a while she drew a deep, shuddering breath and lay back on the pillow. She turned to look at the barred windows, and her expression grew thoughtful. She began to wish she had a novel to read. It would be pleasant just to lie here and read.

A key sounded outside the door. She turned her head and saw a large woman with a square, homely face entering. She wore a nurse's uniform, and on her head the small starched cap seemed frivolous.

"And how are we feeling this morning?" she asked.

"All right."

"Good. That's good." She retucked the foot of the bed with automatic gestures. "Doctor will be with you in a moment. Meanwhile, is there anything you need?"

"Yes, I'd like something to read, and—if I'm going to be here for a while, I wonder if you could have this phone disconnected?"

The nurse looked up quickly. "What phone?"

"This phone. I want it disconnected."

"Oh—" the nurse said slowly. "Yes, well, I think perhaps you should talk to doctor about that."

"I intend to."

The nurse straightened up from the foot of the bed, and there was something different in her eyes, a hint of sharpened speculation, and something else. Pity? Could this big, ugly woman pity her?

The nurse left then, and Kristie heard her outside, locking the door.

THE END